FATAL CONFLICT

FATAL CONFLICT

Matt Hilton

SEVERN
HOUSE

First world edition published in Great Britain and the USA in 2022
by Severn House, an imprint of Canongate Books Ltd,
14 High Street, Edinburgh EH1 1TE.

Trade paperback edition first published in Great Britain and the USA in 2022
by Severn House, an imprint of Canongate Books Ltd.

severnhouse.com

British Library Cataloguing-in-Publication Data
A CIP catalogue record for this title is available from the British Library.

ISBN-13: 978-0-7278-5075-1 (cased)
ISBN-13: 978-1-4483-0899-6 (trade paper)
ISBN-13: 978-1-4483-0900-9 (e-book)

Typeset by Palimpsest Book Production Ltd.,
Falkirk, Stirlingshire, Scotland
Printed and bound in Great Britain by
TJ Books, Padstow, Cornwall

ONE

A droplet of sweat hit the scalding metal with a hiss. Tess Grey took a step away and swiped more droplets from her brow with the back of her wrist. She adjusted her footing, ensuring she was fully balanced, and safe from even an accidental caress of the searing metal. The air shimmered before her.

She judged her next move. Decision made, she acted. Her actions were fluid and quick, and she delivered them with confidence. The corresponding hiss and wafting steam brought a feral grin to her face. She watched bubbles erupt, then pop, and leave tiny craters in the surface of her concoction. She wielded her utensils like a master swordsman, slicing under then flipping her creation on the skillet. She stepped back again and once more dashed sweat from her brow. Boy, the smell was wonderful, but it was hot in the kitchen.

Tess was making ployes, fluffy pancakes that were indigenous to Maine. It was hardly the most exotic dish she could rustle up, but ployes were versatile and satisfying mouthfuls. They were a staple diet of the French Acadian exiles who once settled in Maine, and she thought they'd be a fitting treat for her fiancé, Po, himself of Acadian descent, albeit he traced his more recent ancestry to the Cajuns of Louisiana. She planned on keeping things simple, and serving the ployes with melted butter and molasses, but had decided on piling up a hearty stack for Po. He stood tall and sinewy, almost to the point of looking lean, but his appearance belied a healthy appetite. He'd polish off the pile of pancakes without a complaint.

She scooped off the test pancake, and was happy with its texture and golden color. She set it aside to eat – cook's privileges – and ladled more mixture onto the skillet.

Minutes later, noises from deeper inside the house caught her attention.

Po was up and about.

She checked the time. Just gone eight a.m.

Her partner often woke with the larks. By now he would've usually been up, showered, shaved and probably onto his third or fourth mug of coffee each taken with a cigarette. Today she'd left him in bed, Po having fallen back asleep, while planning on treating him to the breakfast of champions. He needed the extra rest and nourishment.

Po stuck his head around the kitchen door. His hair was damp, looking darker. He finger-combed it off his forehead. 'You think I've time for breakfast?'

'We have to keep your strength up,' she reminded him, and flipped another pancake onto the growing pile. 'Come on over, sit down and tuck in.'

'I can't. I gotta git goin'.'

'What do you mean?'

He aimed a nod towards the front of the house where his Ford Mustang was parked. 'I can't believe you let me sleep so late. I promised Chris and Jazz I'd be at the diner at eight sharp.'

'So ring them and warn them you're going to be a little late. You need to eat some breakfast if—'

'I'll have them rustle up somethin' for me at Bar-Lesque.'

'Po,' she said, and nodded at the ployes she'd stacked up. 'I made these special.'

'Special, huh?' He picked up one of the pancakes, rolled it and stuffed it in his mouth. He munched down as he headed across the kitchen. He said something around the batter that sounded like, 'They're more than special, they're lovely, Tess.'

'They're even better lathered with butter and molasses,' she called after his retreating back. She set down her spatula to the sound of the front door closing behind him. The temptation to fist her hips was strong. Instead she shook her head; the fool man had a habit of frustrating her, but admittedly rarely deliberately.

She wasn't mad at him. How could she be under the circumstances?

Po had interests in several companies around Portland, Maine. He owned Bar-Lesque. It was once a strip-joint, a dive bar, and the domain of creeps and criminals. Nowadays, under his influence, the bar had been converted into a retro-style bar-diner, and had earned a reputation for great food and good service. It had been turning a decent profit, until the pandemic hit and the world almost came to a halt. To try to squeeze down the pandemic curve, lockdowns of huge swaths of the country had occurred, and Maine's hospitality industry had taken a savage kicking as a result. Big-box and grocery stores had been allowed to remain open, but restaurants, diners and public bars had all been ordered shut. Over the summer, some restrictions had been lifted, the latest of which allowed the reopening of some venues albeit under strict Covid-19 safety measures and at a much-reduced capacity. His bar and restaurant managers, Chris and Jasmine, were desperate to get Bar-Lesque up and running again while current restrictions allowed, and Po must assist every way he could. Po wasn't averse to rolling up his sleeves and helping with the physical stuff; any excuse to get out of the house, he took it. During the enforced lockdown he'd been like a caged beast and was on the verge of going stir crazy.

He'd once been incarcerated in Louisiana State Penitentiary. He had already spent a good portion of his adult life held in a cage, and was not enjoying a return to form. Here he was surrounded by the comforts of home but his ranch remained a gilded cage. Given he could assist with the reopening of his diner, he had jumped at the chance. Tess on the other hand was stuck 'working from home'.

Her skills as a private investigator weren't in high demand, not while most folks were ensconced indoors. Crime had not disappeared because of the pandemic; it had mostly gone underground, or was hidden behind closed doors. Once this was over with and the world returned to some kind of normalcy she suspected that her trade would experience a boom time, but for now philandering partners were unable to cheat, and had most likely turned their frustrations on their long-suffering spouses. She felt a twinge of concern; domestic violence was probably at an all-time high and not a subject to be taken lightly.

She eyed the stack of ployes. Enough was enough.

She turned off the heat and set aside the smoking skillet.

There were far too many pancakes for her to eat alone, but by God she was going to try, her waistline be damned. If all had gone to plan her waist would soon be expanding exponentially, and she would be eating for two.

She laid a hand over her abdomen, imagining that a miracle of biology was taking place under her fingers. A shadow crossed her mind: it would be nothing short of a miracle if, this time, she were pregnant.

Sitting, she dragged the ployes towards her, and jostled over the butter dish and a squeezable bottle of syrup. She arranged them all in easy reach, then selected a fork and knife but the dark thought wouldn't fade. She pushed the food aside, her appetite gone.

She left the pancakes growing cold in the kitchen as she cut through into the adjoining sitting room. Po's ranch-style property was upon a lot alongside the Presumpscot River, a sprawling home built across one level. Tess had commandeered one of the spare bedrooms for an office, in which Po had set up a computer desk and filing cabinets. She'd been cooped inside too long: she grabbed her laptop and took it outside. She sat on the porch swing. Sunlight slanted through the trees that surrounded her. Shimmering dapples danced across her bare arms as she tapped keys on the laptop. It was early still, but the sunlight held warmth: she couldn't feel it. The rush of white water over the nearby Presumpscot Falls normally made a pleasing soundtrack: to her ears now it sounded like static and put her teeth on edge.

'Stop with the negativity, goddamnit,' she scolded out loud. 'This time it's going to be different.'

Her intention was to log onto an online tool, one tracking her menstrual cycle to pinpoint her time of highest fertility . . . or its lack. Tess was in her mid-thirties now. She had enjoyed a healthy sex life since her college days, but had practiced safely, using contraceptives for most of the time. Her career as a sheriff's deputy had taken precedent over pregnancy, and besides, she had never been in a relationship with a partner with whom she'd have liked to raise a child before Po. It was only a few months ago that she'd stopped taking the birth-control pill. It had never occurred to her that she might struggle to conceive.

Her email icon drew her gaze. She had unread mail. Habitually, she tapped the icon and was taken to her inbox.

TWO

Joshua Brogan set the gun down on the table as if it were no longer a threat. It was a deliberate move, intended to show how little regard he had for Bob Wilson, and how little he feared him, and how much Brogan should be feared instead.

Wilson's tongue flicked at the corner of his mouth as he stared at the pistol. Sweat shone on his forehead. His fingers stayed put, arched on the tabletop where he'd been warned to keep them. The gun was in grabbing distance, but even if he beat Brogan to the weapon, it wouldn't stop the other man behind him from shooting him dead. Twice the other's gun muzzle had touched the base of his skull, both times eliciting a cringe of terror from him.

Brogan shook his head as if remorseful over their respective predicaments. 'Tell me where to find Anthony and we'll leave you alone. You can go back to whatever you were doing before we arrived, safe, untouched . . . alive.'

'Tony's my brother, man,' Wilson whined. 'You can't expect me to tell you.'

'I can and I do.'

'But he's my bro, my *little brother*. I can't give him up.'

'Let's get some facts straight, shall we? You might have the same whore as a mother, but you don't have the same father. You weren't raised in the same houses; hell, you weren't even raised in the same towns. He's only your half-brother by the weakest connection of blood; but he's a fully paid-up, card-carrying, lying, thieving piece of shit. Think about that, Bob, and decide if he's worth protecting when the price you'll pay is with your life.'

'Jeez, c'mon, man, there's no need for this kinda talk,' Wilson said.

'You think I'm just making idle threats, Bob?'

'You don't have to threaten my life. There's no need, not when what Tony has done doesn't warrant it. You aren't gonna risk going to jail over *that*.'

'You make his crime sound trivial, unimportant. It tells me you're underestimating what I'm prepared to do to you. Choose a hand, Bob.'

'Uh, whaddaya mean?'

'It's not a difficult instruction. You've two hands, pick one of them.'

Wilson glanced at his right hand. The second gunman leaned close and chuckled in his ear, 'Pick wisely, Bob. If that's your jerking-off hand you might want to choose the other one.'

Wilson gave a double take, then looked again directly at Brogan. The gun still lay between them, within lunging distance. Wilson was fooling himself if he thought he had a hope of getting to it first. Brogan had placed his hands on the tabletop, his fingers spread like the legs of a giant arachnid. Self-inflicted tattoos decorated his knuckles and each of the first phalanges of his fingers. A human skull leered from the back of each hand.

Wilson's left hand crept forward a hair's breadth. He halted, blinked at Brogan. 'Wh-why do I have to pick a hand?'

'Would you rather I made you choose a knee, or worse, one of your nuts?'

'I'd rather you forgot whatever it is you have in mind and get outta here. I told you already, I don't know where Tony is.'

'You didn't tell me that,' said Brogan. 'You said I couldn't expect you to tell me where he is.'

'Well, that's the thing, man. I don't know where Tony is. You may as well leave. Go on, get outta here.'

'There you go again, disrespecting me by not taking me seriously.'

'I'm not, I'm just—'

Brogan snapped his hand over Wilson's and dragged it across the tabletop. Wilson jerked up in reaction, but the other gunman leaned closer, stuck the gun under his ear and Wilson got the message. Resistance would not be tolerated. He slumped down, chewing his bottom lip, his gaze locked with Brogan's. Brogan held the trapped hand in place so that Wilson was forced to remain bent at the waist. The gun was now only mere inches from Wilson. Brogan's gaze didn't slip as he transferred his grasp to Wilson's wrist and dragged out his arm a bit further. He rose to his feet without releasing his captive. Wilson made the mistake of keeping his gaze locked with Brogan's, and missed Brogan scooping up the gun. Brogan dug the muzzle deep into the flesh at the juncture of Wilson's thumb and index finger. He caressed the trigger and the hammer slammed home.

Shock yanked Wilson's hand free. He bucked back in his chair, yelping in terror, and in anticipation of the pain yet to come. He drew his hand close to the tip of his nose, eyes almost crossing as he goggled in dismay at the bullet wound . . . of which there was none.

Brogan laughed as he stood, holding the gun out from his side. 'You actually believed I'd be stupid enough to put a loaded weapon within your reach?'

The second gunman interjected. 'Before you get any crazy ideas about fighting us, Bob, my pistol is definitely loaded. D'you get me?'

Wilson was confused. He had fully expected to find a hole blown through the web of his thumb. He'd expected blood and agony. Instead he shivered and more sweat broke out along his hairline and poured down his face.

Brogan ejected what was obviously an empty magazine, and swapped it for a full one from his pocket. He slid it home into the pistol's grip and tapped it secure in his palm. He thumbed back the hammer, but kept his index finger outside the pistol's guard. He wagged the gun at Wilson. 'Are you going to take me seriously from here on?'

'I was already—'

Brogan lunged around the table. He swung the pistol low, and Wilson might've thought it was to avoid a misfire harming him: but that wasn't it. Brogan deliberately fired, and the bullet went through Wilson's instep, exited through the sole of his shoe, and continued into the floorboards. Wilson howled, and danced away on one foot, the other casting droplets of blood everywhere. Brogan looked at his companion, gesturing with the gun for Wilson to be returned to the seat.

A hand on his collar, Wilson was dragged back to the table and forced to sit. He gasped and moaned, craned his neck as if it would help disassociate his brain from the pain in his foot. Brogan remained standing, again pointing the business end of the pistol to one side: he knew that Wilson was no less terrified of it now, and more so of the man wielding it.

'You brought that on yourself,' Brogan chided, as Wilson again mewled at the agony in his foot. 'But I think you've learned your lesson and won't underestimate me a second time. Now how's about you tell me where to find Anthony, and as soon as you do that you can get your injury looked at.'

'I . . . I've told you already . . . I don't know where Tony is. Whoa! Whoa! Please don't hurt me again!'

Brogan stepped aside, having lunged in at first. Wilson held up both palms, warding him off. Brogan was tempted to put a bullet through both palms and proclaim that Wilson's wounds were stigmata. He resisted the urge.

He tapped the pistol's barrel on Wilson's head, causing him to scrunch his eyelids and shy away. 'If you don't know where he is, then tell me about somebody who will know.'

'If I tell you, do you swear you won't shoot me again?'

'You have my word.'

Wilson made a show of thinking, face contorting with the effort. He held up a trembling finger. 'There was this guy that Tony mentioned a few times, said that he had thrown some work Tony's way. Maybe if you pressed him, he'd be able to tell you where Tony has gotten to since.'

'Give me this guy's name.'

'What are you going to do to Tony when you find him?'

'That shouldn't be your concern, Bob. Besides, you've already proven your loyalty to him isn't as strong as you first made out. What does it matter to you what happens next?'

Wilson chewed his lip a moment longer. Brogan knew he'd already folded and his actions now were an act, one designed to ease his betrayal of his brother. Brogan allowed him a few seconds more, then again clunked the gun's muzzle on his head to motivate an answer.

'Jeez, man, I'm just trying to remember, and ensuring I get things right. This man you have to go see next, he can usually be found at an autoshop called Charley's, up the road apiece in Portland.'

'He owns the place?'

'If he does, it isn't his name over the door. No, this guy's a southerner, goes by the name of Peabody or something like it. I know that he was giving Tony a few hours a week; my brother's a decent grease monkey, y'know.'

'Peabody, huh?' Brogan glanced over at his buddy, and saw that his pal was nonplussed. His partner had conducted business in Portland before, and knew most of the criminal movers and shakers, and those that required a certain amount of caution to deal with. Whoever this Peabody was, he wasn't on his buddy's radar; kind of indicative that he was nobody to worry about. 'He sounds like a wuss.'

THREE

Exercise in any form should have been an alien concept to Jerome 'Pinky' Leclerc. He towered over most men, was thick at the waist and his legs were as tubular as tree trunks: sweat stood like bullets on his high dark-skinned forehead and his eyes slightly protruded at the effort. A man of his stature and girth had no business walking without the assistance of sticks, let alone moving at the brisk pace he'd set. But Pinky's appearance belied his physicality. He suffered a condition that periodically bloated his legs, but he was otherwise fit and healthy. He was prone to surprise those that assumed him to be slow and cumbersome, and especially those that deemed him a target for their derision. Many a would-be bully had learned to their peril that you didn't poke Pinky Leclerc without suffering swift retaliation.

He was a man of other contradictions.

He was an ex-convict, an ex-gangster, and an ex-illegal arms dealer: the emphasis on *ex*, he kept telling himself. In his mid-forties he'd enjoyed an epiphany, one that had caused a paradigm shift in his lifestyle choices, and had seen him relocating from Baton Rouge, north to Portland, Maine, to be nearer the two people he loved most in the world. If not for Tess and Po's influence, he could only guess at where he might be by now, and no scenario he conjured was a pleasant one. He was under no illusions: his villainy would have grown if left to do so. At the helm of a criminal empire, he'd have become a man whose face he couldn't meet in a mirror, or by now he might've been slain by a rival. Even after abandoning his old ways, attempts had been made on his life; things would have been much worse if he'd stayed in his enemies' crosshairs. Here in Portland, he could enjoy a brisk walk in the morning sunshine without constant fear of execution.

Instead of his Baton Rouge mansion, he now lived in Tess's tiny upper-story apartment above a curios and antiques shop on Cumberland Avenue. The small but homely apartment suited him, and gave access to the nearby fifty-five-acre Deering Oaks Park, which suited him even more. The public park boasted sports facilities, a playground and large pond, and ordinarily was home to Portland Farmers' Market, though that had been somewhat affected by the current pandemic. The loosening of some of the restrictions would soon mean the reopening of the market and bring more visitors to the park. For now Pinky had the expanse of grass and trees mostly to himself. He strode out, pumping his elbows as he headed for the bridge over Deering Oaks ravine. A young mother ambled towards him, pushing a stroller in which burbled a plump toddler. Pinky smiled and nodded in greeting, and the girl made pains not to acknowledge him, turning her face aside and feigning interest in the empty children's splash pool below. Maybe it was his lack of a face-mask that had perturbed her, except he knew he was making a concession for her behavior. There was presently a lot of division in the country, with skin color being used as a weapon by both sides in their presidential campaigns. Being in the minority in Portland, Pinky had noted he was subject to more attention than before – it was a weird time to be black; some of the attention verged on sycophantic, some was blatant hatred, and none of it was welcome. Pinky was not a delicate soul, so the young woman's actions didn't bother him. He was not about to let her spoil his mood.

Sunlight and shadow danced together on the paths, a light breeze stirring the treetops. The sun's warmth was on his skin, and he tilted his face towards it as he picked up pace. Beads of sweat trickled behind his ears and down the back of his neck. His T-shirt held the moisture, and it cooled. With each step he felt hotter air wafting up from his body; each step was one more step towards a higher degree of fitness. If he kept this up, soon he could begin jogging a route around Deering Oaks Park without causing irreparable damage to his knees.

He was simply dressed in T-shirt, jogging pants and sneakers. As a concession he'd added a Gore-Tex harness strapped over one shoulder, which carried a few necessary items. He had his cell phone, doubling for now as an iPod, and some folded cash, as well as an ID card, because it was not uncommon for a black man in a hurry to be stopped by the local cops. As he stepped out towards the pond his cell phone began ringing. He pulled it out of its holder, read the caller's name on the screen and grinned.

'Hey, Nicolas!' He was still unused to Nicolas Villere's nickname despite everyone else calling him Po. 'What d'you want, I'm busy, me?'

'You're busy?'

'Sure I am. I'm taking my permitted daily constitutional, me.'

'You're breathing heavily. Can I hear your big feet slappin' the sidewalk?'

'Yep. I'm doing laps around Deering Oaks Park, and I'm letting nothing spoil my flow.'

'Just let me check . . . yeah, I called the right number. But who is this pretending to be my best friend? The Pinky Leclerc I know does not jog.'

'Least he didn't before this damn lockdown gave him reason to, eh?' said Pinky. 'I've put on about twenty pounds already and I ain't having none of that, no more.'

'Didn't y'hear? Lockdown's bein' relaxed in a day or two, and you'll be able to mix with the rest of society again. How'd you like to enter my and Tess's bubble?'

'Sounds kinky.'

'It isn't. Man, you must be going stir crazy by now. I know I am. It's time you saw a friendly face.'

'Tess's face I can take, not so sure about your ugly puss.'

'Take it or leave it, it's the best I can do.'

'I'll take it, me.'

'How'd you care to expend some of that wasted energy on helping me get the diner shipshape and ready for tradin'?'

'Will Chris and Jazz be there?'

'Yup, both of them.'

'Then count me in. Y'know, there's neither of them that's hard on the eye.'

Po snorted. 'Can't say as I noticed.'

Who was he kidding? Chris and Jazz had the good looks of 1950s movie stars. Pinky was gay, and Chris's pretty boy looks appealed to him, but he could also appreciate a beautiful woman when he saw one, and Jazz was ravishing. Somehow Po felt he might somehow be dishonoring Tess by admitting how gorgeous his restaurant manager was, so wouldn't say.

'He-he!' Pinky vocalized his humor in words, one of many strange speech traits. 'I need something prettier to look at than your brutish Neanderthal mug, Nicolas.'

'You're in Deering Oaks Park,' said Po, changing the subject swiftly, 'you anywhere near the exit onto State Street? If so, I'll pick you up.'

'I'm nearer the Deering Avenue end of the park, but anyways, you don't expect me to go mixing with beautiful people while sweating like a hog? I gotta go home first, me, and shower.'

'Maybe Chris will find you more appealing when you're dripping in sweat.'

'Doubt it. An' sure as hell he won't enjoy my new manly scent. I stink like road-kill, me. I need to shower, Nicolas, and then I'll be happy to come help at Bar-Lesque.'

'I'll swing by Park Avenue, get you there and I'll drop you back home.'

'How long will you be? I'm only a fifteen-minute walk from home, as is. If you're going to be longer I'll—'

'Gimme two minutes and I'll be with you, podnuh.' Po ended the call.

Pinky put his cell safely in the Gore-Tex holder, and struck out again for the exit. He didn't smell anywhere close to as bad as he'd made out, but he'd put in enough effort that his shirt was soaked through, and likely would smell before day's end if he continued wearing it.

The vintage Ford Mustang was waiting by the time Pinky exited onto Deering Avenue. Po had stepped out of the muscle car to smoke.

'Maybe you should throw those things in the trash and join me on my next jog,' Pinky announced.

Po sent a torpedo of smoke into the heavens. 'I like to smoke. I don't like to jog.'

'Doesn't look as if you need to jog, you. How's it everyone else in Maine has put on pounds during this lockdown except for Nicolas Villere?'

'Maybe the nicotine keeps me lean.'

'Then light me up one of those, you.'

Po stubbed his cigarette underfoot, then kicked the stump into a storm drain. 'Your fitness regime trumps mine, Pinky. Keep at it, podnuh, I'm proud of you.'

Pinky backhanded sweat from his forehead. 'You're proud of a wheezing, quaking mound of sweaty blubber?'

'Don't put yourself down, Pinky; I don't hear you wheezing.'

They chuckled together as they got in the car. The passenger seat was still slid back on its rails from the last time that Pinky had been a passenger. 'I take it you and Tess haven't gotten out too often either?'

'We've barely left the house in months. Those Zoom meetings are fine, but it's so good to see you in the flesh, Pinky.'

'Ain't it, though? This sure beats having to shield.'

'That's a point. You want me to mask up?'

'You've made me put up with your ugly face all these years, you, now you want to hide it?' Pinky flapped long fingers. 'If I'm joining your bubble, we'll be close enough to smell each other's halitosis, us, so how's a mask going to help?'

'Yeah, that's what I figured too.'

Po aimed the Mustang at Cumberland Avenue. Before they reached Pinky's place, Po's cell phone began ringing. He tapped the button to pair his phone with his car's stereo system. Having not looked at the phone screen he expected it to be Chris or Jazz enquiring about what was holding him up, or maybe Tess with some errand she wanted him to run: it was none of them.

'Hey, Po,' said a man who sounded as if he gargled with battery acid each morning.

'Geoff, whassup, bra?'

Geoff Audley worked indirectly for Po. Charley, of Charley's Autoshop, managed the place and had his name over the door, but the business was owned by Po. Geoff was one of a few mechanics that Po had been able to keep working throughout the pandemic, others he'd had to furlough, or pay off entirely.

'Charley asked me to call you,' said Geoff in a rasp. 'You know how he dislikes using the phone.'

Pinky was familiar with most of the guys at the garage. Charley, old enough now to be enjoying retirement down in Florida, but clinging desperately to the job he loved, was allegedly one of the best mechanics Po had met, and yet, conversely, he was rubbish when it came to using any type of modern technology. Still, surely he wasn't so useless he couldn't make a phone call he'd delegated to a man whose throat had been riven by cancer.

'There a problem at the autoshop?'

'There was a couple of mugs in here just now, looking for somebody called Anthony Vaughan . . . Wasn't that that guy with the bad eye? Tony whatshisname?' – Geoff checked his assumption with somebody alongside him, likely Charley – 'Yeah, Tony One-Eye. When they were told he didn't work here any more, they demanded to speak to somebody called Peabody, a southerner by all accounts. Charley made them no wiser, though he guessed they musta misheard your nickname when folks round here still called you Po'boy.'

'They still around?'

'They left, but they warned they'd be back.'

'Hey, Geoff, just tell Charley to take the phone will ya.'

There was some fumbling and whispered urging before Charley came on, sounding a bit out of breath. 'Hey, Po! Sorry, but you know I don't like these new-fangled cell phones and stuff.'

'I'll get you over your aversion yet, even if it means draggin' you kickin' and screamin' into the twenty-first century,' Po promised. 'Tell me about these guys.'

'They're bad news.'

'Yeah, I got that; otherwise you wouldn't have had Geoff call me. Tell me about them.'

'Couple of wannabe hard-asses, you know the type. Thought they could walk in here and throw their weight around; I ensured I was holding a heavy wrench when I was talking with them, let them know I wasn't taking any of their shit.'

'They were looking for Tony, huh? They say why?'

'Nope, only that they wanted him bad.'

'And then they demanded to speak with me?'

'Nah, they said *Peabody*, but I think they musta gotten their wires crossed somewhere, seeing as you're the only southerner round here.'

'Peabody,' Po echoed.

Pinky chuckled under his breath. 'Could've been worse, could've been Peckerhead.'

Po ruminated a moment, before concluding, 'So whoever it was sent them after me doesn't know me well.' He checked the clock on the dash. It was almost 9 a.m. 'Listen, I've got to run by the diner, but I'll be with you in the next hour.'

'You don't need to come over, son,' said Charley, 'I'm not afraid of trouble. And besides, I've still got my hand on a wrench. Those guys come back and start throwing their weight around, I'll show them the error of their ways.'

'I only need to open up shop. Chris and Jazz can handle the rest without me. I'll be there soon' – he glimpsed over at Pinky and received a nod, all thoughts of showering first having fled – 'and I'll bring backup.'

FOUR

Tess showered, then dressed in fresh clothing, and again went out onto the porch and sat in the swing. In the kitchen the ployes had gone cold. She had left her laptop sitting on the porch swing, and she settled it on her thighs as she tucked her feet under her backside. She looked at the emails on her screen, not a single one of them held a promise of employment, nor an ember of excitement.

She powered down the laptop, setting it aside on the swing.

She stared into the middle distance, barely aware of her surroundings. Lately she'd found herself sitting in a similar way, her usually sharp mind busy doing nothing, almost as if a blanket of cotton wool muffled her. She thought of her condition as Covid fog – nothing dangerous, only a condition brought on by weeks of home arrest and tedium. Much more of this inactivity and she'd probably turn to stone, as if she was under the petrifying gaze of a gorgon. She needed something to occupy her mind, a puzzle to solve, a quandary to get her teeth into. She stood and jumped down from the porch, and walked aimlessly across the front yard. She bent and plucked a weed that had broken through the crushed shells that formed a hardstand for Po's car. If she checked, she'd bet there were dozens of weeds. For now gardening was not a solution to her boredom. She rubbed the extracted weed between her palms, crushing it into a green mush, then headed back towards the house to wash the pulp from her hands.

Tires on crushed shells drew her attention and she watched a dark blue but otherwise nondescript panel van pull into the spot usually reserved for Po.

Two figures sat in the cab, and the one in the passenger seat greeted her with a wave. Tess raised her own hand in acknowledgment, and immediately regretted it: her palm was still green with mulched vegetation.

As the van's passenger door opened, and a man swung out she moved to greet him. She'd barely taken a step when the skin prickled between her shoulder blades. She'd been so pleased to see another human face that she'd allowed caution to slip.

She stopped and took a closer look, first at the van, and next at the man approaching, regarding her with a beaming grin. His features were amiable enough, but there was a gleam in his eyes that looked too feverish. He held out his hand as if it were an offer to shake in greeting.

Tess took a step backwards to retain distance, holding up a finger to stall him, and she dug a surgical mask from her hip pocket and pulled it on, one-handed. The man got the message. He stopped in his tracks, and lowered his hand. He shrugged, indicating he hadn't come prepared with a facemask. He gestured towards the van, as if the driver might be able to help, and Tess's gaze fell on the back of his hand. It was covered by what appeared to be a self-inflicted tattoo, the skin almost entirely blue, as were the digits to the first knuckle. His other hand was similarly inked, she saw, and when she again checked his face she could tell he'd undergone a procedure to have tattoos concealed – only partially successfully – beneath the outer corner of his left eye. She knew enough to recognize a gang or prison tat when she saw one. She must not be judgmental; her lover and their best friend had both served considerable sentences in prison and they'd since proven to be the best of men.

'How can I help you?'

Po's house was at the end of a road, and the Presumpscot River bordered his land; you only reached his house by design, rarely by accident. She wondered which had brought these men to the house, and still couldn't shake the feeling she should be more careful around them.

'I was hoping to speak with Nicolas Villere.' The man took a look around at their surroundings and nodded appreciatively. 'This is his place, right?'

'Who are you?'

'The name's Brogan, ma'am, but I don't suppose that will mean anything to Mister Villere. We aren't acquainted: I hope he might be able to help me find a mutual friend.'

The small hairs on the back of her neck bristled. 'Nicolas isn't home, although I do expect him back soon.'

'Would you mind if we waited here for him?'

'You've given me your name, and a reason for wanting to speak to Nicolas, but not why you need to find this friend.'

'Yeah,' said Brogan and offered her a conspiratorial wink, 'the subject's kind of between me and Villere, y'see?'

'Is that right? Then you'll understand when I ask you to leave and wait elsewhere. I don't want to appear unduly rude . . . *but*. What with the social distancing rules and all, I think it's best if you go somewhere else and I'll tell Nicolas you dropped by. Want to leave me your cell phone number and I'll have him call you when he gets home?'

'How's about you ring him now and have him come home?'

'He's driving, he won't answer his cell phone while he's driving.'

Brogan stopped dead. He didn't speak, he didn't move. He only appraised her, and again she noticed that strange feverishness in his gaze. She wondered if he was high on something, amphetamine or cocaine perhaps, but if so, his behavior didn't fit with his sudden stillness.

Finally he broke away to look over at the van. The man at

the steering wheel stared back, his mouth pursed in silent question.

Tess took another subtle step away. Her stomach cramped. She had worked in law enforcement for long enough, and dealt with enough suspicious people to know when their behavior was dishonest. These men showing up uninvited at the house felt decidedly wrong.

'Why do you feel the need to lie to me, miss?' Brogan's amiable look had not fallen from him, but his tone had altered. Apparently he was not a man disposed to being lied to.

'In what way am I lying?'

He gestured at the house. 'Villere isn't due home soon, and I'm betting he would answer his cell if he saw it was you calling.'

He was correct on both counts, but Tess wasn't going to admit it. 'I'll ask again that you leave and wait elsewhere.'

Brogan smiled. 'You're a lone woman, and we are strangers to you, and you've every right to be worried about us showing up like this. It's all right for you to say so, miss, and I'd respect those as reasons for asking us to leave. But I must say, I'm offended that you've outright lied. Lies are totally unnecessary.'

Tess didn't need to explain her actions to this stranger. It was enough that he and his pal had turned up uninvited on Po's property with dubious intent, let alone that Brogan had then challenged her over her choice of words. 'I'm going to ask you once again to please leave and wait elsewhere. If you'd like to leave your details I'll have Nicolas contact you when he gets back, otherwise . . .'

Brogan leaned in and exhaled sharply. It was intentional intimidation, using her fear of viral transmission against her. He sneered when she drew back, turning her face aside. 'Otherwise *what*? What exactly do you think you can do?'

'OK,' said Tess sharply, 'I've heard enough. Leave right now, or I'll call the police.'

'Here's a better idea. Call Villere. Get him back here.'

'I'm calling nine-one-one.' Her phone, forgotten for a few minutes while she'd plucked weeds, was lying on the porch swing alongside her laptop. She backed away another step then turned swiftly to vault up the steps onto the porch.

'You aren't.' Brogan grabbed for her.

Tess's head was yanked back torturously. Brogan's fingers were entwined in her hair. He dragged her away from the house. A croak escaped her. Her body threatened to seize, to give in to a stronger force. Tess couldn't allow it. She spun, her face bleached of color, and kicked at his shins. He retained his grasp on her hair, but danced his feet back, laughing, as if her reaction was all a bit of fun. Tess was dragged after him, bent awkwardly at the waist to avoid her hair ripping out at the roots.

The second man got out the van. He was bald and older than Brogan, maybe fifty pounds heavier too. He could easily have scooped up Tess while she struggled to free her hair, but he didn't approach further than rounding the front of the van. He held a pistol: when he had a gun, he didn't have to help physically subdue her to demand compliance. He pointed the pistol at her, even as Brogan withdrew his fingers and allowed her to stand straighter. Brogan shook some yanked strands of hair from between his fingers as he stared directly at her. Tess pushed back her now unruly locks, so that she could clearly see her enemies.

'That was totally uncalled for,' Brogan told her.

'You don't say?' She tried taking a subtle step back, but the gunman shook his big head at her and wagged the barrel of the pistol.

'Let me get that cell phone for you.' Brogan smiled and nodded as he by-passed her and stepped up onto the porch. His faux joviality grated on her senses. She knew that well-mannered sociopathic criminals were at home in the pages of fiction novels and movies, but rarely in reality. Yet here one was.

Brogan tossed her the phone. 'Call Villere, have him come back.'

'No. You've just proven you have bad intentions towards him. There's no way I'm having my man drive into a trap.'

'I only want to speak to him, to ask him the location of a mutual friend.'

'After *this*? You expect him to help you after what you've done to me?' She held his gaze once more. 'You really don't know my fiancé, do you?'

FIVE

The Ford Mustang's tires whistled over asphalt, only making sharper squeals when Po took corners too fast and tight. On several occasions the car's rear drifted as he took longer curves, but they were controlled maneuvers to get home faster than if he drove at the speed limit. Because of the lockdown there were few vehicles on the roads, so Po practically had a free run. Pinky clung to the door handle, or braced a hand against the roof to stop from tumbling into Po's lap, or worse, out of his open window: his girth wouldn't allow either, but the forces did their best to achieve both. If not for the urgency he'd have laughed at the fun wild ride.

Po wasn't laughing. His teeth were clenched and his eyebrows knitted so tightly they formed an arrowhead. He had abandoned his visit to Charley's Autoshop, and to Bar-Lesque, the instant that Tess had rung his cell phone with news of the armed visitors to their home. Other than a knife he carried in a sheath tucked into his high-topped boots, Po was unarmed, but news that the strangers had guns didn't slow him. Pinky was totally unarmed, but hadn't questioned Po's decision to return home with haste.

As they approached Po's house they were on high alert, watching for the gunmen. Po throttled the Mustang up the road that dead-ended at his property. If the gunmen were nearby, then they had to have taken their van off road and down by the Presumpscot River. He brought the car to a controlled halt, though the tires sunk a tad deeper into the crushed shells than normal, and kicked some up behind the trunk in a pink and grey fan. Po was out of the car in a second and taking long strides towards the house. Tess waited, seated on the swing on the porch. She got up to meet him, while Pinky also extricated his bulk from the muscle car. Po's head was on a gimbal, his eyes darting as he sought foes. Tess ducked under one arm and leaned against his chest. He hugged her briefly, without ever lowering his guard.

Pinky backed from the car, watching the entrance gate, expecting to see the van come barreling in at any second.

'Where are they?' Po demanded.

Tess stepped out from under his armpit. She held out a piece of cardboard. 'They left, but the main guy – he calls himself Brogan – said to give you this.'

Po checked out the handwritten note on a torn off-strip of cardboard: it looked as if it had come from a Dunkin' Donuts box. Tess didn't have to read the words again as she was obviously familiar with them.

Let's meet, Brogan had written, *with no funny business. I only want information on Anthony Vaughan. You have my promise.*

'Who is this joker?' Po scowled. 'Just like that, he comes here and threatens you, then thinks things will be OK between us? The fool has another think comin'.'

'You see where he says you have his promise?'

'Yeah. Sounds kinda weird, y'ask me.'

'He's deliberately being obtuse . . . see, he warned me that if you didn't answer his terms, he'd be back and *that's* his promise.'

Also written on the cardboard were instructions for where and when Brogan expected Po to show up: the parking lot adjacent to Widgery Wharf at 11 o'clock. He had chosen what would ordinarily be a busy public place, but in current times the wharves were as deserted as everywhere else in Portland. Nevertheless, Brogan had made an effort at showing his willingness to meet at a location neither party could normally go armed, not without alerting too many witnesses and bringing down the police on them.

'What time have we got?'

'Five after ten,' Tess said, after a quick glance at the time on her cell phone. 'What? You're seriously considering meeting him?'

'Don't see how I can avoid it, Tess. Would you rather I let them come back here again, bringin' fresh trouble to our door?'

'I got the make and model of their van, plus their license number; I could have Alex put out an APB and have them pulled in.' Alex Grey was one of Tess's brothers, and a serving police officer with Portland PD.

'No, hold off on involving the cops, will ya.'

'Why? Those thugs shouldn't be allowed to behave like this.'

'I agree, but I'd like to know exactly why they're lookin' for Tony, before they get chased off.'

He touched her hair. She had made an attempt at straightening it, but there was an incriminating lock or two sticking out. 'Besides, that sumbitch laid his hands on you, and I ain't lettin' that go.'

'You're forgetting that Brogan and his friend were armed. They had pistols, Po.'

'So go get your grandpa's gun for me and it'll help even things up.'

Tess kept her grandfather's service revolver locked safely in a gun box, only rarely taking it out when it was absolutely necessary. Judging by her expression, it surprised her that Po had suggested giving it to him.

He flicked a hand at their friend. 'It ain't for me. Brogan and his pal have no idea about Pinky. Give him the gun and he'll be my ace card.'

'While I'd normally agree to giving Pinky the gun, I'd rather it was me who went with you.'

Po shook his head.

'Don't give me any chauvinistic bullshit about me being a girl and possibly getting hurt,' she warned. He knew better. Tess had proven to be as resilient and tough as any man he'd ever fought alongside. 'I'm coming with you, Po.'

'I wouldn't suggest anything less, but those guys know about you. They won't know about Pinky until we need him to show his hand.' He turned his attention on their friend. 'You good with my idea, podnuh?'

'I'm up for anything, me,' Pinky grinned, ''specially if it means getting out and about for a few hours. No disrespect intended, pretty Tess, that apartment of yours is nice, but I'm going la-la looking at the same four walls, me.' He held out his palm as if she was able to slap the revolver in it that instant. 'Gimme it, and I'll show those bums they messed with the wrong crew when they messed with you.'

'Why do I feel this could be a bad idea?'

Po shrugged. 'You don't have to come. You can wait here, stay safe, and I'll be back the instant I know Brogan and his pal are no longer a threat.'

'What, and miss finding out what the hell's going on? You know me better than that, Po. I'm aching to find out why they're looking for this Vaughan guy, even if we've to pry the answers out of them at gunpoint.'

SIX

A trio traveling in one vehicle might attract unwanted attention from law officers keen on enforcing the social-distancing rules brought in to help control the pandemic. To avoid any awkward situations with the local PD, and for obviously strategical reasons too, Po took Pinky back to Cumberland Avenue to collect his own car. Pinky was still garbed in sweat-dampened exercise clothing, but there was no time for a shower and change of clothes. He jogged up the creaking stairs, entered the upper-story apartment, and was out of sight for less than a minute before re-emerging, and carrying a heavy-looking gym bag to his SUV. He pushed the bag into the front passenger footwell, then got in the driver's seat. He flicked a salute, and started the car.

Po left, returning to collect Tess. Pinky headed directly to the wharfside to get set up; Tess had assured Po that by the time he got back she'd have dressed and gotten ready for a showdown with Brogan. When he again drew the Mustang to a halt in his front yard, he saw that she was good to her word: she'd dressed in cargo pants and a brown bomber jacket over a sweatshirt, and she wore sneakers, and, her hair had been dried and styled – the evidence of where Brogan had grabbed her hair had disappeared, but it was still indelibly ingrained in Po's mind.

Tess settled into the passenger seat, even as she pulled on a cloth mask, covering her from chin to bridge of the nose. It was a pointless exercise as far as controlling the virus went – the two were intimate, eating, sleeping, making love together – but it would help dissuade any questions from overzealous Covid-19 enforcement officers who might spot them.

'You got what you need?' Po asked.

She puffed out her mask, tapped the bulge in her purse, and he took it that was where she'd put her grandfather's service revolver: after some more deliberation it had been decided that having two weapons was better than one, the reason for Pinky fetching a gun from his apartment.

Tess shifted in the seat, and he noted the movement of her lips under the mask. 'Say again,' he encouraged.

'I called Jazz and told her you wouldn't be joining her this morning. She was fine with it, said they'd already gotten in with Chris's keys and have the prep well under way.'

'Great.' He hadn't gotten back to Charley at the autoshop since announcing he was on his way. 'Do me a favor, will ya, and let Charley know I've been sidetracked.'

He could have made the call himself, using the hands-free facility between his paired phone and car, but his mind was now fully on the meeting with Brogan. There was no room in his head for distractions. Tess took out her cell phone and brought up the number for the autoshop. Po spun the Mustang around in the drive and set off. Ordinarily it would take fifteen minutes to drive to the wharves; that would leave little time for getting in place before Brogan's arrival. The bonus of a literal lockdown meant the roads were much quieter than usual, with only key workers out and about. Po put his foot down, intending shaving five minutes off the usual journey time. He completed the drive in nine minutes; fortunate not to have been stopped by either of the two patrol cars they'd passed. It paid to have a recognizable car, a future brother-in-law in the local PD, and a retired sheriff's deputy sergeant onboard.

Po parked on an adjacent pier. The Cushing's Island ferry usually ensured that the lot there was filled with cars, but not that day. There were few other vehicles in evidence, reminding him it was sometimes equally important to have an unrecognizable car. He left it partially hidden from those on the adjacent wharf by a red-brick building housing a savings bank. He checked all around for Brogan's van, trying to find it from the brief description Tess had given. She had a much clearer idea of what it looked like, and she had also memorized its license tag. He checked with her for any sighting. She shook her head, and walked alongside him clutching her purse against her side.

Po had surmised that Brogan would've ensured he was in place to witness Po's arrival. He had believed the man, or his pal, would've had the sense not to park their van exactly where Brogan said they'd be waiting at eleven o'clock. For his part in maneuvers, Pinky had agreed to park further down the commercial strip and make his way to Widgery Wharf on foot. Perhaps that was what Brogan had in mind too, because there was no sign of their van on the expanses of concrete that made up the parking lots serving Chandlers, Widgery and Union Wharfs.

'What time we got?'

Tess dipped her spare hand in her pocket and took a brief glance at her cell phone. 'Ten minutes.'

'The punks are playin' things tight.'

'I think they're already here.'

'You're probably right, but where?'

'Look.' Tess made no attempt at disguising her interest. In fact, she had to go on her tiptoes and crane, to get a better view of what had caught her eye. 'That van way down there, where the old wooden pier begins. It could be Brogan's.'

'You think?'

'It's the same model and color blue. I'm as sure as I can be from all the way back here.'

Po nodded. He had the advantage of being a head taller. He could see several trucks and vans parked at the entrance to the pier; beyond were old wooden sheds and mountains of stacked lobster cages waiting for the time when more of the fishing fleet would put back out to sea. The van appeared empty.

His gaze withdrew along the wharf, taking note of the few cars parked alongside the owners' corresponding boats. There were no signs of life. He glanced down at Tess. She chewed her bottom lip, frowning hard. It was her first time in this part of town in months and its deserted aspect must feel weird. He didn't like the sensation either but didn't allow it to slow him. He aimed for the blue van, confident that Tess would accompany him all the way. She hadn't put away her cell phone: she must have hit Pinky's number, and now spoke loud enough for him to hear. Her mask hid her subterfuge well.

'The van's located on the working pier of Widgery Wharf. We

can't see its occupants but they must be nearby. How close are you, Pinky?'

'I'm close, and got you both covered.'

'Cool. I'll leave my cell on so you can hear what's going on.' Tess slipped her phone in her breast pocket. 'You still hear me?'

'Loud and clear, me. You want to give me a safe word, pretty Tess?'

'I think you'll know if and when the crap hits the fan,' she assured him.

Tess had to double-time to keep up with Po. He walked with the gait of a prowling big cat but his long legs carried him across the ground surprisingly fast. Already they'd halved the distance from where Tess had first noticed the van. Closer now, she affirmed it was Brogan's van. She spoke the license tag aloud from memory, and Po squinted, confirming the details against the plate on the van.

They closed in on the van, alert to any movement. Other than the birds overhead, there was none.

'Want to wait here and cover me?'

Tess slid her hand into her purse and gripped her revolver, but continued on, walking alongside him. Once they reached the van, she halted, quickly checking the empty cab, then turned and placed her back to the hood while she scanned the nearest parked trucks. Po also perused the stacks of lobster pots, and the nearest ramshackle work sheds. He rapped three times in quick succession on the panel van. He stepped back and to one side, ensuring he was a target and not Tess. It also allowed her to cover him without fear of catching him in crossfire.

The door on the side of the van slid open on squeaking rollers. A big bald man stepped down onto the pier, working one knee to get it to move more freely – he must've been sitting with his legs bent sharply for a good few minutes at least. The next figure hopped down spryly, and with a grin on his surprisingly youthful features. Po had pictured an older man, being that Brogan was the obvious leader of the two. Po checked out the hands of both men: neither held pistols, but they were only seconds away from being able to draw and aim them. He stepped in sharply, and his fists blurred as he struck three piston-like strikes into the jaw of the bald man. The flunky was knocked back against the open side door, and then his already weakened knee gave way and he sat down hard on the stained planks of the pier. His mouth hung slack and his eyes rolled, on the verge of unconsciousness.

Po readjusted his angle, and he could have easily blasted a series of punches in Brogan's face, but that was not his immediate intention. Instead he jabbed an index finger in Brogan's direction and the guy flinched, threw up his hands, but laughed, as if everything was all a case of good-natured banter. 'You're gonna get that next,' Po warned, but Brogan's eyes shone, and he rolled his tongue in his bottom lip. He clapped his tattooed hands like a trained sea lion.

'Tactfully handled, Villere,' Brogan chortled. 'Bravo!'

Po exchanged a glimpse with Tess. Was this guy nuts?

Tess drew the revolver far enough from her bag to show it to Brogan, without making it obvious to anyone else she had him under guard. Spotting the gun had no effect on his mood.

'I mean it, man,' Brogan went on, nodding enthusiastically at Po. 'Those were some Chuck Norris-style moves you just pulled on Walsh. Are you a black belt, Villere, or something else?'

Po ignored his questions. The asshole didn't deserve polite conversation after manhandling Tess the way he had. However, it was difficult raising his ire enough to strike Brogan when he was acting so affable. Po snarled, more to galvanize himself into an appropriate response. 'Are you soft in the goddamn head?'

'I promised there'd be no funny business if you came here and met me. I'm only living up to my side of the bargain.' Brogan checked out Walsh's semi-conscious state. He grinned lopsidedly. 'I'm unsure how I'd describe *that*; would you define that as funny business?'

'You also *promised* my fiancé you'd be back to hurt her if I failed to show. Nobody touches her, d'you hear?'

'I didn't say I'd hurt her, only that I'd be back.' He stared at Tess, challenging her to disagree. 'I told you how important it was I spoke with your fella.'

Tess coughed in scorn. 'You dragged me around by my hair, you stopped me from calling for help.'

'And you barked my shins, kicking me like that. I'd say we're even.'

'We're nowhere close to even,' growled Po.

'She was going to call the cops, Villere. Look at us, man' –
Brogan again cast an amused grin at his fallen companion – 'do
any of us really want the cops sticking their noses into our
business?'

'This is how you conduct business, is it?' Po said. 'With violence
and threats?'

'I guess I'm not unique, eh?'

Walsh rubbed his hands over his face, groaning deeply. Po hadn't
used full power in his blows, but enough to shake his brain inside
his cranium; it'd be a few minutes yet before Walsh was able to
think clearly. Despite that, Po gave Tess a quick glance, which
she deciphered without question. She stooped down and checked
Walsh for weapons. She found his pistol in a shoulder holster
under his jacket. Po stood ready, should Brogan decide then
was a good time to reach for his own gun. The young man only
watched as Tess stripped Walsh's pistol, dropped the magazine,
and ejected the round from the chamber. She threw the component
parts inside the panel van.

Brogan shrugged at her. 'We don't need guns to parlay.'

'Who says we are parlaying?' asked Po.

Brogan wagged a finger between them. 'I thought that was
what we were doing. You have some info I need, and I'm happy
to reward you for it.'

'There's nothing you have that I want,' said Po. 'Truth is, I
came here with one intention only, and that was to beat some
manners into you.'

'I think we've gone beyond silly threats, don't you? I mean,
you beat Walsh like a drum, and yet you haven't laid a finger on
me. Admit it, your curiosity about why I'm seeking Anthony
Vaughan has been piqued.'

'Why is it so important you find him?' Tess asked.

Brogan chuckled again. 'Oh, I see now. It isn't you whose
curiosity is piqued is it, Villere?' He turned and eyed Tess directly.
'You're the boss woman. Are you the one who wears the pants in
this relationship, miss?'

Po struck Brogan with frightening speed. The man, stunned, sat
down hard in the van's open doorway. Po loomed over him, fists
cocked. 'You want to throw aspersions on my manhood again?
Come on. Stand up and I'll knock you on your goddamn ass again.'

Tess grasped Po's elbow. He was riled, only a second away from shrugging her off. Brogan was a nut job, and a cheeky son of a bitch too. When Po knocked out Walsh, it was a strategic tactic designed to take the dangerous triggerman out of action, now he wished he'd beaten Brogan's face to liver instead. He'd missed his moment now that Tess wanted to interrogate him.

Brogan touched fingertips to his mouth. They came away glistening redly. 'Was there any need for that?'

'Why's it so important you find Anthony Vaughan?' Tess countered.

'Because it's my goddamn job,' Brogan said, and in an instant his demeanor had changed from faux joviality to seething. He stood, and it came as a surprise to Po when Brogan flicked his bloody fingers out, and from his sleeve appeared a concealed knife – obviously it was affixed to a sliding mechanism attached to his forearm. He aimed at Po, even as Tess swore under her breath and brought up her grandfather's revolver. Po rocked from one side to the other, even as his nearest hand darted to grasp or knock Brogan's weapon skyward.

Glass exploded next to Brogan. A second later it was as though somebody punched the van's metal wall; it buckled, and a hole appeared at the center of the delve. Brogan dropped, as did Po as the silenced rifle sent a third bullet into the van. Before the young man could recover, Po dipped to his boot, came out with his own knife and lunged, spearing the point at Brogan's throat.

SEVEN

Tess had longed for some kind of activity to shake her out of the funk she'd fallen into. She had needed something to engage her mind, to get her blood pumping through her veins, and whether she'd admit it to Po or not, she'd thought that Brogan's arrival was just what the doctor had ordered. She loved to solve a mystery, and why the man was chasing Tony Vaughan needed to be answered. When Po had been adamant about meeting Brogan's terms and coming here to the wharves, she'd been secretly excited at the prospect; no way on earth was she going to stay at home and miss the action. She'd expected raised voices and perhaps a punch or two thrown in anger. But never had she expected the situation to devolve into a blood and guts knife fight.

And rifle fire!

Reacting to the imminent threat to Po's life, Pinky had let loose with a volley of three shots, smashing glass and holing the van. His action was shocking in one respect, but necessary and had the desired result. Brogan flinched for cover, but then Po had his knife out and the situation had degenerated further. Tess knew from experience how adept he was with a blade, and feared the fight would end now with blood drawn. Both men postured and swayed, seeking an opening, and then Po darted in.

Pinky's rifle was top end, and was fitted with a suppressor. The retorts were dull thwacks, heard from a distance separated by concrete and wooden shacks. The trio of shots was not in earshot of any witness other than those beside the van, and it was all their saving grace. Tess hoped to bring the fight to swift conclusion, and probably the most direct would be to fire a warning bullet from her grandfather's revolver. However, doing so would have the opposite result to Pinky's warning rounds, as her gun would be heard far and wide and would attract attention. Tess acted, and it was all she could think of to halt Po from opening Brogan's throat: she grappled Po's knife hand, forcing her fiancé aside. She brayed at Brogan to quit the madness and her voice must have held more assertiveness than she felt, because the man staggered in place and lowered his knife hand: he visibly wilted. He took a clumsy couple of steps backwards and again sat down hard on the van's step. He blinked, surprised by the rapid turn of events, even though they were partly of his making.

'Let me at the son of a bitch!' Po snarled, and he sidestepped so that he could get past her.

Risking Brogan stabbing her in the back, Tess got between them, and forced Po to move back. She was careful never to point the revolver at him; simply holding the gun posed a danger. But it was too early to put the gun away: Brogan was still armed with the wrist-knife, and most likely with a pistol.

'This has gone far enough,' she snapped, despite Po's actions being wholly a result of trying to protect her. She aimed her next words at Brogan. 'This is ridiculous! You said it's your job to find Anthony Vaughan; yet here you are acting like a small-time hood. How does it help anyone by resorting to violence like this?'

'I wasn't the one to throw the first punch,' Brogan said, sounding weary.

'You manhandled Tess,' Po snarled over her shoulder, 'that was the first aggressive move.'

'I was wrong. I was worried she was about to call the cops and reacted . . . well, I reacted out of panic. The way I did just now.' He held up the blade, shook his head at what he'd almost resorted to doing. 'I drew my knife out of panic. I'm sorry. I was wrong. I'm . . . I'm gonna put it away now.'

'Yeah, you do that,' Po snarled, 'or it'll end up sticking out of your skinny ass.'

'Po?' Tess cautioned. Things had de-escalated nicely, it wouldn't do for her man to send everything avalanching into chaos again.

He held up an apologetic hand. 'Put away your blade and unstrap it from your arm. Do that, and I'll put mine away too.'

'Deal,' said Brogan.

'Where's your pistol?' asked Tess.

'You already took it away from Anderson.'

Thinking back to when they'd first arrived at Po's house, Tess now recalled that it was Anderson Walsh who had come out of the van, toting a pistol. Brogan hadn't showed one then, or since. But she couldn't take that chance.

'I need to search you. Unless you allow me to clear you of any weapons, we can't continue.'

'Not politely, at any rate,' added Po.

'I can reassure you I'm not carrying.'

'Just remember,' Tess cautioned, 'that we've a friend out there who is very good with a rifle. He fired three times and missed, each of those shots was intended to miss. He won't miss if you pose a threat to either of us again.'

'Where is he?' Brogan wondered. The angle and trajectory of the gunfire suggested a location on a nearby pier of the mysterious sniper.

Tess declined to answer. Neither would she utter Pinky's identity for now, not while their friend was still their ace card.

'Just know that he's nearby and has you in his sights.'

Brogan squirmed uncomfortably. He gestured to show he was at his most unthreatening as he braced the tip of his knife against the van's step and forced it back on its sprung lever. The knife clicked home, again hidden by his sleeve.

'Take it off,' Po ordered.

Brogan unbuckled the contraption from around his forearm, and following a nod from Tess he tossed it into the van alongside Walsh's disassembled pistol.

'Stand up and turn around,' Tess instructed.

Brogan did so, and Po patted him down, brisk and methodical. He stepped away, nodding. Brogan was unarmed. Po turned his attention to Anderson Walsh. By now the man was sitting up, holding his ringing head in his hands: he gave no resistance as Po went through his pockets, then swiftly patted him down.

'Stay where you are,' Po told the man, then as an afterthought added, 'you're better off where you are. Brogan, you sit on the van step again, and no funny business.'

'Funny business was never my intention, remember?'

Po flapped open a wallet he'd taken from Brogan's pocket. The younger man's eyes widened, but he controlled his response this time. Po read the name off several bank and credit cards: Bryce W. Brogan.

A driver's license and several other ID cards confirmed Brogan's identity. Po next checked out Walsh's ID: his full name was Anderson Wayne Walsh. He flashed both wallet contents at Tess and briskly brought her up to speed. Both men's details showed addresses in California, not Maine. Nothing in either man's wallets hinted at their employment statuses and definitely not who sent them to find Anthony Vaughan.

Tess always believed the adage, 'if you don't ask you don't get'.

'Who are you working for?'

'Are you a cop or something?' Brogan appeared genuinely interested. 'It's just you have that look about you, and your manner-isms are those of a cop, too.'

'You came to our house and threatened me. I'd've thought checking out who you were messing with was the first thing you should've done.'

'Yeah, that was my bad,' Brogan accepted. 'We got a lead about some dude called Peabody and from there traced him to your partner.'

'Freakin' *Peabody*,' Po muttered darkly. 'How'd that name lead you to me?'

'One of those mechanics down at your shop, he followed us out after that old Charley character kicked us out. For a few bucks he put us right about where we'd gone wrong with your name' – he eyed Po – 'it's actually Po'boy, right?'

'Wrong,' said Po, and caught a frown of misunderstanding from Brogan.

'Regardless,' Brogan went on, 'he steered us right with your *actual* name – Nicolas Villere – and I was able to pull up your address easily enough.'

'Quite the dogged detective, huh? And you thought it permissible to go there and try threatenin' my girl?'

'I only ever wanted to talk.'

'Bullshit,' said Po.

'We're talking now, right?'

'We're talking,' Tess agreed, 'but I'm still waiting for an answer to my question: who is your employer?'

'Can't really say.'

'I take it your silence isn't out of client confidentiality.'

'Let's just say that Tony Vaughan wronged somebody he shouldn't have, and now he must make amends.'

'You think we're going to allow you to hurt him?'

'I'm not going to hurt him. Not purposefully. It's only my job to locate him, and take him back to face the music.'

'That's why you've a spring-loaded blade up your sleeve, huh?' Po said cynically.

'What's he allegedly done?' Tess pressed on.

'Nothing alleged about it.'

She wagged a finger between Brogan and Walsh. 'You're supposed to be some kind of detectives?'

Brogan laughed at how ridiculous her question sounded.

'They're a pair of goddamn criminals,' Po offered.

Brogan was more astute than he'd first made out. 'You guys seem to know what you're doing. I've pegged you as an ex-cop' – he raised an eyebrow at Tess – 'but not you, Villere. You're something else, right? One thing I know for sure, you're not a simple mechanic. You guys *are* some kind of detectives, right, but you're the *private* type?'

'Let's just say you should be happy we chose to deal with you personally rather than get the cops involved. You'd be going to jail for drawing your knife.'

'I think having a sniper blow holes in our van levels out my indiscretion, yeah?' Brogan's grin had crept back in place. Tess was unsure if it was an act to disarm her, or if the man genuinely found the situation humorous. 'And look at poor ol' Walshy. He's gonna be nursing a sore chin for days.'

Po eyed the man he'd knocked out dispassionately.

'Thing is,' said Brogan, 'I'm not the type to hold a grudge, and I hope you guys can be big enough to forgive and forget too. See, my reason for asking you here is I have a proposition to make.'

'If it's about us finding Vaughan on your behalf, then no dice,' said Tess.

'Hmmm. You didn't even hear how much I was going to offer. Is business so good at the moment you can turn work down that easily?'

'You couldn't pay enough to make us want to work for you,' said Po.

'You might be surprised.'

'Isn't going to happen,' Tess added.

'It's a shame. From what you've shown me here I was certain you were the guys for the job.'

'What?' Po spat between his feet, a signal he was losing all respect for Brogan. 'This was some kind of job interview? Bullshit, bra.'

'You don't want to work for me,' said Brogan, and he set his mouth in a humorless grin, 'fine. So, at least from here on, don't work against me, huh? You knocked Walsh on his ass, and you put me in my place, let's call it quits right now, and move on. What do you say?'

'As I already said,' Tess replied, 'we won't allow you to harm Anthony Vaughan.'

EIGHT

'So, there's no imagining a day ahead where you back off and allow Brogan to hunt down Tony Vaughan,' said Po with a wry twist of one cheek.

'You know me too well. We don't owe Tony anything,' Tess said. 'We could be sticking our noses in business we'd be better staying clear of. But, somehow, I don't believe Brogan when he says he wishes Tony no harm. His were not the actions of a rational person.'

'I might have enflamed the situation, goin' in heavy-handed like I did.'

'As you pointed out, Brogan was first to grow aggressive when he came to the house and threatened me.'

'Yeah, I still regret beating Walsh when it was Brogan that laid hands on you. I should've done a number on his fool head instead, then chased the son-of-a-bitch outta town.'

They had left Widgery Wharf, having first watched while a semi-competent Anderson Walsh drove the van and Brogan away. Back at Po's Mustang, Tess asked Pinky to meet them at Bar-Lesque, rather than blow his cover by joining them there on the pier. Po had driven them to his bar, conscious of a possible tail, but spotting none. He was still of the opinion that Brogan was a rank amateur when it came to his investigative skills. He was unsure that Brogan was as lackadaisical as he made out though, and believed that his unassuming nature was a well-developed act designed to lower the guard of potential enemies. Those tattoos on the backs of his hands were troubling, as was the faint scarring on his face: the scar denoted a past Brogan was determined to keep from the general populace. The probability he'd get a second opportunity at straightening out Brogan was pretty damn high.

Only a few select bulbs lighted Bar-Lesque and there was a dry funky smell inside. The atmosphere was reminiscent of the dive bar it once was, before Po had taken over and reinvigorated it.

The diner had been closed far too long, but thankfully was on the verge of reopening. Life was about to return. Chris and Jazz and a couple of the other servers they'd drafted in to help beavered away in the background, but their voices were muted, the soft clatters and knocks they made distant enough not to intrude. The sound of Pinky entering via one of the rear service doors was a cacophony by comparison. The previously silent sniper was vociferous with his greetings for the staff he hadn't seen in months. Po thought their big friend was probably fighting a strong urge to hug everyone to within an inch of their lives.

He joined them at the table Tess had commandeered well out of sight of the front window, and forgot about socially distancing by sprawling in the same booth. Behind Pinky, the staff had momentarily fallen silent. For a second Po thought he might have brought his rifle inside with him, but that wasn't it. It was the simple fact that the trio were back together again, seated in their regular spot that had given Chris, Jazz and the others a moment for reflection: some sort of normalcy had returned after months of lockdown weirdness.

Pinky threw up his hands. 'Maybe me shooting was a bit over the top, eh?'

'You aren't kidding,' said Tess. 'We're lucky there were no witnesses otherwise we could be going to jail.'

'I've been locked up too long as it is, me. Don't want to go back because I got a jittery trigger finger.'

'We all acted out of sorts,' Po admitted. 'I let my fists fly before we had any answers and caused things to go haywire. To be fair, Pinky, I'm glad you fired when you did, otherwise I might've done somethin' to Brogan I'd really regret.'

'He's a weird one, him.'

'He's an oddball, but not to be underestimated. Nobody wears one of those spring-loaded knives unless they're prepared to use it, and probably has done so in the past.' Po frowned, thinking that he too carried a concealed knife, and under the correct circumstances was prepared to use it. Did it make him a bad person too? He shook off the thought. 'You notice the tats on his hands?'

Tess nodded, and grabbed a bunch of napkins out of a dispenser. She dug out a pen from her bag and began doodling. She drew several of the more prominent tattoos she'd noted on Brogan's hands. She pushed the napkin towards Po. 'Gang-related?'

'I'd say so, but I'm unfamiliar with the tags.'

Pinky craned over to inspect her doodles. He indicated one that resembled a human eye with a cross where the pupil should be. 'That one there's familiar. There was a guy in the pen had that tat. You remember him, Nicolas, that guy from the West Coast I shared a cell with for a while?'

Po remembered. Pinky was deliberately being tactful; he didn't want Tess to know how a vicious punk had repeatedly violated the young and vulnerable Jerome Leclerc. After Po had stepped in to protect him from another attack, said cellmate had gotten the message. Po often wondered if, in Pinky's adulthood where he no longer required Po's protection, he had found and paid back that rapist son of a bitch. It was a subject of their past they had not revisited after renewing their friendship all these years later.

'There must be some kind of law-enforcement database I can access where known gang tags are recorded,' Tess suggested. 'I'll look into it, see if I can find out whom Brogan pays fealty to.'

'Looks as if he's had tats lasered off his face,' Po said. 'Y'ask me, the tattoos we can't see would say more about Brogan than the ones we can.'

'Did you make a note of their IDs when you checked them out?'

'Only the basic details. Names, ages—'

'Addresses?'

'West Coast,' Po said, with a glimpse of confirmation to Pinky's earlier point about the prisoner's gang tag. 'Los Angeles. Can't recall street addresses.'

'You don't need to be specific. It's enough knowing that they've traveled all the way across the country to find Vaughan. It tells me that whatever he's done it's worth their while, and the expense, of sending hunters all this way after him. At this time, with all the travel restrictions on, Brogan's risking things with the cops. Again, it gives some idea of the seriousness of what Vaughan has done.'

'You're assumin' they recently traveled here from California. That might not be the case. They could be from nearer by, and just chasin' Vaughan for an unpaid debt for all we know.' Po didn't put much faith in his own words. Brogan and Walsh weren't going to this much trouble over a couple hundred dollars' worth of unsecured debt. 'But they probably have; they've been running around town, making no bones about who they're lookin' for, and their methods have been a bit over the top, y'ask me. That strikes me as they'll do whatever's necessary to get their man and don't plan on hangin' around afterwards.'

'Brogan said he intends "taking back Vaughan to face the music." Sounds to me as if he plans on abducting him with force.'

'That guy's a psycho, him,' Pinky reiterated. 'I was listening through our cell phones, Tess, and heard what he had to say. I'm telling you, his brain isn't wired up the way normal folks' are.'

'Yeah. He blows from hot to cold in a second. He's erratic, and prone to do the unexpected.'

'It's not a bad thing knowing what we're up against,' said Po. 'If we are on guard to the unexpected it won't take us by surprise.'

'So I guess we're all in agreement?'

'About finding Vaughan and protecting him? Yep, I'm in.'

'Despite what he might've done?' Tess pressed.

'We can always reassess the situation once we know what the hell he's done to ruffle Brogan's feathers. If it turns out he's the worst kind of crap, you can always push the job towards your brother Alex.'

'Tony worked for you, Nicolas,' said Pinky. 'Did he strike you as the kind of man who'd turn out to be the worst kind of crap?'

'I barely knew him. When he was at the autoshop he kept his head down and worked hard, and as far as I know, Charley had no problems with him. I think I can get the measure of a man's true nature quick enough and thought he was OK, but who knows? In private, the guy could've been a serial killer for all I know.'

Pinky rolled his neck. 'We've had our fill of serial killers. How's about we assume Tony isn't going to pay back our kindness by trying to cut off our faces and parade around in skin masks?'

Po laughed at the gruesome image. 'Yeah, that kinda sours the idea of rushing to help him, doesn't it?'

'Was Tony on the books at the autoshop?' Tess pondered.

'Yeah. Everything about the garage is above board, even when it comes to the casual workers.'

'So you'll have a last known address for him?'

'I'll call Charley and have him dig out Tony's personnel file. That's if the old coot decides to answer the damn phone.'

'It's unlikely we'll find Tony where he's supposed to be living, but it's a start.'

'Something I might be able to find out is his next of kin details. The shop can be a dangerous place to work, so Charley always takes the name of an emergency contact. Chances are we'll have more luck picking up his trail from there.'

'Great idea. In the meantime, I'll get on with trying to identify those tattoos.'

Pinky grinned. 'In the meantime I'll just sit here looking pretty, me. Man, but isn't it great getting the gang back together again?'

NINE

B rogan turned his face aside, hiding the faint smile he wore for Anderson Walsh's discomfort. His helper stood before the mirror, dabbing at the puffed-up, discolored skin on the side of his mouth. Walsh hissed and grunted and manipulated the flesh with some trepidation. 'I'm lucky not to have a broken jaw,' he moaned, and Brogan's lips stretched a tad more.

'You've taken worse beatings. Stop grumbling.'

'I've taken worse, yeah, but I probably deserved those. Why'd Villere swing at me when it was you he had the beef with?'

'You're the bigger, meaner-looking guy; he beat your head like a piñata to both show that he could, and to take you out of the equation for a few minutes. So he could then concentrate on intimidating me.'

'It's unlike you to be intimidated, Bryce.'

'I wasn't intimidated in the least.' Brogan flashed a sneer. 'I just said Villere concentrated his attempt on me.'

'Who the hell is he anyway? Thought he was just the owner of a garage, and that was it. He handled himself more like a pro fighter.'

'You don't think people can be business owners and fighters?'

Walsh shrugged, and it was apparent he didn't really care. He was clutching for a reason why he'd allowed himself to be caught flat-footed and get knocked on his ass so easily.

'Villere knows how to handle himself,' Brogan said. 'Did you see that knife he drew from his boot? He doesn't use that for getting the gunk out from under his fingernails.'

'So he's a dangerous son of a bitch, and not to be underestimated? Message received and understood.' Walsh again gently kneaded the flesh on his jaw, wincing and hissing. He probed with the tip of his tongue at a molar. 'Goddamnit! I think he cracked my tooth.'

'Well, that should motivate you to kick his ass when you get the chance.'

Walsh nodded at the suggestion, but there was little enthusiasm behind the gesture. Brogan could tell that Villere had placed wariness in Walsh's heart, and that could prove problematic when they faced off with him again.

'It should be different next time.'

'Yeah. No way will he catch me napping again. Son of a bitch won't get the chance to cold cock me and take my gun away.'

'You were lucky Tess only disassembled it and threw it in the back of the van rather than off the side of the pier.'

'Tess, huh? You got on first name terms with them, then?'

Brogan grinned. 'I overheard Villere call her by her given name. I also sussed them out and it seems like Tess is some kind of investigator, maybe even a private eye.'

'Jeez. You think we haven't dropped a huge dump on ourselves by involving a private eye?'

'I asked her to work for me.'

'Say what?'

'I thought you'd come around by then, but you must've still been cuckoo. I asked them to work for me, to find Vaughan. They turned me down flat, but that's OK. See, it was only to put the idea in their heads that they *want* to find him too. All we have to do is sit back, wait till they do all the leg work and then swoop in and take Vaughan off their hands.'

'How can you be certain they'll look for him?'

'Nothing's ever certain, Anderson, but I have a feeling that Tess and Villere are the intrepid type, and this goddamn lockdown has almost squeezed the life out of them. They're desperate for some action and I just threw them a line and reeled them in.'

'That's pure speculation.'

'Agreed. But think about it. They came to the meeting at the pier. Granted it was partly because Villere was pissed over me manhandling Tess, but they came prepared for more than just a fistfight. They brought a goddamn sniper with them! I'm telling you, those aren't the moves made by your average Joes.'

'More the reason it was probably a bad idea involving them.'

'Bad or good, it's done. You're rightly concerned. That's a good thing. It keeps you alert. But if you're worried about the numbers being against us, you needn't fret about it. I'm going to have Josh and Randall join us. They've concluded that business with Bob Wilson now, so they can come help us here.' Brogan grinned at the thought of doubling their manpower. Next time he went head to head with Tess and Villere, it'd be him holding the upper hand. He didn't know who Villere's sniper was yet, but with the addition of his brother Josh and Declan Randall they'd be the ones to outflank and outmaneuver the gunman.

'How do you think Josh's going to take you involving a private eye in the hunt? Don't you think he's gonna be pissed?'

'He's my elder brother, not my boss. I don't need his permission to do any damn thing I want to do.'

'Regardless, he'll still be pissed.'

'It'll make up for him steering us wrong when he sent us after *Peabody*. I'm betting that if we'd asked around about "Po'boy" Villere we'd have been warned about blundering into a confrontation with him the way we did. Goddamnit if Randall hasn't done business here in the past; I'd bet he's heard about Po'boy and could've given us a heads up if Josh hadn't gotten the wrong name.'

'Josh got the name Peabody from Bob Wilson,' Walsh reminded him, 'and probably had no reason to think it was the wrong one. He didn't steer us wrong on purpose.'

'Agreed, but he still owes us one, and if he's pissed about me taking the initiative with the private eye, then it's just deserts.' Brogan wiped the back of his wrist across his mouth, and dead-eyed Walsh. 'You done here?'

Walsh took a final check in the mirror, and seemed reasonably satisfied that his jaw was aligned as before. 'I think I'm good to go.'

'It's about time. We should've been outta here in a couple of minutes. At least we can be reasonably assured we didn't trip a silent alarm, eh?'

It made difficulties traveling across country but there were some benefits of a national lockdown. Many buildings that would be full of activity were closed, empty of workers, offering places for Brogan and Walsh to lie low. Using his wrist blade, Brogan had jimmied the lock on a door of a small boutique shop special-izing in clothing for babies and toddlers. The owner had removed most of the stock and taken it to a more secure lockup, Brogan guessed. The security arrangements were non-existent beyond the cheap mortise lock that had easily succumbed to a little leverage. They'd used the shop's tiny bathroom and Brogan had allowed Walsh what he deemed ample time to pull his thoughts together. Brogan had rifled through the shop, seeking anything useful, and had discovered a crate of bottled water under a counter. He'd helped himself to several bottles, stuffing them in a large paper bag.

'We need to find somewhere more permanent to use,' Brogan said as they exited the building. He pulled the door to. The lock was obviously broken, but with the door settled back in its jamb the break-in would go unnoticed until the owner's next visit.

'There are bound to be holiday homes spread all over the coast here,' Walsh suggested, 'and with nobody allowed to travel they should be empty.'

'Yeah, I was thinking the same. We can't just choose any old place though, we have to be careful and not attract attention.'

'We didn't do that already?' Walsh exhaled sharply.

'Quit with your damn negativity, will you? I'm kind of enjoying the hunt, and your constant moaning's doing its best to spoil my mood.'

'Sorry, man, but my sore jaw and bust-up face has taken some of the shine off the trip for me.'

Brogan grinned at his pal's discomfort.

Their panel van was parked out of sight of the main road, hidden beyond a stand of trees and untended brush. Villere's hidden sniper had put bullets through the passenger window, blowing it into tiny nuggets that still littered the seats and floor, and had also punctured the body of the van. At a glance the holes were unremarkable, so it was unlikely they would attract attention unless a cop, for instance, made a closer inspection. It was summer, and hot enough that people drove with their windows rolled down, so the broken window wasn't an issue.

'Clean off that broken glass, will you?' said Brogan as he eyed the glass-strewn seat. 'I'll call Josh and Randall, and have them meet us.'

'Are we going back into town?'

'That's the plan. We can't just hide away and hope Tess does us the service of calling us and letting us know where she's found Vaughan.'

Walsh snorted again. Brogan was his superior, but that didn't mean he was expected to take constant sarcasm.

'You really hope to tail them and then swoop in once Vaughan breaks cover?'

'Yeah. But before you ask, no I don't expect us to be able to follow them in this van. They'll spot us in seconds. We need some new wheels. Something less obvious we can follow them in.' Brogan thumped his knuckles against Walsh's shoulder. It was supposed to be a gesture of camaraderie, but he punched hard enough to make the bigger man flinch. 'Following them will be easier once Josh and Randall get here and we can switch out the cars.'

'How d'you suppose we get another car going? I don't know about you, Bryce, but it's been decades since I hotwired a car. These modern cars . . . there's no way.'

'We don't need to hotwire a car. Pick a house, Walsh, any house with a car on its drive' – Brogan held up his hand and with a flick of a hidden switch his levered-knife sprang out several inches beyond his fingertips – 'and I'll convince the homeowner to hand over its key.'

TEN

He pulled down his neckerchief, worked his gummy mouth, and moved quickly from the grocery store to where his car waited. His eyes darted, checking for any sign he was being observed, but except for an old mutt that watched him from beyond a wire fence, he went without witness. Pulling down his mask was probably not the best of ideas until he was back at the car, but its cloying warmth smothered him, making it difficult to breathe. He knew that the sensation of choking was actually the first effects of panic, and that the smothering sensation was all in his mind, but he couldn't fight it. He was gasping by the time he threw his weight down on the driving seat and reached to crank up the air vents. It was hot and stuffy inside the car despite leaving the windows wound down, and he pitied Leah who'd had to suffer the stuffiness while he was inside the store. She stared over at him. Above her face mask her brown eyes looked huge and every bit as trusting in him as before. He wished he shared her faith in his ability to keep her safe.

He handed over the large paper sack containing their provisions and Leah set it between her feet without inspecting what it contained.

'You OK?' he asked.

'I'm fine. You don't look so good, though.'

'I'll be OK in a minute. I just need some air. Once we're moving again . . .'

'Where are we going this time, Tony?'

Anthony Vaughan said, 'The only place I can think of for now. We need to lie low for a few more days, then we'll move on once we know it's safe. You don't have to worry, Leah, I won't let them catch us.'

'I believe you'll do your best to stop them, but it isn't a promise you can make. Don't put that kind of pressure on your shoulders.'

He reached across and grasped her hand. 'I love you, Leah. I'd die for you . . . you know that, right? If it comes to it I'll sacrifice myself before I let them get their hands on you.'

Leah's head tilted and her dark hair fell over her forehead, shielding her eyes. She wore a facemask sporting a printed design of huge red lips and sparkling white teeth. In profile her mostly disguised face looked unearthly, grotesque even, like something glimpsed in a horror movie. Vaughan shivered, but gave her hand a second supportive squeeze. She nodded but gently withdrew her fingers. She had faith in him but not the same level of love he had for her.

Vaughan started the car and was grateful when the blowers blasted air over him. Sweat trickled down the back of his neck. He pulled out and drove north along the coastal highway, heading back to the cabin they had hidden in for the past few days. The cabin was small and decrepit and lacked modern comfort and conveniences. For now it was their only recourse, as Vaughan had almost come to the end of the ideas he'd had for escaping their pursuers. They'd come all the way across the country, fleeing back to his childhood stomping grounds, but he knew that the Brogans would've pursued them, and he didn't know where to turn to next. When he claimed he'd sacrifice his life for hers he meant it, but obviously he'd prefer that he didn't have to.

'Will they ever stop chasing us?'

He looked across at Leah and squeezed her a smile. 'Sure they will. We just have to keep moving and sooner or later the effort and expense will outweigh their need to find us. That or something more pressing will take priority and they'll drop their search for us. We'll have to be careful still, and not make any mistakes that attract attention, but I'm confident that we'll make it and life will return to some kinda normalcy.'

'I'm tired.'

'You should rest when we get back to the cabin.'

'I mean that I'm tired of running, tired of being constantly afraid. I'm so tired I feel sick to my stomach. Don't you, Tony?'

'I'm OK,' he lied. 'Like I said, I just need a little fresh air and I'll be fine.'

'When we get back to the cabin *you* should rest,' she argued. 'You haven't slept properly in a week and you need to eat too, and get a real meal inside you. You're not going to be any good to either of us if you drop dead from fatigue or starvation.'

He nodded. She had a point. He was running on fumes by now, but he'd meant it when he said that he'd die for her if he must. By that he meant he'd take a beating, a bullet, or even Bryce Brogan's knife in his heart, not simply keel over dead. 'I promise I'll get some shut eye once you've taken your nap.'

'I don't need to sleep yet. Let me watch over you for a while, instead of the other way around.'

In his chest he experienced a faint buzzing sensation, and knew it was adrenalin shooting through him. He tried convincing himself it was only his way of preparing to defend Leah, but he was lying, the sensation was fear. 'What if they come when I'm sleeping?'

'Then I'll wake you, Tony. You can't go on like this. If you don't sleep you'll crash and burn. What if it happens when you need to be at your most alert?'

She was right, but how could he simply lie down and go to sleep when at any second they could be found? Leah said she'd awaken him, but by then it could be too late. 'I'll sleep, I promise you, but only once I know you're safe.'

'I'm still capable of keeping an eye out, and watching over you, Tony. I've problems, yes, but they don't include being responsible and doing my fair share. I want to help you to help *us*.'

'What kinda guy would I be if I didn't agree, huh?'

'Then it's settled,' she said, and again offered him a huge brown-eyed stare. 'Once we get back you're going to rest, and I'll keep watch.'

'OK. Deal. I'll rest, but you have to promise me that you won't let me sleep too long.'

'A couple of hours at most.'

The cabin was hidden from view of the coast by acres of dense woodland. A turn off from a back road allowed access, and once Vaughan had pulled in he stopped the car to drag a thick chain across the opening. Hanging from the chain was a hand-painted sign that read: *No Entry. Private property.* The signage would mean nothing to those pursuing them, but at least it would serve to deter any random visits from passers-by. Vaughan got back in the car and drove them deep into the woods to the cabin. They'd moved in a few days ago, before that he'd visited the hunting/fishing cabin the previous year while holding down a job in nearby Portland, but before that it had been decades ago. Vaughan didn't know his daddy, but growing up he'd had plenty of 'uncles' and it was one of those male friends of his mother who'd owned the cabin back then; these days Vaughan had no idea who had ownership, but during this statewide lockdown he was confident they would go undiscovered.

He shielded Leah while she got out the car. He was taller, wider than her. He ushered her inside the cabin and watched her seat herself in a corner away from a direct view of the single window in the room. He returned to the car and fetched the groceries he'd recently bought and carried them inside. Leah hadn't moved when he returned to her side.

'I'll rustle us up some food,' he suggested.

'You're supposed to be getting some rest, Tony,' she reminded him, and nodded him over towards the couch where he'd spent the last few short naps he'd taken.

'Aren't you hungry? I'm famished.'

'I'm hungry, but I'm capable of making us both a meal,' she said. 'D'you want me to make us something? I can have it ready for when you wake up.'

He thought about it. His breathing had returned almost to normal, but his gut still buzzed from the anxiety of being outside and potentially getting spotted by their pursuers. His heartbeat fluttered. Several times he'd had to swallow acid that crept up his throat. He was as much in need of a decent meal as he was for an entire night's unbroken sleep. 'I'll close my eyes for a little while, then I'll make us something.'

'Tony, why won't you trust me to do even the simplest of tasks?'

'I want to look after you.'

'You *are* looking after me, but I can still do some tasks to make life easier for you.'

He nodded at her wisdom. What harm would there be in allowing her to help? She understood by now how much he loved and valued her, and allowing her to help by rustling up some bacon and eggs at the cabin's rudimentary stove wouldn't change her worth in his estimation. 'OK,' he decided, and he gripped her shoulder and gave it a gentle squeeze. 'You sure you can manage without me?'

'Go on, lie down and close your eyes. I'll call you when it's ready.'

He lay on the couch as instructed, listening to the soft noises Leah made as she pottered at the stove. Sleep rolled towards him like an avalanche and Vaughan fought it for a few seconds. A worm of unease sat at the back of his mind, and if he could he would've slept with one eye open – an impossibility, he was blind in one eye.

ELEVEN

Most investigations Tess undertook began with the basics. She preferred to dot the i's and cross the t's before racing off, but Po had a different style completely. He followed his gut, and his nose, and if they took him off on a sharp angle from Tess's carefully designated path he didn't hold back. Tess was mostly happy allowing him his brash investigative process because it could sometimes get results the way in which her own methodical style could too, only much faster. While she followed data and information she could access at the tap of a computer key, he had sped off in his muscle car, with Pinky riding shotgun. They'd gone to the autoshop to personally oversee the digging out of Anthony Vaughan's personnel file after Po recalled that it was one of his workers that'd taken cash from Brogan in exchange for Po's real name. Tess imagined that a dressing down about the importance of loyalty was on the cards for the mechanics at the autoshop.

She had used her laptop to log into databases she had access to through her periodic subcontracting work to Emma Clancy's specialist inquiry firm – whose main client was the Portland district attorney's office – and she set some programs running to search for Anthony Vaughan: by drilling down specific information she could usually determine a target's activities and movements, but for now he appeared to be avoiding using any debit or credit cards and if he had access to a phone or the internet he was using them anonymously. Also she had set an image reverse-search function to try to identify the origins of Brogan's tattoos. She fully expected that the FBI had a database of such gang affiliation tags but if it existed she couldn't get into it, not legally. She hoped instead that the reverse-search function she'd added to her computer would throw up some connections within a few minutes.

She checked for Vaughan through the major social networks: on the run he'd be a fool to keep his social platforms up to date, but she'd known people unable to resist checking into their Facebook or Twitter accounts despite being subjects of a manhunt. She struck out; if Vaughan was ever one to have a social media account it was not recorded under his name. She checked local news websites, and then expanded her search, but the only mentions Vaughan got were historical by several years, when he'd been involved in petty crimes while under the influence of alcohol. She searched for him more recently in California where he must have been staying after leaving his job at the autoshop. She found mention of a person bearing his name, but it was not the man Po described to her. This other Anthony Vaughan was ten years Tony's junior, and being of Vietnamese heritage was the wrong race and skin color. Tess also searched for him using his shortened forename, and even by his slightly ridiculous, and un-PC nickname of Tony One-Eye. Surprisingly, the latter was the only one to return a hit.

Tess followed the hyperlink and read the story, only to discount this One-Eye as the man she was searching for. She sat back and gave the laptop a slight nudge of disgust. She was seated in the same booth as before at Bar-Lesque. While she waited for the other programs to return their findings she could make some telephone calls to certain individuals who might be able to assist in her search, including a couple of contacts she still had in the Cumberland County Sheriff's Office and in Portland PD. As she brought up her contacts list on her cell phone, she hit the button to shut down her screen and placed it on the table before her. Jasmine Reed placed a jug of freshly brewed coffee and a pair of mugs down in front of Tess. 'It's time for this girl to take a break,' she announced, her words meant as much for Tess as her own needs.

Tess gave the diner a cursory check over. 'How're things going with the prep, Jazz?'

'All good up until now. I've asked Chris to prop open a couple of doors though to get rid of this funky smell. The extra noise from outside won't disturb your work, will it?'

'I doubt it.' Tess didn't need to cock an ear to tell there was very little sound filtering in from outside. The streets were mostly devoid of traffic and there were few pedestrians about. When she thought about the lockdown, she wondered how Vaughan had managed to travel across country from California without being pulled over by the police. It gave her an idea for another search process she could program into her computer, but discarded the idea. Also, she might be able to pull on a contact in the DMV to find a car registered to Vaughan, one for which they could search for around Portland, but again she doubted that he'd be stupid enough to be driving his own car.

Jazz poured them coffees. Tess accepted a mug gratefully. Jazz flopped down on the bench opposite.

'Boy am I out of shape,' she sighed as she drew down her dust mask and allowed it to hang under her chin. 'This enforced time off isn't good for anyone, let alone for somebody prone to eat too much chocolate while bingeing Netflix.' Her raven hair hung awry over one ear and her usually crimson lips were lacking lipstick. Jazz was one of those women who could carry off the bedraggled look and still look terrific, while personally Tess felt she always looked frazzled. Eating chocolate and binge-watching box sets on TV was a kinder lifestyle to Jazz than it ever would be to her.

'It has been tough on a lot of people,' Tess said sagely.

'You can say that again. Some more than others, eh? We're fortunate not to have lost anyone close to us through this damn virus.'

'It's not over yet,' said Tess and immediately regretted her negativity. She waved away her remark. 'No, let's be optimistic, shall we? They'll find a vaccine, a way out of this, for sure?'

'For sure. I'm only glad we're returning to some sort of normality soon. This place has been shut too long, it'll be good to get some life back in here.'

'We're only allowed fifty per cent capacity?' Tess asked, though she already knew the answer.

'Better than zero capacity. I can't wait to get back to work.' Jazz eyed the laptop on the table. 'At least you're able to do something now. Working from home must've been difficult in your line of business.'

'I've had very little to do since the pandemic took hold. In fact, this is my first time in town since I don't know when.'

'Mine too. What are you busy with? It is OK for me to ask, right?'

'Missing person. Actually, that's not right. This person isn't missing, they're deliberately in hiding.'

'If anyone can find them it's you, Tess.'

'It's not easy when they don't want to be found. And if I'm being honest, I'm not entirely certain I'm fully committed to finding them.'

'Why not?'

'This guy appears to be a criminal being pursued by other criminals after doing them wrong.'

Jazz shook her head. 'It's not like you to be judgmental, Tess. You stuck to your guns and found me, even after everyone else had written me off as a wild child runaway who deserved everything I got. If you hadn't looked beyond the BS and saw me as a potential victim I *would've* been murdered. No doubt about it. So would those other girls that were being held alongside me.' Jazz paused to drink deeply from her coffee.

Tess returned her steadfast stare over the rim of her own steaming mug. She lowered the mug. 'You're right, of course. It has been a weird time to live through lately, and I've hated being cooped up at the house for days and weeks on end. Trust me I won't let this go: I'm going to grab the first clue I find to this guy's whereabouts and hang on as if it were the tail of a bucking bronco.'

'What has he allegedly done to these other criminals?'

'That's the thing, we don't know and the people looking for him wouldn't say.'

'I see why you might be reluctant to throw in with him when he could be ten times worse than the people he's hiding from.'

'He used to work for Po, and Po said he thought he was a decent guy. Ordinarily I'd trust his instincts, but none of us can truly know what's going on in another person's mind, or what they might be capable of. Until I know otherwise, I guess you're right and give him the benefit of the doubt.'

'Either that or you grab one of those criminals and let Po and Pinky twist his ears until he tells you exactly why they're after this guy.' Jazz smiled to show she was joking, eliciting a laugh from Tess.

'We kind of tried that already.'

'Jeez, it's your first time out of the house in months and already you've been in a tussle with some bad guys?'

'Twice.'

'You're kidding me?'

'And it isn't even lunch time yet.'

'If you'd said so I'd've brought you something over a bit stronger than coffee.'

Tess picked up her mug. 'I'll stick with coffee for now. I've probably drunk far too much liquor in the past few months than can be healthy.'

Jazz eyed her again, this time with a softer gaze. 'Yeah, maybe it's time to lay off the bottle for a bit.'

Tess winced. 'It's not as if I've turned into a lush during lockdown, just . . .' She halted mid-track. 'Wait a minute. What do you mean by "for a bit"?'

Jazz smiled, and stood. She pulled up her mask again, covering her to the bridge of her nose. Her eyes still twinkled with whatever was on her mind.

'What?' Tess pressed.

'You know *what*,' Jazz teased, and she turned to go back to work. She stopped and looked down at Tess. 'Maybe you shouldn't tussle with any criminals for the next six months either.'

'Hey! What?' Tess stood sharply.

Jazz tapped her abdomen gently and waggled her eyebrows. She turned away, leaving Tess standing lost for words.

Tess looked down at her belly, saw that it extended slightly over the top of the waistband of her jeans. 'I've put on a few pounds during lockdown, Jazz, show me anybody that hasn't.'

Jazz giggled from back in the kitchen somewhere. Tess took a step after her, but the back door banged open grabbing her attention. Po entered, followed by Pinky. Both men were without their masks and Tess knew that they'd probably gone to the auto-shop in the same car. Pinky had joined their social bubble for real now. She met them as they walked towards her.

'You up for a quick road trip?' Po asked.

'Where to?'

'Down York Harbor way.'

'Got a lead on Vaughan?'

'I've a lead on his next of kin. Half-brother by the name of Robert Wilson. He lives on the south side of the York River. If anyone might know where Tony's hidin' it could be his brother.'

'Depends on how badly he wants to stay hidden. I mean, if you're in hiding, the last people you tell is anyone you care about. Right?'

'Not everyone thinks that way.' Po was correct, some fugitives and victims believed the ones they could rely on most were family, and often they were right. But they didn't consider how they could be putting their loved ones in danger from those hunting them. Just as she and Po were about to do, she suspected that Brogan might already have squeezed Robert Wilson for information on his half-brother's whereabouts.

'We'd be fools not to go and speak with him,' she announced. 'If we take the turnpike we can be there in an hour.'

Pinky wagged a finger between them. 'You guys got this?'

'Sure thing,' said Tess with a glance at Po for confirmation.

'Yeah, we've got it,' Po added.

'Good, I hear a hot shower calling my name, me.' Pinky dragged out the collar of his shirt and sniffed the warm air rising from under it. He gagged. 'I stink like cheese, me.'

Tess thought he smelled perfectly lovely, but understood Pinky's words as his way of bowing out gracefully. He was conscious of the old adage that three's a crowd, and that Tess and Po probably wanted some time together: she remembered how he used to jokingly call himself 'the three-hundred-pound gooseberry in the back seat'.

'You're welcome to join us,' she said, meaning every word.

'Cops will probably pull us over if they see us traveling together. You and Nicolas have a valid reason to be out, me I'll just catch myself a fine.'

Po patted their friend on the shoulder. 'Soon as we're back in Portland we'll give you a call.'

'Sounds like a plan.'

Po checked out the booth where they'd sat earlier. Tess's laptop and purse and various other items were scattered across the table. 'Need any of that stuff with ya, Tess?'

'All of it. Gimme a minute and I'll be ready.'

Her estimate was off by a couple more minutes, but shortly she joined Po at his Mustang. He'd already started the engine, and as soon as Tess was settled he peeled away from the rear of Bar-Lesque, heading south for York Harbor.

TWELVE

Tess knocked on the door, then, as an extra measure, she pressed the doorbell despite it hanging off its mounting. She heard a corresponding chime from within the small decrepit house but no other sounds. At her feet was a package, left propped against the doorjamb by a courier with too many deliveries and not enough time on their hands. A delivery slip had been wedged between the door and frame: there was no traditional letterbox slot. There was a pane of semi-opaque glass. Through it Tess could have sworn she'd noticed movement, but it could have been her own dim reflection, or that of the trees swaying in the breeze behind her. She knocked again.

Following US Route 1, Po had driven them to York Harbor in under an hour. Because there were only essential workers traveling the roads he easily shaved a half hour or more off their usual journey time. At York Corner, Tess had pulled up a map on her cell phone and guided them to Robert Wilson's address. The house sat on a small lot alongside a tiny industrial park next to the river. Few of the companies were open for business, and none that were in earshot of the house. Wilson's place was as remote as it possibly could be while being surrounded by small towns and highways.

Tess knocked a third time, rapping sharply on the pane of glass. The harsh snaps of her knuckles on glass resounded through the house. She called Wilson's name. No response.

After driving up to the house, Po had alighted his car to follow Tess towards the front porch, before angling off to make a perusal of the yard. It was weed-choked and overgrown shrubs dominated the grounds. An older model Chrysler sat under an awning on the side of the house. Po had gone to it and laid his hand on the hood. Judging by his nonchalance, the engine under it was cold and Po had moved on, strolling around the back. She heard him knock on a rear door, the sound filtering through to her at the front. He tried a door handle and she winced at his boldness.

On the drive down they had considered the possibility that Brogan and Walsh had visited Wilson before them. Knowing how they operated Tess wouldn't put it past them to have tried forcing Vaughan's whereabouts out of his half-brother. Perhaps they had hurt him. It was little wonder that Wilson refused to answer his door to another couple of strangers, perhaps expecting more violence. Following a similar thought process Po had possibly deduced that Wilson was inside and in need of assistance. Tess tried the front door handle, and the lock popped open, the door swinging inward under the slightest of nudges of her fingertips. She called out Wilson's name. 'We're here to help,' she added. 'Are you hurt? Holler out if you can, so I know where to find you.'

She waited at the threshold.

Nobody answered.

Po applied more pressure, and the backdoor scraped open, dragging on the floor. It was doubtful that Wilson regularly used the back door. From what she could see, he'd put as little time and effort into maintaining his home as he had his garden. She felt air waft through the house as Po fully opened the door. The smell was sour and she held her breath as she leaned inside. She exhaled as once again she called Wilson's name. With her next inhalation she smelled something antiseptic but it failed to conceal the coppery sourness she'd first detected.

'Po, do you smell blood?'

'I smell crap,' he answered from the depths of the house. 'Must be the cleaner's day off. Fact is, the cleaner musta taken off a couple of years judging by this mess.'

Her partner approached along the hall, on high alert as he moved from one door to the next.

'No sign of Wilson, though?'

'Nope.' Po paused at the nearest open doorway. His face grew pale. 'Tess, you'd better take a look in here.'

'Is it Wilson?'

'Nope.'

She entered the house. The vinyl floor sucked at her soles. She joined Po at the doorway and looked into the kitchen. It was apparent that some kind of disturbance had taken place: a chair was upended, and a table had been pushed across the floor to butt against the kitchen counters. Items on top had tipped over, and a pool of cold coffee dripped off the table to spatter the floor. There were small droplets of a more vivid color too, and larger smears of blood showed where a wound had bled more profusely. Bloody cloths and sponges had been dumped in the sink, and an open bottle of disinfectant sat on the drainer. Somebody had been cut, and had attempted to staunch their wound at the counter. Had they gotten the bleeding under control, then headed off to hospital? If so, why was Wilson's Chrysler still parked outside? Had his injury been so debilitating he'd called for an ambulance?

She glanced down and spotted where a shoe had tracked a smear of blood into the hall. She nodded at it and Po was on it like a hound. He followed the trail further into the house, to a closed door. He'd ignored the door on his first perusal, denoting it a seldom-used walk-in broom cupboard. He looked at Tess, and she returned his stare. He held up a cautioning finger, and stood to one side of the jamb. He reached for the handle, and after another glance to check Tess was out of the direct line of fire. As the door swung open, a howl of desperation accompanied it.

Robert Wilson wasn't hiding in the cupboard. He erupted from another doorway – this one to a bedroom – where he must have been concealed from Po. He clutched a baseball bat in sweaty palms, and his face was as pale and slick as a fish's belly. He swung for Po's head. Po ducked and the bat knocked a lump out of the wall beside him. Po rose from his semi-crouch, left elbow spearing up to slam Wilson's sternum and force the man backwards. Po lunged and kept him moving until he crushed him against the doorframe. Wilson wailed again, and tried to turn the baseball bat on Po's neck and shoulders.

Tess grabbed for the flailing bat and missed.

Po headbutted Wilson.

The bat fell from lax fingers as Wilson's knees failed. He sank down, groaning, and would have ended seated on the grimy floor, but Po grabbed him and dragged him up. Tess gave way, backpedaling so that Po could manhandle Wilson into the kitchen. Po shoved him down with his back to an open space on the wall. Wilson had come around from the butt in the face: he stared up fearfully, mouth stretched wide in anticipation of more violence. He was missing teeth at the front, and weirdly he wore only one shoe. His other foot was wrapped in a towel that had been secured around his ankle with duct tape. The towel was sopping with blood.

Po jabbed a finger. 'You'd best stay down, bra.'

'I already told you everything I know,' Wilson cried, 'why'd you have to come back again?'

'Dunno who you think we are,' Po said, 'but we ain't them.'

Wilson cringed. Po was on high alert, almost buzzing with energy as he fought down the urge to fight. He ran his fingers through his hair, then checked his fingertips for blood. Perhaps the blow from the bat had come closer to striking his head than Tess originally thought. His fingers were clean. He growled a curse; the bat had come closer to caving in his skull than he appreciated.

'You OK?' she asked.

'Totally.'

Tess turned her attention back on Wilson. He had drawn in his injured leg, and cradled his knee. Sweat stood on his forehead like pearls. His face was marked from where Po headbutted him, but she saw now that his missing teeth had nothing to do with being beaten, he was simply missing some dentures. His foot troubled him, and little wonder.

'What happened to you?'

'Your buddies hurt me.'

'I told you already,' said Po, 'we ain't with those guys. You're talkin' about Brogan and Walsh, right? A blond guy with tats on his hands, and another bigger lummox?'

Wilson nodded at the descriptions.

'They were here demanding to know where to find your brother?' Tess ventured.

Wilson bit his bottom lip, quite a feat while missing his front teeth.

'You flew off the handle there before we could explain,' Tess said. 'We aren't here to hurt you, we're here to help.'

Wilson gingerly touched the fresh chafe on his face.

Po sniffed. 'You tried to bash in my brains with a Louisville Slugger, whatcha expect me to do to you, bra?'

Wilson had the good sense to look regretful. 'I'm not a violent man. Not usually. But, well, a man has the right to defend himself, right?'

'Yeah, I guess it works both ways.'

'You thought that we were with those other men, those that hurt you before,' Tess said, 'but we're not. I can see how you must've been afraid when we showed up and how you thought you had to fight back.' She looked down at the blood decorating the floor. Whatever was done to him earlier, it had put the fear of death into him. Under the circumstances his actions were understandable. 'What happened to your foot, Robert?'

He creased his brow at her familiarity.

'Do you prefer to be called Bob?'

'I'd prefer you to get the hell outta my house and leave me the hell alone.'

'Keep a civil tongue in your mouth, bra,' Po warned.

'Why the hell should I? This is my house and you're unwelcome here. I'll talk how the hell I like in my own goddamn home.'

Tess said, 'Help us with a few answers to our questions and we'll leave. Or, if you like, we can get you some help with your foot. What happened to it?'

'I stubbed my toe,' he said, but Tess wasn't fooled by his sarcasm.

'Were you shot, Bob?'

An answer was unnecessary. She'd noticed the hole in the floor where the bullet had exited his sole.

'You must be in agony? Probably you're in shock too. You need medical assistance, Bob. Let us help you.'

'It's just a damn scratch. I've got the bleeding stopped and it'll heal by itself. I don't need no medic. I don't need your help. Just get outta here, and leave me be.'

Tess crouched. She met his gaze and told him the grim facts. 'If there's only soft tissue damage, then you're probably right. Your wound will heal and you might get away with a limp for the rest of your life. If the bullet hit anything major, a blood vessel, a nerve, or a ligament, for example, then you're in for a world of hurt. If it broke bones, and has sent splinters of them into your flesh, or maybe a fragment of shrapnel came off the bullet, then the likelihood is your wound will become infected. The poison will spread rapidly. You'll be lucky if your foot isn't amputated, maybe even the entire leg . . . do you know how quickly gangrene takes hold? If you contract sepsis then there's little hope for you. You *do* need a medic, Bob, and you *do* need our help. We'll help you, all you have to do is help us to find your brother.'

'How do I know you're not with those others, and you're only trying to trick me?'

Po sneered. 'By now I'd have shot you in your other foot or worse.'

'My name's Tess Grey,' Tess said, as she stood, 'and I'm a private investigator. My partner here is called Nicolas Villere.'

Wilson squinted up at Po, and it was possibly the first time he'd taken note of his physical appearance. 'Villere? That name's familiar. Yeah, that's it, you're that southerner who employed Tony last year, ain't you?'

'That'd be me.'

'Shit,' said Wilson. 'Now I know why you're here. You came for payback for giving your name to those assholes.'

'If you're the one who told them I'm nicknamed Peabody, then you got it all wrong.'

'Yeah, it was me. I was sure that was what Tony called you.'

'It still brought those punks to my home, and they threatened my girl.'

'So now you want another piece of my ass?' Wilson cringed at the agony flaring through his foot. More beads of sweat broke out on his forehead.

'I already got payback for that.' Po meant during their meeting with Brogan and Walsh at the pier, but Wilson misunderstood. He touched his sore face again and nodded in agreement.

Again Tess crouched and met Wilson's gaze. It was important to continue being forthright with him. 'We believe that Tony's in genuine danger from the men who hurt you. We hoped that you could tell us where to find him, so we can help protect him from them.'

'What did you say your name is?'

'Tess. Tess Grey.'

'Well, Tess, I'll tell you what I told the asshole that shot me. I don't know where Tony is. Period.'

'You sent them to my autoshop,' Po said.

'I had to give them *something* or who knows what they might've done next. You said it yourself, man; I didn't even get your name right. So no harm, no foul, eh?'

'Except harm was done. Those sons of bitches tried roughing up Tess.'

'I can't be held responsible for that. I just gave them a name I'd heard Tony mention – the wrong name, as it happens – so they'd let me be. I'd already been shot in the foot, I was terrified that tattooed sumbitch was about to start on the rest of me.' Wilson suddenly halted mid-flow. He blinked in confusion, as he looked first to Po then to Tess. 'Say, how'd you guys get here so quick?'

'How do you mean?' asked Po.

'I take it you came down from Portland? It's only a couple of hours since those assholes left. They can't have gotten there and alerted you this quickly about me.' He grew fearful again, cringing back against the wall. 'This is a trick. You can't be who you claim to be. You're only pretending to care about what happens to Tony or me. Go on. Get away from me. Get the fuck outta my house!'

'Calm down, Bob,' said Tess. 'I am a private investigator from Portland. And this is Nicolas, my partner. You know we're telling the truth, but I can understand your confusion and mistrust. You say it's only a couple of hours since Brogan and Walsh left; how can that be possible? Are you sure you didn't pass out and lose some time?'

'I'm in too much agony to pass out! Since those assholes left I've been trying to stop the blood leaking outta me!'

'Not possible,' Po echoed Tess. 'Brogan and Walsh were in Portland since early this morning. Whoever it was that was here, it wasn't them.'

'But the tattooed guy . . . I'm sure I overheard the other call him Brogan.'

Tess described his tattoos.

'That's him.' Wilson touched below his eye. 'And he had a burn scar here where he's had something removed.'

'Sounds like our Brogan,' Po admitted. 'But we know it can't have been.'

'You're right,' said Tess. 'There has to be others looking for Tony, and they were directing the ones we ran into in Portland.'

'You were following that lead with Brogan's tattoos. If they indicated some kind of gang affiliation, I think we can assume his homeboys were here, Tess.'

'Where have they gotten to now?'

'They left,' said Wilson, 'and that's all that I care about. I also want you two outta here. Go on, like I said, and git.'

'I'm not leaving until I know you've had that wound looked at,' said Tess.

'My health's not your concern.'

'I won't have your death on my conscience. I wasn't kidding about the seriousness of leaving a gunshot wound untreated.'

'You expect me to go to hospital? If I do that the cops will be called. That tattooed guy warned that if I involved the cops he'd come back and finish the job.'

'He won't have to come back, podnuh,' said Po, 'when the gangrene will do the job for him. Listen to Tess, she knows what she's talkin' about.'

'I can't go to hospital. Don't you get it?'

'Then let me help you,' said Tess. 'Let me clean and dress your wound for you. In return you can help us to help your brother by telling us how to find him.'

'I don't see how I can help when I've no idea where Tony is.'

'You'd be surprised by what you do know, it's just you haven't given it any thought yet.'

'It's true,' said Po. 'Torture doesn't work the way most people think it does. You tell your torturer what you think they want to hear, not the actual truth. It'll be different when you actually comply and speak with us of your free will.'

'Come on,' said Tess, extending a hand. 'Let's get you seated more comfortably and I'll take a look at that wound for you.'

Po righted the upended kitchen chair and moved it so that it was situated where Tess could move freely between Wilson and the kitchen sink. Without any bidding from her he delved in cupboards, seeking anything useful. To the already open bottle of disinfectant he added table salt, a clean jug, and a bunch of paper towels.

'OK,' said Tess to her patient, 'while I'm doing this, you concentrate on what you know about Tony and where he might have hidden out.'

'I can't promise anything . . .'

Po offered his hand, a gesture that had fallen out of practice during the pandemic, and when Wilson took it, he hauled him up and guided him into the kitchen chair. Wilson hissed and grimaced, and took care to keep his weight off his injured foot. While she administered to his wound, and Po stood sentinel over them both, Tess was aware that Wilson's tongue was growing looser.

THIRTEEN

Tony Vaughan jerked upright, gurgling out a shout of alarm. He swiped away the hands grasping him. His body fizzed with adrenalin, his stomach flipping, as he scrambled to gain his footing. He couldn't stand. He was trapped, his legs bound, and he couldn't extricate his feet. He croaked in dismay, and again wrenched to escape the hands now pressing down on his chest.

'Tony! Relax. It's only Leah.'

He heard and recognized her voice, but he was still traumatized by his abrupt awakening. He struggled, and this time got his right leg free of whatever was holding him, and he thrust at the floor, trying to stand. The couch he had fallen asleep on moved, legs screeching across the uneven floor.

'Tony,' Leah again said, 'we're safe. It's only me.'

Vaughan's blind eye affected his depth perception; mostly he'd gotten used to compensating for his lack of binocular vision, but sometimes he struggled to make sense of objects close by. He couldn't make out Leah's features beyond a dim blur, and her body was an amorphous blob. Her fingers on his pounding chest weighed a ton apiece. He shuddered and fell back.

'Wh-what's wrong? Why'd you w-wake me up like that?'

'I only shook your shoulder,' Leah explained. 'You must have been dreaming . . .'

'I . . . I don't remember dreaming.'

'You were talking in your sleep. You began getting agitated and I thought you were having a nightmare. I tried to wake you gently but—'

'I overreacted?'

'You might say that,' she said, and he could see her clear enough now to recognize a timid smile. 'But it's understandable.'

'No. I'm not much use to either of us if I'm going to panic like that when they do come.'

'Don't put yourself down, Tony. You were having a bad dream, that's all, and when I touched your shoulder you reacted to whatever was troubling your sleep. Anyone would've done the same.'

Therein lay the rub. In his dream, despite claiming not to recall it, he was in the clutches of their enemies, and while they flayed Leah alive for their amusement, the Brogan brothers forced Vaughan to watch. Anyone else would've fought them tooth and nail, not stood watching, too cowardly to save her.

He was doing himself a disservice, because it was different in real life than in his dream. He might stand ineffectually in a nightmare, but he was the only person to extend the hand of assistance to Leah, despite the fact he'd earned a death sentence. Actually the death sentence wasn't solely through helping Leah escape, it was the manner in which he'd financed her rescue that ensured a posse of killers would chase them across the country.

He was sitting on the couch, with Leah beside him. She was side-on, bent over to stare at him earnestly while he gathered his wits. He shivered still and his mouth tasted of spoiled meat. Leah patted his hand gently. He wished to turn over his hand and interlace their fingers, but was unsure how she'd react. If she pulled away, it would rip his heart open. He must be satisfied with her soothing touch for now. His legs had never been bound; he'd fought against a blanket that Leah must've placed over him after succumbing to sleep. It was a knitted woolen thing, heavy. It had caught his feet, made it feel as if he was fighting against bindings, but he'd finally managed to kick loose. The blanket now lay in a heavy puddle around his ankles.

'How long did I sleep?'

'Most of the afternoon.'

'I thought you were going to wake me after two hours.'

'I was, but you were so deep in sleep I thought it best to leave you. I only shook you now because of the nightmare.'

He could smell the food she'd cooked, but the aroma was stale and cool. 'What happened to lunch?'

'I'll make us something else.'

'Did you eat?'

'I ate, but I'm hungry again. Jeez, these days I'm always hungry.'

'Think you could rustle us up a pot of coffee? I'm parched.' Again he was conscious of the awful taste in his mouth. Back when he used to drink, he'd wake from sleep with a sore head and a mouth that tasted almost as bad as it did now. If he didn't know otherwise he'd swear he'd had a skinful of liquor last night. While helping Leah he hadn't allowed a drop of alcohol to cross his lips.

Leah stood, and Vaughan found he was reluctant to have her leave. He fought the urge to reach after her and pull her back down. He'd asked her to make him coffee, so had nobody else to blame. She moved to the kitchen, and he forced himself to get a grip. He exhaled several times, while rubbing his unshaven face with the palms of his hands. He stood shakily, and went to the front window. It was summer, the sun was out of sight to his left, but he could tell by the slant of light through the nearby trees that there were several hours of daylight to come yet. He wasn't checking for how long he'd slept, but for anyone lurking at the tree line. The window didn't allow a panoramic view. He stumbled over to the front door and pulled it open. Outside it was hot and airless. Even the trees stood still. He listened. Distantly he could hear the ocean foaming against the cliffs. He heard traffic on the highway to the west, so faint that it almost blended in with the crashing waves. If a vehicle drove up the private road it might be difficult hearing it until it was too close to the cabin for comfort. He checked around, his eyes darting as before: his blind left eye moved in its socket, but saw nothing but the most vague of shadows. He took care to pivot on his heels to compensate for his lack of peripheral vision, checking where a fully sighted individual might miss the obvious. Nobody he could spot lurked in the woods.

He listened again. Birds twittered merrily in the treetops. If anyone was creeping around, the birds would know, and they'd either kick up an alarm or fall silent. He felt sure that they would alert him if danger were closing in. In the next second he knew he was fooling himself. He wasn't that alert that he could constantly monitor the behavior of the damned wildlife! He moved from the threshold, planning on circling the cabin and ensuring everything was in order around the back. Leah exited the cabin and watched him, her hands on her hips. He moved back towards her.

'Leah, you have to stay inside, otherwise somebody might see you.'

'Somebody might see you, Tony,' she countered. 'Where's the difference?'

'I'm not as recognizable now.' He had shorn his hair close to the skull, and shaved off his beard and mustache. Even with a few days' stubble on his chin again, he barely resembled the bohemian-looking figure he'd struck while out in California, but anyone who really knew him would still recognize him. His change of appearance might buy him a few seconds but wouldn't stand up to scrutiny. There was little he could do to hide his distinctive eye: he was blinded as a kid, in a reckless attempt at jumping his cycle over a stream. His Evel Knievel-style stunt had saw him crash and burn, and scoop his eyeball out of its socket on the handlebar of his bike. Back then the surgeons saved the eyeball, if not his full vision, but it was now a scarred, milky orb that occasionally turned some people away in revulsion. He'd thought about wearing dark glasses to hide his injury, but wearing shades could be conspicuous in its own right.

'I don't look much like I did back home, either,' Leah pointed out. She'd dyed her normally fair hair the deepest brown and had cropped her locks into a short boyish style. Her bangs still hung long enough to mostly conceal her eyes. She was indistinguishable from the girl he'd first met in California, where even her build had totally changed from sylph-like to verging on rotund. He doubted anyone would instantly recognize her, and even her mother might have to make a double take. To Vaughan she was lovely, whatever her current appearance.

'We just can't take the chance of you being spotted.' Vaughan strode towards her, hands poised to guide her back indoors. 'Come on, let's get inside and have some of that coffee.'

Leah moved to where the sunlight cut through the nearest tree-tops and heated a patch of the ground. She stood in its glow, her head thrown back, eyelids scrunched shut as she relished the warmth on her skin.

'I'm so tired of hiding inside,' she said, without opening her eyes. 'I need the sunlight, and fresh air, otherwise I might get sick.'

'We can't afford for you to get sick,' said Vaughan. 'But we can't risk you being spotted either.'

She turned and appraised him. 'Tony, who's going to recognize me way out here in the boonies?'

'We don't know how close they are. For all we know they could be out there, in the woods, just waiting for the right time to come in and grab us.'

'That's pure paranoia talking.'

'Maybe, but it's also what's kept us out of their hands. I swear to you, Leah. Like I said, we just have to hang on a bit longer, stay hidden, and they'll lose our scent. Once the time and expense outweigh what they hope to get back they'll move onto bothering somebody else.'

'Sometimes I wish we'd just left and didn't touch a cent.'

'Yeah, in hindsight that might've been best. I'd've found a way to finance your new life without having the dogs sicked on us.'

'Maybe we can give it back?'

'We've talked this over before. We can't give back the money and hope for them to let us off scot-free. They'll still want to punish us, make an example outta us. Way I see it, we may as well keep the money if they plan on hurting us for taking it in the first place.'

'It could be years before they stop hunting,' Leah sighed. 'I mean, when will the time and expense outweigh finding us?'

'They'll give up,' he stressed. 'They can't keep it up for ever.'

'I don't see it,' said Leah. 'A million dollars is strong motivation for them to keep looking.'

'Yeah,' he agreed, and hoped she didn't realize he'd railroaded her into his way of thinking. 'And they might be out there right now, watching us, ready to pounce. So let's get back inside again, huh?'

'OK, you're right.'

'Once the sun's down and it's a bit cooler we'll come outside again,' he promised, 'when there's less chance of being seen. And besides, it will be more comfortable for you then.'

She nodded at his wisdom. He lent her his hand on her elbow. Leah waddled alongside him, one hand cupping her heavily swollen belly.

FOURTEEN

Seated opposite each other, glowering and grinning in turn, the Brogan brothers shared more than a passing resemblance. Nobody would take them for twins, which they weren't, but most folks would deem them siblings, or cousins. On further study their differences became obvious. Josh Brogan, ten years older than Bryce, had a square face, lined by experience, and his fair hair tended towards silver at the temples and through a central cowlick that stood up on his forehead. By comparison, Bryce retained some youth in his features, though he was in his early thirties and not the twenty-year-old he was often mistaken as. His hair was fair, but longer, a result of lockdown and having not visited a barber in months. Bryce's face was unlined by age, but he bore more scars than his big brother did. Most noticeable was the one under his eye – of which Josh also carried a similar scar – where the removal of tattoos had been bodged by a back-street plastic surgeon. Josh's tattoo cover up had been more successful, but had still left him with an untanned portion of skin in the general shape of the tattoo. The tattoos decorating their hands could be concealed beneath gloves when necessary, hidden with all the others decorating their torsos and limbs. Josh regretted allowing a needle to mark his face, especially when the allegiance it signified was historical, and meaningless to him these days. Rather than to the tattooist, Bryce rued the day he visited the quack doctor to have his gang tag removed: there was part of him that remained loyal to his old compadres first, stronger than to his current employers. Josh had to occasionally remind him that it wasn't their old pals back in the 'hood who were now financing their lifestyles, or who demanded quality returns on their investment.

Josh was seated on a low leather easy chair, his knees splayed. He sat bent forward at the waist, his elbows between his thighs, hands clasped. As he stressed points to his younger brother his hands jerked up and down. Bryce sat on an equally low couch, on the opposite side of a small circular table on which stood cups of take-out coffee. He too splayed his knees, but his upper body was thrown back, one arm bent behind his head. He appeared relaxed to the point of lackadaisical, and couldn't care less for his brother's points of view. Had he been anyone else, his attitude would have gotten Josh's goat by now, and it was highly likely he'd have shot him in the nuts, but this was his little brother, and Bryce often got away with behavior other men might die for. Case in point: Bryce had involved a local private investigator in their hunt. Ordinarily Josh would've boiled over at his stupidity, but this time, he saw how Bryce's plan to have Tess Grey find Vaughan for them held some validity. Their pal Randall wasn't so sure, and had made his concerns plain when hearing that the 'Peabody' lead had panned out, and the man was actually Nicolas 'Po'boy' Villere. Po'boy, he cautioned the brothers, had built himself a reputation as a man not to be messed with. These days, partnered with Tess Grey, he was on the side of the angels, but mess with them and he could bring down fire and brimstone.

'He kicked Walsh's ass,' Bryce conceded, 'but I don't think he's as dangerous as Randall claims. He hit Walsh with some sneaky shots, otherwise Walsh would've handed him his skinny ass.'

'I'm not so sure about that,' said Josh. 'From what Randall tells me, this Po'boy dude can throw down with the best of them. He handled you too, bro.'

'That's not what happened,' Bryce sneered. 'I'd've gutted him if not for some guy with a rifle. The son of a bitch had a bead on me and would've dropped me. I decided that retreat was the better part of valor. Besides, it got us talking, and I know I piqued the detective's interest. I can guarantee you, Josh, we just need to stick close to her and she'll lead us to Vaughan.'

'Maybe you're right. But you haven't exactly made it easy for us. They know both yours and Walsh's faces now, and will be watching for you. We look enough alike that they might make the connection if they spot me. That only leaves Randall to stake them out.'

'We need to get more feet on the ground,' Bryce said.

'You got a bunch of minions on call, little brother?'

Bryce shrugged aside the question. 'We can buy help here as well as anywhere else.'

'I'll ask Randall, see if he has any contacts we can pull on.'

'I've been thinking about putting out the call to the locals. If anyone can help us find Vaughan it's those who know the lay of the land. I'm betting that Villere has made his fair share of enemies around here, and they're keen to have a dig at him.'

'Randall says Villere's respected around here.'

'By respected he means feared,' Bryce corrected him. 'But fear doesn't trump need. Drop enough dollars in a junkie's lap and they'll cut Villere's throat on our behalf.'

Anderson Walsh pushed indoors. He stood for a few seconds, acclimatizing to the dimness inside the room. As they had at the children's outfitters, they had taken over a closed business premises in which to hold their meeting. Used books stuffed shelves all around where the Brogans sat in the reading nook. As at the first boutique, this second-hand bookstore didn't boast a burglar alarm, and it was unlikely anyone would turn up to check on the dog-eared stock too often. Bryce had been confident enough of privacy that he had switched on the power to the shop's coffee machine and gotten it working. Walsh fed a paper cup under the spout and pressed buttons. Once his steaming brew arrived, he carried it over and stood looking down at the brothers over the cup's rim.

'What's the plan, guys?'

'The plan hasn't changed,' said Josh. 'We find Vaughan and we make him pay.'

'Yeah, that's a given. Just wondered if there was something you wanted me to do to help move things along.'

'When we need you to do something, I'll tell you,' said Bryce. 'Why ain't you outside doing what I already asked you to do?'

Walsh held out the coffee as if the answer was obvious. 'I'm thirsty.'

'Take it outside with you,' Bryce ordered, 'and keep a look out. We don't want the cops rolling up on us while we're cornered indoors.'

'I haven't seen another car in the past twenty minutes,' said Walsh.

'Then somebody is due to arrive. Go do as I ask and watch out that it isn't the law.'

Walsh swigged coffee, but did as instructed, walking for the exit.

'Tell Randall I'd like to speak with him,' Josh called after him. As Walsh pushed outside, Josh Brogan eyed his younger brother. 'You treat that guy like dirt, I'm surprised he'll do anything for you.'

'I pay him well. For the right amount he'd suck my dick if I told him to.'

Josh's face contorted in revulsion. 'D'you have to be vile? It's so undignified.'

'Just stressing my point. Besides, Walsh needs guiding with a firm hand now and again. He can be a lazy ass if I let him get away with it. If I hadn't made him go back outside, he'd have happily parked his butt and spent all afternoon dozing.'

Randall entered. His eyebrows arched in question as he approached the brothers.

Josh sat back, looking up at his helper. Walsh was a bit slow on the uptake, but the same could never be said for Randall. He was as sharp as a tack, and Josh often sought his counsel. 'I need you to get on your phone and see how many guys you can round up to come help us.'

'Wouldn't normally be a problem,' Randall said, 'but I don't know how many will respond under this lockdown.'

'I bet every one of them is champing at the bit to get their hands dirty again,' said Bryce.

'Possibly. But they're probably also worried about being under scrutiny if they're the only ones traveling around.'

Josh held up a hand to forestall any further argument. 'You're possibly right, Randall, but until you ask you won't know for sure what's in anyone's mind. Tell anyone willing to help that I'll pay him well, and if he's the one leads me to Vaughan I'll give him a fat bonus.'

'The same goes for me, right?'

'Of course, my friend. I'll also pay you a finder's fee for each man you bring onboard.'

'How many do you need?'

'I don't have an open checkbook,' said Josh, 'so don't go bringing me coachloads.'

'Lemme see what I can do.' Randall took out his cell phone and began scrolling through his contacts. He wouldn't have many folks from hereabout in his list, but he only needed a single conduit into the local underworld and that would lead to as many people as they required.

'I need to ask again about this Villere guy,' said Josh, and Randall looked up from the phone's glowing screen. 'D'you know who might have been his back up at the pier? Bryce here said a rifleman was covering him.'

'I don't have a personal clue, but I'm betting once I get talking with some of the locals they'll be able to tell us.'

'Yeah, get us a name. I want to know who we're up against.' As Randall wandered off to make calls, Josh returned his attention to his brother. Bryce still sprawled on a chaise lounge as if he was some kind of diva. 'It's one thing letting the private investigator lead us to Vaughan, but taking him from her hands might prove difficult.'

'Wasn't going to offer them the opportunity to resist us,' said Bryce, 'I fully intend taking him. Villere and Grey won't get a chance to stop us, and neither will their pal. We won't be playing around next time we meet them, Josh. We go in hard and fast, neutralize the opposition and take what's ours. Soon as we have Vaughan we leave this pissant town in our rear-view mirrors.'

'Soon as we have Vaughan *and* Leah,' Josh corrected him.

'Yeah, sure, we'll grab Leah too. That goes without saying, bro.'

'Sometimes it's as if she's meaningless to you,' Josh said.

'You're not wrong. When she chose Vaughan over me, she became nothing in my eyes.'

'She's pregnant.'

'Who cares?'

'You should. Vaughan wasn't around to impregnate her, so the kid isn't his.'

'Ain't mine neither, brother.'

Josh sneered in revulsion at what Bryce's words suggested. 'She has betrayed us, Bryce, but it doesn't change who she is. You don't have to like what she has done but you can still show some goddamn respect for your daughter.'

'I've no respect for any white girl that lies down with a subhuman.'

FIFTEEN

'You tried. It was the best you could do for him. If his foot rots, it's on him, not on you, Tess.'

Po was back at the wheel of his Mustang, with Tess riding shotgun. She had frowned all the way since York Harbor to Kennebunk before Po offered his take on proceedings.

'He could die if he doesn't get help, and then it will be on me.'

'He won't die.'

'He could. He's in shock. I managed to clean and dress his wound but I don't know if there's any shrapnel still in his foot. Or if any of his bones were compromised. If his wound gets infected—'

'He'll seek help.'

'He's too afraid of Brogan to go to hospital. The doctors must report gunshot wounds, there's no way around it, and he's terrified that Brogan will come back to finish him off.'

'I had a word in his ear while you were cleanin' yourself up,' said Po, 'told him to do himself a favor, go to the hospital and play dumb. He wasn't the sharpest knife in that kitchen, they'll believe him if he tells them he shot himself in the foot.'

'He doesn't own a gun.'

'Are the doctors gonna check?'

'If I was the cop called in, I'd want to know all about the alleged firearm.'

'Not all cops are as astute as you musta been in the job.'

'It's a moot point. Wilson isn't going to go to hospital, so we needn't worry about him lying about how he managed to get shot.' She shook her head. 'Maybe we should call the cops and send them round to his house; he'll be more inclined to seek help once the matter's taken out of his hands.'

'If you gotta do it, then do it.'

'I promised him I wouldn't.'

'Then keep your promise.'

'If *you* call them then I'm not breaking my word.'

'I ain't calling the cops.'

'Call the medics,' she encouraged him. 'You could do it anonymously, just say you heard a disturbance and somebody calling out in pain.'

Po fell silent.

'He had you swear you wouldn't, didn't he?'

'Yeah, while you were getting cleaned up.'

'Seems to me a lot was said while I was washing his blood off my hands.'

'You took your time.'

She had too. She had washed Wilson's blood off her, then washed once more, before liberally sanitizing her hands and forearms with the remains of the bottle of disinfectant. Even after three attempts she still felt unclean. So she'd sanitized again. She had no intention of carrying Covid-19 – or any other disease – home with her.

'What else did you guys talk about?'

'He apologized for coming after me with that baseball bat. Made me feel kinda bad about headbutting him, y'know? He also said sorry for sendin' Brogan to the autoshop, but he said it was all he could think of to do at the time. He said he believed his life was in real danger, and Brogan proved it when shootin' him in the foot. Apparently he'd already played a nasty trick on Wilson, pretendin' to shoot him through his hand, before shootin' his foot for real. Under the circumstances, I don't blame the guy for gettin' Brogan off his back even if it sent trouble our way.'

'It links the actions and consequences of today into some kind of order, but the timeline is still crazy wrong to me. Brogan can't have been in two places at the same time . . .'

'I thought we'd already established it couldn't have been the same guy, just another of the gang with similar tattoos,' said Po.

'We did. I mean how we keep on referring to Brogan, as if he had a personal hand in everything when he couldn't have. We need to differentiate between the two to make things simpler.'

Po shrugged. Apparently he had no trouble keeping both men, and their actions, as separate entities in his head. Tess supposed she was needlessly complicating an already infuriating situation: infuriating because she still had no clue why Tony Vaughan had attracted the wrath of gun- and knife-men all the way from the west coast.

* * *

Po drove them through the town of Bartlett Mills. The highway was lined on both sides with fast-food outlets, banks, nail and hair salons, all of them deserted. It was eerie, reminiscent of a scene in a post-apocalyptic movie. When Tess thought about it, they were in a time of uncertainty with this terrible disease, and who knew how bad it could grow next. They were nearing halfway back to Portland, and she wished that Po had chosen the turnpike after all, because at least on the interstate the affect of the pandemic on their surroundings wouldn't seem as obvious.

As they approached the southern end of Portland, Tess referred to the scribbles she'd jotted on a notepad after leaving Bob Wilson's house. They were prompts for places to look for his half-brother Tony – after she'd asked about Anthony, he had put her right, informing her that his brother had never used his full given name, except for on official documentation. Some of the locations were old apartments he'd stayed in, and old haunts and drinking dives, as well as the homes of some old pals whose couches Tony had used to sleep off hangovers in the past. None seemed to be appropriate hiding places but she should dot the i's and cross the t's. She directed Po towards the first of the dozen or so possible places Tony might have taken cover.

Tess knocked on doors, Po stayed in the background, watching over her from the socially distanced margin of the curb. Mostly, while answering Tess's questions, several of those people she spoke with looked over her shoulder at Po, squirming under his scrutiny. Some of those who might otherwise have given her a hard time paid her due respect because of her lurking guardian angel. The consensus was that nobody had seen or heard from Tony Vaughan in the past year, others told her he'd moved to the west coast, and some were genuinely clueless. Within another ninety minutes, she'd struck through with a pen all but one lead on her list and was ready for changing tack.

'Where now?' asked Po, as she got back in the car.

'We need a fresh approach.'

'Agreed, but we ain't done with the first yet.'

She read the final name and address off her list.

'Gabe Stahl works for me,' Po responded, 'at the autoshop. When I think back, Gabe and Tony got pally before Tony left. Maybe when he came back home he looked up his old pal.'

'He didn't let his own brother know he was back,' said Tess.

'Half-brother,' Po corrected her. 'According to Wilson, he and Tony weren't close as boys, and they grew more distant as adults. Before he went missing, Tony only paid lip-service to his relationship with Wilson. After they had a few drinks I'd bet he told Gabe secrets he never told Wilson.'

'If you think it's worth following up on, then let's do it.'

'Tell me his address again.'

Tess read it off her list. Gabe Stahl's home address was in an upmarket suburb of neighboring Falmouth, on the promontory of land at the mouth of the Presumpscot River. From his front windows he'd have a beautiful view across Casco Bay to the state park on Mackworth Island.

'You must be paying him too much if he can afford to live near Mackworth Point,' she said.

'He earns every dollar I throw his direction,' said Po. 'Gabe's a hell of a mechanic and a good worker and worth every cent.'

'I didn't mean to undervalue your profession.'

'My profession, huh? I have to wonder what that is these days, but can't claim to be much of a mechanic any more. I have my fingers in too many other pies . . .'

'Entrepreneur?'

'Jack of all trades,' he countered, and offered a sly grin.

'Sidekick.'

'Partner,' he corrected her, and got no argument.

SIXTEEN

terminus of a leafy road at ranch. There wasn't a boat er was dotted with leaf litter been used in several months d access wouldn't be required muscle car abreast the entrance to red to climb out. There were three vicinity and she was unsure which was Stahl's. Po shrugged; he had never visited Stahl's home. He got out the Mustang, checked mailboxes and then jerked a thumb at the house on the right of the pier. 'I should be the one to do the talking this time.'

She deferred, it made sense for him to approach Stahl for information. 'I'm coming with you,' she added.

'Sure thing.'

Po pulled up his neckerchief to cover his mouth and nostrils. Taking his cue, Tess jostled her facemask into place as she followed him up Stahl's drive to the front of the house. It was early evening, but daylight prevailed and would do so for a couple of hours still. There were no lights on inside the house that Tess could see, and no other hint of life beyond its walls.

'Was Gabe working today?' she asked.

'Yeah, but the shop closed at five. He should be home by now.'

Ordinarily Po couldn't be certain where Stahl went after work, but with the current rules he had little choice to go anywhere. He could be grocery shopping, or had maybe even stopped off elsewhere to take some permitted exercise, but otherwise he shouldn't really be out. It was ironic that she expected Stahl to follow the rules to the letter when she and Po were flouting them: if challenged, she would argue that Vaughan's life could be in danger, giving her and Po valid reason to seek him before it happened. Of course, any cop would be perfectly justified in reminding her that the responsible thing – within or outside a time of pandemic – would be to inform the police about Brogan and pals, and let the cops do their jobs. The officer would be correct, but it was a Po had pointed out after their violent run in with Brogan Walsh; there was no imagining a day ahead where she'd bac and allow Brogan to hunt down Tony Vaughan.

Po indicated a car parked alongside the house. He expound, but Tess took it he was confirming he recogn Stahl's so he must be home. Po angled for the fron pulled open the screen. He rapped knuckles directly of glass. Tess kept a safe distance, and watched as so he wouldn't invade the space of anyone openii checked for movement beyond the windows ove yard.

'Does Gabe have a wife and children?'

'Nope. Confirmed bachelor.'

'It's a nice family home.' She was unsure how she'd answer why family homes were on her mind, one with ample bedrooms for several children. But Po didn't ask, he rapped on the door again.

When there was no response, he glanced back at her, then shamelessly reached for the door handle. He tried it and the door popped open. He gave it a gentle nudge, and leaned across the threshold. 'Yo, Gabe! It's me, Po Villere. You home, podnuh?'

Stahl didn't answer.

Déjà vu assailed Tess. There was no comparison between this lovely home and Bob Wilson's neglected house, but there was the same vibe about them. She experienced that same sense something horrible had occurred inside, and that an ambush was about to be sprung. She hissed in caution as Po took a step inside. He wasn't displaying the wariness he had at Wilson's, and she feared his head being cracked by a baseball bat.

'Yo, Gabe?' Po tried again. 'You home, buddy?'

She rushed for the door and gave it another series of hard knocks. The sounds resounded throughout the house. From above their heads came a soft thump, followed by shuffling footsteps across a floor.

'Who is it?' a tremulous voice called.

'I'm looking for Gabe,' Po answered, because it was apparent that the person wasn't Gabe Stahl. Tess would put a bet on the voice belonging to an elderly man.

'What do you want with him?'

'There's nothing to worry about,' Po called up the stairs. 'I'm his employer. Gabe works at my autoshop.'

'That doesn't give you the right to waltz into his home uninvited.'

'You're right. I thought there could be somethin' wrong and was only checking Gabe was OK.'

'Why'd there be anything wrong?'

Po peered at Tess, unsure how much he should divulge. She interjected. 'Hello, sir. My name's Teresa Grey. I'm a specialist investigator following up on a missing persons case and thought Gabe might be able to help me. My partner here's telling the truth, he is Gabe's employer, and his friend.'

'So let's get this straight, pal,' said the old man directly to Po, 'you're the owner of a garage or you're partnered with a *specialist investigator*?'

'I can be both.'

At the head of the stairs a figure shambled into view. He was elderly as Tess had assumed, and lacked mobility, attested to by his shuffling gait. It was evening, but early to be dressed in pajamas and a housecoat unless it was the old man's usual attire. He peered over the rail, eyeballs enlarged behind thick lenses. The man's hair was long, white, and sparse and even in the dimness his lined face had a yellowish caste.

'You must be Gabe's da?' said Po.

'His what?'

'His da. His daddy.'

'Yes, I'm Gabe's father.' The old man didn't proceed down the stairs, for which Tess was thankful. His legs didn't look as if they had the strength to carry him. He clung to the banister and stood eyeing them with his mouth hanging open in question. 'You're that southern fella my boy mentioned owns Charley's.'

'That's right.'

'Gabe speaks well of you.'

'Happy to hear it.'

'Sir,' said Tess as the old man wobbled at the head of the stairs. 'Do you need to sit down? I'd hate to see you fall.'

'I'm fine. Just setting my feet so's I can see you better. You're looking for a missing person, you say?'

'The guy used to work alongside your son at my partner's garage,' she explained. 'He left, went west, but allegedly has recently returned to Maine. We wondered if he'd been in touch with Gabe since he got back.'

'What's this guy's name?'

'Anthony Vaughan.'

'Wait a minute! Are you talkin' about Tony One-Eye?'

'You know him?'

'Not too well, but I remember when he was a buddy of Gabe's.'

'Has Tony been in touch with Gabe to your knowledge?'

'To my knowledge, huh?' The old man coughed out a laugh. 'I might look senile but I still have my wits intact.'

'I meant no insult,' said Tess, smiling behind her mask, 'it was just a figure of speech.'

'Girl, I'm only pulling your leg. To my *considerable* knowledge, Tony One-Eye has not been in touch with my son. But that's not to say that he hasn't. Gabe moved me in here so's I wouldn't have to spend this darn lockdown alone, but I'd've been as well sitting put where I was before. I rarely see Gabe, and when I do he hasn't much to say to me. This' – he wriggled his fingers over his chest to indicate his presence in the house – 'is more about him having a sense of duty than any affection for his old man.'

Tess took out a business card and placed it on the third stair up. 'When Gabe gets home can you tell him we called by and have him call me on that number?'

'I might be asleep when he gets back.'

'I don't want to put you to any trouble,' Tess said. 'But I'd really appreciate your help. Now, I think we've overstepped our mark and come in here when we could be risking your health. We should leave, Po,' she ended her announcement quieter, for Po's ears only.

Po grunted in acknowledgment, but so there was no misunderstanding, he held up a thumb to the old man and said, 'Remind Gabe he has my number too.'

'Will do. You saw yourselves in, may as well see yourselves out again. Make sure the door's fully shut behind you, don't want any stray cats getting in and peeing all over the house.' Without another word, Stahl senior turned and shuffled away, lost in seconds in the dimness of the upper floor landing.

Tess and Po exited the house. Po pulled the door tight behind him, then shut the screen door, and jammed the bottom in the frame with a short jab with his boot heel. 'That should do it.'

Tess took out a small bottle of hand sanitizer. She offered it to Po, and he held out a palm. She dispensed a small puddle into his hand and he washed away any contact with the door handle and screen. Tess also sanitized her hands, although the only thing she'd touched was with her knuckles when she knocked. You couldn't be too careful with touch contact though, and again she thought she didn't wish to carry any disease back home with her. Wilson's house had been unsanitary, Gabe Stahl's wasn't, and yet his elderly father was decidedly sick: his skin color was down to jaundice, probably due to an acute kidney or liver problem.

A motorcycle rumbled towards them. The rider wore a full-face

visor, and it reflected the lowering sun. Po stood between the
motorcycle and Tess. However, there was nothing cagey about
the rider's posture as he brought the bike to a stop and set his feet
on the ground. He threw open his visor to greet them.

'I haven't done anything wrong at the shop, have I?' Gabe Stahl
asked as his opening gambit.

'Take it easy,' Po said, 'there's no problem, Gabe.'

Stahl eyed Tess. He knew her from the several times she'd
accompanied Po to his autoshop. He also knew what she did for
a living and was cautious.

'What're you doing here? Is my dad—'

'Like I said, there isn't a problem, Gabe. We're only looking
for your old pal Tony,' Po said.

'Tony Vaughan?'

'Who else?'

'Haven't seen or heard from him in over a year. Son of a bitch
still owes me a hundred bucks.' Stahl climbed off the motorcycle,
and reached to unstrap a bag from the pillion seat. He held it up.
'I had to go to the drug store for my dad's meds. You been here
long?'

'We spoke with your father,' Tess said, to gauge his response.

Stahl jerked his head, and glanced towards what was obviously
his father's designated bedroom. 'You went inside the house?'

'Door was open,' Po lied. 'We heard movement and called out
to you, but got no reply. Thought perhaps you'd had an accident,
so we checked. You don't have to worry about your da: we got
nowhere near him, so there's no fear of us spreading the virus
to him.'

'Your father spoke to us from the upper floor,' Tess stressed.

'So you didn't get beyond the hall?'

'That's as far as we got,' Po confirmed. 'Don't know what
you're concerned about, Gabe. I'm in and out of the shop and I
don't see you running for the hand sanitizer each time.'

'It's just that my father's vulnerable, y'know. I've been shielding
him from outside contact.' He again shook the bag of medication,
to stress *his* point. He scuffed at the ground. 'I'm sorry, Po. Maybe
I shouldn't act so ungrateful. Thanks for checking up on me, but
as you can see . . .'

'You certain Tony hasn't been in touch?'

'Is he in some kinda trouble?'

'Why d'you ask, bra?'

Stahl nodded his helmeted head in Tess's direction. 'Thought perhaps he'd gotten himself in some bother with the law.'

'Nope. Unless you know somethin' about him that we don't.'

'I haven't seen him in a year, and don't expect to either, not while he still owes me money.'

Po squeezed out an understanding smile, and then flicked a wave of goodbye. 'Thanks for your time, Gabe. See you back at the shop, huh?'

'Yeah, see you.'

Stahl began pushing the motorbike the last few yards towards the house. He didn't look back, so didn't see Tess watching him with a frown before she turned abruptly and followed Po back to the car.

Inside the Mustang, she looked across at Po. 'You do realize you are employing a bare-faced liar?'

SEVENTEEN

Pinky watched the Ducati motorcycle zip past. He gave it only a few seconds to gain distance before pulling out of the side street and falling into its wake. Po had described Gabe Stahl's clothing and his red bike when asking him to conduct surveillance on the big house near Mackworth Point. Tess and Po would've tailed the motorcycle, except Stahl was too familiar with Po's muscle car and would spot them easily. He would possibly recognize Pinky if he got too close, but not Pinky's SUV. Pinky drove with more urgency than usual; keeping a motorcycle permanently in sight on these leafy, twisting streets was almost impossible. Things proved a little easier when Stahl got on the highway, although he gave the bike throttle and exceeded the speed limit frequently. Pinky sat back a couple of hundred yards, happy to follow at a distance while Stahl beat a path north.

'It doesn't look as if he's going to slow down till after Yarmouth, him.' Through the SUV's hands-free system Pinky updated Tess

and Po over his cell phone. Po followed Pinky, too far back for
Stahl to spot the muscle car in his mirrors. 'I think we can assume
he isn't on a run for some takeout pizza.'

'Definitely seems to be on some kinda mission,' Po replied.

'Maybe he's just taking a drive to clear his head, him.'

'It's a possibility. But we don't think so. Tess and me are on
the same page; Gabe was rattled when we asked about Vaughan.
He denied seeing or hearing from him, but he was lying through
his teeth. He looked about ready to crap his pants when he learned
we'd been inside his house. We wonder what he's hiding in there.'

'Now would be a good time to go and take a look,' Pinky said,
'while Gabe's out. I could keep an eye on him, me, and let you
know if there's any danger of him coming home while you're
searching.'

'Conduct an unlawful search of his premises? Absolutely not,'
said Tess.

'You said you'd been inside his house once, why not a second
time?'

'His sick elderly father is at home,' Tess reminded him. 'It was
one thing entering before we knew he was there, it's totally different
now. Especially now it's growing dark. The old guy could have a
heart attack if he hears us creeping about downstairs.'

'I guess you're right, pretty Tess. FYI, we're passing Todds
Corners,' Pinky claimed, changing tack abruptly to his latest
update on his and Stahl's location. 'Could be heading all the way
up to Brunswick, him.'

'Stay with him,' said Po. 'Even if he drives all the way to
Bangor.'

'I don't think that's likely, me. He's just taken a right onto . . .
hold on while I get a look at a road sign . . .'

'He's gone into Freeport?' Po suggested.

'You've got it, Nicolas. He's slowing, him, but it doesn't look
as if he's for stopping just yet.'

Pinky's prediction proved correct. Part of the way through town
Stahl took a hard right towards Mast Landing. Stahl kept going,
and once he was beyond the town limit signs, he again sped up,
seeming determined to reach the nearby coastline.

'Could get a bit obvious I'm tailing him if he stays on these
back roads,' Pinky announced.

'These roads don't go on much further,' Po reassured him, 'not unless you were right and he's only out for a ride to clear his head. He could circle back and follow one of the minor roads down the coast. If that's the case, we'll just back off and pick him up again back home.'

'OK, I could've saved you some breath, Nicolas. He's slowing down. I'm going to stop otherwise I'll have to pass him.'

Pinky slowed the SUV, rolling it to a stop at the roadside. Tess had mentioned earlier that it was growing dark; he'd been driving without the use of his headlights on, and only now realized how much the gloom had moved in. The proliferation of trees helped the darkness edge in closer. Three hundred yards ahead, Stahl had stopped and dismounted his motorcycle. Pinky watched him unclip a chain and throw it aside. He pushed the bike forward, rolling it beyond the chain before returning and securing the chain across the entrance to a side trail.

'I've no idea what he's up to, but Stahl just went off road,' Pinky said, hearing the distant grumble of the motorcycle as Stahl drove it into the woods. 'D'you want me to follow him?'

'See if you can see a sign or mailbox or somethin',' Po asked. 'But don't try followin' him in your SUV. If he spots you back in the woods he'll know for certain you're after him.'

'Gimme a minute.' Pinky took the SUV along the road, and slowed adjacent to the entrance to the trail. A thick, rusted chain blocked it and a sign proclaimed: *No Entry. Private property.* 'There's a sign to deter trespassers, but that's about it. No other hint there's a house back there in the woods but I'd guess so, me.'

'Yeah, I'd agree.'

In his rear-view mirror Pinky watched the Mustang prowl into view.

'That's me about two hundred yards ahead of you,' he said.

'I see you. Maybe you should move, in case Gabe comes back.'

'I can still hear him moving deeper into the woods. But you want, I'll move, me. Join me at the next pull in?'

'Lead the way, podnuh.'

It made sense to clear off from the exit, but not too far away that they'd miss when Stahl – or perhaps even Tony Vaughan – left the property. Pinky chose to stop on a passing place in the narrow road and got out of the car. The air was still and heavy with the lingering warmth of the day, and from somewhere over his shoulder he could hear the shushing of waves on a pebble beach. The tires on Po's Mustang crunched his arrival. Tess and Po got out and joined Pinky.

'What do we think?' Tess asked.

Pinky smirked. 'For all we know Stahl's supplier lives back in those woods and he's come out here to replenish his stash.'

'Far as I know, he doesn't use,' said Po. 'But I could be wrong.'

'I was kidding, me.'

'Yeah, but you might be closer to the mark than you thought. There's possibly nothing to be gained from following Gabe out here, but my gut's tellin' me otherwise.'

'Mine too,' admitted Tess. 'I was never one to believe in hunches before, but I've learned to trust my instincts, guys.'

'I'm for going in and takin' a look,' said Po, 'but if we run into Gabe on his way back, it'll kinda give the game away that we tailed him.'

'Why should that bother us when it's obvious he was lying to you before?' asked Pinky.

'If Vaughan isn't back there, we'd lose the one person who might lead us to him another time. I'd rather Gabe never learns we followed him here.'

'Agreed,' said Tess.

'D'you want to hang tight, wait for him to leave and then take a look see, us?'

'I could go in and recce the place on foot,' Po said. 'I'm confident neither Gabe, nor anyone else, will spot me.'

'When you go off on your own you always get into trouble,' Tess warned.

'Mostly I manage to get myself out of it again,' he smiled. 'Besides, it's not as if I'm gonna run into any bad guys, is it? I'll go take a look, see if I can get eyes on Vaughan and if I do I'll call you and you can come on in. Won't matter if Gabe knows he was followed then, right?'

Tess shrugged.

Pinky was unsurprised by her nonchalance. It was apparent that they had already considered Po entering and surveilling the area before they'd gotten out of the car. 'You should park that beast outta sight, you, then Tess can join me in my car. You don't want

Stahl coming out while you're still in there, and spotting it.'

Po took his advice without comment. After grabbing her stuff Tess joined Pinky in the SUV. She flipped open her laptop and brought up satellite images of the area. She zoomed down tight, just as Po padded back towards them out of the deepening gloom. He came up to her open door and looked inside.

'I'm surprised you got a signal way out here,' he said.

'There aren't too many places around here where you can't get a signal these days.'

She showed him the image on the screen. It was a bird's-eye view of the roofs of a cabin and outbuildings, nestled deep in the woods. 'According to the scale, it looks as if this building is about half a mile away' – she looked up from the map, back at it again, then pointed – 'in that direction. I'd say it's easily twice that distance if you follow the road, but I think it's still your best option.'

'I can easily duck outta sight if Gabe comes back my way. I'll hear him long before there's a chance he'll see me.' He reached in and touched her hand. 'Don't worry, Tess, I'm gonna be fine.'

'You damned well better had be.'

'Watch your skinny white ass, you,' Pinky added, 'I don't want to have to come in there and drag you out.'

With that, Po turned about, and jogged across the road. He hadn't made it as far as where the chain hung across the trail entrance before the darkness swallowed him.

'That's the second time today I've been struck by déjà vu,' said Tess. 'How is it this pattern of Po leaving us sitting on our thumbs while he runs around the woods keeps on repeating, Pinky?'

'Ha! He's never happier than when he's running around the woods. He thrives on this Daniel Boone crap, him.'

'I suspect you're right.'

'You needn't worry about him burning himself out, if that's what's on your mind. He's getting older – man, aren't we all? – but there's still plenty life in the old dog yet.'

'I want him to be around to see his children grow up.'

Her words gave him pause. He eyed her across the breadth of the SUV. With the doors shut and the engine off all was in darkness. Her eyes reflected the last ambient light of sunset. They glistened like pools of mercury.

'Hey, what's up with you, pretty Tess?'

'I'm fine.' There was an unfamiliar croak in her voice.

His blood went cold. 'Is there something wrong with Nicolas I need to know about?'

'Oh, God, no! It's nothing like that, Pinky. He's as healthy as a bull. It's just me. This damn virus, it has me worried for us all. Po, you, my mother and brothers, I don't know what I'd do if it took any of you.'

'We'll all get through this, you'll see.'

She wagged a finger between them. 'We shouldn't be doing this, sitting so close, breathing each other's air.'

'I don't got the 'rona, me,' he quipped.

'I can't swear that I haven't. Today I've been around people I should've avoided like the plague . . . literally. Any one or more of them could've been infected, and I could've given it to you, or to Po.'

'I think you were more in danger from Brogan's concealed knife than you were from him sneezing on you,' he said. 'Try putting those concerns to the back of your mind, Tess, they aren't worth dwelling on.'

She scrubbed at her eyes with the heels of her thumbs. 'Phew. Don't know where that came from,' she said, her voice trembling. She sat taller in her seat. 'I'm OK, Pinky. Or I will be in a minute.'

He gently squeezed her knee, and she nodded slightly in gratitude.

'I'd've squeezed your hand,' he said, 'but then we'd have to sanitize, us.'

'Speaking of which . . .' She took out a small bottle of hand sanitizer and offered him a squidge.

She put a generous drop in her own hand then washed. He too slowly interlaced his fingers and rubbed his palms, humoring her. She was probably correct to worry about the damn disease, and being an overweight black man, he had extra cause to take note of the simple hygiene rules designed to keep them safe. It would be ironic that his life had been defined in many ways by violence, with people trying to hurt or kill him, and yet a microscopic bug could be the thing to take him out. 'Here, gimme another blob of that stuff, you.'

Tess shook her head in mock dismay, then leaned across to dispense fluid on his palm.

A distant sound halted her.

She jerked up her head and stared at Pinky. In the dark, he could sense all her fears and concern for Po had struck her anew. He voiced her unspoken question, though he already knew the answer. 'Was that a gunshot?'

EIGHTEEN

He listened to the faint sounds Leah made in her sleep, watching over her from an old easy chair brought here years before by his 'uncle'. The old leather was cracked, the upholstery sunken, so it was uncomfortable. But the chair had a priority position from where he could see through the open bedroom door, while also keeping a watch through the front window. In the cabin's sole bedroom, Leah lay atop the single bed, blankets thrown askew. She was overheated, and had lamented the lack of air conditioning or even a ceiling fan – common facilities in homes she had grown up in, but not so much in northern fishing and hunting cabins – before undressing down to her underwear and kicking aside the blankets. To preserve her modesty, Vaughan had crept into the room after she fell asleep and draped a corner of a blanket over her pelvis, but since then it had slipped, or been thrown aside. He took care where he looked, but there was an unmissable feature: her swollen belly was a shiny mound at the center of the bed. Droplets of sweat shivered on her flesh with each gentle snore. He didn't have to watch her so closely, but he felt he should. He had taken on the duty of guardianship, and would not ignore the responsibility. Having checked on her, he again looked outside. He'd arranged the curtains so that he had chinks to see out of, while he'd be concealed to anyone outside. Unless he got close to the window it made having wider views of the woods impossible.

Paranoia assailed him.

He jerked upright and lunged to the curtain, thumbed it an

inch wider and peered outside. Night had fallen at last, and the air was growing mercifully cooler, but it had also made the gaps between the trees only marginally lighter than the inky black of the trees. It was easy to imagine that every shadow hid one of his hunters, stealing in to surround him and cut off any escape. He conjured eyes staring back at him from behind bushes and tree trunks. No way on earth was the view from the window enough to check that Leah was safe. He went to the door and opened it a crack, then stepped outside. He trod on hard-packed dirt, for which he was thankful because it deadened his footfalls. He made a rapid circuit of the cabin, and returned to the door. His first task was a quick check inside, ensuring nobody had slipped indoors while he was around the back. No lurker greeted him. Leah still slept, tossing and turning a little but not waking. He turned and again spied all around, his gaze lingering on the most likely hiding spots.

He wondered what it was that had stirred the small hairs on the back of his neck and brought him jolting out of the easy chair. He was paranoid, yes, but there must have been some stimulus that tickled his senses. He walked out from the cabin, peering to where he'd left the car concealed between two slowly collapsing outbuildings. He moved around the car, crouching at each to touch the fully inflated tires. The doors and windows were all secure, as was the trunk and hood. From what he could tell the vehicle had gone unmolested during the few hours it had been parked out of his sight. He'd arranged it with the hood out, ready for a speedy getaway if necessary. But whom was he kidding? If the Brogans and other henchmen surrounded the cabin, how was he ever going to get a heavily pregnant girl into the car and out of their clutches before they swarmed in?

He'd have to fight their way clear.

He held up the revolver he'd taken to holding while he sat guard. Sometimes he forgot the gun was in his hand, it had become a familiar weight over the days – and especially the nights – that they'd been on the run. It was a Taurus 856, a six-shooter. Three of the chambers were empty; the others contained .38 Special cartridges. During the pandemic, and the recent social upheaval and fall out, there'd been unprecedented demand for guns and ammunition, and it had grown seriously difficult for him to lay his hands on the correct ammo. The gun, he knew, would have more worth as a visible threat than it would enable him to fight a path through his pursuers. Besides his lack of firepower, he doubted he could kill a person in cold blood. Under pressure, running for their lives, to save Leah and her unborn infant, yes, he could fire the revolver, and if it took down an enemy then so be it. But to look a man dead in the eye and pull the trigger . . . he wasn't confident he could go to that extreme, even if Leah had warned him he must. Her father, Bryce Brogan, would not flinch if their positions were reversed. He'd kill Vaughan with pleasure, she'd warned, and her uncle Josh, whose moral center was virtually as twisted as her father's, would act only a fraction of a second slower.

He pushed the revolver in his pocket. Headed away from the car and stationed himself at the edge of the clearing that served the cabin as a front yard. Really it was simply an area cleared of brush, once used as extra parking for more than one truck, and for the boat his proxy uncle once owned. The underbrush had reclaimed most of the yard, but some was bare dirt like at the front of the cabin, so there was still occasional foot and vehicle passage. For now though, they were safe from discovery by whoever now owned the place: he couldn't even swear that his mother's ex-boyfriend – Uncle Roger – was still alive, never mind coming up here to hunt, but chances were he did still visit. Surely that old chair would've been gotten rid of by new owners?

To hell with Uncle Roger! His mom's old squeeze turning up was not a major concern. He was out here trying to determine what the hell had gotten him riled a few minutes ago, and he was allowing an old chair to dominate his thoughts! Concentrate, he warned himself, or you may as well suck on the barrel of that revolver and pull the trigger and save the Brogans the effort.

With more clarity, he stood alert. He could hear the distant ocean, and the creak and groan of the woods around him, and he heard something else, and realized that at the edge of his hearing the buzz of an engine had impeded for several minutes now. It wasn't unusual to hear traffic on the surrounding roads, but this engine had a different oscillating timbre than what he'd grown used to, and he suddenly understood why: the vehicle was cautiously closing on the cabin following the winding route through the woods, in one instant louder than the next as the trees intervened.

His breath catching in his chest, he spun around and raced to the cabin. He banged inside, throwing the door wide enough for it to slam the interior wall. Coupled with his footsteps and the shout now erupting from his throat, Leah awoke with a shriek and kicked backwards on the bed to put her spine against the headboard. She clutched at blankets that had already slipped off her, aware now of the vulnerability in her lack of dress.

'What's wrong?' she squeaked.

'Somebody's coming!' Vaughan croaked as he rushed to her side. 'You have to hide before they get here.'

'Where, Tony? Where is there to hide?'

He span about, at a loss. Except for attempting to squeeze under the bed there was nowhere else she could feasibly hide, and she was in no fit state for crawling on the floor. He grabbed one of the fallen blankets and thrust it into her hands. She wrapped it around her shoulders as she scrambled off the bed. He saw discomfort contort her features, the stress she was under was unhealthy for her and her unborn. But there was nothing he could do to alleviate it at that moment. He must conceal her somewhere safer. He held out a hand to help her, but Leah was oblivious. Instead, he grabbed her discarded clothing off the floor and stuffed it under his left armpit. He swerved past her and beckoned her to follow.

Wide-eyed, she waddled from the bedroom into the open living space. There was the poorly equipped kitchen with an old table and chairs, the easy chair and the couch on which Vaughan had slept, and little else of note. There was a back door though, and Vaughan led her to it, hoping to conceal her in one of the dilapidated outbuildings before the vehicle arrived.

'Who is it?' Leah hissed. 'Who's coming, Tony?'

'I don't know. But they can't discover us here. If it's one of your father's men—'

'It could be anyone. Why are we assuming it's somebody dangerous?'

'We have to, if we intend to stay ahead of them.'

Outside, he went ahead, and gained the corner of the cabin. He ducked out for a second, checking for intruders. The engine sound was much louder, and he now knew it for that of a motorcycle.

He urged Leah to him, and bent to place his mouth close to her ear. 'Go to the nearest shed and hide inside. The car's right next to it, and you know where the spare set of keys is.'

'I'm not a good driver.'

'You'll be good enough,' he assured her, 'if it comes to it. Only get in the car if something bad happens to me, you understand?'

She nodded. He handed her the bundled clothes. 'Try to get dressed if you've time, but you must be quiet when that motorcycle arrives.'

'What are you going to do, Tony?'

'I'm going to try to make it look like we aren't here. But the car's a sure-fire giveaway. If things go wrong, I'll do my best to give you a chance to escape.'

Leah chewed her lip. Her forehead was awash with sweat. In her underwear, she was incredibly vulnerable. 'Go on inside,' he urged, 'and try to cover up.'

She went inside the sagging outbuilding, and he heard a muffled curse as she bumped into something in the dark. He cringed at the racket as whatever she'd nudged fell and clattered on the ground, bringing down more loose items. Thankfully her muttered apology meant she was unhurt, and the motorcyclist too distant to hear the noise. Vaughan backtracked to the cabin, entered the rear door and quickly swept through the room, ensuring the lights were switched off and their few belongings were out of sight from anyone peering in through a window. He closed the drapes he'd strategically arranged, but there was an inch gap at each side he could do nothing about. He gathered up the remainder of the provisions he'd purchased earlier and shoved them out of the way behind the couch. He went to the door and ensured it was shut, and threw a bolt for good measure. Done, he again left by the rear door, pulled it closed behind him and then darted to the right, moved adjacent to the cabin and crouched in the underbrush. The Taurus was back in his hand.

The motorcyclist approached with extreme caution. He creeped the bike the final hundred yards, and only stopped once he'd scanned all around. His visor made it impossible for Vaughan to recognize him, but he could sense the rider's wariness through his body language. The son of a bitch had expected to find Vaughan there, he was certain, and meant him harm.

Paranoia!

Vaughan bit his lip.

Pay attention to your senses, he warned. Paranoia had been his ally in this case, because without it the rider would have been upon the cabin before he'd had an opportunity to move Leah.

The rider dismounted and switched off the engine, but left the headlamp on, so that it illuminated the front of the cabin. Vaughan attempted to read the man's features beyond the visor, but the backwash of light made it an impossible task.

The biker peered over at where Vaughan had strategically parked his car. He looked again at the cabin, seeking any signs of life. Then the biker moved forward.

Vaughan's thighs were on fire. He had been crouching in one position in the underbrush too long, and his muscles screamed in protest. He tried to adjust his stance, to keep his shoulders square on to the biker as the man crept forwards. Something crunched underfoot.

The sound was faint, and should've been indiscernible to a person wearing a padded helmet.

The man turned and stared directly at him.

With Vaughan at the edge of the headlamp beam, crouching in the grass, it would have been difficult for the man to define his shape, but his senses must have been on high alert too. The biker cocked his helmeted head, spotted the amorphous shape several yards away and jumped in reaction. He stumbled, letting out a yelp and Vaughan echoed his cry.

Unconsciously, Vaughan had already thumbed back the hammer on the revolver. His yell transposed to a jerk on the trigger and the gun barked. The biker recoiled, spun in an ungainly bundle of flailing limbs to the ground. In the next instant he began scrambling, on hands and knees, then rolled over onto his backside. He kicked back, arms raised to pull off his helmet.

'Don't move! Don't move!' Vaughan raced forward, aiming the revolver. Dust kicked up all around the biker, hanging in a cloud of swirling motes in the headlight beam. 'I said don't move another fucking inch!'

His bullet had missed its target. Vaughan was much closer, bent over the downed biker now, but he was unsure if this time he could pull the trigger. If he could, his aim was affected by the quaking of his body, and he wasn't confident he'd hit the biker. He needed his captive to obey him, and fear the gun and the man behind it. 'Stop moving, *goddamnit!*'

The biker ignored the instruction, and continued to tug at his helmet. Vaughan coughed out an oath, stepped in and kicked the man in the chest. The downed man cursed in agony, but gave his helmet a final wrench and tossed it aside in the dirt. Vaughan crouched low, trying to enforce his point by jamming the revolver under the man's chin.

'For fuck's sake, Tony, it's me, your old pal, Gabe!'

Vaughan withdrew, his mouth dropping open. His good eye blinked like the beat of a moth's wings. The revolver was again forgotten in his hand as he stared down in confusion at his friend. He hadn't seen him in a year, and he had grown out his hair and beard, but it was unmistakably Gabe Stahl.

'What are you doing here?'

'Looking for you, Tony.'

'But if you found me . . .' Vaughan felt his stomach flip, and was in real danger of needing to run to the outhouse. He spun about, seeking *others*.

'I'm alone,' Stahl tried to reassure him. 'I'm the only one who knows where you are, buddy.'

'But *who* sent you?'

'I wasn't sent. I came looking for you. I guessed you were in trouble, man, and look at *this*. Kinda proves my point, yeah?'

'You shouldn't have come.'

'Maybe. But I'm here. C'mon, Tony. Can I get up off my ass? And for Christ's sake, put that damn gun away, will ya? You almost took my head off with it already.'

Vaughan glanced down at the revolver. He shook his head. He wasn't going to lower his guard until he knew for sure why Stahl had sought him; was he here as an agent of the Brogan brothers, a friendly face to lull him into a trap? He aimed the gun directly at Stahl's heart. 'Tell me the goddamn truth. There's a reason you came looking for me, and I want to know why.'

'I came to warn you that you're being hunted.'

'I don't need warning. I know it.' Vaughan fixed him with his good eye, seeking any sign of deceit. 'Did you speak with the Brogans?'

'I've no idea who they are.'

'They didn't have you lead them here, to help capture me?'

'No, man, I came here to help.'

'Then tell me, who's looking for me, Gabe?'

'You remember Po Villere?'

'Course I do.'

'He's looking for you, and so's his woman. Tess Grey. The detective.'

'Why?'

'You tell me. What the hell did you do, buddy?'

NINETEEN

P o dropped to a crouch the instant the gun barked. He was under no illusion; had the gun been fired at him there was no hope of dodging the bullet, but the first shot could have missed and more incoming. When the gunfire wasn't repeated he straightened to almost his full height, but ensured he kept some tree trunks between him and the cabin. He was still several hundred yards away from where Stahl had finally brought the motorcycle to a stop and had no clear view of what was happening in the clearing. Maybe he'd lied when questioned about Tony Vaughan earlier, but Po thought Stahl was a decent guy and good worker all the same, he'd be sorry if he'd been gunned down.

He'd be sorrier again if Stahl was the one who'd shot somebody dead – most likely Tony Vaughan – but didn't credit that scenario.

Stahl had been nervous driving towards the cabin, and he'd halted several times, standing astride the idling bike as if contemplating his next move. The stops had given Po opportunities to catch up, so too had the winding road Stahl followed, while Po was free to cut corners through the low-lying underbrush. Now that Stahl had reached his destination Po needed to get much closer to have any hope of seeing or hearing what was happening. He began a cautious advance, and was brought up short within a few steps. In his shirt pocket his cell phone vibrated. Taking cover behind some thicker brush he took out the phone, unsurprised to find Tess ringing him.

'What's up?' he asked barely above a whisper.

'You're alive, then?'

'You heard the gunshot, huh?'

'Yeah, we did. Is somebody shooting at you?'

'No. The gunshot came from up by the cabin, I'm still a ways off. I guess whoever's in there takes their privacy seriously and fired a warning shot at Gabe.'

'Is it Vaughan?'

'Like I said, I'm still a ways back, so can't confirm it's him yet.'

'We were just about to drive in and rescue you.'

'I want to look and see what's going on first. If I get eyes on Vaughan I'll call you. Somebody's gotten his hands on a gun, Tess, so be careful.'

'*You* be careful.'

He ended the call and shoved the phone in his pocket. Momentarily the blue light from the screen glowed softly over his heart, a target for a gunman if he wasn't careful. He put his hand over his cell, as if pledging allegiance to the flag. Once the glow disappeared he felt he could move on.

He followed the road for approximately thirty seconds, and when it doglegged to the north-east he cut through the woodland that the road was forced to curve around. Once he was through the woods he came to the edge of the road again and knelt down, camouflaging his human shape with the bushes. The cabin and outbuildings shown to him on the aerial photos lay ahead. They were all in darkness, no lights behind any of the windows. The scene itself was lit, the beam of Stahl's motorcycle casting the oversized silhouettes of two figures on the cabin. Both men spoke with exaggerated hand gestures, and one of them, Po could tell, still clutched a snub-nosed revolver in his right hand. For now, though, it seemed there was no immediate danger of further violence. The gunshot must have been a misfire from the lack of fear that Stahl now showed the gunman.

It was some time since Po last saw Tony Vaughan. If it were Vaughan facing Stahl, then he'd changed his appearance since he worked at the autoshop. He was about thirty pounds slimmer and had lost the shaggy hair that Po was familiar with. It stood to reason that he'd attempt to change his looks while on the run, but there was another reason for shedding all that weight, and Po wondered why.

The men's voices didn't carry well. He only caught one in every four or five words, but what he could tell was that there was more incredulity between the two than animosity. Minutes had passed since the gunshot. Stahl had already forgiven his old friend for taking a pop at him with the gun. After more gesticulating, Stahl moved towards Vaughan, and they gave each other a manly shoulder-to-shoulder one-armed hug. Stahl returned to the motorcycle and set his helmet on the seat. He switched off the headlight. He left the motorcycle on its stand and returned to Vaughan, who instead of walking to the cabin, began towards one of the outbuildings. Spotting the car nestled between two of them, Po initially thought he was going to it, but he opened the door on the shed nearest the cabin, and said something Po couldn't hear. Stahl watched his pal, now with his hands hanging immobile at his sides. Stahl's body language gave a hint at what to expect: he stirred, straightening an inch or two to present himself clearer to the person emerging from the darkness of the shed.

It was difficult defining who emerged. They were smaller than the men, but seemed squatter, rotund almost. It wasn't until the person took another step past the threshold that Po realized they were draped by a blanket, giving them the broader shape. Vaughan stood close to the person, protective of them, but also a bit awkward in their presence. Stahl raised a hand in greeting, and received a bare nod in response. Vaughan offered a hand that was ignored, and the person began an uncomfortable shuffle towards the cabin. It was a child, Po saw, or a young woman at most.

For a reason unknown to Po, the trio didn't enter the cabin through the front door. They disappeared around the back, but he was unconcerned that they were going to slip away into the woods. He waited, and within a minute saw a light click on inside. A dim shadow passed behind the curtained window, and Po guessed somebody was peeking out, checking for other unexpected visitors. Po remained exactly where he'd hidden. There was further movement, and this time he caught actual movement of the drapes as somebody – probably Vaughan – took another glimpse outside.

The guy's nerves were on edge, but maybe for good reason, considering he was being spied upon. Under these conditions Po doubted Vaughan would welcome the intrusion of a private investigator sticking her nose into his business, despite Tess's good intentions.

He backed away, retracing his passage until he was distant enough that his voice wouldn't be heard, and importantly the glow from his screen wouldn't be spotted. He rang Tess.

'Following Gabe was the right thing to do,' he announced.

'You've seen Tony?'

'Sure have, but I'm having second thoughts about contacting him directly. It was Vaughan who fired that gun. I'm unsure how he'll react if we approach him, and I'll be damned if I'll risk you being shot when you're only tryin' to help.'

'What are you thinking, Po?'

'We stand down tonight, and tomorrow I go back to Gabe and ask him to act as a middle man for us. He can speak to Vaughan, explain your intentions and we'll take things from there.'

'It's not a bad suggestion, but what if Vaughan has been spooked by Gabe's arrival and he takes off?'

'He'll no longer be our problem. He'll be in the wind, and Brogan will leave town. Problem solved.'

'Problem exacerbated,' she replied. 'You don't expect me to stop looking for him even if he leaves Maine?'

'I guess not.'

'But for now you should come on back.'

'I'm more inclined to stay put and keep an eye from a distance. I'd hate to think Brogan finds Vaughan while I'm sitting with my feet up at home.'

'You can't sit out here all night.'

'Why not? Don't know about you, Tess, but I'm just about crawlin' up the walls from being stuck indoors. A night camping under the stars sounds real agreeable just about now.'

'You must be insane.'

'Was goin' to ask you to camp out with me. Not like you'll be lyin' in a hole in the dirt, we'll have the car and its roof over our heads.'

'I'd prefer our home comforts and our own bed.'

'You haven't tried the back seat of the Mustang yet,' he said.

'Hey!' Pinky piped up in mock horror. 'Did you guys forget I was here or something, you? I'm about to burst into flames, I'm blushing so hard.'

'I haven't forgotten about you, Pinky. In fact I have a job for you too, podnuh.'

'So now I'm your podnuh when you have some chore for me to do?' Pinky joked. 'Tell the truth, you don't want a gooseberry hanging around and cramping your style.'

'Gabe's daddy is sick. The old man said they ain't close, but I don't think Gabe will leave him alone all night in that big ol' house. I need you to follow Gabe when he leaves here and make sure he gets back safe and sound.'

'You think Brogan is on to him and Gabe's in danger?' Tess asked.

'I doubt it, but it's better bein' safe than sorry, right?'

'There are days when I still struggle with the concept of good guy or bad guy, me,' said Pinky. 'Remind me again why it matters that we protect a guy who blatantly lied and went out of his way to avoid helping us.'

'The day you don't need to ask is the day you'll be one of the good guys,' Po said deadpan. 'For now you must still have one foot planted on the dark side.'

Pinky chuckled. 'You can rely on me. Tess's going to have to wait with your car in case Gabe comes out before you get back.'

'You OK with that, Tess?'

'I haven't agreed to camping out yet.'

'Wouldn't have suggested it if I wasn't confident you'd say yes,' he said, and that was the matter closed.

TWENTY

What some criminals wouldn't do for money could be counted on one hand, Josh Brogan thought. He surveyed the motley bunch rounded up by Randall thinking that his money would have probably been better spent taking out a wanted ad for Vaughan in the local newspaper. But that old cliché concerning beggars and choosers couldn't be ignored; these men were the best Randall could do at short notice, and Josh appreciated his friend's effort. By comparison, his brother was unmoved by the trouble Randall had gone to. He outwardly insulted those hired to assist them, then laughed sarcastically at their poorly subdued outrage. To Bryce these people were expendable, but to Josh he wanted his money's worth out of them, so he would attempt to keep them happy and motivated. He was paying them well, and he had reiterated his promise of a cash bonus should any of them be instrumental in leading him to Tony Vaughan.

One benefit of employing local crooks was their access to available properties. Breaking and entering currently unused business premises held risks that Josh could do without. He wouldn't find Vaughan, or the misappropriated cash, while constantly dodging the local cops. One of the men drafted in by Randall unlocked the door to his bait and tackle shop and allowed the Brogans to set up a base in the adjoining warehouse. The building came with a bathroom and an area converted to a kitchen: it consisted of a fridge, microwave, ancient coffee maker, and a battered table and chairs. It was not what he'd call plush accommodation but Josh had no intention of sticking around Portland for any longer than he must. It was inevitable that sleep would take him before the problem of Tony Vaughan was resolved. He would be happy bedding down in a sleeping bag on the floor of the kitchen, or out in the back of the van where his brother and Walsh had slept for the past few nights.

Four men had joined the search for Vaughan. They were locals and known to each other but not well. They were friends of friends, and that was usually as close a connection as was required to get a job done, but Josh would have preferred if they were an outfit, a sole unit used to working together. He guessed that each of these men would cut the others' throats and steal their payments if they thought they could get away with it. It didn't matter, it wasn't as if Josh was organizing a bank heist, he only needed a few tough guys to take some of the heat if it came to a showdown with Po Villere and his woman. Two of the thuggish men had already expressed desires to take out Villere. The second two could barely conceal their fear when they heard the name of their potential enemy, but greed overcame fear and they stuck around. Josh was sure they couldn't be counted on, but they'd make cannon fodder if and when it was needed, so he kept them employed. Besides, he needed somebody to conduct surveillance, and they could take the scut work and free up those willing to confront Villere. One of the tougher sons of bitches owned this bait and tackle shop, and was called Elvin Collins. Elvin held delusions of grandeur about his importance to the success of the Brogans' mission, and had already suggested being their guy in Maine should they wish to expand their operation into the north-east. Josh was happy allowing him the fantasy for now while he required a roof over his head and somewhere private to hunker down and make plans. Once this was done, he'd drop Elvin quicker than a lukewarm dog turd.

Bryce Brogan waltzed inside the warehouse, whistling tune-lessly. He grinned at his big brother, then sidled over and squeezed into one of the chairs at the kitchen table. Josh had a jug of coffee on the go, and Bryce reached for it and poured a mugful. He used Josh's cup.

'You should've gotten a clean mug,' Josh cautioned him.

'Why? You got the 'rona, Josh?'

'I wouldn't know if I were asymptomatic, and that's the problem with this damn disease.'

'You ain't sick, bro,' said Bryce, then tapped the side of his own head, 'except up here perhaps.'

'Kettle calling the pot?'

'I'm not *plain* crazy, I'm *uniquely* nuts.' Bryce grinned again. His teeth glistened, but his eyes were flat and dull. 'My quirkiness is what makes me so lovable.'

'It's what makes you insufferable,' Josh corrected, and a spark of genuine humor in Bryce's gaze rewarded him this time. Seriously, Bryce was joking about being insane, but Josh knew it for the absolute truth.

'All I'm saying is you shouldn't be so reckless. This virus is a bad one, Bryce, and not to be sneezed at.'

'If that's a play on words, it's the worst I've heard in ages. I'm not afraid of catching the bug. Why should I be? A few hours ago there was more chance of me catching a rifle bullet and I didn't let that worry me.' He swallowed the entire mugful of coffee in one long swig, then clunked the mug down on the table. 'Every day is a day nearer to death, bro. I've made peace with the inevitable.'

'Personally,' said Josh, 'I don't fancy ending my days gasping for oxygen on a ventilator.'

'You don't have to worry about that, Josh. Y'know that guys like us don't die in hospital beds. Neither will the likes of Tony Vaughan, or Po'boy Villere.' Bryce contorted his wrist and his concealed knife sprang from under his sleeve. He gripped the handle and made a twisting motion with his hand. 'Tony will get his when I catch up with him. If Villere tries me again, there'll be no holding back this time. Not now I know who his guardian angel is.'

'You've identified the rifleman?'

'You sound surprised. I'm not totally useless without your guidance, big brother. I got a name and an address. I've dispatched Walsh to go over and keep watch and let me know when Villere's pal shows up.' He upended his elbow, so that the knife tip dug into the table, and used the leverage to push home the blade into his sleeve. 'When he does, I'm gonna pay him a visit.'

'Tell me about him.'

'What d'you want to know? He's some nigger boy goes by the name of Pinky. I mean, how dangerous can he be with a faggot name like that?'

'He knows one end of a rifle from the other. Maybe you shouldn't underestimate him, Bryce.'

'This time he'll be the one ambushed. Trust me, Josh, he won't get his hands on a rifle before I open him up and hand him back his guts to carry.'

'Killing him goes contrary to your plan of getting the detective to find Vaughan for us.' Josh caught and held his brother's gaze again, letting him think about the consequences of murdering 'Pinky'.

'Or it will galvanize her to try harder.'

Josh shook his head. 'By killing her friend you'd be attracting serious heat from the cops, and we don't want them involved until after we've caught Vaughan and Leah and are out of here.'

Bryce frowned, but nodded at Josh's superior wisdom. 'Tell you what, brother. You're right, and I'm big enough to admit when

I'm wrong. But I'm still gonna have my five minutes with the asshole. I don't have to kill him immediately, and I just thought how he can help us prod Tess Grey into action.' He took out his cell phone and checked for messages – he expected an update from Walsh, Josh assumed. There were no messages. Instead, Bryce composed further instructions to his helper and hit send.

'Any word from Villere's place?' Bryce asked after slipping away his phone.

'Nothing yet.' Josh had sent the two anxious locals to keep watch on the approach to Villere's home. The southerner was yet to return with his partner to the ranch, but Josh was confident they'd do so before much longer. From there onward Josh wanted a 24/7 tail put on them, because he was certain Grey would make it her mission to find Vaughan. He'd had no personal interaction with either of them yet. Bryce had formed an opinion based on anger, frustration and not a little embarrassment, so Josh was careful not to be taken in by his skewed version of them. Elvin Collins had given him another version of Po'boy Villere, one where the displaced Cajun was blown out of proportion to a point where he'd almost resembled a superhero. A quick online search had given Josh enough of an idea that Villere, and especially his partner Tess Grey, had attained equal levels of hero-worship and notoriety due to their antics. They were dogged, and capable, and probably best avoided at all costs. Ordinarily Josh would heed his own advice, but if he'd to admit which scenario he was most wary of he'd choose attracting Villere and Grey's attention sooner than return to California empty handed: he had a higher chance of surviving a run in with Villere and Grey.

Bryce splashed more coffee into the stained mug. He held up the jug to Josh, an eyebrow cocked in question.

'I'll pass. I'm going to try to get some shut-eye, and that won't happen with caffeine leaking out of my ears. Has Walsh taken the van?'

'No. He used Randall's car 'cause Pinky would recognize the van.'

'No problem,' said Josh. 'I won't be sleeping on the floor here then. Gimme a shake as soon as you hear anything, brother.'

Bryce checked the time. 'It's still early. You're going to sleep?'

'I haven't closed my eyes in almost forty-eight hours, Bryce. I'm surprised I haven't fallen over before now.'

Bryce tossed the van's keys across the table. Snatching them out of the air, Josh showed he was more alert than he'd made out. He doubted he would be able to get any decent rest, but to lie down with his eyes closed for an hour would help.

'Try not to upset the locals while I'm asleep, huh?'

TWENTY-ONE

Seeing a friendly face brought some relief but Vaughan remained guarded. There was only so much that he would divulge to Gabe Stahl. The more Gabe knew – no, the more about the money he knew – the less Vaughan could trust him. Stahl was a good guy, a good friend, but he was also prone to human frailties. If he knew that Vaughan was sitting on almost a million dollars, it would test their friendship to breaking point. Vaughan thought there wasn't a man alive, discounting perhaps some holy lama sitting on a mountaintop in Tibet, that couldn't be tempted by the kind of money he had stolen. As good a man, as good a friend, that Gabe Stahl used to be, avarice could change him if he heard about a mountain of cash for the taking. Vaughan used to drink to excess, and when he was on the town with Stahl, his pal matched him drink for drink, woman for woman, and card game to card game. Stahl worked hard and played harder back then, and Vaughan didn't believe he'd changed in the past year. He'd bet he still owned that big old house overlooking Casco Bay, and the mortgage that went with it, and was struggling to juggle his standard of living with his incoming dough: at present, some people were losing their jobs, or working for less pay, and Vaughan doubted it was a boom time for mechanics when most cars and trucks were sitting idle on people's drives and in parking lots. Greed could turn Stahl against him, but so too could disbelief if Vaughan didn't share a plausible reason for being on the lam.

The bone of contention was coming up with a believable story that explained why Vaughan was prepared to shoot a stranger dead.

'That was a misfire,' Vaughan explained.

'Why'd you need a gun to begin with?' Stahl countered.

'I told you, Gabe. I'm protecting Leah. She was in a violent relationship, and I was afraid you were her baby daddy and you'd turned up to try taking her home. The gun was just a visible deterrent. Seriously, man, if I'd realized it was you I'd never have picked it up.'

Stahl wasn't buying it. 'You know you can trust me with the truth, Tony. I'm here to help you, man, so I should be allowed to know what I'm getting into, right?'

'You're my buddy, and it was good of you to come to warn me, but it'd be best if you leave and forget you saw me.'

'See, I'm finding it difficult accepting what you're telling me.' Stahl checked out Leah, who had sat without speaking on the couch, chin buried in the blanket she'd wrapped up in. He tried drawing her attention but she ignored him, as if his presence was an anomaly that she could dispel by strength of will. 'What kind of guy would chase you all the way across a continent even if you are having his baby? He sounds like the type who'd care less about a kid than he does about you.'

'You don't know how badly he'll try to get her back,' Vaughan said.

Stahl scrunched his forehead. He studied Leah once more, then Vaughan for confirmation. 'Tell me the truth now, Tony, is the kid yours?'

'What? No. Jesus, Gabe, Leah's just a kid herself. Holy crap, I care for her, but not like *that*.'

For the briefest of seconds Leah glanced up at her self-styled protector, and an emotion flickered across her features that was difficult to read.

Stahl shrugged grandiosely and then clapped Vaughan's shoulder. 'I had to ask, man. See, I thought maybe you'd got her in trouble and it was her daddy chasing after you.'

'You wouldn't believe how far you are off the mark,' said Vaughan, trying not to squirm at the uncomfortable prickling of his flesh: Stahl couldn't be allowed to know how close to guessing the truth he'd come. 'The thing is, her ex-boyfriend could be closer than we think and could've followed you here.'

'How would he know to follow me?'

'You said he's got a private investigator, and Po Villere was asking about me. Maybe there's other old friends he has trying to figure out where I am too.'

'You *were* the subject of BS at work today,' Stahl laughed dryly. 'Some of the guys were trying to figure out where you'd gotten to, but I kept myself to myself. Was surprised when I got home and found Po and Tess waiting for me, especially when they admitted being inside my house. Thought they'd come across the stolen booze I'm storing in my utility room – don't forget, Tess Grey used to be a deputy, and I wouldn't trust her not to bust my ass.'

'I don't know what she'd do; I never met her. I always liked Po though and find it hard believing he'd be bothered by you hiding some stolen beer.'

'I'm not just talking about a boosted six-pack of Bud, Tony; I've got the contents of a delivery truck piled next to my washing machine. I'm just holding the stuff for a buddy, as kind of a favor, y'know. He was supposed to collect it when things cooled down but then this virus hit and everything stopped, so it isn't safe to try moving them. He's promised me a cut when he gets around to selling them on, I just don't know when it'll be now.'

Vaughan shook his head in exasperation. Stahl always had been a good man, a good friend, but he had human frailties: gullibility in this case. 'Sounds to me like you're being used, buddy.'

Stahl smiled slyly. 'Don't get me wrong, Tony, the number of boxes dropped off at my place won't tally with those that leave. I've made sure I've already profited from the deal.'

Perhaps, Tony thought, 'good' wasn't the perfect way to describe Gabe Stahl after all. He had admitted double-crossing and thieving from a buddy he was supposedly helping. What was to stop him betraying Vaughan as well? No, he wouldn't allow any dark thoughts concerning his old friend. Stahl had come looking for him out of concern, so he was a decent enough guy, and still a good friend. 'How did you know to come out here, Gabe?'

'Didn't take much figuring out. Couple of times we hit the bars hard, we came out here to carry on the party afterwards. Ha! Don't you remember the time we stayed here all weekend with those sisters we picked up at that bar on Fore Street?'

'I guess so.' Vaughan flicked an apologetic look at Leah. Not that he need apologize about having a good time before meeting her, let alone having sex with another woman. She was his ward, not his girlfriend, and neither was she naive. Her pregnancy showed she was aware of what lovers got up to in bed together. 'I just didn't think it'd be obvious I'd hide here.'

'Wasn't obvious to anyone but me. You can relax, Tony, I didn't tell a soul where I was coming.'

Vaughan went to the window and peeled open the drapes. He pressed his face close to the gap. He shuddered out a sigh, could barely suck in the next breath. Panic had not fully subsided, neither had his breathlessness.

'Chill out, dude, I wasn't followed,' Stahl reiterated, and again clapped Vaughan's shoulder in camaraderie. 'If anyone had followed me and they're as dangerous as you say, they'd have kicked the door in by now, wouldn't they?'

For the first time, Leah spoke directly to Stahl. 'No. Kicking down doors isn't their style.'

'So what are you worried about?' Stahl directed his question at Vaughan. 'They arrive, wave that piece under their noses and tell them to fuck off.'

Again it was Leah who answered. 'You have no idea who we're up against.'

'Some pissed-off guy, angry at you for ditching him and worried you'll come after him in court for child support? He sounds like a complete shithead to me.'

'If only,' she muttered and sank back into her own world.

Vaughan checked her out. Her eyes were bulbous and she chewed her bottom lip. Signs she too was concerned with the ease by which Stahl had found them.

'We'll move on in the morning,' he reassured her. 'For now try to get some more rest, Leah.'

She didn't answer, only shuffled away and pulled the bedroom door shut behind her. Vaughan exchanged glances with his old pal. 'I can't fault you for trying to help,' he said, 'but you don't realize the trouble you might have gotten into, Gabe. Seriously, man, you should leave while you still can.'

'How many times can I say I wasn't followed, buddy? Listen, I'm here, and I'm offering to help. If there's anything I can fetch for you or Leah, y'know, even like a doctor or somebody that knows—'

'No! No doctors.'

'She's ready to pop, man!' Stahl checked out the decrepit confines of the old cabin. 'This place is fine for partying or sleeping off a hangover, but for Christ's sake, Tony, you can't expect that girl to give birth here. She needs to go to hospital.'

'We can't risk it.'

'Then come with me to my house. At least there she can make herself more comfortable—'

'No.'

'Tony, you can't—'

'I said "no", goddamnit. Listen to me, Gabe. You have to go, and for your sake and ours tell no one that you saw us.' Vaughan grasped his pal's elbow and steered him towards the door. Stahl walked with him, and Vaughan made sure they didn't slow until they were back at the waiting motorcycle.

Stahl took his helmet off the seat and squeezed his head into it. He threw up the visor and looked in earnest at Vaughan. 'This has nothing to do with somebody chasing his pregnant girlfriend. What's going on, Tony? Why are you really so afraid, man?'

Vaughan said, 'It was good seeing you again, Gabe, but please don't come back.'

He waited until the sound of the motorcycle engine had diminished before returning to the cabin. All the while he clutched the revolver in his sweating palm.

TWENTY-TWO

Following Gabe Stahl during the return trip proved more problematic than on the journey out. For starters he drove his bike more aggressively: on the way to the remote cabin Stahl must've been assailed with caution so had taken his time while thinking over his approach. On the way back there was no such trepidation, and added to that, it was later in the evening and even fewer vehicles were on the roads. Pinky had to fall back or risk giving the game away. At first he was frustrated, before realizing he had no reason to sit tight on Stahl's tail, not when he knew

where he lived. All he needed do was follow at a sensible distance
and check that Stahl had made it safely back to the house and his
sick father. So he slowed down and allowed Stahl to rocket on
ahead.

Back in Falmouth again, Pinky cut across the promontory
following the surface streets towards Mackworth Point. It was eerily
quiet in the neighborhood. He crept by Gabe Stahl's house and
spotted the motorcycle parked on its kickstand. Stahl's car was
where he'd left it earlier. Inside the house, several rooms were lit,
including one on the upper floor where Stahl senior probably spent
his days and nights. He was happy that Stahl was home, untroubled
by Brogan or anyone else, so his job was done for now.

He drove back to the highway and cut across the river into
Portland, heading home to Cumberland Avenue. He wondered how
the stakeout back at Vaughan's hidey place was going. Tess had
made it sound as if the prospect of camping out was an awful
idea, but Pinky had read her mood as easily as Po had: she was
literally loving being back on a case after months of house arrest.
They'd been together for months now, pent up inside Po's ranch;
Pinky made a bet that they'd fallen into torpor, as he had before
deciding to do something about his health. Sitting guard over
Vaughan would give them purpose and should be good for their
souls. Having been around and about today, his mind active
throughout, it had both enlivened Pinky but adversely had also
wiped him out. Tonight he might sleep, but it would be with one
ear cocked to his cell phone.

Pinky currently lived in Tess's apartment, situated on the upper
floor above an antiques and curios shop. The ground and
upper floors had private access and facilities. A set of wooden
steps climbed the side of the building to the door to the apartment.
Alongside the steps there was room to park two normal-sized
vehicles on a sloping concrete ramp. Pinky's huge SUV dominated
the space as he bumped over the low curb onto the slope. Before
getting out, Pinky sat a moment, checking the reflection in his
rear-view mirror. He had only the barest of angles on the car sitting
at roadside directly opposite. Pinky had lived on Cumberland
Avenue for a number of months now so was familiar with his
neighbors' cars. This car was not one of them. Ordinarily, the
presence of an unfamiliar vehicle wouldn't be cause for concern,

but under lockdown measures it was the first he'd noted in weeks. Add to that the fact there was a figure seated inside and it was enough to have Pinky's primal senses tingling.

He purposefully avoided looking at the car and its occupant as he stepped down from his SUV. Its hood pointing up the slope, the driver's position was on the left. Pinky had to walk around the SUV's hood to gain the steps up to the apartment. Pinky peered through the windshield, between the seats and out the back window. He spotted the pale blur of a face turned to observe him, while he would be effectively concealed by the SUV and the reflection of a streetlamp off its back window. Simply because the person in the car had turned to watch him wasn't proof positive that Pinky was under surveillance, but he'd learned to trust his instincts. Past the car, he mounted the steps and danced up them without looking back. At the top there was a small landing. Pinky fiddled about with his keys, and took a sidelong glance at his observer. From his higher vantage, he could tell that the person in the car had to bend to see under the car's roof.

Pinky took a glance over his shoulder at his SUV, formulating his next move. The rifle, his only available weapon in the SUV, had been deconstructed to its component parts and locked in a box in a hidden compartment in the trunk. He couldn't reach, rebuild and load it before he'd either scared off his watcher or been gunned down himself. He had other weapons inside the house: handguns kept prepped for the inevitable day his enemies came for him to ensure he never returned to Louisiana to reclaim his criminal empire. He unlocked the door, swiftly stepped inside and firmly closed it behind him. He strode directly to the first of the guns he'd secreted about the apartment and felt better with a Glock 17 in his hand. He went to the nearest window and posed himself to see out to the street below. The unfamiliar car and its occupant were nowhere to be seen.

'Now where'd you go to, huh?'

He adjusted position several times, confirming that the car hadn't been moved to another spot nearby. Whoever had been parked suspiciously across from Pinky's apartment had gone, and he had to consider they were the actions of somebody totally innocent of any wrongdoing. No, Pinky didn't live in a world where he'd ignore the obvious. He moved to other rooms in the apartment

and peeked out the windows there too. Each gave different views
along Cumberland Avenue. The car had disappeared. No, he still
wasn't prepared just to let it go as an anomaly.

He returned to the front door and stepped out onto the landing.
No sign of the car. He kept the Glock down, concealed by one
sturdy thigh, and descended the steps to the ground. He rounded
the corner and stood outside the shop. From there he had a good
view for hundreds of yards each way along the avenue. There were
other cars and the occasional van or truck in sight, but he knew
them all. He shrugged his wide shoulders. Was about to give up
when he caught the dim red glow of a light from between two
vans parked about fifty yards away. He could hear the low grumble
of an engine. Frowning, and clutching his weapon he began a
march towards it.

The same car as before came back into sight. Pinky still couldn't
be certain that he was the object of the driver's attention, but the
chances were high. He was of a mood to find out. He strode
towards the car, bringing up the pistol so that there was no misunderstanding about his intentions. He was still ten yards short when
the driver must have spotted him. The engine roared and the car
peeled out, coming close to taking the rear fender off the van in
front. Pinky lurched out into the street, but could only watch as
the car made off at speed. It didn't slow as it took the next corner
and sped towards Congress Street.

Pinky watched a moment longer. He was standing exposed, with
a pistol in his hand. Not the best image he could portray on the
leafy street. He pushed the Glock into his waistband and pulled
his sweatshirt over to conceal it. He retreated to his house, thinking
furiously. He checked he hadn't missed any other watchers on the
street.

He phoned Tess the moment he was back inside his apartment.

'Something odd just happened,' he announced after she
answered.

'With Gabe?'

'No. This was back home. When I arrived somebody was waiting
here for me.'

'What did they want?'

'Who can say? They took off like a cat with a firecracker tied
to its tail.'

'Brogan?' Po piped up.

'Wasn't him. Least I don't think so. I didn't get a clean look at his face, me.'

'What about his pal Walsh?'

'Your guess is as good as mine, Nicolas. Like I said, I didn't get a clean look at him. He was a white guy, but that's all I'd put my money on.'

'He took off after he knew you'd made him?' Tess asked.

'Nah, he only moved along Cumberland Avenue. He took off when I went after him and showed him my piece. Uh, by "my piece", I'm talking about my Glock, pretty Tess, not—'

'Don't worry, Pinky, I got what you meant.'

'But now I've this horrible picture I can't shake outta my head,' Po laughed. 'I've seen you in the shower, podnuh, no wonder you scared that guy off.'

Pinky grunted in mirth, then frowned, not totally sure if he should be insulted or not. Tess saved him the trouble of asking: she must have given Po a playful jab of the elbow because they both laughed and exclaimed like a couple of courting teenagers.

'Thing is,' Pinky went on, 'he's gone now, and nobody's taken his place. Maybe I stumbled onto a burglar casing out Mrs Ridgeway's shop downstairs and spooked him when I waved my Glock.'

'Maybe,' said Tess, sounding unconvinced.

Pinky didn't credit his own theory but who else could've been out there? When he'd sniped at Brogan and Walsh with his rifle, they'd no idea who he was, and he doubted they'd found out his identity since. If they held a boner for what had gone down at the pier it would be with Po not him, surely?

Po had grown serious again. 'If you don't feel safe there, go up to my place and let yourself in. You've still got the spare key I gave you, right?'

'I'm not allowing anyone to chase me outta my home, me,' said Pinky. 'If he comes back, *I'll* be waiting and *he'll* be sorry.'

'We should come back and keep an eye out—'

Before she'd done speaking, Pinky cut Tess off.

'Don't you dare, girl! I'm big and ugly enough to protect my own ass, me. If anything happens to Tony Vaughan 'cause you're here when you guys could've protected him from Brogan I'll never

forgive myself. No, you sit put and keep an eye out for him. I'll
have one ear on my phone, an eye on the street outside and my
Glock under my pillow.'

'You're sure you're gonna be OK?' Po asked, fully serious again.
'If there's any trouble, and I mean *anything*, you call us, right?'

'F'sure.'

Pinky ended the call. He meant what he'd promised Po, but
what could his friend actually do if something bad did occur? Po
was currently about a twenty-minute drive away and by the time
he'd gotten back it'd be all over but for the bleeding.

TWENTY-THREE

Tess considered Pinky's call, peering across at Po while he
too ruminated over their next move. He'd driven them onto
the wooded property surrounding the homestead, then
secreted the muscle car off road but with a good view of the trail.
Any vehicle traveling to or from the cabin would have to pass
them. She now wondered if they were in the best location they
could be.

'If you want, we should go back and make sure Pinky's OK.'

Po shook his head. 'It's like he said; he can look after himself.
Vaughan and the girl inside the cabin need our protection more
than he does. If anything happens to Tony while we're gone—'

The practicalities of their situation demanded that they stayed
put, not go haring back to Portland. Pinky hadn't sounded too sure
of his watcher's motive, but who could know?

'How quick can you drive us back if Pinky needs us?'

'Once we're on the highway I could get us to Cumberland
Avenue in under a quarter hour, that's obeying the posted speed
limit. On these roads, with nobody to slow us I could shave off
five minutes.'

She nodded at his estimated journey time. Even ten minutes
was too long, and an eternity for Pinky to endure under violent
conditions.

'Tell me again about this girl,' she said.

'Don't know what else I can add.'

'Humor me. Pretend I'm a knucklehead and need telling twice.'

'She was hiding in one of the outbuildings next to the cabin,' Po said. 'I figured that Tony moved her there when he heard Gabe's motorcycle coming. The cabin lights were doused and they'd used the back door rather than the front. I think Tony hid her, then ambushed Gabe, firing a warning shot at him before realizing who it was.'

She agreed. If Gabe Stahl had foreknowledge of Vaughan's location, and was helping him hide, Vaughan would not have acted aggressively when Stahl approached. But he'd hidden the girl and prepared to defend. Who was she? It mattered not, only that the presence of a girl added to the necessity to protect Vaughan, and now her, from Brogan and his henchman.

'You said she looked young.'

'It was dark, but Gabe had left on his bike's headlamp. I could make out enough of her features to tell she was a kid.'

'By kid you mean a child?'

'To me, anyone under thirty looks like a kid,' Po admitted. 'But no, not a little child, I mean she was late teens or maybe in her early twenties. No more than that though.'

'You said at first you took her for a boy.'

'It was the cropped dark hair and round face, the stocky body. My first impression was I was lookin' at an obese boy, but it came obvious she'd draped her figure in a blanket to disguise it from Gabe.'

'Who is she?'

Po said nothing.

'Her presence changes everything. I vowed to help Tony on the understanding that he was in danger from Brogan. What if Tony *is* the bad guy here?'

'Y'ask me, the girl wasn't being held prisoner.'

'Did they look . . . involved?'

'In a romantic relationship?' Po turned down his mouth, thinking about it. 'They looked awkward together, and she refused his offer of help when he tried to give her his hand. Who could say for sure?'

'Why's she with Tony, and why was he prepared to shoot somebody to stop them finding her?'

'I guess we won't know until we go and ask.'

'You've changed your mind about having Gabe act as a middleman for us?'

'Nope, but what if we have Pinky fetch Gabe here, and we make the approach tonight instead of tomorrow?'

She thought about it for only a few seconds. Actually, if they followed his suggestion it would serve to protect Pinky from harm too. If he was out of town, he was out of Brogan's reach.

'What about Stahl senior?'

'He looked frail, but not helpless. Now that Gabe's checked in on him, I'd say he'll be fine to be left alone for a few hours. As soon as Gabe's done here, I'll have Pinky take him home again.'

This case was unlike any she'd worked on before, with having no clue yet what Vaughan had done to attract Brogan's ire, and now whom the mystery girl was he appeared to be protecting, or why. Tess experienced a trickle of adrenalin, an uncommon sensation for months now. It felt good. 'Let's do it.'

They must time their plan for it to work best. Pinky should already be waiting outside the Stahl house when Po asked Gabe for his assistance, giving Gabe less time to consider and perhaps turn down his request. Po took out his cell phone and brought up Pinky's number.

Pinky was more than happy to assist. Tess suspected he would be, as despite pretending otherwise he'd been disappointed at being given the job of chaperoning Stahl home but had left in order to allow them some privacy. She guessed that the last thing he wanted to do was stay cloistered in his apartment again, anticipating the return of the mysterious watcher who might never show up. Within minutes of Po's call, their friend was back in his SUV on route to Mackworth Point. Po looked for Gabe Stahl's cell number in his contacts list.

'We should warn him about what happened to Bob Wilson,' Tess said.

'Why should it concern Gabe?'

'Just so he knows what he's getting into if he agrees to help us.'

'Tess, I wasn't going to give him a choice. If he still wants to work for me, he'll have to do this job for me.'

'Don't you think that's a bit of a low trick?'

'It's a practical and necessary move. Besides, Brogan will have no idea of Gabe's involvement, so we needn't worry about him ending up with a bullet through his foot.'

'Don't tempt fate.'

Po waited until Pinky was again sitting at curbside near Stahl's front door, near to the boat ramp where Po had parked earlier. Pinky sent a brief text message to say he was ready. Po rang Gabe Stahl's cell number and promptly received notification his call could not be connected. It wasn't the end of the line. He used his phone's internet connection to search for an online telephone directory. There was a landline listed at the big old house at Mackworth Point. Po rang the number and heard the ringtone this time.

'Whatever you're selling, I don't want it,' a voice grumbled a second after the phone was picked up. As was often the case, most calls Stahl received on his landline these days were from touts, scammers and market researchers.

'Gabe, it's me, Nicolas Villere,' said Po. 'I need you to do something for me.'

'Po? Watcha doing calling me at this time of night?'

'It probably doesn't take much figuring out, bra. I still need to speak to your old pal, Tony Vaughan.'

'Yeah, can't help you there, Po.'

'I know where he is, but I need you to open the door to negotiations between us.'

'You know *what* . . . Shit! How'd you find him? Did you—'

'My girl's a private investigator, finding missing people's her specialty,' Po said, bending the truth. It was best for now that Vaughan didn't suspect they'd had him under surveillance since the afternoon. 'Fact is, we're sitting watching his place now, but we don't want to approach him unannounced and spook him. He could have an itchy trigger finger: who knows what he might do.'

That last part was going a little too far for Tess, but Po shrugged aside her frown of caution. Stahl must have considered the way in which Vaughan fired a warning shot though, because he said, 'Yeah, you should be careful. Wouldn't like him to hurt you by accident, boss.'

'So what d'you say, podnuh? You gonna help me?'

'I'm home, getting the old man ready for bed.'

'I'm sure your da's capable of tucking himself in, Gabe,' Po said. 'From what he said earlier he regularly gets by without you.'

'He said that, did he?'

'As near as damn it, or words to that effect.'

'I'm not supposed to be going out. Lockdown rules state—'

'Don't give me any of that crap, Gabe. We both know you've been around town plenty times you shouldn't have been. Besides, there's mitigation about being away from home if it's to help the vulnerable or to protect them from harm. If you're with us you'll have a legitimate reason for being out. It's like we told you this afternoon, we only want to help Tony.'

'What *exactly* do you want from me, boss?'

'I want you to convince Tony that our intentions are good.'

'Why would he listen to me?'

'Because he didn't kill you when you drove up to his cabin on your motorcycle earlier.'

'You saw that?'

'I was there,' Po admitted, again without alerting Stahl he'd been followed. 'Tony fired at you but obviously not to hit. Once he recognized you he dropped the aggression and took you inside the cabin with his girl. He musta trusted you to keep his secret when he allowed you to leave again.'

'See, that's the thing, Po. I swore I'd keep his secret. Now you want me to break his trust.'

'No, I want you to do the opposite. I want you to build it, and to extend that trust to Tess and me.'

'But how can I trust you when—'

'Don't insult my integrity, Gabe. You've worked for me for some years now, have I ever given you cause to mistrust me?'

'No, but . . . well, there was how you snuck inside my house earlier.'

'There was no sneaking, Gabe. We only checked everything was OK.' Po looked across at Tess, now was the moment he intended coercing Stahl with his threat about his employment status. She still didn't like what he had in mind, but he was right when pointing out it was both a practical and necessary move. 'You still want a job to go to—'

Thankfully, Stahl butted in, taking away the necessity to bully him into complying. 'How am I supposed to get Tony to trust you?

He wouldn't tell me what kind of trouble he'd gotten in and practically kicked me out. I take it that it's bullshit about Leah's baby daddy chasing them, right?'

'Leah?' Po asked, and exchanged looks with Tess again. 'That's the name of Tony's girlfriend?'

'That's what he called her. But she isn't his girl. Not like that.'

Tess couldn't hold her tongue any longer. 'She's pregnant?'

Stahl had obviously expected her to be alongside Po because he was unfazed by her question. 'Not that I'm any kind of expert, but she looks ready to go drop at any minute.'

'So we should move fast. I've a friend waiting for you outside,' Po informed Stahl. 'You know Pinky Leclerc, right? You've seen him with me at the shop.'

'Yeah, I know Pinky. There's not much chance of missing him, is there?'

Tess wondered if he meant because of Pinky's skin color, or his sexuality, and didn't approve that Stahl had referenced either. But then again, Pinky was larger than life, in his looks and his actions: he wouldn't be missed in a packed room. Not unless he wished to be.

'Pinky's gonna accompany you here,' Po went on, 'and will soon have you back home again. I only need you to mediate between Tony and us. Once we're in, you can leave.'

'Do I have a choice?'

'Nope.'

'If I don't go with him, what's Pinky gonna do?'

'Come with him and you won't have to find out.'

'I'll come.'

TWENTY-FOUR

Pinky barely knew Gabe Stahl. On the few occasions Pinky had attended Charley's Autoshop it had been with Po, and they'd usually sequester in the cramped office at the back, a room decorated with ten thousand oily fingerprints and air impregnated with perished rubber. The times he'd been there, Pinky had kept his visits short. He'd seen different mechanics at work on various vehicles, and had gotten to nodding terms with some of them. Stahl had always been one of the more distracted workers, paying Pinky less than passing notice before.

As Stahl exited his home now, he stared directly at Pinky, who waved him over to the SUV. Pinky watched the mechanic approach. He had the same clothing on as when Pinky shadowed him earlier – denim jeans, a baggy green T-shirt, neckerchief and tan boots – but was missing the full-face visor and helmet. Stahl had longish straw-colored hair that stuck out at the sides and was sparse at the top, and a short straggly beard. He looked like one of those surfer dudes from out west, skin tanned to leather and hard-bodied. Equally Pinky thought that if ever Shaggy gave up ghost-hunting, *Scooby-Doo* would have a reasonable replacement in Gabe Stahl.

Stahl bent at the waist to see inside the car.

'You getting in or not?'

'I told Po I'd come,' said Stahl. 'Hasn't he let you know?'

As soon as Po ended his call with Stahl he had indeed dropped him a snappy message to say Stahl was on his way out. 'Did I knock down your door and drag you out?'

'No, but—'

'Would I have asked you to get in if I wasn't expecting you?'

'Should I pull up my mask?'

'D'you intend robbing a bank, you?'

'No.'

'Just get in, man.'

Stahl settled into the front passenger seat. He scanned around, taking in details. His fingers twitched, and Pinky thought he wanted to touch and twist the controls on the dash. The mechanic was so attuned to his work he couldn't help inspecting the SUV. His twitchy hands stayed in his lap.

'You're worried about catching something from me you can put down a window, you.'

'I'm fine.'

'You're as jumpy as a tweaker on withdrawal.'

'I just don't know what to expect, man.'

'Nicolas explained, yeah? You're needed to make an introduction so's Vaughan doesn't come out blasting. That's all. Job done and I'll bring you back home after.'

'I should take my bike.'

'You don't trust me to drive you safely?'

'No, it's just—'

'I'm black?'

'No.'

'I'm gay?'

Stahl frowned briefly.

'Don't worry, you,' said Pinky. 'You aren't my type.'

He started the engine and pulled out from the curb. Stahl looked over his shoulder at the house, or maybe at his motorcycle sitting on its stand. He lowered his head, muttering into his straggly beard.

The SUV meandered across the promontory, and once they hit the highway, Pinky put down his foot and the car gathered speed. Stahl still muttered and jerked like a meth addict. He was worried, maybe about betraying his pal, Vaughan, and Pinky understood that. He too would feel terrible if he'd given his word to Po or Tess only to break it within hours.

It was late enough in the evening that even the usual weight of traffic would've diminished, during lockdown where only essential workers were supposed to be out, the roads were mostly deserted. However Pinky took occasional glances at his mirrors. It was force of habit from years of criminal behavior. He noted a vehicle sitting some distance back on his tail, notable because one headlamp was slightly dimmer than the other. Pinky noted its presence on the road, but for now was unalarmed.

Beyond Yarmouth he caught sight of the same car in his mirrors. It wasn't yet cause for concern. They were on a direct route up the coast to Brunswick, with Augusta and Bangor beyond, a well-traveled road. Most cars in his wake had probably been there since they'd left Portland. This car was only notable due to the discrepancy in intensity of its lights.

In Freeport, Pinky took a right.

'How'd you know where you're going?' asked Stahl.

'Say what?'

'I haven't given you any directions, and you haven't got a satnav or nothing else. How do you know where to go?'

Pinky tapped his forehead. 'I've a natural homing device up here, me.'

'Did Po tell you where to come?'

'Don't you think we've been talking for hours, us?'

What difference would it make for the man to know the truth when he was already suspicious? Po had asked Stahl to mediate between them and Vaughan and build trust; could he be expected to do his best when his own trust in them was being severely tested? Pinky thought about admitting following him earlier, but snapped his gaze on his mirrors again.

Stahl said, 'I'm not stupid. I know that—'

'Hold that thought.'

'Uh?'

'We're being followed.'

Stahl looked over his shoulder. 'I don't see anybody.'

'You won't yet. We came around a bend.'

Pinky watched his mirrors.

'There he is,' he said, as a car came around the now distant corner. One headlight was brighter than the other.

'Who is it?'

'I don't know, but I've an idea.'

'He isn't gaining,' said Stahl. 'How d'you know he's following us?'

'He's been behind us since Falmouth. Unless he works for L.L.Bean, I doubt he has a reason to follow us out here.' L.L.Bean's corporate headquarters was based in Freeport, and the company had several other warehouses and factories dotted around the area. 'I should've been more on the ball. I disturbed somebody watching for me outside of my apartment earlier.'

'You think it's the same guy?'

'What are the odds against?'

'Is he following you or me? Did he follow you to get to *me*?'

'I don't know,' Pinky replied honestly. 'Why would he be after you . . . to get to Vaughan?'

'Why else?' Stahl rubbed furiously at his eye sockets with the heels of his thumbs. He sat for a few seconds with his mouth hanging open, feeling totally useless. Then his arms flapped like Kermit the Frog's. 'Oh, shit! If he followed from Falmouth then he probably knows where I live. What if—'

'Calm down,' Pinky warned, 'before you have an aneurism.'

He dug for his cell phone and tossed it to Stahl. 'Get Po on the line.'

Stahl fumbled, pushed and poked at the screen. 'I can't find his number.'

'OK, quit panicking, you.' Pinky would have made the call without all the messing about, but preferred to concentrate on driving. If he slowed or stopped to find the number it could prompt some kind of response from the one following. He preferred any response was under his terms and not his enemy's. 'It's under "Nicolas", not "Po". If you don't see it, bring up my call list and it'll be the most recent number.'

This time Stahl was able to find Po's number and he stabbed a fingertip on it. 'Hold that towards me so's I can hear,' Pinky instructed.

'Pinky? You close?' said Po without preamble.

'I'm close, but we have a problem, us.'

'What's up, bra?'

'Got myself a tail.'

'Same guy as before?'

'Has to be, right?'

'D'you feel in imminent danger?'

'No. He's staying back, my guess is he's following to see where I'm going before he makes a move.'

'So don't stop. Keep moving and draw him after you.'

'That was my intention, but it makes delivering Gabe to you kinda difficult.'

'It does, but not impossible. Here's how we're gonna play it, Pinky.'

Pinky listened while Po outlined his plan. He glanced in his mirrors. 'OK, I think that will work, except the situation just changed. I've not just one vehicle; there are now two after us. And they're coming fast.'

TWENTY-FIVE

Bryce Brogan had wakened Josh with the news that Anderson Walsh had been made by Pinky Leclerc. Not only had Leclerc spotted Walsh, he'd chased him off with a pistol. Bryce was flinching with poorly retrained anticipation, keen to get to

Cumberland Avenue and have things out with Po Villere's sniper.
It took some convincing him not to rush in but Josh finally got
through to him.

He hadn't expected to sleep, but exhaustion had taken him.
Josh, foggy-headed and aching from having lain in the back of
the van, had to get his act in order before Bryce followed his
initiative and possibly blew everything.

First, Josh had the two locals pull off their stakeout of Villere's
home to take over surveillance on Pinky's apartment. If Pinky
had made Walsh it might press him into some kind of action they
could capitalize on: no sooner had the two locals gotten set up
than Pinky left home in his SUV. Pinky was alert to the vehicles
he'd become familiar with – the blue van and now Randall's car
– but the locals were using their own cars. They followed him to
Falmouth, keeping well back while he picked up another guy from
a big old house on the sea front. The locals shadowed Pinky and
his new friend out of the city and up the coast, taking turns to
follow so as not to alert them. In the meantime the Brogan brothers
mobilized the others in their team. Walsh was sent after the locals,
adding to the convoy on Pinky's tail, because Josh was convinced
that they were answering a summons from Villere, and he had
reason to believe that the Cajun had possibly found Vaughan. It
was speculation, but why else would there be maneuvers underway
so soon after Pinky spotted Walsh?

Elvin Collins gave them access to a van and pickup truck. The
fourth man drafted in by Randall was called Eamon White;
he was instructed to follow in the blue van while the Brogans each
took one of Collins' vehicles, Collins sitting shotgun alongside
Josh in the company van, while Randall accompanied his brother
in the pickup. Together, they had a rolling convoy of six vans and
cars on the road, an ample force to tighten a noose around him
wherever Pinky led. Josh coordinated the team over walkie-
talkies he'd had the presence of mind to supply them with. The
radios were set to a dedicated channel, but there was always
the possibility of eavesdroppers. Then again half of what Bryce
said over the airwaves would sound like the ramblings of a maniac.
He sounded nuts at the best of times, but over the radio it was as
if he'd found a new pulpit for his weirdness.

Pinky dragged them up through Yarmouth, and then further

north into terrain unfamiliar to Josh. Collins told him that they would soon reach Freeport, a town whose name meant nothing to Brogan. After Freeport, Collins went on, Pinky could forge on towards Augusta or to Brunswick. He was relieved when their point man reported a hard right turn in Freeport that would take them into the coastal woodland bordering Maquoit Bay. Josh sensed they were nearing their destination. He urged further caution from the point man, aware now that Pinky could spot a tail much easier on these back roads. In fact, it'd be better if the two locals closest to Pinky leapfrogged their vehicles so that it was never the same car behind him twice. He ordered the second car to speed up and take over point. Anderson Walsh, now not too far behind the two locals suggested he too join in the leapfrogging, and Josh saw sense in that. He gave the go ahead.

'I'm moving in,' Bryce announced. 'When it's time I want to be the one to take that fucker down.'

'Whatever you do, don't blow it for the sake of getting revenge on Leclerc,' Josh cautioned. 'I think we're close enough to Vaughan now that I can smell him. Allow the nigger to lead us to Vaughan and Leah, and after he's yours to do with what you wish, little brother.'

Josh and Collins were sat near the back of the convoy – only Eamon White was behind them in the blue van – and in a more fortunate position than Josh would've first assumed. Collins was familiar with the roads thereabout and directed Josh across country, taking narrow service trails through the woods to get ahead of Pinky. Apparently the main road made a large loop and turned almost fully back on itself as it neared the coast, but many locals knew about the shortcuts. Josh commanded White to follow so they could set up a rolling barricade with both vans if need be. Once they made it to the main road White was instructed to wait on a wide passing place for further instruction. Josh kept the van emblazoned with the shop's decal rolling, now directly towards where Pinky's SUV had reportedly slowed to a crawl.

'I think he's suspicious of being followed,' Bryce reported over the walkie-talkie.

'He has a good right to,' Josh answered. 'I warned you not to blow things, brother, by getting too close.'

'Chill, Josh, I'm still a-ways back from him. I think he's just being cautious because he must've spotted the lights on one of the other cars and he's now slowed down to check them out.'

'Remind me who is now on point,' said Josh.

'I am.' It was one of the locals, whose name Josh couldn't recall off the top of his head.

'Be more specific.'

'Davenport.'

The man's entire name now came to mind: Richard Davenport. The other local in their team had introduced himself as Heck Bury – but asked to be called by his nickname of Huckleberry.

'Davenport,' Josh said, 'are you confident that Pinky hasn't seen your face at any time today?'

'I've always been set well back. Huckleberry and me kept swapping out so's we were never too close for any length of time.'

'Yeah-yeah. Good. So here's what to do. Pinky's grown suspicious about being followed, so I need you to get right up on his tail, and then make it look as if you're keen on getting past. Once you're past him, I want you to hit the gas and make off and leave him in your dust. That should put his mind at ease about being followed.'

'What if he won't let me pass?'

'For Christ's sake, show some goddamn initiative, will you?' Bryce hadn't the patience of his older brother, and besides, he still found fun in baiting the local guys. 'Make him move aside, you goddamn idiot!'

Josh cut back in. 'Bryce has a point, Davenport. If you must, make things look as if you're pissed about being held up, and force your way past if you have to. I want Pinky to believe you're no threat once he watches your taillights disappear ahead.'

'OK. I'm speeding up now.'

Josh waited for approaching two minutes before Davenport came back on the radio sounding breathless.

'I'm past and have kept going, what do you want me to do now?'

'We should see him any minute,' Collins said, peering intently through the windshield for any hint of the approaching vehicle.

'Just keep moving,' Josh told Davenport, as he pulled the van to a stop, 'and you'll soon come up on us. I'm in the bait-shop van, with the lights off. Whatever you do, don't fucking hit us head on. Huckleberry, what's happening?'

'The SUV's slowed even more. It's crawling along. If I keep moving at this speed I'll be forced to pass it too.'

'Fine. That's what you need to do. Get past him, and keep moving.'

'Wait up, the SUV's just gone dark.'

'What do you mean?'

'I thought it was just taking a corner but then all the lights went out. I can't see any glow on the trees or anywhere else.'

'Shit, Huckleberry, I need eyes on that car right now!'

'Wait up, Josh. Panic over. The SUV's lights *are* on. The woods must've hid them for a few seconds or something. Do you still want me to pass?'

'Yeah, but don't show any interest in its occupants when you do.'

'OK, I'm speeding up.'

Josh had to endure another interminable couple of minutes of radio silence before Huckleberry spoke once more. 'OK, I'm past. What now?'

'Keep going and wait for further instruction. Walsh? Pinky knows your face and your car, so keep well back. Bryce, you're up, little brother.'

'Already on him,' said Bryce, jovial again. His happy mood lasted all but a few seconds. 'Shit! He's just taken off as if his fat ass is on fire! He knows we're after him, Josh.'

'Goddamnit!' Josh snapped a look at Collins, seeking a suggestion for his next move.

Collins said, 'Hate to say it but I think we've been played and led on a merry dance. If he gets back onto Flying Point Road, he can use the coastal tracks to get back down to Falmouth again without having to touch the highways. He could have easily kept somebody without local knowledge outta the way for an hour or so.'

Collins' theory made sense. Pinky had deliberately drawn away his watchers and led them on a wild-goose chase around the countryside and Josh had an idea why: so that Villere and Grey could make a play of their own and spirit away Vaughan and Leah.

'Davenport, Huckleberry, I want you to get your asses down to that house in Falmouth where Pinky collected his passenger. Eamon White, you got your ears on?'

'I'm here.'

'Follow them back to Falmouth, I want you to stand by and give them help when they need it, they're gonna need the van.'

'What do you want from me, brother?' Bryce demanded. 'If Pinky's been playing us for fools, he's not leading us to Vaughan, so that makes him fair game. I'll skin his hide and force him to tell us where Vaughan is.'

'I don't know about you, Bryce, but I've about had my fill of Maine. It's time to get on with the job we came here for.'

'That's music to my ears, big bro. Stand by, cause me and Randall are gonna push his fat butt right into your faces.'

TWENTY-SIX

Tess was within fifteen feet of Po when her fiancé grabbed Gabe Stahl, slapped a palm over his mouth to stifle any complaints and dragged him backwards from the road. A small wire fence, a boundary marker rather than a security feature, separated the verge and woods. Po barely slowed, performing a high-stepping motion backwards, and yanked Stahl up and over in the next motion. There was a drainage ditch just inside the fence line. Immediately Po flattened Stahl to the ditch's bottom and ensured they couldn't be seen from the road.

Pinky, having slowed to an almost imperceptible crawl while Stahl slipped out under the cover of darkness, now flicked back on his SUV's lights and gunned the engine. Within seconds a car caught up and the driver hit the blinkers to pass. Pinky kept the SUV moving and the car had to put two wheels on the shoulder to get past. Its tires kicked up a curtain of grit and grass divots. Some battered the windshield of the SUV, but Pinky just kept gamely on. The car headed away into darkness.

Another vehicle swept along the road. Tess made out the shape of a pickup truck with big tires and a long cargo bed. There was a decal on the doors and hood but in the dark she couldn't define it. Pinky waited for the pickup to gain on him, then hit the gas and the SUV surged ahead. He drove as if chased by the devil, with the sole intention of making his enemies pursue him. Even if Pinky made it back to Portland, their window of opportunity to move Vaughan was short. It would only be a matter of time before Brogan discovered the rouse and understood their reason for sneaking Stahl out from under his team's noses. The bad guys would return, in the understanding that they must have been in grabbing distance of their prey, to conduct a rapid search of the nearest properties. As the crow flew Vaughan and the pregnant girl were less than half a mile away. The chained access route to the cabin was one of very few trails nearby that Brogan would need his people to check.

Tess stayed low as the pickup roared past, but raised her head enough to watch the snippet of activity in the cab. She saw the same man that'd roughed her up that morning – Bryce Brogan – accompanied by a burly, shaven-headed fellow she hadn't spotted before. Counting the two cars that had already gotten past Pinky, it seemed that Brogan had doubled the numbers of his team at least, because none of the drivers she'd seen was the man knocked out by Po at the wharves. In the pickup Brogan had one hand on the steering wheel, the other clutched a cell phone or some kind of hand-held radio. He was hollering orders judging by the determination on his face. Then he was past and Tess could only watch as the pickup's taillights flared as Brogan tapped the brakes to safely negotiate a corner. She turned her head and spotted another car whizzing in pursuit. This time a face she recognized was behind the steering wheel: it was Anderson Walsh. In the backwash of dim light from the car's dashboard his jaw looked swollen and discolored.

Tess checked for Po, and saw that her fiancé had also spotted Walsh. Po wore a feral grin, happy to have bruised more than the thug's ego. He held Gabe Stahl down, ensuring he was hidden from Walsh's view. Once the sounds of racing engines diminished Po assisted Stahl to stand. Tess couldn't hear exactly what was said between them, but Po thanked the mechanic for helping. Tess moved through the tall grass at the edge of the ditch, and then crouched, watching both directions along the road. She urged Po and Stahl out of the ditch. Thankfully the dry spell meant that they weren't soaked by filthy ditch water. Po aimed a finger through the darkness, and Tess helped by waving Stahl to follow her. The

Mustang was only a hundred feet or so back amid a copse of trees, parked out of sight of the main road. Tess was sure that Vaughan and the pregnant girl hadn't managed to slip past them unseen in the meantime.

'We have to move quickly,' she told Stahl as he stumbled to a halt beside her. 'It's imperative you get Vaughan's trust and he hears us out before those guys come back again.'

'Where's the cabin? I'm lost.'

'You're not lost,' Po said, coming up swiftly behind him, 'you're with us and we know exactly where we are.'

Speak for yourself, Po, Tess thought because she'd gotten a little turned around while Po had driven them to the rendezvous with Pinky. However, she was confident that her partner was cognizant of his exact location and which way they must go. For her part, she could find the car easily enough, after that, well, it was Po's party. 'Follow me,' she told Stahl, and turned for the woods.

'Whoa! Get down,' Po warned, and this time he was closer to Tess than to Stahl. He grabbed her and they both dipped low, even as Stahl took a lurching dive onto his belly. No sooner had they hidden than a large van prowled by, going in the opposite direction to the others. It was near enough that Tess saw that the van was decorated similarly to the pickup Bryce Brogan had been driving; it was fair to assume that those in the van were part of the team seeking Vaughan.

'Lookit,' said Po.

At first Tess was unsure what had alarmed him. There was a huge, burly, bearded guy in the passenger seat, but he wasn't the one that'd caught Po's attention. She peered at the driver and understood. He looked like an older version of Bryce Brogan, down to the tattoos on his hands and neck, and the scar under his eye, visible as the man turned his face to scan the terrain.

Tess turned her attention from the driver to the van itself. Closer and lit by the backwash of its own headlamps off the trees, she could make out the design on the doors and side panels: it was the stylized image of a fish fighting a hook and line. She picked out the words 'bait' and 'tackle' and a Portland address. She committed the details to memory, though there was no way of saying if the company owner was involved or not – for all she could tell the van and pickup had been stolen by Brogan's crew.

Correction, *The Brogans'* crew, because it was apparent that the driver of the van was a close blood relative to Bryce Brogan, likely a brother.

The van continued along the road, retracing the route the others had all taken. This elder of the Brogan brothers was wise to the possibility of a trick and was seeking anything suspicious before joining the rest of the gang in chasing Pinky back to the city.

'Now we know how Brogan managed to be in two different towns at the same time,' said Po as the van disappeared around a distant bend.

They had guessed that a lookalike of Bryce had been the person to torture Bob Wilson, culminating with the shooting through his foot. This was confirmation of their theory but also of something worse. Whatever Vaughan had done to attract them it was enough to bring at least four hunters all the way across the country in pursuit. The obvious was that he owed them money, but now, with the inclusion of both brothers, Tess tended to lean towards the notion his crime was more personal. When the expense outweighs the value of possible recovery a chase usually peters out, but when the stakes are personal the pursuers can remain dogged till the bitter end. She suspected that the Brogans wouldn't be leaving any time soon, not without taking their pound of flesh.

With the van out of sight, but still undoubtedly sweeping the area, it was time to get moving. Po urged Stahl up again and they began a rapid trot through the woods. Tess followed, keeping one ear cocked over her shoulder for sounds of pursuit. Back at the Mustang Tess waited until Stahl was sequestered in the back seat, then got in alongside Po. Po started the car, and drove without lights. The forest floor was uneven, littered with fallen debris from past storms, but the Mustang's thick tires crunched them to mulch. They made it back to the road and Po picked up speed. Within minutes he'd taken them to a dogleg in the road, and another plot of closely grouped trees. He stopped the car so that it was mostly concealed from view of those in the buildings a few hundred yards away. Tess made out the geometric shapes of the cabin and several smaller outbuildings as denser shadows in the night. A faint glow came from behind the curtains in one room in the cabin.

'Last time I was here, Tony ambushed me from that field over there,' said Stahl, indicating a patch of long grasses surrounding one side of the cabin.

'He doesn't seem to be out there now,' said Po.

'How can you be certain?'

'I can't, but I'm reasonably sure he hasn't heard us comin' this time. That motorcycle of yours, it sounds like a goddamn hornet in a coffee can and can be heard from miles away.'

On the way there, Pinky had explained to Gabe Stahl what was needed of him. He'd come around to the idea of acting as a go between, but now that he again faced the cabin his enthusiasm had slipped. He nervously wiped his mouth with the back of his hand as he peered beyond Po's shoulder at the dim light behind the window. 'What if Tony gets spooked when I show up and shoots again?'

'He's not going to shoot if you announce it's you.'

Tess wasn't as certain as her partner. After Stahl showed up earlier, it had shown how vulnerable to discovery Vaughan was; she'd bet that his nerves had been strung as tight as tripwires since Stahl left. He could be expecting more visitors and this time his warning shot might not miss. 'Don't get too close to the cabin before calling out. Give Tony plenty opportunity to see and hear who you are.'

'I intend to.'

'We'll follow you,' said Po. 'But it's probably best you get outta the car now and begin walking in. Remember, we only need you to convince Vaughan we're here to help.'

Once Stahl was walking tentatively towards the cabin, Po rolled the Mustang forward. He turned on the low beams so that they weren't deemed to be sneaking, and to limn Stahl in their glow so he'd be recognizable. Stahl raised his hands in the air in surrender.

Tess's gaze roamed beyond Stahl to the lit window. She watched for movement, the shifting of a shadow that would indicate somebody had moved the drapes to observe Stahl's approach. There was nothing evident, which was surprising considering that Vaughan or the girl must have heard the Mustang by now. Earlier, Po had reported, they had fled the cabin via the back door; was that the case now with Vaughan leading the pregnant woman on foot into the woods behind the cabin?

Stahl called out.

There was no reply.

He called out louder, and even brought his hands down to clap sharply. 'Yo, Tony! It's me . . . Gabe. I'm with Po Villere and Tess Grey. We're here to help. Don't shoot any of us, man!'

Vaughan didn't shoot. But neither did he come to a window or to the door to greet his friend.

'Maybe one of us should go around the back,' Tess suggested.

Po continued to peer over the steering wheel. He brought the car to a stop, but allowed the engine to idle. His gaze scanned the field of tall grasses, but as before he seemed to believe nobody lurked in ambush this time. He turned his gaze to the outbuildings. Tess caught his exclamation at the same time she heard the cough of an engine turning over. A car, its lights suddenly dazzling, lurched out from between two sagging sheds, on a collision course with Gabe Stahl. He yelped, took a leap and landed in an unceremonious heap in the dirt ten feet away from where the car swung a tight turn and headed for escape.

'Son of a bitch!' Po hit the gas and it jumped towards the rapidly moving car. The driver, undoubtedly a panic-stricken Tony Vaughan, was probably prepared to ram them, but to do so would also write off his getaway car. He tried swinging around the Mustang instead, but Po whipped the front fender into the back end of Vaughan's car and pushed it in a tight arc. The car spun out, kicking up a cloud of dirt and gravel. Before Vaughan could get it moving, Po adjusted the steering and used the entire front of the Mustang as a battering ram. He moved the car steadily and with determination, forcing Vaughan's car into the long grass, and then jammed it to the bole of a tree.

TWENTY-SEVEN

Tess was bewildered. But she acted on instinct too. She jumped out of the car and ran to cut off any escape for whoever was in the back of Vaughan's car. As she blocked passage, arms spread, she saw her partner lunge out too. Po skidded across the sloping hood of the Mustang on his butt, and ended up alongside the open driver's window where Vaughan was already trying to get a bead on him with a revolver. Po grabbed Vaughan's wrist and battered it down on the window frame. Vaughan yelped and released the revolver. It slid off the hood, lost for the moment, and that was best for them all. Po grabbed Vaughan by the collar of his jacket and dragged him bodily from inside the car. He manhandled him, hopped down to the ground and then yanked Vaughan after him. He tossed Vaughan down in the dirt with little sympathy for the man's exclamations of pain.

Tess was more tactful as she opened the door and helped the woman out. The young woman was frightened, and in some discomfort, but otherwise she was unhurt by Vaughan's rash escape attempt. She blinked in question as Tess lowered her eyes to her massively swollen belly.

'Is your baby OK?'

'I . . . I think so,' the woman whispered. She put her hands on her abdomen, fingers fluttering across its expanse as if she could read her unborn child's condition by touch alone.

Po had employed his heavier car to immobilize Vaughan's, but he'd done it in a controlled manner that shouldn't have caused any harm to the mother or her unborn baby. Yet Tess couldn't help a pang of regret that force had been used. She looked for where her partner had taken control of Vaughan and was glad to see he was helping the other man stand, and there was no animosity shown by either man. A gasping cough brought Stahl to mind: he stood, brushing at the dirt on his shirt and the knees of his jeans. He winced and checked his palms for abrasions. He'd come close to being hit by Vaughan's car, but other than scraped hands he was probably uninjured. The girl began to sidestep away from Tess. Surely she wasn't going to try running away?

'Please hear us out,' Tess said, holding out a hand to the woman. 'We don't intend you harm, we've only come to help you and Tony.'

'I don't know who you are,' the girl rasped, her voice barely above a whisper.

'When Gabe was here earlier, he told Tony we were looking for him, but not why. Believe me, we have nothing to do with the Brogans, in fact, we're here to help you escape them.'

'You're here to help?' Vaughan guffawed at the inanity. 'So that's why you guys just rammed us into a goddamn tree?'

'That was on you, Tony. You made me bash up my ride stopping you from doing something stupid. Trust me, if I didn't think you were worth helpin' I'd've let you drive into the hands of those scumbags that're chasing you.' Po stabbed a finger towards the coast road. 'There's a bunch of guys riding around out there trying to find you.'

Tony cast a scolding eye on Stahl.

'It wasn't my fault, Tony, man. It wasn't my idea to come back.' Stahl nodded at Po, then Tess, to show who was responsible. 'They asked me to speak to you on their behalf, to get you to trust them. You should, man. Po ain't kidding about how many people there are after your ass.'

Tony got the gist of the situation fast enough. 'If you hadn't come here, the goddamn Brogans wouldn't have followed.'

It was a valid point. In trying to help them, Tess and Po had drawn their hunters much closer to Vaughan and the girl than before.

'It's happened, get over it,' said Po. 'We're here to offer help and you'd be a fool to turn it down.'

'We were doing fine without you. Goddamnit, Po, I know you're a good man, and you want to help but, man . . .'

'You heard him just now, Tony,' said the woman. 'We're surrounded and you'd be a fool to turn down an offer of help.'

'The alternative is that I call the police,' Tess suggested, knowing full well she wouldn't. 'I've a duty of care to you now, knowing how you and a heavily pregnant young woman are being threatened with harm. You'll let us help you, or I'll call the cops and put your welfare in their hands. Of course, then you'd have to explain why you have a gang of criminals from California chasing you.'

Po eyed the getaway car. Its engine had stalled when he'd crushed it sideways into the tree. Mechanically it would still work fine, and the scrapes on its sides weren't as noticeable as they could have been. He looked past the car's shell to what it must conceal. He mustn't have spotted what he expected because he left Vaughan standing under his own power, and ducked to peer inside. Tess knew from when she'd helped the girl out that there was nothing much inside the car. Po grunted once, then moved around the tree to reach the back end of the car. He hit the button to release the trunk.

'That's only our personal things in there,' Vaughan said. He looked jittery, one eye rolling wider in its socket than the other: Tess recalled he'd cruelly been nicknamed Tony One-Eye by the guys at the autoshop, but understood why. His blinded eye was shrunken, the eyelid nipped tightly with scar tissue. He'd given himself a badly executed haircut, and his cheeks were hollow, his lips tight and verging on blue. When she thought about it, Vaughan looked sick. His clothing hung like sacks on his lean frame.

Po sifted through the trunk, lifting and moving a few hastily packed bags, and laid his hands on a canvas holdall hidden under the rest.

'Leave that be,' said Vaughan and lunged after Po.

Stahl's gaze darted between Vaughan and Po, then he started after his friend. Tess tensed, unsure what was coming next, but preparing to react.

Po unzipped the canvas bag, delved inside then pulled out a wad of used bills. In that handful, Tess guessed he clutched a couple of thousand dollars. 'Jeez, Tony, did ya win the Mega Millions lottery or somethin'?'

'Holy shit!' Stahl wheezed, and took another step forward. Vaughan elbowed Stahl in the ribs not too gently and frowned at his old friend. Stahl rubbed at his mouth, greedily this time, as he goggled at the canvas bag chockfull of bills. 'I've never seen that much money in my life.'

'It's blood money,' Vaughan growled, 'and should be burned.'

'You gotta be joking,' said Stahl. 'Say the word, brother, and I'll happily take it off your hands.'

'I said it *should* be burned, but it's not gonna be. It's for Leah, and for her baby when it's born. People have died for that money, but it will give Leah and her baby new lives.'

Po shoved the wad of bills back inside the bag and tugged the zip closed. 'What was your plan, Tony? Drive till the tires fell off your car then set yourselves up wherever you stopped?'

'There's plenty cash in there for new tires when we need them. I don't see any need for us to stop.'

Vaughan's plan sounded ridiculous to Tess. 'Then you've a skewed sense of responsibility towards Leah's unborn child.'

'Yeah, I didn't mean when the little one is born, I'm talking about the next few days. You just stopped us leaving, we were gonna travel to a safe place where Leah can give birth.'

'The way things are looking,' said Tess, 'there's nowhere on this continent you can drive to where the Brogans won't follow.'

Tony scuffed his boot in the dirt. Leah looked at him with her mouth pinched. She said, 'I warned you they'd never stop searching. This lady here just confirmed it. If nothing else, they're tenacious.'

'Insidious more like,' Tony added, and clutched unconsciously at his chest.

'Your safest bet is to stick with us, we'll give you protection and when the time comes we'll get you both to hospital for the medical assistance you need,' Tess said.

'Leah's gonna give birth the way women have for millennia, without the need for doctors or midwives. I've read up on it and know how to help her.'

'That right, Tony?' Po asked sarcastically. 'Whatcha gonna do, podnuh? Bite through the umbilical cord the way they did back in the Stone Age?'

'What about you, Tony?' Tess pressed on. 'If you don't mind me saying, it looks as if being on the run has played havoc with your health.'

'I'm fine,' said Vaughan, appearing the opposite. At a guess, Tess would say he was malnourished and dehydrated at best, and was dying of a horrible untreated malady at worst.

'Brother,' said Stahl, 'Tess's right. You look like a three weeks old dog turd left out in the sun.'

'I haven't really had time to consider my needs lately.'

'You can say that again. Maybe instead of thinking about new tires, you should buy some soap or deodorant, 'cause you stink like a three weeks old turd as well.'

Vaughan dipped his chin but couldn't conceal his smile. Po grinned openly. 'Y'see why I asked you to act as a go between, Gabe? If I'd said that, I'd bet Tony would be insulted. Comin' from you it raised his spirits.'

It was impressive how men's crass banter could break the ice where logic and common sense could fail. Tess was dug in, prepared for a lengthy battle on her hands to get Vaughan and Leah to comply with her suggestions, but here was Vaughan already comfortable in the presence of his old work buddies. Leah had dug her chin into her collar, choosing silence as her best policy. Tess wondered if she'd been raised in an environment where her role was to be seen and not heard. Leah glanced at her, caught her staring and offered a weak smile: her face was flushed and Tess noted how wide she'd settled her feet.

'Do you need to sit down a moment?'

'Before I fall down?'

'Here.' Tess offered a hand again and Leah took it. Her hand, as diminutive as the rest of her when discounting her swollen belly, was as delicate as a child's but on closer inspection Tess noted the scars on her fingers and backs of her forearms: Tess knew cigarette burns and razor cuts when she saw them. This young girl had endured torment that no child should suffer, either by her own hand or those of others. Tess led Leah around to the Mustang and helped her slide her backside onto the back seat.

Vaughan studied his car. 'Ramming it like that just made my car too conspicuous to drive. But nowhere near as conspicuous as your muscle car, Po. I should just load Leah back into mine and get the hell outta here while we have a chance.'

'Weren't you listening when I told ya that you're surrounded? We're unsure how many people the Brogans have rustled up but we counted four cars, and I'd bet there are others we didn't see yet.' Again Po indicated the nearby coast road. 'We've a friend helpin' us: Pinky Leclerc. He's dragged some of them after him, but just before we got here we spotted one of those Brogans prowling about in a van.'

'Which of the Brogans is it?' Leah asked.

'We don't know his name, we've only met the other one – Bryce – before now.'

'Uncle Josh,' Leah intoned. 'Bryce is my father.'

'What? The Brogans are your folks?'

'You choose your friends,' said Leah, 'you don't choose your family. Actually, that's not true. It's why we're running and they're chasing. I chose to escape my family forever, but they just won't let me go.'

Stahl nodded at the holdall in the trunk, and couldn't resist a furtive lick of his lips. 'You ask me, it isn't you they're chasing, it's the nest egg you guys stole to finance your new lives.'

'Then you'd be wrong,' said Leah with resignation. 'If it was only Uncle Josh after us, it would be different. Probably we could give back the cash and he'd let us get on our way, but not my father. He's crazy, and he will take my running away personally. Don't let him fool you with fake charm, he's a fully-fledged psychopath and incredibly dangerous.'

'From what we learned your uncle ain't the gentlest of souls either,' said Po. 'Tony, Josh Brogan dropped in on your brother Bob before coming here, and he tried torturing your location outta him.'

'Shit! No . . . is Bob . . . *alive?*'

'He's alive but hurt. Josh shot him through his foot and left him to bleed, terrified that Josh is gonna come back and finish the job.'

'Oh, man, no. Bob wouldn't even have a clue where I am. I deliberately avoided getting in touch with him to protect him from the Brogans. Hell, man, how am I gonna make this up to him?'

'Making amends with your brother is something for later,' said Tess. 'We dressed his wound and made him as comfortable as we could. He refused to go to hospital. Hopefully his injury will heal without complications and he's back on his feet soon. For now we have to worry more about getting you guys to safety and stopping the Brogans from hurting anyone else.'

TWENTY-EIGHT

Pinky's role in the plan verged on craziness to him. He had successfully dropped off Gabe Stahl and led some of the followers after his SUV but once those actions were completed he wasn't exactly sure what his next move should be. Tess and Po were back there in the boonies, unarmed and potentially facing a number of desperadoes and Pinky felt as if he were running away. The sensation didn't sit well with him, but it was what had been asked of him so he kept going for the duration he had those headlamps in his rear-view mirror. Earlier two of the cars had gone past him on the minor roads along the coast, an attempt at persuading him that they weren't following him. Other cars had fallen into line to pursue him, no less a large pickup truck with chunky off-road tires and a spotlight rack above the cab. Somewhere during the chase he must have passed one of the cars that originally went ahead, because again the point car in the pack was the one he'd initially noticed with the dimmer headlamp.

Getting around Freeport had proven easy enough. A residential street had taken him along the eastern edge of town and back onto the winding road that hugged the coastline below where the Harraseeket river emptied into the ocean. Pinky had lived in Tess's apartment for a good while, but for months now had barely traveled any distance – trips out for groceries or to a pharmacy were as far as he could boast – certainly he had not driven out this far. He had a bare notion of where he was but knew that if he kept moving he'd meet the highway at some point. He had disdained the highway earlier, but fully intended using it to gain distance on his pursuers as soon as he could. Not that he'd continue fleeing towards home. He was the only one armed with anything more powerful than Po's boot knife, and now regretted not taking the few extra seconds to toss his Glock to Tess after Stahl got out. His rifle remained in its safe box in his trunk's hidden compartment. If it were his choice, he'd halt the SUV and force his pursuers to stop at gunpoint, show they were messing with the wrong guy. Fighting these people was permissible if he was cornered or an innocent life was imperiled. Alas they had to behave within the boundary of the law, so cold-blooded violence was not Tess's, or even Nicolas's, way and while Pinky worked with them he was compelled to flee. His best play was to assist his friends when he wasn't the Pied Piper with a bunch of rats scurrying after him.

The road wound through hilly terrain, dotted with brush and great stands of trees. Gullies off the hillsides ordinarily drained rainwater into the sea, but the warm spell had dried up most of the streams. His tire noise changed each time the SUV spanned one of the narrow valleys. He only periodically spotted the lights of the following vehicles. He sped up incrementally, not making it obvious he was accelerating away. The narrow road came to an intersection. Pinky slowed and his gaze darted both ways. He almost missed the car parked at an oblique angle in the gateway to a forest trail. It sat far enough back that it wasn't visible until he was committed to the turn, and by then he was fully in view of the watcher. It was the first car to have overtaken him prior to dropping off Gabe Stahl. Its wily driver had stayed ahead all this time, then waited here in ambush. If the man was armed he could poke out his gun and blast Pinky as he drove by. Pinky grimaced in frustration, forced to continue past but also happy not to be shot to death. He was again tempted to turn around and confront his watcher, but no doubt the others would be upon him in the next minute and events could turn deadly. The watcher didn't fall into line immediately: apparently he had the means to update his pals via a phone or radio. The first lights to appear in Pinky's wake was the one with the dimmer lamp. Oddly, it did not come after him but turned and he saw its rear lights recede as it continued south. The next car to appear was possibly the pickup truck and it too went south. Lastly, the car edged out from the gateway and followed the others.

'What messed-up game is this you're playing, you?'

He stood on the gas pedal and the SUV rocketed.

Pinky took the car through several turns, fully intent on finding a way to return to his friends. He hit the brakes and the SUV slewed and sent up smoke off the overheated tires. The obvious had struck him: the latest watcher had spotted that he was alone in the car, and realizing he had dropped off Stahl someplace they had sped off to gain leverage over them. He rapidly turned the SUV, and reversed roles with his previous pursuers. He had his Glock clipped under the SUV's dashboard, in easy reach. He felt for it, because the rules of engagement could be about to change.

He used the buttons on his steering wheel to call Po's cell phone. His buddy didn't answer, so he switched to Tess's cell. She did pick up.

'Tess,' he said without any of his usual eccentric speech patterns, 'I think they're going after Gabe's father.'

'What . . . how?'

'I made a mistake and let myself be seen alone. They know I must've dropped Gabe off somewhere, but they're not coming back. They've taken off at speed towards Falmouth. I dunno . . . what if they know about the old man, and try to use him to manipulate his son?'

'We have to call the police and get him protected.'

'But what if I'm wrong?' Pinky chewed his bottom lip. 'Maybe I've gotten it all wrong about what they're up to. If we call the cops, won't you have to explain why the old man's in danger? It'll spoil any plans you have for helping Vaughan without incriminating us all.'

'So what's the alternative? We've just gotten our hands on Vaughan and his heavily pregnant companion. If we leave them to rush back to Falmouth—'

'No, don't do that. I'll try catching them and stopping them from getting to Gabe's dad.'

'Pinky, you can't. You'll be outnumbered and—'

'Don't worry about me. I won't risk my ass, at least not too much. If it's definite what they have in mind, I promise I'll call in some back-up, me.' He'd slipped back into the role of the larger than life Pinky Leclerc, but he couldn't fool Tess. She knew him well enough to know he was exhibiting bravado when in reality his anxiety was about to go through the roof. He ended the call before his vocal tone raised a few octaves. He wasn't afraid per se – his anxiety wasn't even for the old man's welfare – it was that the frail old dodder could be used against his friends and that didn't sit well with him one bit.

Pinky had no idea if the bad guys had headed directly for the highway, but it was where he planned on going. He intended getting back to the house at Mackworth Point as quickly as possible.

Surprisingly, the first vehicle to heave into view was none of the three he'd spotted following him earlier, it was the blue panel van that he'd shot at with the rifle at the wharves. It must have been trailing the others, but exited the intersection while Pinky was rocketing in the opposite direction. They'd probably need the van for transporting their hostage if he'd guessed their plan correctly. Well, he would happily put paid to that notion. He aimed the large SUV after the van.

In a straight competition, the van was probably heavier and had an edge on brute force, but Pinky didn't try matching it. The SUV was more maneuverable and had a lower center of gravity. He used those factors as he powered in and touched the van's rear left fender with the SUV's front right. It was barely more than a caress at first, but once he had contact, Pinky turned the SUV an inch or more to the right. The reaction was more than equal to the nudge he'd given the fender, down more to the driver's over-reaction than to the laws of physics. The van swerved, first one way then the other, then it careened, almost toppling over as its wheels mounted the shoulder. The driver again over-corrected the steering, and Pinky eased on his brakes to allow distance between them. The van's rear end juddered, slewed again and Pinky heard the eruption of air as one of its tires blew. The van toppled the other direction and this time gravity got a grasp on it that there was no escaping. Pinky stood on his brake pedal as the van crashed on its side but kept skidding along the road. It slammed something on the shoulder. Outcroppings of boulders dotted the ground on either side of the road. The van partially concertinaed while its rear swept around and wedged crosswise in the road. Pinky had taken the van out of commission but effectively had also blocked his route. He cursed more vehemently than normal. He disembarked the SUV, clutching his Glock, and had to clamber around the van on the churned-up shoulder to get to the cab.

A stranger lay stunned in the front, surrounded by sundry items thrown from the glove box and other compartments when the van tipped over. His seat belt had saved him from being thrown from the van but also served to constrict him now. Pinky stared at him through the veined glass of the broken windshield, contem-plating. He'd expected to see the bald man that Po had knocked unconscious earlier, but it wasn't him; this was some other asshole that'd made the mistake of making an enemy of Pinky. Pinky thought about shooting him, but even in anger he rarely succumbed to the basest of his instincts. The guy was unconscious and probably unfit to trouble anyone for days, so Pinky left him and headed back to his SUV with another dilemma. Should he ram the van out of his path and continue on this path or retrace his route and seek another way to the highway? He chose the former.

The SUV's tires plumed more smoke as he employed the big car again, this time as a bulldozer as opposed to a ram. The van screeched along the asphalt, then its body shrieked as it buckled under duress. Pinky reversed and then swung the SUV onto the opposite shoulder and rode past. He glanced over at the cab. The driver was still unconscious, and oblivious to what had happened. Leaving a crashed van blocking a road could bring police to the scene, but Pinky thought it would be an age yet before anyone stumbled over the wreckage. Other than the cars of his enemies, he hadn't spotted another road user since his first drive through Freeport. Once the police arrived it would be unlikely that the driver would still be hanging about to answer their awkward questions. It was doubtful that what had happened to the van would be connected to him, or to Tess and Po, so he was unconcerned by his decision to halt it, in fact he was tickled pink with the result.

TWENTY-NINE

Finding she was wrapped up at the center of another maelstrom of madness was not unusual to Tess. Over the last few years, since she first hooked up with Po to conduct a manhunt in the swamps of Louisiana, she had become embroiled in violent and frightening incidents she wouldn't have believed before. Even when she was a law-enforcement officer she couldn't have imagined that she would be taking on serial murderers, hitmen, a vicious family of militants, or any other of the dangerous foes she'd faced since. Never let it be said that Maine, allegedly the state with the lowest crime rate in the US, would be a boring place to work for a private investigator.

She had listened to Pinky's update with a sense of bewilderment. How did the Brogans know about Stahl senior, or that they might be able to leverage Gabe into giving away Vaughan's location through him? They must have been conducting surveillance on Pinky via several sources, not only through the man he'd chased from his apartment in Cumberland Avenue. They must have shadowed Pinky, watched him collect Gabe and somehow spotted the infirm old man at his house.

Gabe Stahl stood agog while Po hauled out the cash-stuffed holdall and swung it underhanded to Vaughan. Vaughan was relieved to not have to fight for possession of his treasure. Leah sat sidesaddle in the Mustang, her feet on the dusty ground outside, knees spread immodestly. She needn't be concerned about covering up. Mouth open, Stahl could barely take his eyes off the bag of cash, he gave the pregnant girl no attention whatsoever. Tess thought that if she checked his eyes they would hold dollar signs like somebody overcome by greed in those old cartoons. He glanced over at Leah once, but only licked his dry lips and returned his gaze to the holdall. Tess didn't think he'd even registered her presence. While he was engrossed in the cash she should keep Pinky's concern to herself. It would only complicate matters if a frantic Stahl demanded to be returned home.

She wasn't happy with her decision to ignore the potential of harm coming to the old man. She caught Po's eye and jerked her head. He got the message; she wished some privacy to speak. He gave Vaughan instructions to load his and Leah's belongings in the trunk of the Mustang, and asked Stahl to help his pal. He joined Tess and she guided him away with a hand on his forearm. As concisely as possible she related Pinky's cell phone call to him. Po tensed when he heard Pinky had gone after the group on a single-handed rescue mission. He didn't comment on its rashness. How could he? Po was guilty of conducting single-handed rescue missions too. He glowered towards Vaughan and Tess knew that he was calculating which of them deserved his support more: his best friend Pinky or a runaway thief. His gaze slipped to the pregnant girl and his brow puckered. His decision wasn't as simple when including Leah.

'Things haven't gone as smoothly as I'd've liked,' Po admitted. Using his car to stop Vaughan and Leah from fleeing was probably the last thing on his mind until forced to do it. Also, fetching Stahl to act as a mediator had become moot, and if anything he was now proving an extra hindrance to moving Vaughan and Leah out of harm's way.

Po checked out the two men. They were whispering animatedly, arms flapping and swiping to emphasize their respective points. Stahl looked on the verge of feverish while Vaughan often scowled and pinched his mouth.

'I can have Gabe take Tony's car and return home while we get the others out of here,' Po suggested.

'Do you think it's safe to take them anywhere right now? It's not as if we can even drive them home to the ranch, or even to my old apartment, because the Brogans already know those places.

Plus, *what*, it's a good idea to send Gabe back to his father when the bad guys could already be there?'

'He should be given the opportunity to go protect his da,' said Po. Tess read the subtext of his words. Po's father had been murdered and Po had not been able to save him. Po avenged his father's death, killing his slayer, and spent half his adult life behind bars as a consequence. He'd taken his punishment on the chin, and would do the same again if any of his loved ones were harmed.

'I agree, but under the circumstances it might complicate matters. Pinky's already gone there to help Mr Stahl, he doesn't need Gabe showing up and need saving too.'

'Maybe you're right, Tess. Gabe's handy with a lug wrench, but I don't think he'd be much use in a brawl. Besides, if we tried sending him home now he'd faint from separation anxiety since getting his eyes on Vaughan's haul.'

'Let's call it what it is, Po. It's stolen money. As Tony made clear, it's *blood money* and people have already died because of it.' She wagged a finger at each of them and then at Leah in particular. 'I'd rather burn the entire bagful before willingly allowing it to kill anyone else.'

'I hear ya loud an' clear.'

Po checked the cabin over with a brief sweep of his eyes. He turned his attention to the outbuildings. 'This place is more defensible than either the farm or Pinky's apartment. Maybe moving them to either place would be putting them in a worse situation than they're already in.'

'At least in Portland we'd only be minutes from a police response.'

'Let's face it, Tess. Your law-enforcement days are well and truly behind you now; you want to involve the cops in this even less than I do.' He smiled ferally. 'Why, I'd say you're spoilin' for a fight as badly as I am, Miss Grey.'

She laughed, a sharp escape of air. She was enjoying getting back in the saddle again, but they had to be judicious about things. She was a private investigator not a vigilante, so there were still rules and regulations she had to obey. She couldn't just go picking a fight with a bunch of gangsters from California and expect the cops to turn a blind eye while they duked it out.

She considered their next move and came up with nothing valid.

The damn brain fog she'd suffered for months was making decision-making particularly difficult. It wasn't good enough. There were people whose lives could be reliant on her so she had to be more decisive. She said, 'What about taking them to Bar-Lesque? There's food and provisions there, bathrooms, and they can sleep in the back office if they want some privacy.'

'I'm not comfortable taking them there either. If the Brogans know about the ranch and the autoshop, they probably know about the diner. I know what you're thinking about it being central and in hollerin' distance of the cops, but I really don't want it to become a warzone, not when we're tryin' to reopen it after months.'

She nodded. Saying no to her under the circumstances was reasonable. 'I'm open to other ideas.'

'I think stayin' here at the cabin could become problematic. Sooner or later the Brogans will come looking, and I'm not sure we can fight them off when we're unarmed. But stayin' put for now beats the alternative: we could leave and run directly into Leah's uncle in that van. Alone he doesn't scare me, but we know him and his brother have other punks at their beck and call . . . we dunno how many guys they have nearby, ready to throw at us. We get pinched between two vehicles on that narrow coast road and there's no way we're drivin' out of the trap. We know that Josh Brogan has a gun and isn't afraid to use it, Walsh also had a gun this morning; it's fair to assume the others are packing too. They want to, they could cut us all to pieces.'

Again, nothing that Po said was contentious. 'If you prefer to wait at the cabin, why load Tony and Leah's stuff in your car? Actually, no, forget I asked that.' Tess scrubbed her fingers through her hair, digging in with the tips of her nails to try igniting a few sparks of inspiration in her fogged brain. The effects of prolonged lockdown had turned her into a goddamned zombie! It was obvious why they'd load their belongings in the car: Po wanted it ready to go in an instant should the worst happen and the Brogans arrived. As a last resort he'd ram a path through the bad guys. She had noted already that discounting the large holdall stuffed with cash, their other belongings were few.

She staggered, and had to catch herself. She exhaled, feeling weak.

'You OK, Tess?'

'I'm feeling a little light-headed,' she admitted. What she kept to herself was how hard and rapidly her heart was beating. 'I haven't eaten much. My blood sugars are probably a bit low. I should've ate more of those ployes I cooked this morning, eh?'

It felt like an age since she'd been flipping pancakes, certainly it felt as if it was days ago and not that same morning. She'd snacked at Bar-Lesque, but that too must have been at least twelve hours ago. Right then, in keeping with her foggy head, she had bare sense of what day of the week it was never mind how long it was since she'd last eaten. However, she wasn't a person to faint for lack of calories, so this onset of weakness was mildly troubling.

'You should sit down.' Po began leading her to the car.

'I'm fine, honestly,' she said, but wasn't fooling him.

Po returned and offered his hand. 'There's no shame in feeling rotten.'

'I'm OK,' she reiterated, and felt droplets of sweat roll from under her hair and down her jawline. There was genuine concern for her in Po's gaze. 'All right, I'll admit to feeling a bit crummy.'

'Is it this damn virus?'

'No, no, it's not coronavirus, it could be—' She halted mid-sentence, because she didn't think it was the time or place for that type of conjecture. 'I'll sit, catch my breath and the dizziness will disappear. Leah's in more need of sympathy than me. We should make a decision, Po, and either get her fully in the car or back indoors.'

He gestured at the cabin. 'I've thought about it and vote for staying put.'

'I've no objection. We should give Leah's uncle time to leave the area. Hopefully Pinky calls with an update on what's happening in town, and it'll help us make a more informed decision on what we need to do next.'

'I'm tempted to call him this instant,' Po said, and Tess instantly felt crummier than before. This time it was because she had become an extra burden for him when he'd already a bunch of people to be concerned for. If it came down to difficult choices, he'd always pick her and Pinky over anyone else, but she'd rather he didn't have to. She mentally hitched up her pants and walked with more determination to the car.

THIRTY

A light burned behind the thick drapes at the upstairs bedroom window. Only a chink between the heavy folds of cloth allowed a dim glow to leak out. Over the door another light illuminated the front entrance. There was not another hint that anyone was home but Bryce Brogan knew that to be untrue. According to Huckleberry and Davenport, they'd spotted a lizard-like old guy with his nose pressed to the upper window when Pinky Leclerc collected Gabe Stahl earlier. It was possible that Stahl senior had moved in with his son for the duration of the pandemic. There was the possibility that little love was lost between father and son, but he was ready to test to what length Stahl would let his father be harmed. Bryce would be first to admit that he held little affection for Leah, but she was still his flesh and blood, and anyone else would get a rise out of him if they threatened her . . . without his permission.

There was nothing to say that Gabe Stahl would, or even could, give up Tony Vaughan and Leah's location, but Bryce shared a similar theory with his older brother, that Stahl had been drafted in by Grey and Villere to assist them in their hunt for the runaways. It was supposition, but why else would Pinky have been dispatched to collect Stahl and deliver him up the coast, where they'd obviously pulled some kind of stunt to drop him off in secret. Both Brogan brothers believed that their prey had to be in spitting distance of where Pinky pulled off the switcheroo, and Josh had stayed up there to conduct reconnaissance while Bryce took on the task of securing leverage. Bryce wasn't averse to storming a stronghold in order to reclaim what was stolen from them, but, more prudent, Josh preferred to get back the money without breaking a sweat.

Bryce keyed the radio. Distractedly he wondered about its range; it had been some time since he'd heard from Eamon White, whom Bryce was waiting for to bring in the van. How far back had the van fallen while the others sped towards Falmouth? Eamon

White better not have booked out on them, Bryce thought. Not because he gave a crap about the man's loyalty, or lack of for that matter, but the van was needed to carry the old fart in.

'White, come in. You got your ears on?' he asked.

The silence was deafening.

'Any of you other limp dicks spotted White lately?'

Beside Bryce, Declan Randall shook his head. 'How to win friends and influence people,' he muttered under his breath.

'You're right,' said Bryce, 'I should show the help more respect. Hey, have any of you *upstanding* dicks seen or heard from White lately?'

There was reticence to answering, but finally Anderson Walsh keyed his radio: 'Can't say I've heard from him since you aborted the idea of pushing that bastard nigger back towards Josh.' Walsh was still carrying a boner for Pinky. Bryce was unsure why his buddy was so pissed with Pinky, considering the shots had been fired to keep Bryce from knifing Po'boy.

'Yeah, I'm saving him for later,' Bryce reminded Walsh. 'Don't forget he's mine. The rest of you, anyone heard from White or not?'

Nobody had.

'Huckleberry, I want you to go and take a look around. We don't want any witnesses calling the cops. Neighborhood like this, the residents are bound to be uptight and paranoid about home invasions.'

'Home invasion robberies aren't something the folks of Portland have to worry about,' Randall sighed, 'not unduly.'

'Nevertheless, I know rich folks and rich folks think guys like us are out to steal their stuff. We are, but that's beside the point, huh?'

Huckleberry keyed his radio. 'I'll attract more attention checking for witnesses than if I sit tight.'

'So sit tight, asshole. Davenport, you do it. Go check the coast's clear.'

'Man, I hate to say it,' Davenport came back, 'but I'm beginning to have second thoughts. Randall, dude, you promised good pay for a few hours' work. You said there might be a bit of a scuffle, but you never mentioned it would be with goddamn Po'boy Villere, probably the toughest motherfucker in Portland. And you didn't mention anything about abducting a sick old man either. I'm sorry, dude, but the pay isn't enough. Not near enough.'

'Why don't you do as I ask, then come see me for your bonus?' Bryce snapped.

'I'll recce the place,' Anderson Walsh offered and Bryce smiled. Good old Walshy, maybe Bryce should pay him more respect because the guy was always willing to come through for him.

'Do it, Walsh. You two other sons of bitches keep your heads down till I tell you what to do.' Bryce again looked across at Randall and briefly pursed his lips. 'These are the type of punks I'm supposed to treat like equals?'

'They're not our equals, Bryce, but they are putting their asses on the line for us and deserve some appreciation.'

'I've to show appreciation to a coward and to a lazy sumbitch? Na-ah, they won't get it from me, Randall. But I must say Ol' Walshy has won me over. Lookit him! He's as eager as a virgin in a whore house.'

'. . . and not conspicuous at all,' Randall wheezed.

Anderson Walsh jogged from between some roadside shrubs, arms swinging by his sides, neck craned forward to make his silhouette smaller. He ducked alongside another overgrown bush at curbside near the front of the Stahl house, then bobbed up for a glimpse of the house. He seemed happy to advance. He darted around the bush and into Stahl's front yard, then moved for the lean-to garage. Walsh disappeared from view, heading around the back and Bryce pictured him bobbing up and down at ground floor windows trying to peep inside.

'What do you see?' Bryce asked over the walkie-talkie.

There was no immediate answer. Evidently Walsh had thought ahead and turned down the volume so he didn't risk alerting the neighborhood. Bryce clicked the send button several times.

Walsh came on, whispering. 'I don't see anyone, but there's a darn mutt barking from nearby. Don't know if I'm the one spooking it or what, but it's going nuts. Want me to pull back outta here, Bryce?'

'You're doing fine where you're at, buddy.' Bryce smiled at Randall, showing he was following his advice about praising his helpers more. His smile was so disingenuous even he felt like a fake. 'While you're around the back, try the door and see if it's been left unlocked.'

'Will do. I'll see if—' Walsh's voice disappeared, replaced by a few seconds' worth of static, the white noise sounding like the rush of water down a flume.

'Walshy, repeat.'

Walsh remained silent.

The barking dog kicked into overdrive, going ballistic. Bryce winced with each high-pitched yap, expecting the dog to raise the neighborhood.

'Walshy, whatever you're doing, stop it.'

The lack of a reply irked Bryce, but he guessed what it meant. He doubted that Walsh had tripped in the dark and knocked his brains out, it was more likely that he'd gotten into trouble and couldn't respond.

'Huckleberry, Davenport, have either of you got eyes on Walsh?'

'Nope,' said Heck Bury.

'Nah,' said Davenport.

'For fuck's sake show some initiative! Move in, see what you can see.' Bryce audibly ground his teeth together. 'Tell you what, if you're thinking of turning tail on us, do it the fuck now, Davenport, so I don't have to waste any more time on you.'

'I've still not been paid, I'm not leaving yet.'

'So get moving and earn your pay, Dickwad!'

Davenport must have been parked closer to the pickup than Bryce realized, because he heard the clunk of the car door, then the rush of Davenport's feet on the asphalt as he hurried to find a vantage from where he could see Walsh. Davenport scurried into the front yard, then headed the opposite direction around the house that Walsh had gone.

'Things are turning to crap.' Randall dipped his hand under his jacket, caressed the butt of his holstered pistol. 'We should leave before it's too late.'

'Really, Randall? Are you prepared to run back home with your tail tucked between your legs? I'm not, pal, no way, no how. I'd rather keep my head on my shoulders than have it put on a stake in the Mojave Desert.'

'I'm not suggesting we give up the hunt for Tony and Leah, I'm talking about dropping this idea with the old guy.'

'Would you argue my plan's validity if I was my brother Josh instead?'

'This isn't about *you*, Bryce, it's about the horrible sense I have that the shit's about to hit the fan.'

'Yeah, well if that's the case I want to be the one throwing the shit at it.' Bryce threw open the pickup door and stepped down to the street. 'Slide over, Randall, and keep the engine running. I'm gonna take a look at what's going on.'

'I don't think that's a good idea, Bryce.'

'Yeah, well I'll take your warning on advisement.' Promptly, Bryce ignored him and headed for the house. There was no jogging or crouching for him. He preferred to hide in plain sight. His arms swung gently at his sides, his head swaying benignly with each step. To an observer he'd appear unthreatening. Concealed in his sleeve his knife was poised for action.

THIRTY-ONE

Tess frowned up at the trio standing around her, two of them awkward in the other's presence. Tony Vaughan glowered suspiciously at Gabe Stahl, while Stahl lowered his eyes, blinking rapidly and licking his lips. Lastly, Po eyed both men with his arms folded across his chest and his jaw sticking out. He looked like a doorman refusing entry to two drunks who'd turned up at a club without their neckties. Outside, Po had had to physically separate them after Vaughan took out his frustration at being found with a verbal scolding of his old pal. Stahl hadn't taken the berating without argument and they'd gotten into a pushing and shoving match. They'd since each apologized for their outbursts, but the atmosphere was still as thick as molasses. Typical male behavior, Tess decided, and turned her attention on Leah instead.

The pregnant girl had reclined on the couch in the living area of the cabin. It was low, and she had sprawled on her side to ease her discomfort. Tess, seated at the other end, almost mirrored Leah's posture. She still felt weak and shaky. Leah wouldn't meet her gaze, but Tess felt it was more to do with the girl's nature than any other reason. Tess reached across and gently laid her fingertips on Leah's knee. The girl blinked at her. Possibly this was the first tender human interaction she'd had in a long time.

'When's your baby due?' Tess asked.

'Any day now.' Leah grunted. 'It's difficult pinpointing when he's due when I can't swear who the father is. How could I with that lot at me?'

Reading the subtext of her words, Tess wondered what hell the young woman had gone through that had prompted her to run for the hills while heavily pregnant. From what Leah intimated, she was being used and abused by several men around the time of conception. 'You were being . . . raped?'

'What other name could there be for it? It definitely wasn't lovemaking.'

'Dear god . . .' Tess turned and glowered up at Vaughan. Oblivious to her anger, he carried on circling around with the other men, lost in their own discourse. Leah caught the direction of Tess's scowl.

'No, no, Tony isn't guilty of what the others made me do.'

'Who are these others?' Tess's database searches had failed to throw up anything pertinent about the Brogans' tattoos, but she still felt positive they were gang-related tags. She'd formed an opinion that said gang were those that had sexually abused the girl on multiple occasions.

Leah wafted a hand in the general direction of the road. Tess took the gesture to mean it was the same people that were chasing her.

'Your father and uncle were—'

'No. It wasn't like that. But they are both guilty of allowing, in fact in my father's case, *encouraging* their clients to use me.'

'He encouraged men to assault you? *Your own father?* What kind of monster—'

'He saw me as an incentive to help sweeten deals; he offered me to the kind of scumbags that found little girls attractive.'

Something sour frothed at the back of Tess's throat. She swallowed hard. 'How old are you, Leah?'

'I'm seventeen. I wasn't seventeen when I was first raped. I was used for *many* years before that.' Leah laughed at the absurdity, the sound more like a shriek of anguish. 'Now I've begun maturing into a woman I've lost most of my usefulness in that regard! I'm surprised my dad has bothered trying to take me back.'

Tess had previously thought it was the holdall stuffed with cash that had brought her father here to Maine, but not now.

'Of course, I know why he won't let me go; I'm his property, and nobody was ever allowed to *take me* without his blessing.' She glanced over at Vaughan and her face softened momentarily. 'Tony put a target on his back the first time he looked kindly in my direction.'

'Is your father a drug-dealer?'

'He has his dirty hands in loads of stuff. But if you're asking if my dad, or my Uncle Josh, is the boss, no, they're not. There are people above them, the real important people. My father and uncle look after some of their affairs in L.A., but their main role is as . . . I guess you'd call them *enforcers*?'

'They do the dirty work to keep the real criminals' hands clean?'

'Yeah. I guess they're in a unique position when I think about it. They don't always work exclusively for one outfit, they hire their services out where they're needed.'

'They both had gang allegiance at one time. The tattoos they have on their hands, and this here . . .' Tess tapped her cheek under her eye. 'This tattoo was significant, right? But they had to conceal it after they became guns for hire?'

'They work for whoever pays them most. Gang tags marking them as white supremacists don't go down well with some of their prospective employers. Uncle Josh had his removed years ago, but my father hasn't been as enthusiastic at covering up his. The joke is my father buys into that racial bullshit: why should he when he has no empathy, and pretty much dislikes anyone of any race or color who isn't *him*? The tattoo here' – now Leah touched under her eye – '*was significant*. It indicated the number of people he killed as part of his initiation into the gang. If the rumors are true' – Leah traced her fingertip from her eyelid down the curve of her jaw, over her collarbone towards her breast – 'he should have a column of figures all the way down to here.'

'It sounds as if we've been fortunate not to be killed in our previous encounters with him.'

There was not an iota of sarcasm in Tess's words, but Leah

shivered. 'I'm not exaggerating. My father's as dangerous as I say, and then some. He doesn't have an off switch; if he wants you dead he'll do everything to make it happen. He won't give up chasing me . . . unless he's stopped. I don't want him to find me, Tess, and I don't want him to hurt Tony. Tony doesn't deserve to be in constant fear, he already has enough to contend with as it is.'

'He's attracted a whole heap of trouble, for sure,' said Tess. 'How is it he came to be your . . . what would you call him, your *guardian*?'

'My friend.'

'Your friend it is. Tony obviously got sucked into some criminal scheme out west after he left Maine. How'd you two cross paths and come up with this idea to flee together?'

'Tony was doing some driving work, couriering and stuff, and unknowingly got drawn into making deliveries for some cartel guys my father and Uncle Josh had signed on with. They kept Tony around, and pretty much used him as badly as they did me, just in a different way. He saw me one day and we got to talking and we became friends. Soon he trusted me enough to say he was planning on leaving and would take me if I wanted to go. He saw how much I was suffering, and what the future meant for me' – Leah stroked her abdomen and winced – 'and my child, and said he couldn't bear to think of us suffering if he could help us escape. It was my idea to take the money; I had access to it where Tony had none. We took off, with Tony hopeful that we'd be more trouble to chase than it was worth, but that was before he fully understood how much I'd stolen. I made the mistake of grabbing way more than I needed. When Tony and me counted it, we gave up nearing half a million dollars and we were less than halfway through the holdall. I guess the money was payment on some deal my father and Uncle Josh were overseeing, and now their clients want it back.'

'Cartel guys?'

'So I heard. When I was being passed around those scumballs they treated me as if I was deaf, dumb and blind, so they sometimes forgot I was there and spoke freely. I heard the term *cartel* mentioned on more occasions than I can count on both hands, but I don't know which specific cartel was being spoken about. Does it really matter which cartel, when they're all extremely dangerous?'

'It'd be beneficial to know who our enemies are before—'

'You know our enemies already. They're my father and uncle, and they're as scary as anyone their clients could send across the border.'

Tess drew in a deep breath. Nausea coiled in her gut, and it had nothing to do with the fear of cartel hitmen. She wiped a damp hand over a damper forehead.

Leah studied her.

Before the girl could comment on her condition, Tess diverted attention to the trio now standing together at the far end of the cabin. She had the distinct impression Po had herded the others aside to allow her and Leah to talk privately. Where there had been tension before, Vaughan and Stahl were now easy in the other's company, bosom buddies again. Tess said, 'Tony's reason for helping you couldn't be truly altruistic. Is there more he wants from you, something he expects from you later, perhaps?'

'You mean after I've given birth and am desirable again?' Leah gave a sharp, scornful shake of her head. 'Tony has admitted to loving me, but he swears it's in a purely platonic way, as if I'm the daughter he never had, or maybe a little sister. He said it might be hard for some to believe, but a man and woman can be friends, sex doesn't have to get in the way. And I believe him. He has and shows affection for me, but he has never tried anything inappropriate, or even laid a dirty look on me.'

Did Vaughan's feelings for her, sexual or otherwise, have any bearing whatsoever on why he'd choose to risk his neck for her? It needn't. Perhaps, as Leah said, Vaughan was a decent guy who couldn't bear to leave her to her suffering. His character raised several steps in Tess's estimation. By contrast, she was unsure how far she'd credit Gabe Stahl: again he was licking his lips nervously, or perhaps greedily?

Vaughan clutched the holdall, hugging it to his chest. It looked weighty, perhaps twenty to thirty pounds, but not as heavy as Tess thought a million dollars would be. She had imagined a much larger stack, but supposed it was down to the denomination of the bills. If they were all hundred- or fifty-dollar bills, she supposed they could be rammed into a holdall. It looked as if Vaughan was struggling to carry it. She studied him in more detail than before, and had an inkling why he might be willing to give his life for Leah's.

THIRTY-TWO

Minutes ago Pinky crouched, his left palm squashed down over as much of Anderson Walsh's mouth and nostrils as possible. Under the pressure of his hand Walsh squirmed and despite Pinky's efforts to muffle them, his cries of dismay were still too loud. Even in the dimness at the back of the house, Pinky had recognized the burly figure and shaved head of Bryce Brogan's second. The punk had come after Pinky for a reckoning, but had fallen short.

'Sorry, you,' said Pinky as he raised his Glock, 'but I can't trust you to stay quiet.'

Walsh's eyes widened in terror and he bucked hard against Pinky's hand.

Pinky slammed the Glock on Walsh's head. He felt him go limp, but only for a second. His prisoner squirmed again, and Pinky supposed that sometimes going easier on a guy wasn't the best option. He'd tried tempering some of the force so he didn't break Walsh's skull altogether, but now he required striking again. He made the next blow shorter and sharper, aiming for the jaw where Po had earlier softened it up. The light went out of Walsh's eyes.

A neighborhood dog was barking so loud that it should've wakened the dead, but Walsh didn't stir. Pinky dragged his now unresponsive captive away from the house and pushed him under the shrubs at the side of the property. Under different circumstances he might've rolled Walsh downhill to the boat ramp and set him adrift towards Mackworth Island. For now, Pinky only needed him out of the picture for a couple of minutes. Already a second punk called Davenport was moving in, trying to be stealthy, but Pinky could hear his rasping breaths as he snuck in. Davenport was soiling his pants, was tight as a bowstring, and therefore very dangerous. Pinky had easily taken out Walsh because his presence was totally unexpected there, but Davenport had been sent to investigate under duress, so wouldn't fall as easily into an ambush. Pinky had heard all on Walsh's walkie-talkie, and it helped him judge how much time he had to deal with Davenport by the radio silence. Soon Brogan would demand to know what had become of his second minion after Pinky knocked him the hell out too.

Moving among the deeper shadows of the trees in the back yard, Pinky stole to the far side from where he'd dumped Walsh. He wished now he hadn't knocked Walsh totally senseless, as his moans could've assisted to draw Davenport to him, leaving him vulnerable to Pinky. But never mind, Pinky preferred to make his own advantages.

As Davenport rounded the house Pinky went stock-still. Davenport's head moved like a chicken's, bobbing and jerking as he tried to see everywhere at once. He scanned the yard, then up at the back of the house. On the uppermost floor light leaked through a chink in the drapes, and Davenport's gaze lingered on it for a long count of three, drawn through the darkness to it like a moth. Pinky judged the pistol in his hand: he could easily shoot Davenport and have done, but that would ensure chaos. Unlike his rifle, this gun wasn't equipped with a suppressor. At first sound of gunfire, the others might turn tail and flee, but he could guarantee the cops would respond. Alternatively the others might attack en masse, and again it was certain to bring the cops. Neither scenario suited. Pinky wished to foil this abduction attempt on Stahl senior without ensuring himself a trip to jail or worse when the cops showed up. Sad to say, but they'd see a black man with a gun and possibly assume the worst.

Pinky's athleticism often surprised people. They saw an over-weight man, and assumed he'd be an unfit lumbering oaf. But as was often the case with guys with fuller figures, he possessed grace and lightness of foot and could jitterbug skinnier dudes off the dance floor. Also he could be stealthy and equally light-footed when hunting. He moved towards Davenport, timing his footsteps to match his prey. Davenport moved obliquely away from the house, trying to spot what had become of Walsh, expecting to spot him coming around the other corner near to the carport. All he achieved was to set off the dog barking again. Davenport sought the mutt, afraid perhaps that it was about to launch at him. Pinky capitalized on the dog's timely interruption.

He swept in from behind, bent over so as not to cause movement in Davenport's peripheral vision. Three yards and closing swiftly, he unfolded, bringing up the Glock so it was held like a hammer alongside his head.

Afraid and on edge, Davenport's senses warned him of impending attack. Whatever had pricked him into action, he spun around and gawped up in the last second before Pinky brought down the gun butt. Instead of it hammering the back of his skull, the gun flattened Davenport's nose and loosened teeth. Davenport collapsed, and as graceful as Pinky could be, he still trampled him underfoot. Instantly Pinky corrected his balance and returned to check on Davenport. He was in dreamland. Pinky stripped the walkie-talkie from Davenport's rictus grasp, and checked for weapons. The man had a belt knife, but no handgun: Pinky almost felt bad about crushing the asshole's face. Almost.

The unseen dog was going apoplectic.

Weak light strobed across the backyard.

Pinky hunched again, lowering to a crouch, while checking for the light's source. Upstairs Stahl senior must have heard the commotion. He stood framed between the opened drapes backlit by a dim glow. The strobing effect had to have been when he was adjusting the curtains for a better view. The old man seemed to be looking beyond Pinky, at some indeterminate point between the house and Casco Bay. Pinky heard the old man's muffled grumble. 'Stupid dog. If I had a gun I'd darn well shoot ya! Now shut it, and let a man sleep.'

Stahl senior continued to glare and holler out of the window, and the dog continued raising hell, but in the end it was the man that yielded. Stahl yanked the curtains shut and retreated further inside the house. Pinky waited a few seconds more before straightening. He checked the approaches on both sides then trod towards the house. Earlier, Bryce Brogan had commanded his minions forwards; Pinky guessed if he was any kind of leader he'd act by example. Pinky checked his gun. It was never a good idea to use the butt as a blunt instrument, it risked damaging the magazine and courting a jammed round, but this time, the gun had been more than a match for the cartilage in Davenport's nose.

He could only approximate how many bad guys had come to snatch the old man. He recalled the blue van, the pickup and three cars. He had taken three players out of the game already, possibly as many as half the team, but he couldn't be certain. He knew there was Bryce and the man they were calling Huckleberry to contend with, but was there anyone else? 'Plan for the worst, hope for the best, you,' he whispered and went to check the back door.

As was sometimes the case in low-crime neighborhoods, the Stahls were lax on their security arrangements: the door was unlocked and opened soundlessly to Pinky's touch. He looked over his shoulder, watching for anyone else before stepping over the threshold into a small anteroom adjoining the kitchen. There was barely room to move for stacked boxes. Pinky squeezed between them and stood a moment in the entrance to the kitchen. There were more of the boxes, plus various other crates and polystyrene containers. They dominated the space and didn't leave much room for preparing or eating dinner. Pinky had housed similar goods in warehouses and lockups he once owned. He guessed Gabe Stahl had a sideline going in contraband to help stretch the wage earned at Charley's Autoshop.

Padding forwards Pinky found the door to the hall and he waited a few seconds, listening. The dog barks filtered in from outside, and there was a faint humming noise coming from somewhere, as well as the occasional click of settling floorboards from overhead. Pinky couldn't discern any sound or hint of movement foreign to the home. He pressed down the handle and allowed the door to swing towards him under its own weight. The hinges squeaked. Pinky caught the door with the toe of his sneaker and again waited. If elderly Mister Stahl had heard the squeak he didn't respond. It suited Pinky that Stahl stayed upstairs for now, and he'd only let him know he was inside the house once he was sure the old man was out of danger. He went silently along the hall, passing the stairs centered to his right and approached the front door, through which Tess and Po had earlier gained entrance. Small windows on either side of the door allowed decent views of the front yard, and the street beyond. Pinky could make out the hood of the pickup truck, parked in the darkness below the branches of a sycamore. He couldn't tell if anyone was in the truck or not. He tried tallying numbers, but again couldn't be certain how many people he'd yet to contend with, beyond Bryce Brogan and Huckleberry.

The best-case scenario would be for Brogan to realize his plan to abduct and use Gabe Stahl's dad against him had been foiled, and to vacate the area immediately. But from what he'd seen and heard of the guy over the walkie-talkie, Bryce Brogan wasn't screwed in tight enough. He expected that Bryce was the all-or-nothing type and he'd continue with his plan. If Brogan attacked the house, Pinky felt justified in shooting the legs out from under him, or even in putting a bullet through his pissant face.

Pinky backtracked along the hall. He halted at the stairs and craned for a view of the upper landing. The window where Stahl senior had berated the noisy dog from was to the far right, but all that Pinky could see towards the middle and front of the house were the tops of closed doors. From his low vantage he had no way of seeing the light bleeding out from under the old man's bedroom door. It was unnecessary: he pinpointed the room because of the sudden garbled soundtrack of a TV cop show. Stahl senior must have turned up the volume to drown out the annoying barks.

The racket from the TV worked two-fold, both good and bad. Good that it overwhelmed any slight noises that Pinky might make while moving through the house, bad that it might do the same for any other interlopers. He darted along the hall again and spied out one of the panes next to the door. As he watched, he noted the slightest of movement of the pickup as if somebody in the cab had shifted their weight. From what he'd gathered already, Bryce Brogan had traveled here in the pickup. Had he sent Huckleberry towards the house while he'd been dealing with Walsh and Davenport? Pinky still had Walsh's walkie-talkie wedged in his trouser pocket with the volume dialed low, and hadn't heard Brogan give out more orders. They could have switched channels when deducing their pals had fallen. Pinky took out the walkie-talkie, and he spun the channel selector dial through a sequence of clicks, waiting a second or two at each channel. If they had switched to another channel, they were keeping schtum for the time being.

Pinky eyed the pickup truck.

'Come on, you,' he whispered, challenging Bryce Brogan to leave its safety and meet him on open ground. However, he doubted he'd be afforded a clean and fair fight when Brogan had Huckleberry as backup. Plus, Walsh and Davenport wouldn't stay unconscious forever. Soon, unless a decisive move was made, Pinky would lose the slight advantage he'd earned in knocking out two of his adversaries.

He turned to look over his shoulder, making a check on the old man, and it was the action that saved his life. Stalking along the dimly lit hallway, his knife poised to slice open Pinky's neck, came Bryce Brogan. As they met gazes, a Jack o' lantern grin split Brogan's face, and he hurtled forward, his knife slashing to part Pinky's gun hand from his wrist.

THIRTY-THREE

'You seen the state of him, Tess?' Po frowned at Tony Vaughan.

Still in command of his bag of loot, Vaughan had slumped down in a rickety wooden chair at the kitchen table. He groaned and dropped his forehead onto his folded arms. The cumbersome holdall slipped off his lap, but it got caught between his ankles and Vaughan nipped his lower legs around it. His hair – shorn it appeared without any guidance from a barber – stuck up in longer tufts at the back where the cutters had missed. Here and there were patches on Vaughan's scalp, bare of hair and the skin reddened and angry. The veins and ligaments in the sides of his neck stood out like the strings on a harp. His clothes, Tess had already noted, looked as if they'd been sourced from a thrift store, where their previous owner had been a much sturdier guy than him. He smelled too, of sweat, and frying oil, and something else that sent a qualm through Tess. Her father had a similar aroma about him in the weeks before he had died.

'He's only half the man he was when he worked at the shop,' Po said.

'He's sick,' Tess agreed with Po's unspoken diagnosis. 'Has he admitted to you what's wrong with him?'

'Nope. Keeps sayin' he's fine and good to go. He's almost good for nothin', not unless you need somethin' to scare the crows off of your corn field.'

'When I lost my dad to bowel cancer,' Tess said, 'he had this smell about him towards the end . . .'

'Yeah,' said Po, and frowned again at Vaughan, this time with sympathy softening the harder lines of his face. 'I caught a strange odor off of him earlier, but couldn't place it.'

Tess would never forget the smell. Her memories of her dad, Michael Grey, were tinged with the scent of his illness. Aromas could evoke nostalgic memories from as far back as a person's childhood, to which Tess could attest; it was horrible and a true pity that the prevalent aroma guaranteed to hurl her decades into the past was the stench of bodily corruption.

'Leah hinted that Tony was sick.'

'She did, huh?'

Tess lowered her voice and nudged him so they both turned their backs on Vaughan. 'Not so much in what she said, but in how she said it. "He already has enough to contend with." I guess she was talking about him being terminally ill. I challenged his reason for helping her at risk of his own life, that it couldn't be all down to altruism, or even to getting his hands on the cash – Leah hadn't stolen it when they formed the plan to run away together. I think he knows his life's limited, Po, and decided to do something decent with what little time he has left.'

'A noble mission.'

'He keeps going up in my estimation.'

'He's asleep,' Po said. Vaughan had fully sunk down onto the table. His head was tilted towards them, his damaged eye still partially open, but watching them blindly.

'Perhaps this is the first time he's felt relaxed enough to sleep in weeks.'

'He was resistant at first, but he knows he can count on us to help. We should let him sleep for now, he deserves some shuteye. Where's Leah?'

She aimed a nod at the closed bedroom door. 'I made her go

and lie down on the bed for a while. We don't want her exerting herself too much. The last thing we need is for her to go into labor. Are you up for assisting her to give birth?'

Po's swarthy features bleached a few shades at the idea. 'Please, God,' he croaked, 'keep that baby healthy and inside of her for a few days more.'

While they talked and the others slept, Gabe Stahl had found a place to stand where he wasn't causing an obstruction. Tess had momentarily forgotten he was there. He again had his gaze set firmly on the holdall nestled between Vaughan's shins. He had a zoned-out look on his face, and slouched, arms folded across his chest. He must have sensed her scrutiny because he turned his head and blinked at her several times. 'What's up?'

She felt they owed Stahl more than he knew. He had no idea that Pinky had gone to his house to stop the Brogans from getting their hands on his father. Again she wondered if she should have said something and given him the opportunity to return home to help. Or if maybe now was the time to send him back. If anything bad had happened she expected a call from Pinky very shortly. If all was well and the abduction halted or aborted, then what harm was there in sending him home? He was once Tony Vaughan's drinking buddy, but it was obvious their friendship had diminished greatly. He wasn't needed in the capacity of a mediator any more, had never been needed for that matter, and didn't owe any of them a thing. If the Brogans were to discover the cabin, and storm it, then they shouldn't endanger Gabe Stahl. She asked, 'What's keeping you here, Gabe?'

'Whaddaya mean?' He glimpsed at Po as if her partner was his jailer.

'If you want, you should leave,' said Tess.

'It's a long walk back to Falmouth.'

'We can't drive you unfortunately, but if you want to take Tony's car, I'm sure he wouldn't object.'

'You mean the car you guys crushed into a tree?'

'There's a few scratches on it,' Po interjected, 'but you know it's still mechanically sound. It'll get you home, Gabe, if that's where you want to go.'

'I thought you were gonna have Pinky drive me back, that idea kinda went to crap.'

'Yep, circumstances changed. So did us needing you here. You don't need to get caught up in any more of Tony's trouble.'

Stahl shrugged off the idea. 'He's my buddy, I'm not gonna abandon him.'

'You do realize how dangerous these guys are that're chasin' him, right?'

'I'd be a punk-assed coward if I ran away from a fight, right?'

'F'sure,' Po said, 'but this isn't your fight. Nobody's gonna criticize you for steppin' out before the crap hits the fan.'

Stahl eyed Tony Vaughan, and his tongue darted to moisten his lips. 'Back in the day, Tony and me would get into some drunken barroom brawls. Neither of us is the handiest dude you'll ever meet, but we toughed it out, back to back, the way pals should. If it comes to a fight I'll get in a few slugs before they put us down.'

'I'm not planning on being put down,' Po replied, 'and when it comes I doubt it will be a fist-fight. We know for certain some of those guys are packing guns; and we aren't. You'll only get in the way, bra.'

'Jeez, a guy kinda knows where he's not wanted,' Stahl grumbled. 'But if it's all the same by you, I'll stick around for now. I'm here for Tony, cause I know he'd do the same for me.'

'Your choice, I guess,' said Po, despite Tess wishing Stahl would just go before anything bad happened.

'My choice,' Stahl agreed. 'There a john around here?'

Po shook his head. 'Can't say as I've noticed one indoors.'

'Maybe it's in one of those outsheds,' said Stahl and approached the door. Po stepped to stall him.

'I don't need my hand holding,' said Stahl, then seeing an opportunity to lighten the mood he added, 'nor nothing else. I'm just going to the can, Po. I need to relieve myself and I don't want to do it here in a bucket in front of your lady.'

'OK,' said Po, 'but be careful and listen out. First sign of trouble and you get back here lickety-split.'

'I swear I won't even waste time shaking off the drops.'

'Gabe, you were right the first time: there are things a man shouldn't do – or say – in front of a lady.'

'My apologies,' said Stahl to Tess. She was nonplussed. Much worse had been screamed at her in the past. Stahl shoved his fingers through his hair, leaving it sticking up on top, reminding Tess of one of the *Sesame Street* puppets. He went towards the door and Po again got in his way.

'Use the back door, Gabe. Going out front it could be directly into a gunman's sights.'

Stahl swallowed hard, and did as suggested.

Po waited until the door was closed and Stahl's footsteps had receded. He looked at Tess.

'Are you certain he can be trusted, Po?'

'He can be around an engine, not so sure about around a bag of money.'

'His demeanor has changed.'

'Yeah, I know.'

'But it's to be expected, right? He's out of his depth and putting on a brave face for us? Rather, for his old friend over there.' Vaughan was still sleeping. Blissfully, by all appearances. His facial muscles had grown lax and his lips were tugged into a smile. He snored faintly into the tabletop.

'I'm gettin' the sense their *old friendship* isn't as strong as what Gabe initially made out. From what I heard them arguin' about, Tony left owing Gabe some small change, and Gabe hasn't forgotten. He actually demanded that Tony pay him back, said he'd enough cash to honor his debt. I thought for a second Tony was going to go for his throat, him having told us the money's for Leah and her baby.'

'I'm sure he wouldn't miss a few bucks,' said Tess, playing devil's advocate.

'It's not the money, it's the principle that counts,' quoted Po.

'Gabe doesn't seem to think so.'

'You watch,' said Po, 'before this is resolved, I'll bet that Tony stuffs Gabe's pockets with money. He was pissed with his buddy's attitude to his debt, but he looks one for turning. He's given himself selflessly to Leah, he'll probably do the same for Gabe.'

'Why didn't you just tell Gabe to take a leak out the back?'

'You know why. I could tell you wanted to talk in private, so I let him go off looking for an outhouse.'

'He's taking his time.'

'Maybe he knows we're talking about him.'

Tess frowned at the door.

'Want me to check on him?' Po said.

'It's probably best that you do it.'

'I'll do a quick recce while I'm outside.'

'Be careful.'

He winked and turned to the door.

'Throw the bolt while I'm gone,' he said.

He opened the door and left. Tess noted the stillness of the forest beyond the cabin. It was late in the evening, approaching midnight. She wondered if and when the night-time creatures came out to hunt, then thought about Bryce Brogan and how the description of *creature* fit him well. Behind her, Vaughan moaned in his sleep. His smile had become a grimace; he was in pain even during slumber. She shut and bolted the door. Went to Leah's room and peered inside. She was asleep on the cot bed, lying with one arm flung out, the other cupped under her swollen belly. She, as Vaughan had, had fallen asleep in the knowledge that they were under Tess and Po's protection. Hopefully they wouldn't give Leah a reason to feel she'd put her trust in the wrong guardians.

Tess closed the door and returned to the far end of the cabin. Vaughan's revolver was sitting atop the cold log-burning stove, casually set aside earlier. After the incident at the wharves, Tess had left her grandfather's service revolver at the ranch before going to Bar-Lesque. It had been a terrible mistake, coming here unarmed. She picked up Vaughan's gun and opened the cylinder. There were three shells, but only two of them live. She tapped out the spent bullet casing and set it on top of the stove. She ensured that when she shut the cylinder, it was with the loaded chambers ready to fire. She thought about putting down the gun, but of them all – discounting Pinky, of course – she was the one with most experience around firearms, so she fed the revolver into her belt at her hip.

Somebody rapped once on the back door.

She approached, but stood a moment.

'It's me,' said Po.

He had returned swiftly from his recce.

She unbolted the door and he stepped inside.

'Where's Gabe?'

'Still doing his thing. He's in one of the sheds. I saw the light from his cell phone. Hoped he wasn't trying to phone his daddy.

I asked and he told me he had the light on so's he could see where he was taking a dump. Sorry for the crassness, but they were his words, not mine.'

'Hear anything more untoward?'

'Nope. I didn't get a sense we're being watched, but I still think our best bet is to sit tight a while longer before we move.'

'I wish Pinky would get in touch. His silence is concerning.'

'Yeah, it makes me uneasy, too. Let's give him another fifteen minutes and if he hasn't checked in I'll ring him.'

Gabe Stahl pushed inside. Tess had neglected to reinsert the bolt after Po had entered. The mechanic came in wide-eyed and chewing his bottom lip. 'If anyone's planning on using the can I'd leave it for fifteen minutes if I were you. Whatever I last ate, it stinks like a dumpster in summer now!'

His gross joke passed over Tess, but not his mention of fifteen minutes, a repetition of what Po had said a moment earlier. She wondered if Stahl had been eavesdropping. On his way out she'd heard his footsteps, but not when he returned. He came further inside, shut the door, then looked immediately towards Vaughan, or more correctly at the holdall between his feet. Tess was also concerned that the next glance he shot was towards the stove, as if checking the revolver was still in grabbing distance. Then the moment had passed as Stahl crossed the cabin, nudged aside the drapes and took a quick peek out of the window. 'Didn't see or hear anything suspicious,' he announced. 'I don't see anything out front, neither.'

'Let's hope things stay that way,' said Tess.

'Yeah,' he intoned, 'let's do that.'

THIRTY-FOUR

I t had been his wish to protect the sickly old man without alarming him to the danger he was in, but there was no hope of that seeing as Pinky fought a pitched battle with Bryce Brogan the length and breadth of the hall. They grunted and cursed, stamped and rebounded off walls. They smashed against the banisters at the foot of the stairs and in a grapple they waltzed down one wall of the hall, pulling down framed photographs and puncturing holes in the plaster. Pinky shed blood, spatters of it that got on the ceiling as well as the walls.

Tess had almost lost a hand to a crazed drug addict with a cleaver, and it had put an end to her law-enforcement career. It had taken her years of rehabilitation, several microsurgeries and many therapy sessions to get it back to normality. Thankfully the wound to Pinky's arm was not as acute as the one that had almost severed Tess's hand, but it was debilitating enough. His fingers slick with his blood, he'd found holding on to his Glock difficult, and it was easier than he'd have liked for Brogan to knock the pistol from his grasp before he could place a shot in the psycho's heart. He had risked his meatier forearm to save his wrist, but in doing so, he'd lost the advantage of a gun: whoever said you shouldn't bring a knife to a gunfight had no freaking idea! Also, his wounded arm was weakened, and the longer they struggled the more he'd bleed and then the remainder of him would weaken too.

Bryce Brogan hissed like a cat, eyes wide and sparkling. Alternatively he rolled his tongue behind his lower teeth and made weird sounds of encouragement. Pinky couldn't say if he was spurring him to try harder or if it was some odd form of self-motivation. Whatever, the son of a bitch seemed to enjoy being locked in a death grapple way too much to be sane. He couldn't match Pinky for size, or brute strength, but he was wiry, fast and unafraid, and that could tip the balance in his favor even before counting Pinky's injury. Oddly – just one of the oddities displayed by the madman – when he could have stabbed or slit Pinky deeply, he'd held back. Pinky had been jabbed and sliced on both arms and legs, but all were minor wounds, except when taken as a whole. Blood made his clothing adhere to his flesh, and dripped with each movement. Brogan wasn't trying to spare him; he was ensuring his torment lasted.

They completed another length of the hall, this time with Pinky in the dominant position where he could cram a shoulder into Brogan's gut and ram him into the wall several times. Brogan laughed with each attempt at crushing the life out of him, and again egged Pinky on with monkey noises. They checked up against the front door, the force of the collision shaking the house. 'Is that all you've got?' Brogan grinned.

'I'm going to rip your goddamn head off, me.'

'Yeah, keep on trying, boy.' Brogan sliced at Pinky's neck with his blade.

Rearing from the knife, Pinky got an arm free and chest-palmed Brogan away. The knife missed, but for nicking his ear lobe, and Pinky couldn't swear if that wound wasn't what Brogan had aimed to achieve in the first place.

Pinky looked for his fallen weapon, couldn't spot it in the dimness.

'Thought you might need a gun to kill me,' Brogan taunted. 'I'm not as easy to shoot when you aren't hiding behind a scope half a mile away, eh?'

Pinky snatched up a small table that had been spared from being wrecked yet. He tossed it at Brogan and the enforcer swiped it aside with his knife. The contraption that was strapped to his forearm aided the knife's strength and stability. It chopped through the spindles on the table, and it flew apart. Brogan tracked one of the flying pieces, watched it ricochet off a wall and tumble through space. He turned back to regard Pinky, one side of his mouth turned up. His smile flickered and disappeared as Pinky's foot found his gut and he was projected backwards down the hall. His butt collided with the lowest steps on the staircase, and he rolled away, gasping for air and not as sharp in his movements as before.

Pinky charged after him, galvanized to speed having won an advantage over his enemy.

Brogan tucked up onto his backside, his knees pulled into his chest and his heels on the rucked carpet. He pistoned his legs, throwing his upper torso away from the kick Pinky aimed at his jaw. Pinky missed, but Brogan gave him a reminder of how dangerous his jabbing knife was: fresh blood beaded out of what would normally prove a trivial scratch to his ankle. It didn't slow Pinky, he continued the pursuit, though Brogan again tried to kick away. Pinky raised a foot and then stamped down, trapping Brogan's right thigh. He clubbed the younger man around the head with his fist, hitting three times in rapid succession and leaving Brogan dazed. The knife swept at Pinky's gut, but this time he had the edge on speed and grappled Brogan's arm aside. He stamped again, this time between Brogan's legs. Brogan groaned in agony, and most of the fight fled him.

'Still think I need a gun to kill the likes of you?' Pinky hissed.

Brogan wheezed at the discomfort in his groin, but managed to laugh. 'Well ain't you the champ, *my Negro*?'

Pinky cursed at the blatant racism, and wrenched Brogan's trapped arm around, trying his utmost to break the limb in two.

Something crashed between Pinky's shoulders. Under attack from an unknown assailant he dropped his hold on Brogan and spun on his heel battering his attacker with a swipe of his elbow: he hit no elusive attacker. He crabbed away from Brogan, aware of shards of ceramic on the floor and recognized pieces of an ornamental horse. Somebody had tossed it at him and hit bullseye. He scanned for any of Brogan's pals racing to his rescue. Beyond the pair of them the hall was empty. Not so the landing on the upper floor.

'Who are you people? What do you think you're doing in my house? Where's Gabe? Get out! Get out!' Stahl senior raised another ornament he had snatched off a nearby cabinet, and he hurled it at Pinky. Pinky dodged aside and it shattered on the floor. Brogan used the moment to slither backwards on his butt, then pushed up. He remained bent at the waist, cringing, still suffering the effects of the stamp to his groin.

'You'd better get the hell outta my house,' Mr Stahl snapped, and he cast around for another missile. 'I've called nine-one-one. The cops are on their way, so you'd best skedaddle or you'll go to jail.'

'The old fart has got a point,' said Bryce Brogan, and Pinky snapped his attention on him once again.

'I could still kill your ass and save you from jail time.' Pinky glanced about, seeking his Glock. He wasn't sure of his abilities to kill Brogan with his bare hands before the knife split him open.

Brogan grinned and held up the blade. 'You're welcome to try, 'cause the same applies. I've had my fun with you, boy; I'll get straight to the point this time.' He wiggled the tip of the knife for emphasis.

'Get outta my house, goddamnit. Don't think I'm afraid of the likes of you punks. I did two tours of Nam and over there I fought some real bad-asses. Get out—'

Pinky filtered out Mr Stahl's hollering, and concentrated on Brogan. In the past few seconds he'd backed up a few steps, seeking escape through the kitchen where he'd sneaked inside after Pinky. Another trinket crashed down, and Pinky felt the sharp splinters of porcelain sting his flesh.

'Goddamnit, you ungrateful old coot,' he roared at the old man, 'I'm here to save your skinny white ass. Would you quit throwing things at me, you?'

He was distracted for a second. When he snapped back to Brogan, the enforcer was limping towards the kitchen door. Pinky darted his gaze around, spotted his gun lying against a doorframe and lunged for it. He span and aimed, but Brogan was already out of sight.

'Mr Stahl, stay the hell up there, keep your head down and stay alive, you,' he shouted as he raced along the hall after Brogan. Whether or not the old man did as instructed he couldn't say, because Brogan kept going, and Pinky chased him towards the pickup. Before he got near, Brogan scrambled inside, flipped him the bird out the side window and then Pinky had to duck to save his ass as a gun came out the driver's side to take a pop at him. Pinky went down on his knees, scrambled for cover, severely tempted to return fire. He didn't waste a round, when there was no way of possibly hitting a target. He put an overgrown shrub between him and the pickup, thankful in small part when he heard the truck rev away through the leafy neighborhood without a shot fired. Other cars joined the exodus, and it was apparent that Walsh and Davenport had regained their senses during his fight with their boss, and they had also made themselves scarce.

He scanned around, checking all of Brogan's team had shipped out. He had been unaware of the driver in the pickup, but discounted him as being the one called Huckleberry: it would've been unnecessary for Brogan to give him orders over the walkie-talkie if sitting alongside him in the cab. Huckleberry must have been driving the last of the three of the cars Pinky had chased here. He slapped for his pocket. He found where he'd stashed the walkie-talkie liberated from Anderson Walsh and thumbed up the volume. He spun through the dial seeking the channel the team were now using, and cursed under his breath. He only caught the tail end of an instruction from Bryce Brogan to his pals: 'Let's get back there, I ain't missing out and letting Josh have all the fun.'

After those fateful words, Brogan fell silent, and so did his pals. Pinky kept the volume turned up, listening for any other hint at what they were up to. He jammed the walkie-talkie onto his shoulder rig, holstered his Glock and reached instead for his cell phone.

THIRTY-FIVE

J osh Brogan had left the van to check out the entrance to the forest trail. He stared down at the ineffective chain strung across the opening and at the hand-painted sign tied to it with plastic garden ties. *No Entry. Private property.* Perhaps it wasn't as ineffective a barrier as he had thought. He'd bypassed the entrance several times already during his search and subconsciously obeyed the instruction to keep out. Without the heads up he'd gotten it was unlikely that he would have breached the meager security and entered the property. He gave the sign a nudge with his boot and watched it swinging back and forward. The rusty chain squeaked with each swing.

'Is this the place?'

'Has to be, right?' replied Josh.

'Haven't seen another place with a chain and hand-painted sign,' said Elvin Collins, leaning from the cab of his van.

'Yeah, that was the point I tried to make.'

Without being told, Collins reversed the van a dozen yards, then swung out and then towards the trail. Josh held up a hand to halt him.

'We aren't going in yet. I promised Bryce I'd give him twenty minutes to get back here first. Besides, we'll probably need more than only the two of us to get the job done.'

'You're armed, I'm armed; a sick man and a pregnant girl shouldn't give us too much trouble.'

'You're forgetting about Villere and his woman, the private investigator. They could be packing for all we know.'

'I haven't forgotten about Po'boy Villere, no way and no how. Doing him over's the reason I'm here.'

Josh returned to stand by the driver's door. 'Things aren't going to stop at *doing him over*. You do realize that when we come back out of here again, nobody in there – except Leah perhaps – can be allowed to live?'

Collins gnawed a moment at his hairy bottom lip, then said, 'Doing him over's a turn of phrase, man; if Villere and his bitch have to be killed, worry not, I'm still with the program. I meant what I said earlier when I offered to be your guy in New England, and am happy to prove it.'

Josh eyed the would-be gangster and thought the big thug should stick to selling chum to fishermen, but unlike Bryce would do, he chose to keep his opinion secret. He indicated he was getting back in the van. 'There's a wide spot in the road back there. We should wait there till Bryce and the others come. Did Eamon White check in yet?'

Collins shook his head.

'Try him again.'

'I just did, when you were scoping out the trail. He's gone silent.'

'I don't like it. I don't think he turned chicken on us, so I'm thinking something happened to him instead. Bryce said that when they got to Gabe Stahl's residence, Pinky Leclerc had beaten them to it and he put up a fight; I've a horrible sense that he had something to do with White's silence too.'

'I don't know this Pinky very well, but from what I've seen he's a fat-assed faggot. I don't think he's capable of taking out Eamon.'

'You forget he's the one pinned down Bryce and Walsh with a goddamned sniper rifle, do not make the mistake of underestimating him. You said you wanted to be my guy in Maine. Well, you'd best start thinking with *this*' – Josh tapped the side of his head, then transferred his hand to his crotch – 'and stop talking through *these*.'

'Man, I'm just saying that I've got your back, if you wanted to go in now.'

Josh said, 'I checked the trail just now. From what I could see there's been some movement in and out of the property over the last few days. There are tire tracks of two different cars, plus, I'd say, of a motorcycle. I can't be certain how many of those vehicles are still there, or if Vaughan has access to any others, but we have to be prepared for anything leaving. So stay alert and don't take your eyes off that trail while I organize the rest of the guys.'

Cowed momentarily, Elvin Collins sat staring over his bunched knuckles on the steering wheel. His hands were large, scarred and weather-beaten. So was his face. His image suited his role as a bait and tackle supplier, but not, Josh thought, a man to be trusted. Once this was over with, he'd already decided that his warning about nobody being allowed to live should be extended to Collins, Davenport and Eamon White. Of the locals, only Heck Bury had proven reliable by keeping his mouth shut and performing his orders without question. Once Bryce joined him and they again had their hands on the cartel loot and his wayward niece, the local punks could serve as a distraction to local law enforcement. Letting the cops believe a fight had erupted between Po Villere and his enemies suited Josh, and gave him and his brother time to skedaddle back west.

He keyed his walkie-talkie, about to check if anyone of the team was in range yet, but released the button. Bryce said that Anderson Walsh had lost his walkie, and Pinky Leclerc most definitely had taken it. He was not about to give his enemies an advantage by blurting his plan of attack over the airwaves. He put aside the radio and instead took out his cell phone and rang Bryce.

THIRTY-SIX

Tess also had her cell phone jammed to her ear as Pinky reported the goings on down at Falmouth. Her blood pressure was almost tipping the scale, but rather than add to her discomfort it gave her a wave of strength and determination she'd lacked for most of that long day. If she could see herself, or cared to think about her appearance, rather than her usual pale complexion her face was glowing with heat, and her eyes were diamond bright in even meager light. Lately she had been feeling a few pounds too heavy, slow and sluggish at times during her enforced lockdown, but this news from Pinky had animated her. She slalomed around the few items of furniture as she listened.

'Jeez, what's got you so fired up?' asked Gabe Stahl as she shouldered past him.

Tess said nothing. She glimpsed at him, but purposefully turned away and caught Po's attention. She shaped her mouth silently at him, an easily recognizable curse, and Po exhaled noisily. He swerved away from her towards the front door and pulled it open a few inches. He listened, then once he was certain his ears hadn't betrayed him, he slipped out onto the hard-packed dirt of the front yard.

'What's going on?' Stahl demanded, but again Tess ignored him. She concentrated instead on what Pinky had to say. Behind her she could hear Stahl pacing and muttering under his breath, and any second now he'd be making enough noise to wake Vaughan. She turned, shushed him, and in response he threw up both his cupped palms, mouth hanging wide in question. She didn't linger on him, returning to the conversation with Pinky.

'But everything's OK at your end?' she asked.

'Mr Stahl's unhurt, just a bit pissed at all these strangers treating his home like a skid-row flop house. I managed to calm him, me, and gotten a promise he won't call the cops till after we get back and explain everything.'

'But how are *you*, Pinky? You said Brogan tried attacking you and cut you with his knife.'

'I'm fine, me. I've fought tougher dudes than him and they didn't mark my pretty face.'

'Seriously, Pinky, I mean it. Are you OK? You sound as if you're hurt.' Several times she had caught a hiss of pain from him, mostly he'd been unaware he was expressing his agony.

'I do? So maybe I'll need a coupla Band Aids to see me through, but I'm OK, me. I'm good to drive if that's what's worrying you.'

'You're coming here?'

'Where else?'

'You're bleeding though.'

'Not much now.'

'Jeez, Pinky, how badly did he cut you?'

'Worse than I'd like. Pretty Tess, trust me, you. I'm good to go. I'm cut, it stings like a sumbitch and I've ruined a good leisure suit, but otherwise I'm still in the fight. Pardon my potty mouth, but sure as shit I am not sitting on my fat ass while you and Nicolas are in danger.'

'We aren't planning on a pitched battle, we intend leaving soon. Po's outside checking now that the coast's clear.'

'I didn't like Brogan's urgency when he made off from here. Plus, I told you what he said over the radio before going silent, me. We have to assume that his brother Josh figured out where you guys are hiding. He called back what was left of the gang to help.'

Let's get back there, Bryce Brogan had allegedly announced, *I ain't missing out and letting Josh have all the fun.* Many reasons for his swift return could be read into those words, but Tess was with Pinky on the assumption that Josh had found them and summoned back his brother and their troops for a full assault.

'Look, you're probably right, Pinky. I need to wake Tony and Leah and get everyone moving. Soon as Po returns I'll get them in the car. If you're coming up here, keep your cell phone handy because we probably won't be around when you arrive.'

'There's no "if"; I'm coming. Damnit if I'm not the only one with a weapon to take the fight back to the Brogans, me.'

Tess ended the call. She couldn't argue against logic that powerful. She had Tony's revolver, with an underwhelming load of ammunition, and Po had his boot knife. As far as she knew, Stahl, Vaughan and Leah had nothing to use as weapons, unless they began breaking down the cabin's rickety furniture and arming themselves with clubs. No, arming them with sticks against guns was a ridiculous idea. It was best to use the advantage of Po's skill behind the wheel of his powerful muscle car and get them the hell clear of the cabin before the Brogans could get their act together. She turned towards Vaughan, and caught Gabe Stahl mid-step towards the table on which his pal rested. Stahl was bent at the waist, twisted slightly over his bent left knee, and Tess was certain it was so he had a better view of the stuffed holdall between Vaughan's legs. He was looking not at the bag though, but directly at Tess. His features had blanched of color. He reached out blindly and jabbed his fingertips into Vaughan's shoulder. 'Hey, buddy,' he said, 'it's time to rise and shine. Got to get yous guys outta here ASAP, dude.'

Long before Stahl had gotten out his words, Vaughan jolted up, blinking for clarity, suffering displacement between his dreams and reality. Again he earned kudos for his character when he first searched for Leah before the holdall grabbed his attention. He stood, dragging up the bag and dumping it on the table, while he opened his mouth in question.

'I'm just about to waken Leah,' Tess told him. 'Gabe's right, it's time to leave, Tony.'

'They're here?' he asked, sounding as if his tongue was too large for his mouth.

'We're unsure, but we'd rather not take the chance. Grab anything else you're taking with you while I bring Leah.' Outside she heard the thrum of the Mustang's engine. 'Po's getting the car ready, once he pulls up we're leaving.'

'Where's my six-gun?' Vaughan asked, and his first impulse was to check Gabe's hands.

'I have it here.' Tess tapped the bulge under her shirt at her hip. 'If there's any shooting to be done, I should be the one doing it.'

'I was saving those bullets for . . .' Vaughan's words petered out and he frowned down at the floor.

Choosing not to challenge him on his plan for the last couple of bullets, Tess moved for the bedroom door and pushed it open. She expected to find Leah sprawled graceless on the bed as she'd been before, but it was empty except for tussled blankets.

'Leah?'

Tess hurtled around the bed, expecting to find the girl slumped on the floor perhaps, or maybe huddled in the darkness in the corner. She wasn't.

Earlier some soft bumps and scrapes had emanated from the bedroom. There had been nothing obvious to alert Tess that the girl was making off, but now she could see that Leah had thrown wide the curtains and the window was shut but not latched. After climbing out – an admirable feat for a heavily pregnant woman – she must have pushed the window shut again, but obviously been unable to set the catch.

Vaughan crammed in past Tess, roughly forcing his way to the window as if it would help him reel in the wayward teenager. 'Where is she? Leah! Where are you?'

Tess grasped him, halting his mad attempt to climb out of the window in pursuit. The girl had fit through at a squeeze, and in his current emaciated state Tony Vaughan might too, but the easier option was leaving the cabin via one of its doors. They bumped shoulders as they exited the bedroom, and then Vaughan was a step ahead and lunging for the front door. He yanked it open and bounded out. Tess, at his shoulder, saw Po bend his knees to a defensive crouch, but only for as long as it took to discard their boisterous exodus as a threat.

'Po,' Tess called, even as Vaughan took several lunges towards the nearest trees, 'it's Leah, she's snuck out and we don't know where she's gone.'

'What the hell, I only left for a few minutes and—'

'I could do without recrimination, Po; I feel bad enough as it is.'

'I know. Sorry. Tell you what, you get the menfolk in the car and I'll take a quick look for Leah. She's big as a whale; with her baby fit for burstin' out . . . she can't have gotten far.'

'I'm going nowhere till I know she's safe, goddamnit!' Tony Vaughan was stricken. His features had looked almost pared down to the bone as it were, now he reminded Tess of a mummified corpse.

'Don't worry, nobody's getting left behind. Po, if Pinky was right and they're coming here, we don't have much time.'

'I'm on it.'

He went alongside the cabin to the small bedroom window. If anyone might pick up Leah's tracks in the dark it would be Po, she thought. Plus, with his long-legged gait he'd catch up with her in no time, supposing she had left a trail.

Po didn't hang around, within seconds she heard him lope away and enter the long grass to the east of the cabin; Leah must have trodden it down as she fled.

Vaughan danced from one foot to the other, desperate to join the search. Tess caught at his arm and made him meet her gaze. 'Po is good at this kind of stuff. We'd only slow him down if we tried helping. Let's leave him to bring back Leah, and do as he asked and get in the car.'

'But she could be hurt and—'

'Po will find her.' She hoped she wasn't making a promise her partner couldn't keep. However, she had faith in him that he'd do everything in his power to return the girl safely to them.

'Why'd she do it?' Vaughan croaked. 'Why'd she run away? Is it me, did I—'

'If you ask me she didn't run away because of you, but for you.'

He couldn't grasp her meaning.

'She'd rather surrender to her father again than watch you hurt by him.'

'Going back to him won't change a thing! If she thinks Bryce gives a damn about her, she's wrong. She's a *body* to be *used*, and that's her only value to him. He's not only interested in getting back the money but punishing us for taking it. He'll murder her baby in order to hurt her, so what will he do with me?' Vaughan started, looking back at the open cabin door. He had dumped the heavy holdall while bounding to the bedroom and then outside with her. 'I don't think it will change anything but maybe I should go and hang the damn cash from a tree and call him to come and get it.'

'Keeping the cash out of their reach is probably your only advantage over the Brogans. Hand it back and there'll be no reason for them to let you live. You're going to have to face reality, Tony. As much as you'd wish to set Leah up in a new life, there's no way you can make your idea work. You should hand the cash over to the police and promise you'll give evidence against the Brogans and their employers. In exchange you should push for a deal that they must protect Leah and her child.'

He shook his head. 'One look at me and the cops will know I'm not gonna live long enough to make it to court. No, Tess, I have to get Leah and the baby somewhere safe and she'll need that cash to establish new identities and lives.'

'But it isn't a workable plan, Tony. Sooner or later—'

'Sooner or later the Brogans will get their due, and then Leah needn't worry about them any more.' His face took on an intensity fed by determination. Tess had to reconsider his earlier words concerning the last bullets in his revolver; perhaps they hadn't been saved to end his suffering, but for an execution of Leah's tormentors. He turned from her, heading back indoors. He didn't get all the way over the threshold before his hands snatched at the doorjamb to stop him staggering. 'Son of a bitch!'

Tess's hand went to the gun in her belt.

Before she could draw it, Vaughan stumbled inside the cabin, and again she heard him curse. She entered, clutching the revolver. She sought what had dismayed Vaughan, and it was the absence that struck her. The holdall filled with cash was missing from where Vaughan had dumped it, and there was no sign of Gabe Stahl. She didn't need the clue of the open back door to deduce what had happened.

THIRTY-SEVEN

Following Leah's tracks into the woods was simple enough for Po. He could see where the taller grasses had been crushed underfoot, the broken and bent stems almost translucent in the gloom. As she had reached the trees she had slipped and fallen, there were depressions in the dirt where her palms had dug in for purchase and helped heave her back to her feet. Nearby the lowest twigs had been snapped off the trunk of a tree, the freshly exposed inner flesh almost glowing to Po's sight. His wasn't a hyper-vision; he was simply attuned to his surroundings. Behind him he could hear Tess and Vaughan conversing, and for a moment thought about hushing them, but instead went deeper into the forest. Once he'd progressed a hundred yards or more he halted. He closed his eyes and allowed his lips to form a loose circle: standing that way his hearing grew more acute. From somewhere on an oblique line to his right he heard the soft crackle of breaking twigs. The sounds could have been made by the local wildlife, except he thought any indigenous animal would've made off the instant Leah, and then he, entered their domain. He moved after her.

Po judged he had barely gone another fifty yards when he was alerted to a muffled shout, and by its direction he thought that Tony Vaughan had cursed. What was going on back there? Probably Tess had stopped him from chasing after the girl and getting lost in the woods. It was doubtful he'd sworn because Leah had returned unexpectedly to the cabin. Po halted again, listening, eyes shut, and caught the sounds of conflicting movement. The one he had taken for Leah moving through the trees was still somewhere ahead, but he could also hear somebody forcing a path through the lower shrubs beyond the dirt road. His first thought was that maybe Tess couldn't halt Vaughan from seeking Leah, and he had set off on his own search. Except that didn't fit with hearing Vaughan's voice from his right back corner only moments ago. Somebody else was out in the woods and it put Po's loyalties at odds. Tess was his priority, but Tess was also able and tough in her own right, whereas Leah – not forgetting her unborn child – was extremely vulnerable. He continued after the girl but slipped out his cell phone and hit Tess's number. She answered almost instantly.

'Have you found her?' she asked breathlessly.

'Not yet. But there's somebody else out here.'

'Yeah, that will be Gabe. He's only gone and stolen the bag of cash and made off on foot.'

'What? The son of—'

'The money doesn't matter. Not right now. It's more important that you find Leah and that she's safe.'

'Gabe – freaking – Stahl,' he growled, 'I trusted that sumbitch and look at what he has done.'

'It doesn't matter,' she said. 'He has gotten greedy, that's all. He probably isn't thinking straight.'

'I never did find out who at the autoshop gave my name to Bryce Brogan, and then there was that thing with his cell phone earlier when he was supposedly using the john . . . if Pinky's right and the Brogans know where we are, is it hard to imagine who tipped them off?'

'We don't know that to be true.'

'Yeah, well, if I come across him in these woods I'll beat the goddamn truth outta him.'

'Forget him, Po. If he has betrayed us, so be it. He can be dealt with another time. Don't let him distract us from getting Vaughan and Leah to safety.'

'I'm going after Leah,' he said, 'be alert to anyone else prowling around in the dark.'

'I will. I've gotten Tony in the car, and we're ready to come to you the second you need us.'

Stahl, if it actually was him, had continued heading away from Po, keeping to the edge of the trail where he could move without getting lost in the wilder woods but without exposing himself on the road. Po ignored him for the time being, heading instead after the sounds of flight from ahead. He seethed at Gabe's betrayal. He had kept him employed and even slipped him a few extra bucks to help tide him over when the pandemic first ground the world to a halt. This was how Stahl repaid his kindness, by mistaking it for gullibility? By giving Po's full name to Bryce Brogan, he had first placed Tess in danger when Brogan had visited their home, and that was before he had given away their location at the cabin in the full knowledge that they were facing seriously deranged and dangerous people. Po couldn't understand why Stahl hadn't tipped off the Brogans earlier after first figuring out where Vaughan was hiding, but it was easy to conclude that he was planning on how to get his hands on the money. Unwittingly they had made things easier for him by having Pinky bring him back, giving him a reason to return and he and Tess had then placed him in easy reach of the loot. Even if Leah had not sneaked off, causing the perfect diversion, Stahl would possibly have found another opportunity to grab the bag: for instance, when Po and Tess were fighting to protect his life from the killers he had summoned!

Tess had warned him not to allow Stahl to distract them from the task at hand. Tess, and by virtue he had too, had pledged to stop Bryce Brogan from hurting Vaughan, and that was prior to learning about the pregnant girl Vaughan was protecting. Tess was correct, finding and securing Leah and her unborn baby took priority over kicking the ass of an ungrateful son of a bitch. He tamped down his anger, took in a deep breath and allowed it to slowly leak out between his teeth. Again he listened, and sure enough, heard the girl blundering in the darkness a short distance ahead. He picked up his pace, and before long could spot movement in the dimness ahead. Leah was moving faster than he would have credited, as if she had a specific destination in mind, but from what he could tell from his earlier prowl through the woods she was moving parallel to the main road so gaining no ground. He thought about calling out to her, to tell her to stop, but doubted she would obey. She was sick of being the toy of demanding men: commanding her to stop might push her to go faster and with her stumbling and getting injured, or – worse again – hurting her baby.

He slipped through the trees, almost wraith-like, barely making a sound. Somehow Leah heard or sensed his presence gaining. She began clawing a path through the underbrush, desperation causing her to gasp with each step.

'Leah, it's only me, Po. You don't have to be afraid, girl, I'm not going to hurt you.'

She kept going. If anything she pushed harder to escape.

'You're gonna hurt yourself, slow down. Let me help you.'

Abruptly she disappeared.

'Son of a—'

Po hurtled forward, but skidded to a halt at the edge of the ditch that Leah had tumbled into. It had been weeks since any substantial rain had fallen, so the ditch was dry. It was fortunate for the girl because she had landed face down and gotten one arm wrapped up in some tree roots: had the ditch been full of flood water she could've perished. As it were, she was in a desperate enough state, considering her present condition. Without pause Po hopped down. He first laid hands on her shoulders, gently keeping her in place while hushing her . . . she was bleating in frustration. 'Keep still, or you might break your arm. You've gotten yourself snagged, Leah. Let me help free you.'

'Please!' she keened. 'You have to let me go.'

'Kid, I'm not your jailer. I only want to help you. Let's get that arm of yours free first.'

'Oww, my arm.'

'Yeah, it could be busted.'

He felt, found that her elbow had been twisted up and back – her left forearm had slipped through the roots during her plunge and got caught, wrenching her elbow into an unnatural position.

'I'm gonna have to wrap arms around your body and lift you,' Po said.

'Please, just get me out. I need to go!'

'Wait up.' Po dipped and drew his knife from its boot sheath. He cut and hacked at some of the thinner roots she had gotten snarled among. He tossed the cut lengths out of the ditch. Setting his knife on the edge of the ditch, he straddled Leah, bent at the waist and slid his arms under her armpits. It was not the ideal posture for lifting a dead weight, but it was the best he could hope for. 'OK, girl, on one.'

He counted down from three, then heaved. Leah cried out. He cringed at her obvious discomfort, but kept lifting. Her arm pulled free and Po straightened, holding the girl to his chest in a bear hug. Freed and upright, she felt insubstantial in his grasp, and it reinforced to him how, despite being in the final stages of pregnancy, she was still a child too. He turned her around, swept an arm under her backside and lifted her to the rim of the drainage ditch. She rolled out of his arms, mewling in pain, and gained her knees. She bent her sprained elbow, her face contorting. Then she cupped her swollen belly, as if straining against the weight of her baby.

Po felt a coldness wash up his spine and into his head. He considered himself knowledgeable, with many skills and abilities, but midwifery wasn't one of them. He scrambled out of the ditch, retrieved his knife and without explaining, he scooped her up in his arms and began a rapid march through the woods towards the cabin. It took a moment or so for Leah to comprehend she was being taken in the wrong direction to where she wished to go, but when it hit, she struggled to get free.

'Let me go! Let me go! You must!' she squealed. 'I have to go. Please, just let me go!'

Po didn't let go, he picked up pace.

THIRTY-EIGHT

It was easy to see why Huckleberry had not joined in on the assault on the Stahl house. While Walsh, Davenport and latterly Bryce Brogan had all descended on the house, he must have been busy scouting the nearby neighborhood. The son of a bitch had found Pinky's SUV parked on a side street two blocks up from the Stahl residence, and he'd gone to town on its tires with a knife or screwdriver. Pinky's car was immobilized. He had no one to blame but himself though, because they'd all seen his SUV and it stood out parked at curbside when everyone else's motors were nestled away on drives or inside carports and garages. He was lucky that Huckleberry hadn't caused more damage to his car, or worse, gained entry and taken charge of the strongbox in the trunk.

Pinky bleeped the locks open, and went immediately to the back. He delved inside and brought out the case in which he kept the disassembled rifle and scope. Locking his SUV again he jogged back to Gabe Stahl's house, thankful that he had taken up a fitness regime because he needed the extra stamina he had gained. He entered the house as if he had a given right, and went down the hall to the kitchen. There he had earlier passed a hook on which there were several sets of keys. He searched, and was about to grab a set for the car resting under the carport, but spotted another fob bearing the Ducati emblem. He grabbed the key fob and bounced it on his palm, then grunted at his plan. He found a backpack in which he shoved the rifle case, and pulled it on and cinched the straps.

'You here again?'

Pinky gave the old man a brief salute as he walked down the hall. Mister Stahl was at the head of the stairs, braced against falling with both arms on the banisters. 'I forgot something, me,' Pinky said, 'but I'm leaving now. You won't see me till I bring home your son.'

'Pah! You know how they say absence makes the heart grow fonder? Well, it damn well doesn't.'

Pinky chuckled at the gruff old curmudgeon and continued to the door. 'How are you on those stairs, you? Maybe once I leave you should throw a bolt or two on these doors, huh?'

'Yeah, right. As if that's going to make any goddamn difference? All these swinging dicks keep on letting themselves inside, it feels like it's freebie night at a damn brothel around here.'

Pinky secured the front door and then approached where Gabe Stahl had left his motorcycle. It had been a few years since he'd ridden one, but he supposed it was like riding any bike; you never forgot, right? The motorcycle was a Ducati SuperSport 950, sleek and powerful, colored fiery red. If he could avoid falling off or running it through a wall the powerful bike should get him back to the cabin in half the time it would take a car. Pinky straddled it, and used the fob to unlock and start the engine. He checked Gabe's helmet for size, and then tossed it aside. Hell, if he was going to ride like a daredevil he may as well behave like one too.

THIRTY-NINE

Tess was ready to help as Po carried Leah towards the cabin, standing outside the door, watching and listening while also beckoning Po to greater speed. Tess held the revolver in her right hand, feeling as if they were woefully unprepared for an assault and that was without the added disadvantage of Leah's injury. She had been alert, keeping one ear on her partner's progress and the other on where Gabe Stahl had made off to: this latter only because she was prepared to halt Vaughan from chasing down his old pal and dragging the holdall back to the cabin, bloodied no doubt. However, she needn't have concerned herself because his priority was not retrieving the cash. He was only interested in Leah's welfare. He pushed out, shouldering Tess aside as he rushed towards Po. On his return to the cabin, juggling the girl in one arm and his cell phone in the other hand, Po had warned her that he'd found Leah but that she was injured. Tess and Vaughan had abandoned the Mustang for now, in favor of getting the girl back inside and on a bed. Po hadn't been specific about what had happened to her, but his tone of voice said it was bad enough.

Leah contorted in Po's arms. He fought her, resisting her attempts to writhe free. Vaughan rushed towards Po, and for a second Tess thought he was going to attempt to wrench the girl out of his grasp. She doubted he had the strength to pick her up, never mind carry her back to the cabin. He staggered in place, and when Po snapped at him to stand aside, he did so, and fell in behind Po. He shadowed them as Po delivered Leah to the cabin and Tess made way so he could lie her down. Po ignored the bedroom; instead he set her on the couch where Vaughan had taken naps in the main living room. Leah struggled to rise. Vaughan crouched, placing his hands on her shoulders and gently forced her down. Leah cried out in pain. But whatever agony had struck her it didn't deter her from trying to rise again. Tess joined Vaughan in attempting to calm her.

'She might've broken her arm,' Po said, 'but I'm more concerned that she has hurt her baby. She took a tumble into a drainage ditch and landed belly down. She's in pain, but won't say what's wrong. At least, she hasn't given me a straight answer the entire way back.'

'Leah,' Tess said, 'you have to help us to help you. Is it your baby? Is it your arm? Which is most troubling?'

Leah's eyes were the size and color of Oreo cookies as she stared dully at Tess. For a moment Tess wondered if the girl's pain had taken her beyond comprehension. However, Leah blinked several times, and fresh tears washed from her and she cried out: 'You have to let me go before my father arrives.'

Tess supposed that she had run away in the misguided attempt at sparing them from a fight with her kinfolk. But it was highly likely that they would come into conflict with the Brogan brothers and their helpers whether or not Leah surrendered to them.

'Is your baby all right?'

When Leah didn't answer, Tess took it that the baby's current health wasn't Leah's immediate priority, which kind of answered her question.

'Let me look at your arm,' Tess pressed.

'Yeah,' Po added from the sideline, 'whatever you do, don't you go pushing that babe out.'

Vaughan tried comforting the girl again, but she turned her face from him, making a squawk of dismay. She raised her elbow for Tess, and her squeal this time was drawn out until it petered away.

'How does your arm feel?' Tess checked it for any malformation of the bones or muscles.

'I need to go,' Leah repeated, 'before it's too late for Tony.'

'Don't you worry about me, Leah,' Vaughan hushed her.

'But don't you see? Now you don't have the money you've nothing to barter for our lives with!'

Tess was reasonably certain the girl's arm was not broken. It had taken a severe twisting, but the bones and ligaments had withstood the fall. In fact, if anything, getting her arm caught in the roots was probably fortunate, as it had slowed her from hitting the ground too forcefully, protecting her baby. Despite her emotional state, it was apparent that there was nothing wrong with Leah's hearing. She must have overheard Tess and Vaughan discovering the theft of the cash after climbing from the window but prior to sneaking off through the coarse grass.

'Goddamn Gabe-freaking-Stahl!' Vaughan spat.

Tess understood his vitriol: Stahl's greed had possibly guaranteed them all a death sentence.

'Why'd he have to do it? Why'd he have to steal the money when I just—' Leah devolved into wails and floods of tears. She wrapped her elbow – proof it was not broken – over her head, as if ashamed by her fragility.

'Greed got the better of him, I guess,' said Po. 'I never saw it in him before now, but apparently Gabe Stahl's as weak as any of us can be where money's concerned.'

'He probably didn't even think things through, only saw his chance when we ran out to look for Leah,' Tess said, 'and grabbed the bag. I mean, what does he expect to do with all that money, just take off somewhere and leave behind his sick old father? Then again, I got the impression there isn't much love lost between Stahl senior and Gabe. Maybe he will abandon his old man and run for the border.'

'If the son of a bitch tipped off the Brogans where to find us, I'd say he was also planning the theft,' Po said. 'The asshole needed a diversion and couldn't anticipate that Leah would make one. He rang them from the outhouse, putting us all in jeopardy so's he can escape with the money. When I get my hands on him . . .'

'Yeah, get in line,' snarled Vaughan.

Too busy to make threats, Tess concentrated on comforting Leah. She was relieved, though possibly not half as much as Po was, that the birth of her baby wasn't imminent. By all appearances her twisted arm was sore but fully mobile. Tess stood, kneading her lower back with her left thumb. She was still clutching the revolver in her other hand. She glanced towards the front door. It stood open from when they had all rushed back inside. They were at their most vulnerable and all standing around with their backs to an open door. Po cursed softly under his breath, because he wasn't usually one to compromise their safety in that way. He swiftly rectified the problem by scooting to the door and taking a check outside. Tess saw him round his shoulders and bend his head forward and knew he was employing the periphery of his vision to check for movement in the darkness; it was a stalking technique he'd taught her. Slowly he straightened up, and Tess partially relaxed.

Vaughan sat on the edge of the couch, leaning around so that he could embrace Leah. She allowed the intimacy; rather she seemed to welcome it. Perhaps through making a selfless attempt at saving Vaughan from further harm she had realized how much she cared for him, not simply as a fellow escapee but as the surrogate father figure she needed and he portrayed. They conversed, her apologizing, him apologizing more. Tess moved away to give them space. She wiped her left sleeve across her mouth. Looked for Po.

He had gone further outside. She found him standing next to his car. Ordinarily during a lull like this she would have come across him feeding his nicotine habit, but he had forgone a cigarette. He was alert to anyone sneaking towards the cabin, and was not about to give an enemy the target of a flaring ember to guide them.

'What do you think, Po?'

'They aren't here yet.'

'I meant about Leah running off like that. She was prepared to surrender for all our sakes; it's some decision for her to have to make, considering she's days from giving birth.'

'She won't give birth if she's killed along with the rest of us. Maybe she ran away to protect her child and not us. It's understandable and I wouldn't hold her decision against her.'

Tess exhaled slowly. She was unsure if she could sacrifice Po for their unborn baby. She loved him too deeply to countenance giving up one for the other. But she supposed that Leah was in a different position, and wasn't romantically invested with Vaughan. If she was in Leah's shoes her decision might be totally different. 'I guess that most of us aren't as selfish as Gabe Stahl,' she said.

'Maybe we judged him wrong, and I don't mean missing the fact he's a damn thief,' said Po. 'We've pegged him for tipping the Brogans off about our hiding place but what if it was Leah? She seemed to have a destination in mind, makes me wonder if she was told where she should run. The thing is, I'm doubtful she'd have made it under her own steam, so it's possible Josh or somebody else was moving in to meet her.'

'And when she doesn't show up?'

'He comes here instead.'

'You think he's out there watching us now?'

'F'sure,' he said, 'but I don't think he has the balls to get any closer. I'd say he's waiting for the rest of the team to get back from Falmouth. That's supposing I'm right and it was Leah that called them.'

'Has she even got access to a cell phone?'

'Beats me, but it'd be easy enough to ask her.'

'Let me ask,' said Tess. 'It won't sound as much like an accusation if I ask her.'

'Feel free. I'm busy otherwise. Oh, and Tess? Why don't you lock that back door and the windows while you're at it, in case we don't get to leave as planned.'

'I think Leah's well enough to move.'

'Me too, but I think we could definitely drive into an ambush now. I'd rather force them to come to us than the other way around.'

'I've only two bullets in this gun,' she reminded him.

'They're enough to put down both brothers,' he grunted. 'I'll do my darndest to keep the others off you so you get to drop those evil fuckers.'

Po rarely cursed as strongly. He was obviously worried about their ability to fend off the bad guys, angry that they were in such a vulnerable position as this.

Tess stepped into his embrace and held him for a few seconds, her chest pressed to his abdomen. She said: 'Y'know, now that the bag of cash is out of the equation there's no reason not to call the police. What's more important now, saving their lives or saving Vaughan and Leah from prison? For starters, I don't think Vaughan's going to be around long enough to worry about going to jail, and it's doubtful there's a judge in the land who will rule against Leah when they hear how much she has suffered.'

'If you think it's best to call the cops, go ahead, but I'll remind you that we'll probably be the ones being arrested, while the bad guys will still be on the loose. I'd hate for them to get away scot-free, only to come back another time when we aren't prepared for them.'

'You think we're prepared for them now?' She chuckled without any real mirth, and again hefted the revolver with its meager load of ammunition.

Po waggled his knife. 'There's more than one way to hunt feral pigs,' he said.

They stepped apart and Po indicated the door. 'Go on, Tess, get indoors. Do as I asked and ensure the place is buttoned up tight. I'd say those log walls will stop most small-caliber bullets, but it's best you keep those guys away from the windows.'

'Need I ask where you're going?'

'I'll lose myself in the dark out here,' he said, which was the very place she had guessed. 'If they try advancing on us, I'll turn the tables on them.'

'All well and good if they try sneaking in through the woods; what if they use their vehicles instead and surround the place?'

'I don't see them trying to knock the cabin down by brute force. Sooner or later they'll have to alight their vehicles if they want to try gaining access, and then they'll be in my domain.'

'What if they all have guns, Po?'

'Let's see how quickly I can liberate one of them.'

'You're enjoying this too much.'

'I'm the pot to your kettle.'

'No, Po, you're the pain to my ass.' She winked at him, blew him a kiss and then swung around towards the cabin. From within she heard Vaughan and Leah talking, the latter punctuating her words with sniffles and sobs. Tess paused for barely a heartbeat, then continued: now wasn't the time to respect their privacy. She headed indoors, paused at the threshold and looked back towards the Mustang. Po had already dissolved into the night.

A shrill yell of pain echoed throughout the woods.

The sound was too distant to be the result of Po appropriating a more powerful weapon than his blade. An animal or bird could have emitted the screech, but Tess knew otherwise. That scream had originated from the same direction in which Gabe Stahl had fled. The mechanic had betrayed them, left them in an untenable position, and yet Tess felt that they were responsible for bringing him back there, and therefore owed him protection from criminals far worse than he. No, that wasn't so. In the next second she saw the terrified face of Leah Brogan and knew her priority was stopping the same hands that had grabbed Stahl from being laid on her.

FORTY

J osh Brogan inspected the holdall, judging its weight to be around twenty-five pounds and in the range to be expected when stuffed with used bills. Without any doubt Tony Vaughan and Josh's niece, Leah, had used some of the cash since fleeing California but he knew for a fact that circumstance did not make for a spending spree. They would've paid for gas, maybe a couple nights in roadside motels, and food grabbed from convenience stores and diners. He decided the bag was possibly only light of a couple thousand bucks and he could live with the loss. If his cartel employers made a song and dance about the deficit, he'd personally pay back the measly amount to them. He put the bag on the ground and jabbed it with his shoe.

'You know that this doesn't belong to you, Gabe,' he said.

'I was bringing it to you,' Gabe Stahl mewled.

'Somehow I doubt it. See, I didn't tell you where I was.'

'I was heading for the way out,' Stahl said, pointing in a random direction, 'and thought you'd be waiting there. I swear to God—'

'Don't waste your breath. I don't believe in any god and you don't strike me as the holier-than-thou type either. I think, if anything, you're a man that doesn't put much stock in the Ten Commandments, otherwise you'd know that theft isn't permissible.'

'I wasn't stealing the cash, I swear to . . . I swear. I was fetching it to you, to save you from having to come take it. I didn't want to see anyone get hurt.'

'I don't believe you suddenly had an attack of conscience, Gabe. You were prepared to sell out your best pal for reward, and you expect me to believe that you didn't want to see him harmed.'

'Tony isn't my best pal. Hell, I barely know him. We drank together, before he got sick, and the son of a bitch left owing me money. But that's beside the point. I'm not a total asshole, and don't want to see him or anyone else hurt. Not when I could pick up the bag and bring it for you.'

Elvin Collins loomed over Stahl, standing with his big knuckles bunched. He had been the one to spring on Stahl and beat him to the ground. But he proved he was not simply about violence, he was thoughtful in his own manner. 'He could be telling the truth, Josh. He called Bryce and promised he'd grab the money for a ten per cent cut, remember.'

'Yeah, I know. Bryce told me, and I told you. *Remember?*' Josh peered down at Stahl. Nobody said he couldn't get up, but the mechanic chose to stay down on his side in the dirt, leaning on one elbow. Stahl's mouth writhed and his eyes were huge. Josh aimed his next words at the thief. 'Why not call me directly?'

'How could I?'

'How did you call Bryce?'

'He gave me his number earlier this morning, at my work place when he first came round looking for Po Villere. I put him right on Po's real name and where he lived, and Bryce said if I had any more helpful information I should call him. He said he'd pay me . . .'

'So you're Bryce's personal snitch?'

'I didn't have your number.'

'The point being, as far as snitches go you can't be relied on.'

'Wh-why not? I did what I promised to do and—'

'Shut up. You're trying to win points for being a good little snitch, but you've known where to find Tony Vaughan all this time, and the only reason you're selling him out now is you thought you could run away rich while the rest of us kill each other.'

'No, I swear. It isn't like that. I only wanted my hundred grand. I took the bag, and was bringing it to you for my reward. My father's ill and we live in a house I can't afford to keep. Once the old man goes I'll have to sell up just to pay his goddamn medical bills never mind my debts. I'll be on my ass, man . . . but not with my ten per cent.'

'I don't know if I should despise you or feel pity for your gullibility.' Josh crouched in front of Stahl, rested the fingers of his left hand on the forest floor. 'You really expected Bryce to hand over a hundred grand to you? You do know where Bryce was when you called him, right? He was on his way back here after visiting your poor old sick dad. He was going to use him to force you into giving up your pal, but he didn't need him. He only had to make an empty promise to pay you and he reeled you in,' he glanced up at Collins, and smiled at his chosen metaphor, 'hook, line and sinker.'

'Is my dad—'

'Not that you actually care about him but your father's fine.' Josh stood, and turned down the corners of his mouth as he studied the thief at his feet. 'I'm afraid I can't say the same for you.'

FORTY-ONE

Within the cabin the sound was muffled enough that it could have been the limb of a tree cracking, or perhaps a stick knocked against another, but Tess recognized the sound: gunfire. She tensed at the finality of the single shot, immediately concerned for her partner, but instinctively knowing that Po was fine. The shot came from the same direction as the yell of pain had minutes ago; she was confident that Po was elsewhere but it didn't bode well for Gabe Stahl. She felt again she should feel sorry for Stahl, but couldn't under the circumstances. Her singular relief was that her enemies now had one less bullet in their arsenal to use against her and her charges.

'We should make a run for it, right now, while they're out there in the woods on foot.' Leah had practically passed out from exhaustion. Tess had been unaware that Vaughan had sidled in beside her until he spoke. Tess was standing to the side of the front window, with the curtains hitched open an inch, and the light behind them doused.

'We can't leave until Po gets back and gives us the all-clear,' she said. 'If that is the Brogans out there, and I've no reason to think otherwise, then it's probable that the others are still in their cars. Po can run a gauntlet much more competently than I could. Plus, if I drive, I can't also protect you and Leah.'

'I'm not totally useless, y'know,' said Vaughan. 'For a one-eyed, ex-drunk with an enlarged liver and failing heart that is.'

She checked he was kidding. She couldn't make out the details of his features in the dark but felt certain he was smiling in self-deprecation. She exhaled in mirth. 'I'd give you back your gun,' she said after a moment, 'but it helps me feel as if I actually have a chance to save you both.'

'Why haven't you called the police?'

'Until the Brogans show their hand, the only crime we can prove is your appropriation of the cartel money. You, and – by virtue of our connection to you – us, would be the ones arrested and taken to jail. Po and I feel it's better to wait until the Brogans initiate an attack before calling in the cavalry.'

'That gunshot a minute ago, that wasn't the start of an attack?'

'I dread to think what it could signify,' she admitted, 'but as far as we can tell it could have been a hunter shooting at squirrels.'

'Or at a weasel called Gabe,' Vaughan corrected her.

She felt him stir, and knew he was building up to a question.

'What is it?'

'I was just wondering . . .'

'About?'

'Why are you doing this for us, risking your lives?'

'It would probably be glib to say: "It's what we do." But, well, that isn't far from the truth. I'm a private investigator by trade, but that isn't true of Po or Pinky Leclerc. It's not unusual for me to take on commissions and some of them might include offering a level of physical security, but that isn't how we became involved here. On his hunt for you, Bryce Brogan thought it wise to try roughing me up for information and that doesn't sit well with my friends or me. He then had the gall to try hiring me to find you . . . you might say we chose to tell him to go screw himself.'

'So you're here to spite him?'

'I'd say we're here in spite of him. We learned things had grown more dangerous when we spoke with your half-brother Bob, and heard how Josh Brogan shot him in the foot. We aren't the type of people to stand idle and allow you or Leah to get hurt.'

'Back then, all you knew about me was that I was a thief.'

'Actually we were unsure what you'd done to have the Brogans chase you across the country, but, well, does it matter? Things changed again when we learned you were protecting a pregnant girl from further abuse. The idea that her own father and uncle allow it, and even encourage it to happen, turns my stomach and tells me how despicable they are. In all conscience none of us could turn our backs on you now.'

'I'm dying, Tess.'

'Yes, we figured you were seriously ill.'

'My internal organs are failing. I could drop from a massive coronary at any time.'

'Why not seek medical help?'

He exhaled slowly. How could he protect Leah, keep her out of reach of her kin, and seek medical help at the same time? 'The point is, I've not much to lose if the Brogans catch up with me, but you and Po, well that's altogether different.'

'When I was with the Sheriff's department, I went to work every day in the knowledge that it might be my last. I still pulled on my boots and clipped on my badge. If we allow fear to rule us our lives aren't worth living. Certainly we wouldn't stand up to be counted when somebody needs our help.'

'You aren't afraid? I'm crapping my pants.' He chuckled in self-admonishment at his coarse choice of words.

'I'm afraid for my friends and for you guys, and, yeah, I'm afraid of losing my life, but I choose to harness it and use the fear to help me fight harder to keep us all safe. When you think of it like that then being fearful can be advantageous.'

'I guess so,' he said. Then after a moment: 'Thank you.'

She didn't feel comfortable accepting his thanks yet. 'You can thank us once we get you and Leah safely out of here, eh?'

Her vision had adjusted to the gloom. Vaughan was a solid silhouette against the darkness. She couldn't see Leah lying on the couch, but the regular soft snores indicated that the girl was still asleep and hadn't moved. Tess returned her attention to the gap in the curtains. Outside, the forest canopy filtered the starlight but she could now make out individual shapes against the deeper darkness. Also, from a good distance off she caught the twinkle of brighter lights and thought a vehicle was approaching along the twisting trail. She quickly calculated how many minutes it might take for Bryce Brogan's team to get back from Falmouth and decided that around a half hour had gone by since Pinky's hurried telephone call, ample time for the bad guys to return in. She had followed Po's advice and ensured that the back door was latched and bolted, and that the windows were securely locked: neither barricade would last against a sustained effort to enter, but for now she need mostly concentrate on defending the front of the cabin. She wondered if she should knock some glass out of the window frame like they did in the movies, in order to get a cleaner shot at the bad guys. Rather, she thought, the night would end better for everyone without any shots fired. She had not been altogether honest with Vaughan when offering her take on treating fear as an ally: if Jasmine Reed's diagnosis of her condition proved true then Tess had more to lose than her own life, and it affected her in a way she'd never known terror before.

Then again, she decided, it gave her even greater reason to fight tooth and nail.

FORTY-TWO

The recovery of the blue panel van, complete with the bullet holes in its sides, was underway when Bryce Brogan and Declan Randall rushed back to rendezvous with Josh. There was a tired county deputy observing as the van was winched onto a breakdown truck, who barely gave them a once-over as they mounted the verge to get past. He had probably drawn the short straw, would do what was necessary to clear the road, but wouldn't go out of his way to do much else: the last thing he probably needed was to ticket a couple of rowdies flouting the lockdown rules. He might not be so dismissive with another three vehicles crawling past in rapid order. Because the other cars were behind their pickup, Bryce called each giving Walsh, Davenport and Huckleberry instructions to find an alternative route back to where they'd left Josh and Collins. They enquired about Eamon White, but Bryce could tell them nothing. Either he'd walked away from the crash, or he'd been taken to hospital by ambulance, or to the coroner's office in a black bag: Bryce didn't care which, only that if he could still speak, he knew to keep his fat mouth shut.

Once they were beyond the crash site, he encouraged Randall to step on the gas. Spotting the single deputy on the scene it made sense to him that law-enforcement officers were slim on the ground around those parts, so there was no fear of being pulled over. Besides, after his tussle with Pinky Leclerc, Bryce's hackles were still bristling, so woe betide any deputy dumb enough to get in his face. Before long they were back on the road adjacent to the coast and were in the lee of the trees where – in hindsight – Pinky had dropped off Gabe Stahl. How fortunate that had been – also in hindsight – when Gabe's greed had not only driven him to call Bryce with Tony Vaughan and Leah's location, but also snatch the holdall and carry it directly into Josh's hands. In one respect Bryce was pissed at Stahl, because Josh would claim it was he that personally recovered the cartel money, and his little brother would be relegated to a minor player in the drama. On the other hand, he was mightily pleased that reuniting the cash with its owners could now be put on the back burner while Bryce dealt with the personal matter of cutting off Vaughan's balls and feeding them to his whore of a daughter.

He directed Randall to watch for the trail leading to Vaughan's hideout, recognizable according to Stahl by a chain and hand-painted sign strung across the entrance. It was not immediately noticeable until he recalled that Josh and Elvin Collins had entered the property already, and on the second pass he spotted the trailhead and a chain and sign unclipped and thrown to one side. While Randall drove the pickup in, Bryce bounced in his seat, barely able to contain his excitement.

'Maybe you should let the other guys know where they need to come,' said Randall.

'Yeah, well maybe I want to keep this fight all to myself.'

'Are you serious?'

'Chill out, Randall, you've been around Josh so long you're beginning to sound as big a pussy as he is.'

Randall sneered at the accusation, but was sensible enough not to respond. In the second or two it had taken for Bryce to insult his brother's right-hand man, he'd also taken out his cell phone and rung Walsh. Once Walsh was on the line, Bryce told him to pass on the location to Davenport and Huckleberry. Bryce then ended the call.

'I'm not sure Davenport, or even Walshy, will be much use in a fight. Pinky Leclerc rung their bells good and hard,' Bryce said to Randall, 'but if nothing else they can be used to draw fire, right? Huckleberry, even with his freakin' stupid nickname, proved he's got something about him by hobbling Pinky's SUV back there. Maybe it's time I should put Walshy to pasture and take on a new sidekick, huh? Whaddaya say, Randall?'

'Better the devil you know than the devil you don't,' quoted Randall, his tone dry. When he couldn't contain a glance at Bryce, he received a wolfish grin for his trouble: Bryce had gotten Randall's double meaning.

'Don't worry,' Bryce added, and the grin morphed into a jaunty wink, 'it's only a few more minutes till you can kiss Josh's rosy-cheeked ass again. Pull over a second and let me check where he's gotten to, will ya?'

Randall brought the pickup to a rolling stop under the heavy boughs of a tree, turning off its lights so that it was practically engulfed by the dark. Bryce spoiled Randall's effort to conceal the truck by using his cell to call Josh, the light off it cast on his face. His spectral features stared back in reflection from the windshield.

'I thought you were waiting till I got back before making a move?' he said the instant his brother answered the call.

'Yeah, well once you said that Stahl had his eyes on the bag of money I suspected he'd try to get past us with it. I had Collins move in, and a good goddamn job that we did; otherwise the thieving shit might've snuck past.'

'So where are you?'

'Where are you?' Josh countered.

'Maybe a couple of hundred yards inside the gate.'

'You've a ways to come then. Stick to the road, it twists a few times then you'll come to a clearing. I'll be there.'

'Did you kill Stahl yet?'

'I've given him something to keep him compliant,' said Josh, 'but he isn't dead. We may have use of him yet. By the way, he still thinks you'll honor the agreement to pay him a hundred grand, so thinks a bullet through his instep is worth it.'

Bryce laughed. He was supposedly the maniac; often accused as being a sadistic son-of-a-bitch, but good ol' Josh could be his equal at times.

'Seen anything of the others yet?'

'Not directly. Gabe tells me that Tony's fit for nothing, Leah's ready to drop the brat, and between them Po'boy Villere and Tess Grey have an antique six-shooter missing most of the bullets. Apparently they're holing up in the cabin like it's the Alamo and we're Santana's troops.'

'We can't make this a sustained siege. We should move quickly,' said Bryce, ''cause there's no telling if they want a fight or if they'll call on the law. There's Pinky to consider, too: I left him alive back in Falmouth, but there's no stopping him calling the police about us.'

'If the cops were going to be called, I'd say it would've happened by now. But you're right. We should get this done, bro. We have the money, but I promised you payback on Vaughan, and I'm a man of my word.'

'I've been thinking about how to punish him. Fucker's dying anyway, so he'll probably thank me for a quick end. Maybe I should pluck out his one good eye and leave him to perish completely blind.'

'If we're doing this,' Josh cautioned, 'we can't leave behind any live witnesses, and that means also going back for Pinky and Stahl's old man. Get at Vaughan, hurt him bad, then slit his throat. I'll deal with Leah.'

'Don't kill her,' said Bryce, 'but if the kid's been born, knock its head against a tree for all I care.'

'I don't intend hurting her, or the baby.'

'Good, she's no good to us if she's a lump of cold meat.'

'Bryce, man . . .'

As he ended the call Bryce laughed at Josh's discomfort. No, despite how he'd earlier thought Josh his sadistic equal, he was not, not by a long distance. He gave Randall the nod to get moving again.

It was too dark to proceed without lights, but the rendezvous site was probably far enough from the cabin they shouldn't be noticed. Randall switched them on again and pulled away. He kept his own counsel during most of the remainder of the journey. Bryce sensed that the tough guy, a war veteran both military and on the streets, was not impressed by his talk of murdering a newborn baby, let alone that Leah's babe was his grandchild. 'It isn't yours, Randall.'

'What isn't mine?'

'Leah's bastard, so you needn't give a crap about it. But if it was yours, you'd fight me for its life, wouldn't you?'

'How do I answer your question?'

'I'd expect you to fight me.'

'Good job it isn't mine, then.'

'Park over there,' Bryce said, changing the subject. 'See next to where that big knucklehead Elvin Collins has left his van?'

Reuniting the pickup and van reminded Bryce that bearing their business decal the vehicles were too identifiable. When they left this place it wouldn't be in either of them. The blue panel van, towed no doubt to impound first, but destined for the junkyard, was no great loss to him. Walsh had purchased it for cash, from a private seller found online when they first arrived out here in Maine, and nothing inside, save perhaps his fingerprints and DNA, could trace it back to him. He doubted that the deputy would try too hard to identify who was responsible for turning over the van in the road, and would possibly put it down to joy-riding kids. Nothing in the scenario would compel the deputy to question the presence of bullet holes, right? And if he did, then so what? Plenty of vehicles got accidentally – sometimes deliberately – holed by lousy shots each hunting season. He guessed he'd make the return trip in the car currently driven by Walsh, while Josh could pal up with Randall again in something of his choosing. Bryce didn't ordinarily value Walsh as a traveling companion, but compared with Randall he was the less insufferable.

Collins was standing guard at the back of the van. Bryce got out the pickup and approached the van.

'Is the holdall in there?'

Collins shook his head. Of course it wasn't, Josh would not let the bag out of his sight now.

'So what are you guarding?' He didn't have to ask. He could

hear low sobbing. 'Josh tells me he shot Stahl through his foot, d'you expect him to try making a run for it?'

The bearded face split in a yellow-toothed grin. 'He's so terrified, he'd crawl back to Portland if we let him.'

'Stand aside, I want to talk to him.'

'Josh said—'

'I said different. Now stand aside.'

Abashed, the bigger man shuffled out of Bryce's path. Bryce announced his presence with a brief drumroll of his fingers on the van, then he popped the lock and swung open the doors. Rows of shelves had been fitted to the van walls, and would ordinarily carry all manner of fishing paraphernalia, but were currently empty. Stahl was seated up near the front with his back scrunched against a partition separating the cargo and cab areas. From his location, the details of Bryce's features wouldn't be clear, so it made sense that he squawked in fear and drew his injured foot closer: maybe he thought Josh had returned to inflict further pain.

'Easy there, Gabe,' Bryce said in a soothing tone. 'I wanted to thank you, buddy, and tell you how you've made our task so much easier for us.'

'I . . . I did as you asked. I told you where to find Tony, and I brought the cash to your brother. Why am I being treated like this? We had a deal, man: you said you'd pay me ten per cent of however much I recovered for you, not *this*!'

Bryce nodded in understanding and agreement. 'I owe you a debt of gratitude, so won't be making you suffer the way my ungrateful brother has. However, the money isn't mine to give you, so, easy come easy go, eh? But don't you worry, when it's time, I'll show my full gratitude: I'll kill you fast and painlessly, OK?'

'What? No . . . Noooo!'

Bryce closed the van doors again. He heard the rumble as Stahl scrambled along the bed of the van, then slammed his palms on the inside of the doors. Elvin Collins still stood close to the van. 'You'd better get over here and do as Josh told you,' Bryce advised him. 'I think you were right about that foot injury, it won't slow him if he gets free.'

'Did you have to rile him up like that?'

Bryce turned and appraised his older brother. Josh had materialized from the darkness to the side of the pickup. He had the holdall secured in a backpack that he had strapped over his shoulders. Had he been lurking, observing and judging Bryce's behavior purposefully before announcing his presence?

'If we're going to use him as a distraction we need him to be noisy. It's one thing keeping him scared but people are more vocal when they're offended. He doesn't know what he's most upset about; that you shot him; that he faces certain death from me; or that we've screwed him out of his reward.'

'I've been thinking about how he can be useful.' Josh turned and walked away to talk privately.

Bryce followed. 'Me too: we could stake him out, cut bits off him and have him scream bloody murder. It's sure to draw out those do-gooders, Grey and Villere. Once we've dealt with them, Tony and Leah are ours for the taking.'

'I wasn't going to go that far,' Josh admitted. 'It's enough that they hear him scream not that we actually need to cut bits off him.'

'Brother, you're a goddamn killjoy these days.'

'And time's against us. We can't waste it on anything lavish.'

'You're right, the longer I spend on Stahl the less time I'll have for torturing Vaughan.' Bryce looked back over his shoulder. 'That asshole in the van's unimportant and won't help us. Collins over there wants to be our man in Maine, have him show his mettle by saving us the effort of slitting Stahl's throat. If we set the scene right, we can make it look as if all of this has been a four-ways beef between Stahl, Vaughan, Collins and Po Villere, with no survivors.'

Josh considered his suggestion, and Bryce allowed a smile to blossom. His brother didn't have a more feasible plan than his.

FORTY-THREE

The twinkling of headlights in the distance drew Po towards an area he'd traversed earlier. He knew from memory that the trail twisted and turned before meeting a natural glade. He supposed it was as good a staging area for an assault on the cabin as anywhere else. He began a slow but steady approach, taking care to stay alert to anyone else in the woods, waiting in ambush or perhaps on a parallel track to his. Within thirty seconds of spotting the headlights they went dark. He didn't alter his gait, but kept a close eye on his chosen path, alert to a twig that would snap underfoot, or an exposed root that could trip him. His knife was drawn already, and held close to his right hip, so that if he was ambushed it couldn't easily be grappled or knocked from his grasp. By this time his senses had acclimatized to his surroundings; he saw, smelled and heard the forest, while other subtler stimulants prickled the hairs on his forearms and dried his mouth. Despite the instinctive warning signs he ignored them and carried on. He was on high alert because of the fight to come, not because a feral predator was about to clamp its teeth around the nape of his neck.

He could see the van and pickup truck parked alongside each other. In the gloom he couldn't make out the decals but was confident it was the two vehicles belonging to a local bait and tackle supplier. He had no way of telling whose business it was, or why the person behind it had thrown in his lot with the Brogans. Then again, he had made several enemies after moving north, some of them with genuine grievances against him while others were only perceived. None of them had grown balls big enough to take him on yet, so maybe they hoped the Brogans would do the job for them.

Besides the vehicles there were people. He counted four men, two of them standing close to the van; another couple had strolled away a short distance while they conversed. One of them was wearing a backpack, and it didn't take much imagination to deduce what had become of Gabe Stahl. That gunshot earlier spoke volumes. Po was unsure how he felt about Stahl's possible demise. The guy had possibly betrayed them, had most definitely stolen Vaughan and Leah's bug-out money, but he wasn't really a bad guy, not really, he simply couldn't resist temptation.

One face lit up, washed by cold blue light. Even at a distance Po recognized the face as Bryce Brogan's. He was talking on his cell phone, and Po surmised that he was coordinating their missing forces. From what Pinky had reported, he had beaten two of them about their heads but they'd survived their tussle with him, but another, driving the panel van from earlier, was probably out of the fight after Pinky helped turn the van on its side. It was difficult putting a finger on the exact number he faced, but counting the four already in evidence, there could be two or perhaps three more combatants closing in. He needed to even the odds more in his and Tess's favor, but couldn't make a frontal assault on the quartet. He sought an avenue of attack that wouldn't get him killed, and leave Tess to weather the storm alone.

Apparently, the others had not arrived yet. Po diverted around the glade, avoiding the men there, and headed through the woods as he had before, cutting out the long winding road with a more direct route to the gate. Once he was well beyond being overheard, he took out his cell phone and alerted Tess to his plan. At his suggestion she got a pot of water boiling on the stove: soon some uninvited guests would be arriving for tea.

FORTY-FOUR

He wasn't an accomplished motorcyclist, and had never been the most aerodynamic of individuals either, but Pinky arrived at Freeport without falling off the Ducati. He did however wobble as he took a tight right turn off Main Street to take him out into the wilder coastline. Heart in his throat, he throttled the motorcycle and took off at speed once more. Every second counted. Seemingly in no time the Ducati was rocketing along a narrow road that was never designed for racing. When he was last there it had been dusk, now it was fully dark. Pinky wasn't sure where it was that he'd dropped off Stahl but felt he could only be a short distance away. He swept around a wide corner and found a stretch of road hemmed on both sides by high hedges. It looked more familiar than the almost uniform backdrop of woodland there abouts. From a far corner he caught the glow of a brake light. He had no way of telling yet who he'd closed in on, but as he hadn't passed another vehicle since Freeport it was likely one of the assholes he'd fought with not long ago. He continued at speed but with more caution: he didn't wish to alert them how close he'd gotten.

When he reached the corner he decelerated and went around
the bend at a much slower pace. He checked and saw that the
car traveling along the road was out of sight, then accelerated
again to the next bend. He repeated the process a few more times,
before he once more spotted the car ahead. He recognized it as
one of the cars that had fled him in Falmouth. He couldn't say
which of his enemies was the driver, but it wasn't Walsh or
any of the Brogans. That left Davenport or Huckleberry, and one
of them was in for a rude surprise. He would prefer it to be
Huckleberry, because it was obviously him that had done a
number on his SUV's tires and was deserving of payback.

Pinky slowed down again, coming almost to a stop. Two
hundred yards further on the car had come to a halt. The driver
was looking for the road that would take him to the cabin. Within
a few more seconds the guy, probably habitually, hit his turning
lights and nosed the car into the correct trail. Pinky sped up again,
but as he got near the road end he stopped and dismounted the
bike, and ran instead. He found a wire fence blocking access to
the property, a barrier that was no match for his weight. He stood
on the uppermost wire and flattened it and toppled the post next
to it to the ground. He jumped over a dry ditch and swerved in
among the trees, guided by the lights on the car that was moving
but very slowly. On his back, his knapsack jumped up and down
with each stride, a reminder that he had brought his rifle, but for
the time being he drew his Glock.

He got ahead of the car, and was tempted to step out and
block the road. Level his gun and blast the driver to death. But
he wasn't a murderer, and besides, it wasn't as simple to shoot
through a windscreen as Hollywood sometimes made out. More
likely his bullets would ricochet and the driver would hit the
gas and mow him down. He timed it so he attacked from
the side. From the edge of the path he lifted a baseball-sized
stone, cupping it in his left palm. He swung his arm and pounded
the front passenger window into glittering shards. In reaction the
driver stamped the brake and the car jolted to a sharp halt.
Before he was over the shock of the exploding window, Pinky
reached across and turned off the engine and snatched out the
keys. He, of course, had the Glock aimed at the driver the entire
time. A small part of him was disappointed that he'd captured

Davenport again, rather than Huckleberry, but *C'est la vie*, he decided.

'You don't know when it's time to quit, you,' said Pinky. 'So let me end this fight for you.'

'For Christ's sake, don't kill me! I have a wife and kids and—' Davenport was broken; tears already pouring down his face. It was apparent he was having second thoughts, maybe third or fourth thoughts, about being involved in the goings-on. His face was mushed, the nose flattened, and both eyes were swollen, turning a nice shade of purple. His upper lip wouldn't have looked out of place on a character from a Simpsons cartoon.

'Wasn't having your face almost stove in enough for you already? I'm getting in the car, me, keep your hands in sight the whole time.'

'Wh-what are you going to do?'

Leaning to give clearance for his knapsack Pinky slid onto the glass-covered passenger seat, and dangled out the keys. 'I'm gonna have you drive me, and you'll take it nice and easy, y'hear? Drive faster than ten miles an hour and I'll shoot you in the balls. That's if I can find them, see I'm betting they've sucked somewhere up your back right now. Never mind, you, I'm sure if I shoot you enough times I'll hit them.'

'I swear to you, man, I want no part of this. I didn't buy into murder! When I found out we were supposed to help give Po Villere a hard time it was bad enough, now they want us to help kill some sick guy and a pregnant lady.'

'Yeah. Tell me who you mean by *we*.'

Davenport rolled off the names of the remaining three locals, none of whom Pinky recognized, but he shelved them away for later. He reached across and inserted the ignition key. He stuck the barrel of his gun between Davenport's thighs. 'Now go on, drive, you, and don't get cocky. He-he!'

The car was barely moving for a minute before Pinky directed Davenport to turn off the road, ordering his captive to drive directly into a thick patch of undergrowth. In the dark with its lights off, the car would be invisible from the road. 'OK,' said Pinky, again taking charge of the keys, 'that's far enough. Now I'm going to get out, and when I tell you to, you're going to get out too. Understand?'

Davenport nodded his head with little enthusiasm. He was weeping fully, and his normal-sized bottom lip quivered.

Once upright at the side of the car, Pinky said, 'You can get out now. Don't try running or anything silly or I'll shoot you in the ass, and leave you for the wildlife.'

'I just want to go home to my family,' Davenport whined.

Gesturing with the Glock, Pinky had Davenport walk to the back of the car.

'D'you have a cell phone?'

'In my pocket,' said Davenport.

'Toss it in the woods.'

Davenport shakily removed a cell phone from his back pocket and lobbed it into the underbrush.

'What about your walkie-talkie?'

'In the car.'

'OK.' Using the key fob, Pinky popped the trunk. He looked inside. There was all manner of crap inside, but enough room for a man whose comfort Pinky didn't care about. 'Get in.'

'How?'

Pinky only raised his eyebrows.

Davenport dithered, and Pinky understood why. He believed that Pinky would have him climb inside the trunk then shoot him dead: he was probably picturing being discovered years later as a mummified corpse surrounded by antique motoring oddities. 'I bet your face hurts?' Pinky asked.

The man touched trembling fingertips to where Pinky had smashed him in the nose with his gun butt. 'It hurts like crazy.'

'Don't you fret, you, I won't hit you in the face again,' said Pinky, and brought down the butt of his gun on the top of Davenport's skull. 'That might smart for a few days, too.'

Davenport folded at the knees, and Pinky assisted him to roll into the trunk space. Pinky shoved away his gun in order to grab the unconscious man's legs and tip him fully inside. He had to cram Davenport into the space to get the trunk's lid shut. He doubted there'd be a way for the man to free himself, and Pinky made a mental note to have somebody come and free him later. If Pinky perished before then, well, so would Davenport, but it was a price he must pay.

Pinky dug around in the car. He found the walkie-talkie easily enough. After the earlier liberation he'd made of one of the radios, the Brogans had stopped using them. He threw it into the woods. Earlier he had taken away Davenport's belt knife. There'd been no other weapon then, but he couldn't be certain there wasn't one hidden in the car. However, after a brief but thorough search of the most likely hiding places, he found none. Davenport, he decided, was not equipped for murder, and had shown he didn't have the heart for it either. Pinky hoped that he could return to release his captive, after all. Done with his search, he retraced his route to where he'd left the Ducati. He mounted the motorcycle, got it going and pulled into the track. There was no indication that an assault of the cabin was underway, so Pinky was relieved he had returned in time to help his friends survive the night.

FORTY-FIVE

The sound of the approaching car brought relief to Po. He had made the correct decision in circling behind the quartet already aligned against them. If he could stop the others from bolstering their forces it would add pressure on the Brogans if they chose to storm the cabin. Without their superior numbers they retained the advantage of superior weaponry, but Tess and her charges were fortified. Once the first shot had been fired by the bad guys, Tess said she would alert the police, and then their priority would be to repel the enemy until the cops arrived. The idea was workable but he disliked that they couldn't deal with the Brogans with more finality. Po's was an old-fashioned view of the world, some might say Old Testament, and an eye for an eye meant what it said to him. He had tempered his violent reflexes after serving time in Louisiana State Penitentiary for exacting retribution on the man who had killed his father, but that wasn't to say he was afraid of a fight to the death. These days, though, he must consider the impact of his actions on Tess, so while it worked, he'd go along with her plan.

He had used brute force to snap off the lower branches and foliage of several trees and had piled them across the trail. He'd next found a fallen log, rotten, but large enough that it might be taken for an insurmountable barrier in the car's headlights. He had dragged it and added it to the pile of broken branches. The barrier was strategically placed immediately after one of the sharper bends in the trail, giving a driver little warning as they drove around the corner. If the barricade didn't fully halt a car it would slow it down.

Po judged the terrain, and went to ground where he was concealed by the undergrowth, but not impeded by it. Once he was committed there was no turning back for him.

A vehicle rounded the trail. It was traveling at pace, but not excessively for the road conditions. Its headlights were dipped, and behind the windshield the driver was an amorphous shadow, giving Po no idea of his identity. He had no idea how capable his enemy was, or how heavily armed. He wouldn't allow doubt to gain control of him.

The driver reacted as Po had hoped. Braking sharply he stopped the car with the front fender nudging the barricade. The car reversed a few yards and then the door popped open, the interior light illuminating the driver as he climbed out to investigate how badly the road was blocked. Po judged the man in an instant and he looked a formidable opponent by any measure. Not as tall or wiry with muscle as Po, the man made up for the deficit with broad shoulders and a burly body. His large, shaggy-haired head sat directly atop the shoulders as if he lacked a neck. He hadn't built that physique in a gym; he had what was sometimes referred to as farm-boy strength and that made him more dangerous than any steroidal poseur. Po didn't know his name, but thought he had seen him around Portland. If he wasn't mistaken, Po had once been instrumental in helping Tess deliver him to the cops after he jumped bail. It made sense that the guy might hold a grudge, and work with the Brogans to serve payback. How many of the others had been hired on the basis they were pissed at him? Po didn't actually care.

Having inspected the barricade, there were two obvious actions to follow. He could try ploughing through, or he could disassemble it so there was no risk to the car. The burly man chose the latter. He crouched to grab at the fallen log, and grunted in surprise when it wasn't as heavy as he'd assumed. He hauled up the log in a bear hug, pivoted with it, allowing it to fall away from his grasp on to the grassy shoulder. He wiped his hands clean of rotten bark, and swung around to grab at some of the smaller branches. He was currently unarmed and distracted. Po took advantage, springing from concealment and launching at the man: he could have easily buried his blade in a kidney, or slit the man's throat with it but it was in its boot sheath.

Some primal instinct jerked the man around, so that the kick Po aimed at him skimmed his outer thigh rather than the groin it was intended for. He gritted his teeth, eyelids flickering as Po's follow-up punches rained on his head. He took long seconds to rally, and didn't fold as easily as most men would have under the barrage of blows. He threw his chest against Po's and caught him around the waist the way he'd manhandled the log only moments ago. He hauled Po off his feet, and employed the same motion to pivot and cast Po away.

Po was not an inert lump of wood. He slapped his palms over the man's ears, grabbed handfuls of hair, and drove the tips of his thumbs into his eyes. The man grimaced, screwing his eyelids tightly to avoid being blinded. He couldn't throw Po off him, so he adjusted his grasp, and began to tighten his hold. His arms weren't those of a muscle-bound freak, they were more like the constricting body of an anaconda. In an instant Po felt the air squeezed from his lungs and the immense pressure on his spine was agonizing. Maybe he'd played things wrong and should have stabbed the brute at first chance. No, this was all just part of the dance. Po rammed his knee into the man's groin. The grip around his body loosened but not entirely: Po kneed him in the crotch a second time. When the guy tried to make space between them, Po denied him, dragging his head forward by his ears and hair and met the man's nose with his forehead. He heard the crunch, and felt hot blood spray as the man gasped in pain. Now Po released him, dancing back and then in again in order to power a kick into the man's stomach.

The guy went down, rolling among the broken branches. Po followed, grabbed a thick branch and pounded the man in the side of his head. The blow was a nasty one, but his opponent was tough and shook it off. He swore vilely, and among the curse words, Po caught his own name. He struck again, swiping from the opposite direction, and this time the man collapsed on his side and didn't rise. Po retreated a few steps, gasping for breath, but kept hold of the impromptu club. He didn't take his attention from his opponent until he was certain he wasn't playing possum.

Po set to the unconscious man. He dragged him off the road – a dead weight compounded by Po's loss of breath – and forced him into a seated position against a thin but sturdy sapling. He stripped the man's laces from his sneakers and tied his hands together behind the tree. Then for added security, he yanked off the man's belt and cinched it around his throat, buckling it over a knob of wood at the rear. On waking, the captive might be able to work his way free eventually, but Po was happy the bindings would hold him for now. Po went to the car and got in. There was a pistol lying on the passenger seat, next to a walkie-talkie. The man he'd beaten had left the engine idling. Po set it rolling, the tires easily crunching a path through the barrier he'd erected, and once clear of it he picked up speed.

He didn't get much warning, the car's engine noise mostly covering its approach, and the motorcycle ridden without lights. In his mirror he caught the low, bulky shape swerving around the liberated vehicle, and a more concerning flicker of motion: a hand rising, holding what must be a pistol. Po jerked the steering wheel to the right, and immediately swerved left, to sideswipe and dismount the gunman who had nowhere to go except directly into the trees.

FORTY-SIX

Of the three stragglers, only Anderson Walsh made it to the glade. He reported that Huckleberry and Davenport had both been on his tail until they had to divert around where Eamon White had crashed the van. Walsh said he'd pushed ahead, but trusted, being locals and more familiar with the area, they'd find their own routes back to the rendezvous site. Elvin Collins corrected him: Davenport and Huckleberry were townies; they'd probably never been in these wild parts in their lives before. They were hardly out in a wilderness, but to city boys it could feel so.

'I wouldn't have bet on Davenport showing up anyway,' Bryce Brogan announced. 'He was chicken shit, ready for booking out back in Falmouth. I'd've given Huckleberry the benefit of the doubt, though; at least he showed some chutzpah by slashing the nigger boy's tires.'

'If Heck shows he shows, but we can't wait for him any longer.' Josh Brogan checked their numbers. 'There are five of us, plenty to finish the job.'

Declan Randall nodded at the bag securely cinched to Josh's back. 'How d'you expect to fight while carrying that around with you?'

'My backpack didn't slow me down in Iraq,' Josh reminded him. 'Usually it was heavier than carrying a million dollars.'

'I only meant that the four of us can handle a couple of unarmed private dicks, if you need to stay behind and guard the money. And what about Stahl? Doesn't he need watching?'

'Stahl's coming with us,' Bryce interjected. 'Josh is right about the backpack. It won't slow him down. Besides, it gives him a kick, letting him play at soldier all over again.' He sneered at his brother, who was visibly offended.

'It was never a game to me,' Josh growled.

'It's almost twenty years since your court martial. They kicked you out, bro; it's time to get over it.' Bryce tapped the sequence of scarred-over tattoos on his cheek. 'I'm proof you don't have to ship out to any ass-end desert to feed your blood lust.'

'No, Bryce, you're proof that strait-jackets are still viable.'

'You've got me, brother! So who else's for showing these mother-fuckers how crazy we all can be?'

'I'm not staying behind. Bryce, I promised you revenge on Tony Vaughan, but I also meant what I said about Leah. Do not hurt her.' Randall moved and stood beside him. Josh looked at each of the others. 'None of you hurt her.'

'Y'know, Josh, you denied being the baby's father to me,' said Bryce, 'but the way you're going on, I'm beginning to doubt your word. You sure you didn't have a little dabble?'

'Fuck you, Bryce, and fuck your sick mind. You treat her like a no-good whore but she's your daughter, and my niece, I'd never touch her like that.'

'What's that saying about the lady protesting too much? Methinks it could apply to you, bro.'

214 Matt Hilton

'You know who the father is, and it isn't me. So shut it, goddamn it, and let's move.'

'Yes, let's.' Bryce flicked a gesture for Anderson Walsh to join him in the van this time. His brother could have the pickup truck. He leaned towards Randall and grinned. 'Start puckering up. Josh's ass is exclusively yours again.'

'What about me?' Collins wondered aloud.

Bryce said something inaudible to him, but in the next second Walsh tossed him the keys to the car he'd arrived in.

The big man eyed the pickup and van briefly, wondering no doubt why he was relegated to the car when both the other vehicles belonged to him. It didn't matter, right? He moved towards the car, even as Walsh brought the pickup alongside him. Bryce wound down the window and muttered something unclear. Collins turned to hear what Bryce said, bending his ear to the window. Bryce's arm darted out and in, and the pickup rolled on without slowing. Behind it, Elvin Collins stood for a moment, shocked at having been jabbed so forcefully under his bearded chin. It was a long pause later before he understood the reality of what had happened, and his hands folded around his throat. Bryce had punctured his carotid artery and slit his throat almost to the trachea. Collins' strength gave out and he buckled to his knees. Blood spurted arrhythmically between his fingers, weaker each time as his heart slowed.

Bryce leaned fully from the pickup to call to Josh who was yet to board the van. 'Just thought I'd save us some trouble afterwards. And besides, that stupid idea about pinning all this shit on Collins wouldn't have fooled anyone.'

FORTY-SEVEN

Tess shivered in anticipation. She was cautiously nervous, but not enough to run away from a fight. As a deputy, and several times since, she had been in worse situations than the one they faced now, and she had used a healthy fear of dying to stay sharp. The rush of endorphins made her stomach queasy again, but she ignored the mild nausea, and instead welcomed the adrenalin that would help rather than hinder once the first punch was thrown or bullet was fired.

Tony Vaughan looked equally anxious, but stood between her and Leah as a final line of defense if the Brogans made it past Tess. He had armed himself with a hammer he had found among the tools his bogus uncle had abandoned while attempting some maintenance chores on a previous visit there. Also he'd slipped a large screwdriver into his waistband. It was heavy, rusty and about nine inches in length. With enough power behind it he could probably force it between somebody's ribs.

Being a non-combatant in the coming battle, Leah had been directed to stay on the couch. She couldn't be protected in the bedroom without splitting their forces. Besides that, there was only one gun between them, and Tess and Vaughan couldn't toss it back and forward through the bedroom door when one of them needed it. Vaughan had pushed the couch into a corner so that its upholstered back was presented to the front window, mostly hiding Leah. The back door was now bolted and further secured by a plank of wood wedged under the handle and against an uneven board in the floor. Vaughan had also rearranged the kitchen table and chairs, forming a barricade of sorts, which wouldn't offer much defense against a bullet but it helped obscure Tess as a target. She could crouch at one end of the overturned table or the other, without being seen from outside.

Tess had arranged other smaller items nearer the front door, front window and next to the stove; they would be weapons of desperation if it came to a violent invasion. Occasionally she'd had to shift them around, keeping them viable while they waited for the Brogans. Her cell phone was on the floor, ready to hit a pre-programmed number to her brother Alex's phone if things grew too hot to handle. Alex was a patrolman with Portland PD, and would be able to mount a rapid armed response in a way she'd find more difficult going via a dispatcher. That was if, she thought with a pang of concern, Alex was awake and on duty.

She was confident that Po was wide awake, and she trusted that he was doing his thing to try to even the odds in their favor. After that first gunshot she assumed had been fired at Gabe Stahl, there had been no more shooting, but that meant nothing. Po was not a gunman, his skills were honed while incarcerated in one of the most violent prisons in the US; they were about close-quarters combat with an emphasis on swift, brutal, overwhelming force. He often quoted the adage that the best line of defense is offence, and having witnessed evidence of its efficacy, she agreed. She hoped that he was taking hell to their enemies, but also that he was totally uninjured: sometimes you could have your ployes and eat them, right?

Pinky was returning to join them too, despite her asking him – actually *telling* him – not to. She was happy he had disobeyed her, the obstinate devil that he was. Time and again Pinky had proven his love of them, and she knew that if it came to it he'd lay down his life to save Po, and now her too. It had to be said that the feeling was mutual.

She looked at her cell phone. It had powered down to save the battery, so she saw only a darkened screen against the dimness of the floor. She trusted that Pinky and her partner's silence was good news for now. Should she heed Po's philosophy and make a pre-emptive strike against the Brogans by calling for police support immediately? It was the wise thing to do, after all. But where was the buzz in that? She had been penned inside far too long, her brain going to mush, and this was the most alive – sick feeling in her belly and all – she had felt for ages. Let things unravel a little more, she decided against better judgement, and she craned to see through the chink in the drapes.

Earlier she'd watched a vehicle approach, its lights twinkling like fireflies among the tree trunks. It stopped and shortly after another rolled in beside it. The cars hadn't progressed for some time but now one of them was on the move and unless she was mistaken a larger vehicle had joined it, probably the van they'd spotted Josh Brogan in, to continue the approach. She judged they were less than half a mile away, so should arrive in minutes at the most.

'OK,' she warned the others, 'it looks as if this is it. Leah, keep your head down, and those blankets piled around you. Tony' – she grinned, hoping to bolster his courage with a joke – 'it's hammer time!'

Vaughan grunted, apparently unfamiliar with 1990s pop culture catchphrases, and he'd no way of seeing her rictus grin either. He possibly had no idea she meant they should get busy. But with his next breath he turned and looked at Leah and said firmly, 'You can't touch this girl.'

Leah was oblivious to his play on song lyrics. But they weren't directed at her; instead they were intended for the awful men who sought to harm her again. Tess's joke had rallied his courage but in a way other than she'd intended. How he got there didn't matter, but Vaughan had some steel back in his stance. He hefted his hammer like an emaciated but still potent Norse god of thunder.

Tess checked the smaller weapons she'd arranged. If the invasion didn't happen soon they'd be useless. Actually, they might not do much physical harm but they could still distract an attacker while Tess gained an advantage, so they were worth the time and effort taken to prepare them. She glanced at the others she'd arranged should an incursion be made via the bedroom window.

Outside the vehicles rumbled to a halt. Vaughan's car was crushed up against the tree where it had been abandoned, but Po's Mustang had been moved to the side of the cabin when Vaughan and Leah's meager belongings had been loaded into it. Whoever drove the pickup swung it around and backed towards the Mustang, in an effort, Tess realized to block it as a getaway vehicle. The pickup came too fast to stop in time, but that was probably an intended consequence. Its towbar rammed the front of the muscle car, rocking it on its chassis and setting off the tamper-proof alarms. Tess couldn't see what damage had been done, but for certain she knew that Po would be extra pissed. Those in the pickup decamped and scuttled back to join the others at the van. Tess counted four figures and wondered where the others had gotten: maybe, she prayed, Po had been successful in taking out half of their numbers alone. It was a big ask, but she had such belief in her partner.

'You inside,' a voice called, 'it's time to parlay. Send out Leah and Tony and you're free to leave.'

Tess could've spat in disbelief.

'Don't come any closer,' she replied, 'I have you in my sights and I'm not afraid to shoot.'

'You should conserve your ammo until you can shoot at somebody worth killing.'

Tess recognized Bryce Brogan's voice, though it held more notes of humor than it had when they captured him at the wharves that afternoon. Standing beyond the wash of the van's headlights all four figures were unrecognizable silhouettes, but Tess believed that one of those recently jumping from the pickup was Bryce. It made sense he'd wish to damage their car after Pinky had put holes in their other van, he seemed the spiteful type despite his faux good nature. The silhouetted figure proved her point by pointing at the man next to him. 'Why don't you aim at him, or maybe this other guy here?'

This time he moved aside so that there was space for another of the men to reach inside the van and drag out a captive. For about a nanosecond she was alarmed that it was Po who had been captured, but she recognized the shaggy hair and beard: Gabe Stahl hadn't been murdered after all. He could barely carry his own weight on one leg, and Tess immediately thought of Bob Wilson's foot injury, and that shooting somebody through their foot must be an act of sadism the Brogans favored. Stahl was shoved down in front of the person she believed was Bryce, and she watched the thug wrap his hand under Stahl's chin and force his head backwards. 'Here you are,' he said, gesturing with his other hand to Stahl's chest. 'Put a bullet right here. Trust me, you'll be doing this thieving piece of shit a huge kindness. If you don't give us Vaughan and Leah in one minute, I'm going to begin cutting him apart piece by piece, d'you hear?'

'I don't care what you do to him. Like you said, he's a thieving piece of shit, and a goddamn Judas. He means nothing to me, so don't think you can use him to force us into anything.'

Stahl wailed about being sorry, that he didn't deserve to die, and Tess had to shut her ears to his pleas for mercy.

Bryce clamped a hand over Stahl's mouth, stifling him. 'Sorry, Tess, but I don't believe a single word of it. I don't believe you're the type to stand by and watch while I peel the hide from him.'

'I guess I'm not. If you touch him, I'll put a bullet between your eyes.'

Bryce laughed at her, sounding genuinely amused at the prospect. 'See, you couldn't even hold out longer than a few seconds. Where's your man?'

'In here with me.'

'Cat got his tongue?'

'He only speaks when he has something important to say. Trust me, right now there's nothing he'd say that you would wish to hear.'

Bryce boasted to another of the men. 'See, I told you he wouldn't be in there. He's out there someplace, hiding like a coward.' He returned his attention to Tess. 'Give me Vaughan and Leah and walk away, Tess. I meant what I said when I asked you to work for me; I'd have rewarded you for finding Vaughan on my behalf. The irony is you've done just that, but now you get paid nothing. Your one chance to salvage your day is to stand down and walk away with your life, otherwise . . .'

'Otherwise you'll kill me too?'

'Exactly.'

'Harm me, and my partner will hunt you to the end of the earth and make you pay.'

'It's a chance I'm willing to take. I'm not afraid of Po'boy Villere.'

'You should be afraid. Ask any of your lackeys who know of him, ask them if he's somebody a sane man wants to make an enemy of.'

'Maybe you should ask them if I'm sane?' he countered and laughed as if it was the funniest line ever.

Another man presented himself by stepping forward. The head-light's glimmer bathed him, and Tess saw that he looked an older, stockier version of his brother: it was Josh. He carried a large backpack on his back, and she had a fair idea of what was inside.

'I'll personally vouch for your safety, Miss Grey,' he called. 'Come out, leave Tony and Leah to us and I promise we'll let you leave unmolested.'

'That's a poor choice of words, *Uncle* Josh,' Tess responded snarkily. 'It's a shame that you didn't extend the same protection to your niece. You're obviously as much of a monster as your lunatic brother. So don't waste your breath lying, just take your blood money and *you* leave, while *you* still have the opportunity. I'm giving *y'all* a minute to get back in your vehicles and go home; otherwise you'll all be going to jail. You know I was once a cop, right? Well, I've got a direct line to the station, and I'm a second from calling them. Think you can storm the cabin and take us all before the cops close in? Think again, because believe me, I won't make things easy for you.'

'Son of a gun,' Bryce cawed, 'if I had any interest in taking a wife again, it'd be a wild one just like you, Tess Grey. Shit, you don't have to be my wife for me to take you, no how. I'm going to make you watch while I cut off Tony's dick then make you suck it, and if that doesn't arouse you, well, fuck it, I'll screw you dry.'

'You seriously are one disgusting individual,' Tess said. 'Why don't you come over here, where I can see you clearly and tell me again how you're going to rape me? I'd blow off your damn dick but I doubt I could hit a target so small.'

'Ha-ha! D'you hear that, Josh? I think she's confusing me with you.'

'Yeah, you crack me up, Bryce,' said Josh.

'It's my cutting wit,' Bryce answered.

He dragged his palm off Stahl's mouth, but before his captive could begin howling for mercy again, Bryce gave a hint at what was in store for him. He swiped his right hand slowly across Stahl's chest. In the dark Tess couldn't see the redness of the blood that sheeted from the slashed flesh, but a vivid view wasn't needed. Stahl screamed in abject dismay.

'Dear god,' Tess croaked under her breath, and she rose a few inches to get a cleaner shot at Bryce. She'd believed he had been bluffing, the same way his threats about raping her had been designed to terrorize her into giving in to his demands. He hadn't been bluffing, so he probably meant what he'd promised to do to her too! She should show she hadn't been bluffing either. However, she had been about shooting Bryce dead. She had no shot, and to waste a bullet would be insane. She dipped down on her haunches and stabbed at her cell phone, bringing it to life. She hit Alex's number and waited for a connection. A bullet had not been fired yet, but the slashing open of Stahl's chest constituted a violent assault: things were underway. 'Alex,' she whispered hoarsely the instant he answered.

'Hey, sis, what are you doing awake at this time of night?'

'There's no time for me to explain, I'm going to pass you to a friend and you must believe everything he says and get here as quickly as possible.'

'What? What kind of mess are you in this time?'

'Just listen to him, Alex.' She slid the phone across the rickety floorboards. Tony Vaughan grabbed it, and began a rushed explanation of the crap Tess had gotten into. She trusted Vaughan to get the desperation of their plight across, and she trusted her brother to mount a rescue mission. She concentrated on the there and then, because in the few seconds it had taken to get things in motion, those outside had moved.

A snapshot showed a bald man dragging Stahl towards the van, while the two Brogans had split up, one going left while the other came in a direct run towards the cabin. A fourth man was slinking to the right. Their intention was clear, the three wanted to assault the cabin in a pincer movement, the two closing in from the sides while she wasted ammo trying to hit the one rushing in. Tess wasn't easily suckered. She drew a bead on the man sneaking to the right, and fired. He clutched at his thigh, staggered and went down on one knee. Glass from the broken window tinkled around her feet.

She duck-walked to the far side of the window. An opportunity to drop the man on the left had been missed. She spotted the bulky backpack and realized it was Josh. Unhindered he made it to the side of the cabin. He could try entering by the bedroom window Leah had snuck out of earlier, or even continue around to try the back door. She looked for Vaughan. He was still urgently whispering directions to Alex. She jabbed a hand, warning him where Josh had gone. More glass shattered. This time it was the blade extended beyond Bryce Brogan's hand that smashed and knocked chunks of glass out of the frame. Tess had one bullet left. It would be well spent on the maniac currently trying to smash his way inside. Instead she went for one of the less lethal options she'd set up. She grabbed the handle of a pan and threw water over him. He howled, staggered away, and Tess reached for another of the pans she had boiled in anticipation. The water was no longer boiling, but hot enough to convince Bryce or anyone else she doused into thinking they'd been scalded. She leaned out through the broken window and cast it after the retreating figure. Immediately she ducked back inside.

A door was being forced, the bolt already twisted out of its socket as a shoulder was repeatedly slammed against the wood.

Vaughan hollered and rushed the back door, stamping down on the foot of the plank, halting its inexorable judder across the floor. If he couldn't stop it slipping then the back door would give fully. A gap was forced at the top of the door, and the barrel of a pistol poked inside. There wasn't a clean target for the gunman, but if he got the door open an inch or two more—

Vaughan yelled and hammered the barrel of the pistol in a frenzy. The gunman foolishly continued to push inside, so Vaughan concentrated on his hand and wrist. The man – Josh Brogan, or perhaps the one she had wounded in the leg – cursed and swiftly withdrew. Vaughan threw his weight against the door, slamming it shut, and he again forced the plank under the handle. All the while he checked on Leah. She huddled under the piled blankets, shaking and praying under her breath.

Bullets cut through the door.

Vaughan jumped away, staggered and fell. He scrambled, and regained his feet, using the back of the couch to brace against. He still clutched his hammer but there was no sign of Tess's cell phone.

It didn't matter.

Alex would come.

But where were Po and Pinky?

Approaching through the trees she spotted the flickering headlights of speeding vehicles. The Brogans had summoned re-inforcements. There was no hope of withstanding a siege with those extra numbers ranged against them.

There was a crash from the bedroom and the scrabbling of somebody forcing their way through the window. Reinforcements arriving or not, Tess couldn't just give up. She hurtled into the room, saw a hunched figure half in and half out of the window. She could shoot, but then she'd have no bullets to stand against the new arrivals. She grabbed up another of the pans she'd prepared, this one heavy and wide, and too shallow to hold water.

FORTY-EIGHT

Po checked the reflection in his wing mirror again, and was pleased that he had given it due notice a few minutes ago, otherwise something horrible might have happened to his best friend: serious injury or death that Po would have been respon-sible for caused by an instant's panic. As the motorcycle drew up alongside and Pinky aimed to blow out his window, Po had launched into a maneuver to smash him headlong among the trees. But another glance in the mirror, checking for the proximity of the gun, cast his gaze directly into Pinky's and both men had aborted their attacks. Pinky dropped his pistol and braked the Ducati so suddenly the bike stood on its front tire for several seconds, threatening to cast him over the handlebar, while Po swerved again away from the bike, giving Pinky space to set it down safely alongside him. Po slowed and then halted the liberated car, and leaped out, jogging back to check on his friend.

Pinky was cut up and his clothing was dusty and splotchy with blood, but he was energized and ready for action. He wore a knapsack strapped securely on his shoulders.

'You OK?' Po asked.

'I'm marvelous.' Pinky grinned abashedly at the near miss. 'But I almost gave you a nasty booboo, me.' He cast around, looking for where his Glock had fallen. He swung his leg off the bike, and again searched, finding the gun in the brush at the side of the trail.

'I almost did the same to you, podnuh. That was too close, Pinky.'

'A miss is as good as a mile to a blind blacksmith,' he replied. 'I'm good, you're good, can we say the same for Tess, though, us?'

A distant shot rang through the woods, the sound ricocheting off the nearest trees. The fight had begun.

'We cannot.' Po didn't wait to check on Pinky again. He knew he was fine and would follow. He took off in the borrowed car. He could possibly get closer undetected to their enemies than before if they thought he was their bullish pal coming to support them. They could make what they would of Pinky on the motorcycle.

Po wasn't keen on firearms, but neither was he a complete stranger to them. He trusted his knife over a gun, but there was a time and place for everything: right then he needed the extra range of a gun. He reached for the one dumped on the seat by the brute he'd bound to the tree. It was heavy, fully loaded.

Pinky was still reflected in his mirrors, but as they approached within the last few hundred feet of the cabin, he slewed away to the left, choosing a different line of attack to the one Po took.

Po wished to drive directly to the cabin and carry Tess and the others out of their attackers' clutches. But nearer he spotted the van and pickup with their bait and tackle decals. A bald man hustled another towards the open back doors of the van. Po recognized baldy as Anderson Walsh, Bryce's sidekick, and his limping captive as Gabe Stahl. To some, Stahl might deserve everything he suffered, but Po couldn't hate him enough to leave him to his fate. And besides, it would be unwise to leave Walsh at his back, from where the man could shoot him to death unchallenged. He aimed the car towards Walsh. Walsh saw him coming, but didn't react to the imminent danger, choosing instead to concentrate on striking Stahl and forcing him inside the van at gunpoint. With Stahl out of immediate harm's way, Po didn't slow the car, he sped up. The front fender picked up Anderson Walsh, tossed him onto the hood and then over the roof of the car.

Confident that Walsh was probably alive but in no fit state to ambush anyone from behind, Po swerved around the van and again sent the car rocketing towards the cabin. Elsewhere he knew that Pinky would be off his bike and arming himself with his rifle. Po looked for somebody else on which to direct his cold fury and spotted Bryce Brogan staggering away from the front of the cabin, swiping at the hot water that had been thrown over him. Po grinned, said *good girl*, as Tess had followed his instruction to boil water on the stove. Po sent the car towards Bryce as he had with Walsh.

He could send Bryce spinning over the roof in a flailing bundle of limbs, but at the final moment Bryce blinked through the stinging heat, and jerked aside, lurching to take cover beyond Vaughan's crashed car. Po hit a skid, sending around the side of the car to impact him instead. Hit on the backside, Bryce was flung face down in the dirt. His back was unbroken, proof of which was how fast Bryce crawled away, then reclaimed his footing. He span, grimacing, face scalded red, with steam rising off his shoulders. He raised his arm, his sprung blade jutted from his hand. In those few seconds Po had slid out of the car. He aimed the pistol at Bryce.

'Seriously?' asked Bryce. 'You're going to shoot me?'

'I am.'

'I thought you favored that knife of yours?'

'I do, but my knife's too good to soil with shit.'

'Huh, just as I thought. You're yellow.'

'I'm a lot of things, but I'm not a coward, and neither am I stupid. I won't be drawn into a knife fight with you.'

Po fired.

His bullet struck Bryce's shoulder. The maniac snarled in agony, and clutched at his shoulder with his opposite arm.

'Actually,' said Po, as he set down the gun and drew his knife, 'I've changed my mind about avoiding a knife fight.'

Bryce withdrew his hand and checked his fingers. They were bloody but not as covered as he feared. He rolled his shoulder, wincing at the burning pain of a flesh wound, but the joint and muscles worked still. Po had shot to injure but not totally debilitate. Bryce lowered his blade, though not in surrender; he held it obliquely across his abdomen, and made a blade of his opposite hand, that he held slightly higher and forward to ward off Po's attacks.

Po adopted a similar stance.

Bryce smiled, and a weird look contorted his features, giving him a devilish cast. 'I'm going to cut you up the way I did your nigger boyfriend.'

'You'd best hope to do a better job than before,' Po replied, 'seeing as Pinky's over there right now about to blow the head off your brother.'

Bryce resisted for a few seconds, but then his gaze darted, to check what had become of Josh.

In that instant of distraction Po attacked.

Bryce slashed in response and their blades clashed, the edges grating against each other as the men strove for dominance. Po disengaged, but only so that he could club at the wound on Bryce's shoulder, further deadening his arm. He backhanded his blade and jabbed it through the meat of Bryce's forearm as the enforcer-for-hire tried for a desperate swing at his gut. Blood dripped from Bryce in several places. Po had cut him, but not yet as badly as Bryce had his best friend.

'Give it up, bra,' said Po, 'you're not in my league.'

'I'll take a stab to deliver one,' Bryce grinned manically, 'are you prepared to do the same?'

'No, because I'm not crazy.'

Bryce lunged and this time he cut a figure of eight with his knife, only to redirect at the end and thrust his knife directly at Po's right eye.

Po ducked, stabbed in and out, and now blood dripped the size of ripe cherries from Bryce's thigh. The enforcer stumbled, his leg weakened.

'I'm warning you, come at me again, and there'll be no holding back,' said Po.

'Fair enough,' Bryce yelled wildly, and attacked, proving he was unafraid of a stab to deliver a killing one of his own.

Both men jostled and jabbed and slashed, danced around in a conjoined pirouette, Bryce less nimble on his feet, and then Po plunged in and knifed him in the thigh again. This time the blood ran like a waterfall. Po backed away.

'That's your femoral artery I just opened,' he informed Bryce. 'Unless you get that bleeding stopped you'll die. We're only talkin' a matter of minutes, bra.'

'It won't take me minutes to kill you,' Bryce snarled, without a trace of his previous faux humor.

Po shrugged. 'All I gotta do is walk rings around you and watch you bleed out.'

'I'm not crippled.'

Bryce tried another lunge, but he was unstable. Po had not only sliced open the artery, he'd cleaved the thigh muscle as he withdrew his knife. Bryce's leg buckled under him and he sat down heavily on his butt. He made pointless slashes with his knife; Po had no intention of approaching. He wiped the blood from his knife and reinserted it in its boot sheath.

'Shit, I *am* crippled,' Bryce corrected himself. He looked up at Po and laughed. He studied the massive injury to his thigh, laughed again but it was strained. 'Talk about asking the obvious: I'm not going to survive this, am I?'

'Nope.'

Bryce shook his head at the finality as he twiddled his hands together in his lap. He raised a finger and tapped an unscarred spot on his cheek. 'I was thinking of having my tats recolored, y'know. I was saving this spot for you.'

He twiddled his fingers again, shaking his head morosely. Then he reared back, swung and unfurled his arm and his knife – detached from the spring-loaded mechanism – speared through the air at Po.

Po dodged and the knife flew harmlessly against Vaughan's abandoned car.

Po retrieved the gun he'd set down.

Bryce croaked out another laugh, growing more pathetic with each one. Already his mottled face had taken on an unhealthy glow in places, as if lit by an inner light as the blood leached out of him. 'You can't blame me for trying to take you with me.'

'I'm going over there,' said Po, and indicated the cabin, 'to usher on your brother to join you.'

A dusty pool of blood covered the earth around Bryce. He no longer had the strength to lift his arms. His hands lay cupped where they fell. His head drooped forward. He had died, or was as near to death as damnit.

Po went to help Tess.

All sounds of battle had faded, but he was confident it had ended in success, as Pinky stood with his rifle canted over his shoulder. A man lay motionless at his feet. From what Po could tell, he wasn't dead, only unconscious, having met the stock of Pinky's rifle. Blood had darkened the man's trousers from a wound to his leg. Wondering if it were Josh, Po leaned closer. It wasn't, Po had no idea who Declan Randall was.

FORTY-NINE

Tess sat with her back to the wall. She breathed deeply, in and out, controlling the rush of endorphins through her body to a manageable level. Slowly she regained her footing and leaned with one hand on the back of the couch. Leah peered back at her, eyes as large as moons.

'Is it over?' Leah whispered.

'Things have gone quiet, I hope that means what I hope it does.'

'Is my uncle dead?'

'No. He's going to survive, but he won't be bothering you again.'

'What about Tony?'

'I-I'm here.' Tony scuttled over. He reached and squeezed Leah's extended hand.

She wept. 'You're hurt.'

'Randall shot me through the door,' he agreed, and touched his side with his other hand, 'but it's not going to kill me.'

'Where's—' Leah caught herself. 'I don't even want to call that animal my father.'

Tess looked out of the broken window. She was relieved to see Po walking towards the cabin, and Pinky standing guard over the man she'd shot in the leg. Beyond them all, Bryce Brogan had folded at the waist over his knees in a wide pool of muddy dirt.

'You don't have to fear him any more,' Tess promised her, but chose to spare the girl the horrid details.

Tess checked on Josh.

He was lying where she had felled him with the cast-iron skillet as he had tried bursting his way inside through the bedroom window. The pan, swung with all Tess's strength and deliberation, had possibly fractured his skull; it had most definitely opened a cut and torn out a hank of his hair. In the minute or so since she had knocked him out, Vaughan had dragged him fully inside, over the bed and onto the floor at the threshold to the living room. The knapsack had been removed from Josh's back. Despite being wounded in his side, Vaughan hadn't hung about before recovering Leah and her baby's cash lifeline.

Josh stirred.

Tess unlatched the front door for Po. He entered, his features set in determination. He checked first her, then their two charges. He frowned slightly at Vaughan's feverish expression, then turned and spotted Josh. He looked at Tess for clarification.

'I hit him with a hot skillet,' she said.

'You've been saving that for me since I walked out on those ployes this morning,' he smiled.

She chuckled. 'I did feel like bashing you,' she admitted. 'Look, he's coming around. Tony has checked him for weapons. I don't know what he intended doing because he came inside without a gun or anything else.'

'You're certain of that?' Po directed his query at Vaughan.

'He had no gun, just a walkie-talkie and a cell phone. I took them away.'

When she was a deputy, Tess wouldn't have taken Vaughan's word that Josh had been fully searched, and would have conducted her own. But there, she felt that Vaughan had more to lose than any of them so would have ensured Josh was no longer a threat.

Po had his own feelings about the matter. He dragged Josh deeper into the room and patted him down with the expertise of one who'd endured similar searches on too many occasions to count. He stood, grunted in satisfaction that Josh was unarmed. Tess couldn't fathom the man's motive for entering without a weapon on hand. Perhaps he had dropped it outside the window after she bashed his head with the pan.

'Got anything I can tie him up with?'

Tess thought about it, and said, 'You could always tear one of those blankets into strips.'

Po puffed out his cheeks.

He bent and pulled off Josh's boots to unlace them.

'Thanks, Po, you've just saved me a heap of trouble.'

The voice brought Po snapping around, and Tess brought up her revolver: one bullet remained.

It was not Bryce who'd miraculously risen from death, but Gabe Stahl who pointed Anderson Walsh's pistol at Josh.

Blood soaked his shirt from a deep slash on his chest and he stood barely on both feet. One he held raised off the floor, and it was apparent why when he stumbled further inside the room. He had been shot through the instep the same way in which Bob Wilson had been. By the direction of his ire, Tess thought that Josh must be the one that had shot both men through their feet. 'Stretch out his leg, Po, I'm gonna do the same to that sadistic bastard as he did to me.'

'Gabe, put down the gun, bra,' said Po.

'You're my boss at the autoshop, Po, but you don't get to tell me what to do in my own goddamn time.'

'I'm not telling, I'm asking.'

'Put down the gun,' Tess also said. 'It's over with, he's not a danger to anyone now.'

'He shot me, so I'm gonna shoot him. Never mind his foot, I'm gonna shoot him through his freakin' heart.'

A rifle barrel tickled Stahl behind his ear.

'You heard my friends, you, now put down the gun.'

Stahl shivered under the touch of the cold metal. He opened his arms, allowing the pistol to hang by his finger hooked in the trigger guard. Pinky reached under his armpit and took the pistol away.

'He still needs shot,' said Stahl, then physically wilted. Po grabbed him and guided him to where the table and chairs had formed a barricade. He reached to right one of the chairs to sit Stahl in.

Josh was not as stunned as he had feigned for the last few seconds. He saw a gap in their defenses and went for it. He rolled onto his knees and palms, and pushed off with his stockinged feet. One foot skidded but the other found purchase and Josh almost dove headlong into the bedroom. Without the encumbrance of the cash on his back, he moved much swifter than he had when trying to break in. He scrambled, but it was not for the window and escape; Pinky could've easily cut him off from outside.

Tess thought that perhaps he'd dropped his weapon when she struck him and it had fallen from his hand, landing outside. She was only partially correct. Josh clawed for a pistol lying beneath the bed. He got his hands within inches of it. Tess had caught up by then, and she had the one bullet left to her. She lined the sight up between his shoulder blades, but had second thoughts, snapping the gun downward. She shot him through the base of his right foot. The pain was instantaneous and shocking, and Josh forgot all about the pistol. Yowling, he rolled, pulling up his injured foot, his knee to his chest. By then Tess had already danced past him and grabbed the pistol off the floor: there were enough bullets in its magazine to slay them all and then some. She aimed it at Josh.

'Here, let me take that.' Vaughan had approached. He held out trembling fingers for the now empty revolver. 'There's no sense in all of us going to jail. If anyone asks, I was the one that shot Josh, and Declan Randall. I'd take credit for knifing Bryce too if I could but I doubt anyone will believe me.'

Po had closed in too. The danger over with he again grabbed Josh, slapped his hands away from his injured foot, and tied his wrists tightly with the laces from Josh's boots. Lastly he dragged the man into the living area again, and forced him to sit on the floor at Stahl's feet. Po handed Stahl one of the heavy pans Tess had utilized as weapons. 'If he moves, give his head another bash.'

'Happy to be of help,' said Stahl.

Leah craned to see her uncle. Josh wouldn't meet her condemning gaze. She said, 'You had the money back, why couldn't you just let us go?'

Josh's voice was a monotone drone. 'Bringing you home was always more important than the money you stole. If we let you go unpunished nobody would fear us any more, nobody would hire us. We couldn't let anybody disrespect us like that and not make an example of them. You know the world we exist in, Leah, if you're perceived to be weak you get eaten alive.'

'Would you really have hurt me, would you have hurt my baby?'

He didn't reply at first, then, lowering his head further, he said, 'Bryce would've. The color of your baby's skin condemned it in his mind. I would have tried to stop him . . .'

'No, Uncle Josh, you wouldn't have. You also suspect who the father is and you won't accept any association with his baby. You have as much bile and hatred bottled up inside you as my father had, it's just you were able to hide your true feelings while he wore them on his sleeve.'

Josh did not deign to answer. He instead looked up at Tess, who still covered him with his own pistol. 'You may as well finish me off. Sending me to prison isn't going to change my fate. My employers still expect me to deliver their money to them, along with Tony Vaughan's head. I promised I would, on the under-standing that if I failed my own head was forfeit. Don't think I'm safe from them behind bars. They'll get to me one way or another.'

'Shooting you would do you a favor,' she said, 'so I won't. You're a monster and you deserve everything that's coming to you.'

FIFTY

T ony Vaughan died four weeks later. He passed away happy, having witnessed the birth of Leah Brogan's child, who the mother named after him. Giving the child his name was a legacy Vaughan had never expected, and it gave him great peace and pleasure during his last days of life. His heart failed in his sleep, and when his half-brother Bob Wilson found him, he was lying in peaceful repose with a smile on his face. Had he survived he would have made a great father figure to Leah's baby, and it was doubtful anyone would note that the color of the baby's skin was at odds with his. Anthony Vaughan Brogan was mixed race, his skin verging on mahogany and his hair black and curly. Before he was even born his grandfather had despised him and would have done anything to disassociate himself from him, to a point Bryce would resort to his murder.

Great-Uncle Josh didn't survive Tony Vaughan even. He had prophesied his death under orders of his cartel employers. His three attackers had somehow gained entry to a supposed secure area of the prison and stabbed him repeatedly with ceramic knives smuggled past the metal detectors for the express purpose of taking a million dollars out of his tattooed hide. He was decapitated and his head forced on a post. Heck Bury and Richard Davenport might escape cartel punishment for their parts in the Brogans' failure, but Anderson Walsh and Declan Randall would live in fear of retribution long after their injuries had healed. Elvin Collins had already paid the ultimate price for associating with Bryce Brogan, and the final man in their group, Eamon White, terrified of going to jail, took his own life before the police could trace him.

Gabe Stahl escaped prison. The mechanic had pleaded forgiveness from them and they had blessed him with it, although Po had given him his marching orders from the autoshop. Stahl had limped away rather than marched, but wasn't overly upset at losing his job, as Tony Vaughan had settled his debt with his old pal, giving him back the hundred bucks he owed, plus several tens of thousands to help him and his ailing father out of the debt-hole Stahl had dropped them into. It hadn't surprised Tess to learn how Tony had bailed out his old buddy, or that he bequeathed some money to Bob Wilson either, because he'd already proven he was selfless and hoped to make the lives of others easier after he was gone.

After the birth of her child, and the few days spent in Tony Vaughan's company, she had moved on, taking her son with her, along with what was left in the holdall after Vaughan had settled his affairs. For their on-going safety, Tess had asked that Leah keep her final destination a secret, even from her and Po. Leah had agreed, but also that she would keep in touch via a Hotmail account through which she would update Tess on baby Anthony's development.

Tess and Po escaped arrest, as did Pinky. To some extent Alex, and his fiancée and Tess's sometime employer, Emma Clancy, pulled some strings with the District Attorney's office, and they were described – alongside Gabe Stahl – as heroes for their efforts in thwarting the murderous attempts on Leah and her baby. Between all involved, certain aspects of the events leading up to the assault on the cabin were not mentioned, no less the bag of money set aside to fund Leah and her child's new life. It was enough that the police believed that Leah was being hunted by her kin because of their history with white supremacy groups, and that they had condemned her to death because she was carrying a black man's offspring. For the time being, Tess thought Leah would stay safe and ahead of any further cartel people sent to retrieve the money; perhaps they would be satisfied with Josh's brutal death and forget all about her.

Pinky kept up his fitness regime, pushing on and ignoring the stitches in his wounds. He lost twenty-eight pounds in the first month, and kept at it.

Tess and Po's world returned to some kind of normalcy. Tess resumed working from her home office. Po got Bar-Lesque up and running, serving customers again albeit at a reduced capacity. But the bar-diner was making money, and gotten Jazz, Chris and their other staff back into paid employment. Last month, Jazz had misread Tess's condition; she had been suffering a milder sickness virus than the one currently killing thousands upon thousands of Americans. But Tess had not been too upset when her period came and she wasn't pregnant. It only meant she and Po could share more intimacy and enjoy trying for a spell longer.

Po had worked on his Mustang, bringing it back to pristine condition after Bryce Brogan had rammed it with the pickup's towbar. He was tinkering under the hood when she went outside to call him in for breakfast.

He entered the house, wiping his hands on a cloth, and served her a smile.

'I've made ploys,' Tess announced. 'An entire stack of them, so I hope you're hungry?'

'I'm ravenous.'

'Sit down. Here,' she said. As he settled at the breakfast counter, she set down a plate with a couple of the pancakes already dished onto it. Under the uppermost there was an unexpected bump. 'If I were you, I wouldn't actually eat those,' Tess added and smiled at his confusion. She used his fork to lift the top pancake. 'Take a look, Po.'

He saw a white plastic device, with a small viewing window midway along its contoured length. Within the window were twin pink lines. He didn't need to ask his nervously grinning partner for clarity on what they signified, but, for sure, she hadn't tested positive for the virus.